商务英语阅读新视野

主　编　戎林海

副主编　张春燕　承晓燕
　　　　戎佩珏

东南大学出版社

内 容 提 要

本书共50个单元,选编了涉及经济、银行、金融、保险、财会、统计、物流、证券、外汇、产品、质量、品牌与商标等文章计50篇,文章内容新、涵盖面广,可有效拓展学习者的阅读面和知识面,使学习者在阅读过程中能更加深入地探究各有关领域,为以后从事实际工作打下较牢固的基础。本书可作商务英语、国贸等专业的教材,也是外经贸人员提高自己更新知识的阅读必备。

图书在版编目(CIP)数据

商务英语阅读新视野/戎林海主编. —南京:东南
大学出版社,2007.8
 ISBN 978-7-5641-0903-5

Ⅰ.商… Ⅱ.戎… Ⅲ.商务—英语—阅读教学
—高等学校—教学参考资料 Ⅳ. H319.4

中国版本图书馆 CIP 数据核字(2007)第 127758 号

商务英语阅读新视野

出版发行	东南大学出版社	
出版人	江 汉	
社 址	南京市四牌楼2号	
邮 编	210096	
电 话	(025) 83793329(办公室)/ 83790510(传真) 83795801(发行部)	
	57711295(发行部传真)/ 83374334(邮购)	
网 址	http://press.seu.edu.cn	
电子邮件	liu-jian@seu.edu.cn	
经 销	全国各地新华书店	
印 刷	江苏兴化印刷有限责任公司	
开 本	787mm×1092mm 1/16	
印 张	15.5	
字 数	401 千字	
版 次	2007 年 8 月第 1 版	
印 次	2007 年 8 月第 1 次印刷	
印 数	1—4000 册	
书 号	ISBN 978-7-5641-0903-5/H · 113	
定 价	25.00 元	

前　言

　　随着我国改革开放的推进与深入,国人踏出国门,与世界近距离接触的机会愈来愈多,国际间的商务交往也愈来愈频繁。为适应这一发展趋势与需求,许多高校愈来愈重视国际商务专业的建设与发展。不少外国语学院在发挥自身特色与优势、努力培养应用性和复合型人才的过程中积累了不少好的经验,与之相适应,商务英语类教程也"日新月异"。应该说业已出版的各种不同的商务英语类教材都有自己的特色,为外向型、应用型、复合型人才的培养发挥了作用。但毋庸讳言,不少教材的内容并不能很好地适应时代的需求:有的内容已显陈旧;有的篇幅容量过小,读过之后有"坐井观天"之感;有的人云亦云;有的编写体例则完全套用了英语精读教材的编写体例——面面俱到,应有尽有。

　　常州工学院外国语学院自1984年开办英语(外贸英语)专业,其毕业生大多在外经外贸外事领域工作,成绩斐然,深受社会好评。在二十几年的专业建设与发展过程中,我们深深感到,要办好一个专业,一个重要的、不可或缺的因素就是要有能为专业教学服务、体现时代要求和行业知识的教材。我们认为,商务英语阅读教程必须真正满足学生阅读面宽泛,知识面广博的要求,使学生在学习和阅读过程中能涉猎不同的学科领域,获取相应的知识,进而为日后的实际工作打下良好的基础。出于这一目的,我们经过一年多的准备,编写了《商务英语阅读新视野》教程。

　　《商务英语阅读新视野》教程共有50个单元,内容涉及经济、银行、金融、保险、财会、统计、物流、证券、外汇、外贸、产品、质量、品牌与商标、合资企业、跨国企业、企业文化、商务交流、国际经济组织、市场营销、全球化、地区化、营销策略与计划、人力资源管理、可持续发展、电子商务以及电子货币等等。绝大多数内容都比较新,体现了学术的前沿性、知识的时代性以及实用性。在这里我们要感谢戎佩珏同志,是她在英国赫尔大学攻读硕士学位期间,有意识地为我们搜集了不少可用的材料。

　　《商务英语阅读新视野》对文中背景知识及相对较难的词语提供了较为详

细的注释，免去了学习者阅读中的查询之苦；书中每个单元都设计了三种练习，一种是问答讨论题，一种是词汇的翻译，还有一种是短文翻译，以方便教师的课堂教学，检查学生的学习效果。书中每两个单元或三个单元涉及一个学科和行业知识。教师在课堂教学中可选一篇精讲，另一篇要求学生阅读自学。

《商务英语阅读新视野》由戎林海教授主编，负责全书的设计、材料的收集整理、全书书稿的审订；张春燕同志负责1～18单元的注释及练习的编写；承晓燕同志负责19～23、27、28、32～37、40～43单元的注释及练习的编写；其余单元的注释及练习的编写由戎佩珏同志和戎林海同志负责。

《商务英语阅读新视野》在编写过程中得到了东南大学出版社刘坚同志和常州工学院科研处徐伟同志的帮助与指导，谨向他们表示由衷的感谢。

《商务英语阅读新视野》既可作外国语学院英语（外贸英语）专业商务英语课程的教材，也可作工商管理学院国际经济与贸易专业课程的教材；既是外经外贸人员以及其他涉外人员提高自己、更新知识的阅读必备，也是英语学习爱好者的自学用书。

由于时间紧，编写仓促，书中讹误之处，敬请专家、读者批评指正。

戎林海
常州锦绣花园未厌斋
2007 年 7 月

CONTENTS

CONTENTS

Unit 1

Scarcity and Efficiency: the Twin Themes of Economics

What is economics? Over the last 30 years the study of economics has expanded to include a vast range of topics. What are the major definitions of this growing subject? The important ones are that economics:

- studies how the prices of labor, capital, and land are set in the economy, and how these prices are used to allocate resources.
- explores the behavior of the financial markets, and analyzes how they allocate capital to the rest of the economy.
- examines the distribution of income, and suggests ways that the poor can be helped without harming the performance of the economy.
- looks at the impact of government spending, taxes, and budget deficits on growth.
- studies the swings in unemployment and production that make up the business cycle, and develops government policies for improving economic growth.
- examines the patterns of trade among nations, and analyzes the impact of trade barriers.
- looks at growth in developing countries, and proposes ways to encourage the efficient use of resources.

This list is good one, yet you could extend it many times over. But if we boil down all these definitions, we find one common theme:

Economics is the study of how societies use scarce resources to produce valuable commodities and distribute them among different people.

Behind this definition are two key ideas in economics: that goods are scarce and that society must use its resources efficiently. Indeed, economics is an important subject because of the fact of scarcity and the desire for efficiency.

Take scarcity first. If infinite quantities of every good could be produced or if human desires were fully satisfied, what would be the consequences? People would not worry about stretching out their limited incomes, because they could have everything they wanted; businesses would not need to fret over the cost of labor or health care; governments would not need to struggle over taxes or spending, because nobody would care. Moreover, since all of us could have as most as we pleased, no one would be concerned about the distribution of incomes among different people or classes.

In such an Eden of affluence, there would be no economic goods, that is, goods that are scarce or limited in supply. All goods would be free, like sand in the desert or seawater at the beach. Prices and markets would be irrelevant. Indeed, economics would no longer be a useful subject.

But no society has reached a utopia of limitless possibilities. Goods are limited, while wants seem limitless. Even after two centuries of rapid economic growth, production in the United States is simply not high enough to meet everyone's desires. If you add up all the wants, you quickly find that there are simply not enough goods and services to satisfy even a small fraction of everyone's consumption desires. Our national output would have to be many times larger before the average American could live at the level of the average doctor or lawyer. And outside the United States, particularly in Africa and Asia, hundreds of millions of people suffer from hunger and material deprivation.

Given unlimited wants, it is important that an economy make the best use of its limited resources. That brings us to the critical notion of efficiency. Efficiency denotes the most effective use of a society's resources in satisfying people's wants and needs.

More specifically, the economy is producing efficiently when it cannot increase the economic welfare of anyone without making someone else worse off.

The essence of economics is to acknowledge the reality of scarcity and then figure out how to organize society in a way which produces the most efficient use of resources. That is where economics makes its unique contribution.

Microeconomics and Macroeconomics

Adam Smith is usually considered the founder of the field of microeconomics, the branch of economics which today is concerned with the behavior of individual entities such as markets, firms, and households. In *The Wealth of Nations*, Smith considered how individual prices are set, studied the determination of prices of land, labor, and capital, and inquired into the strengths and weaknesses of the market mechanism. Most important, he identified the remarkable efficiency properties of markets and saw that economic benefit comes from the self-interested actions of individuals. All these are still important issues today, and while the study of microeconomics has surely advance greatly since Smith's day, he is still cited by politicians and economists alike.

The other major branch of our subject is macroeconomics, which is concerned with the overall performance of the economy. Macroeconomics did not even exist in its modern form until 1935, when John Maynard Keynes published his revolutionary *General Theory of Employment, Interest and Money*. At the time, England and the United States were still stuck in the Great Depression of the 1930s, and over one-quarter of the American labor force was unemployed. In his new theory Keynes developed an analysis of what causes unemployment and economic downturns, how investment and consumption are determined, how central banks manage money and interest rates, and why some nations thrive while others stagnate. Keynes also argued that governments had an important role in smoothing out the ups and downs of business cycles. Although macroeconomics has progressed far since his first insights, the issues addressed by Keynes still define the study of macroeconomics today.

The two branches—microeconomics and macroeconomics—converge to form modern economics. At one time the boundary between the two areas was quite distinct; more recently, the two subdisciplines have merged as economists have applied the tools of microeconomics to such topics as unemployment and inflation.

Notes to the Text

1. swing: swinging movement, moving to and fro 摆动,变化
2. Eden of affluence: Eden 原意指《圣经》中人类始祖亚当和夏娃最初居住的伊甸园,Eden of affluence 指物质极为丰富的社会乐园。
3. given: taking something into account 考虑到(此处为介词)
4. Adam Smith: 亚当·斯密(1723—1790),苏格兰社会哲学家和经济学家;著有《国民财富的性质和原因的研究》,简称《国富论》,提出了自由竞争市场经济理论,是古典政治经济学的代表。
5. John Maynard Keynes: 约翰·梅纳德·凯恩斯(1883—1946),英国经济学家;著有《就业、利息和货币通论》,是现代西方经济学最有影响的经济学家之一。他不但是一个理论家,而且是一个实践家;曾在英国财政部工作,任《经济学杂志》主编,英国财政部巴黎和会代表,主持英国财政经济顾问委员会工作,出席布雷顿森林联合国货币金融会议,并担任了国际货币基金组织和国际复兴开发银行的董事。

Exercises

I Answer the following questions.

1. What is economics?
2. What are the two key ideas in economics? Why is the subject of economics important in the present world?
3. Can you describe an Eden of affluence briefly? Is economics useful in such a world?
4. What are the two subdisciplines of economics? What's the key difference between them? Are they absolutely isolated from each other?

II **Write out the equivalents of the following words and expressions.**

1. ups and downs
2. budget deficits
3. distribution of incomes
4. economic goods
5. market mechanism
6. utopia
7. 政府开支

8. 通货膨胀
9. 金融市场
10. 贸易周期
11. 劳动力成本
12. 经济福利
13. 微观经济学
14. 宏观经济学

III **Translate the following into Chinese.**

But no society has reached a utopia of limitless possibilities. Goods are limited, while wants seem limitless. Even after two centuries of rapid economic growth, production in the United States is simply not high enough to meet everyone's desires. If you add up all the wants, you quickly find that there are simply not enough goods and services to satisfy even a small fraction of everyone's consumption desires. Our national output would have to be many times larger before the average American could live at the level of the average doctor or lawyer. And outside the United States, particularly in Africa and Asia, hundreds of millions of people suffer from hunger and material deprivation.

Unit 2
The Three Problems of Economic Organization

Every human society—whether it is an advanced industrial nation, a centrally planned economy, or an isolated tribal nation—must confront and resolve three fundamental economic problems. Every society must have a way of determining what commodities are produced, how these goods are made, and for whom they are produced.

Indeed, these three fundamental questions of economic organization—what, how and for whom—are as crucial today as they were at the dawn of human civilization. Let's look more closely at them:

- What commodities are produced and in what quantities? A society must determine how much of each of the many possible goods and services it will make, and when they will be produced. Will we produce pizzas or shirts today? A few high-quality shirts or many cheap shirts? Will we use scarce resources to produce many consumption goods (like pizzas)? Or will we produce fewer consumption goods and more investment goods (like pizza-making machines), which will boost production and consumption tomorrow?

- How are goods produced? A society must determine who will do the production, with what resources, and what production techniques they will use. Who farms and who teaches? Is electricity generated from oil, from coal, or from the sun? With much air pollution or with little?

- For whom are goods produced? Who gets to eat the fruit of economic activity? Or, to put it formally, how is the national product divided among different households? Are many people poor and a few rich? Do high incomes go to managers or athletes or workers or landlords? Will society provide minimal consumption to the poor, or must they work if they are to survive?

Warning: in thinking about economic questions, we must distinguish questions of fact from question of fairness. Positive economics describes the facts of an economy, while normative economics involves value judgments.

Positive economics deals with questions such as: Why do doctors earn more than janitors? Does free trade raise or lower wages for most Americans? What is the economic impact of raising taxes? Although these are difficult questions to answer, they can all be resolved by reference to analysis and empirical evidence. That puts them in the realm of positive economics.

Normative economics involves ethical precepts and norms of fairness. Should poor people be required to work if they are to get government assistance? Should unemployment be raised to ensure that price inflation does not become too rapid? Should the United States penalize China because it is pirating U. S. books and CDs? There are no right or wrong answers to these questions because they involve ethics and values rather than facts. They can be resolved only by political debate and decisions, not by economic analysis alone.

Market, command, and mixed economics

What are the different ways that a society can answer the questions of *what*, *how and for whom*? Different societies are organized through *alternative systems*, and economics studies the various mechanisms that a society can use to allocate its scarce resources.

We generally distinguish two fundamentally different ways of organizing an economy. At one extreme, government makes most economic decisions, which those on top of the hierarchy giving economic commands to those further down the ladder. At the other extreme, decisions are made in markets, where individuals or enterprises voluntarily agree to exchange goods and services, usually through payments of money. Let's briefly examine each of these two forms of economic organization.

In the United States and most democratic countries, most economic questions are solved by the market. Hence their economic systems are called market economics. A market economy is one in which individuals and private firms make the major decisions about production and consumption. A system of prices, of markets, of profits and losses, of incentives and rewards determines *what*, *how and for whom*. Firms produce the commodities that yield the highest profits (the *what*) by the techniques of production that are least costly (the *how*). Consumption is determined by individuals' decisions about how to spend the wages and property incomes generated by their labor and property ownership (the *for whom*). The extreme case of a market economy, in which the government keeps its hands off economic decisions, is called a lasses-faire economy.

By contrast, a command economy is one in which the government makes all important decisions about production and distribution. In a command economy, such as the one which operated in the Soviet Union during most of the 20th century, the government owns most of the means of production (land and capital); it also owns and directs the operations of enterprises in most industries; it is the employer of most workers and tells them how to do their jobs; and it decided how the output of the society is to be divided among different goods and services. In short, in a command economy, the government answers the major economic questions through its ownership of resources and its power to enforce decisions.

No contemporary society falls completely into either of these polar categories. Rather, all societies are mixed economies, with elements of market and command. There has never been a 100 percent market economy (although nineteenth-century England came close).

Today most decisions in the United States are made in the marketplace. But the government plays an important role in overseeing the functioning of the market; governments pass laws that regulate economic life, produce educational and police services, and control pollution. Most societies today operate mixed economics.

Notes to the Text

1. pirate: to illegally copy and sell another person's work such as book, design, or invention 非法翻印, 非法仿制; 盗版
2. alternative system: 可选择的体系, 另一种体系
3. lasses-faire economy: 自由经济 (lasses-faire 自由, 放任, 不干涉)
4. polar: completely opposite in kind or quality 完全相反的, 正好相反的

Exercises

Ⅰ **Answer the following questions.**

1. What are the three problems of economic organization?
2. What does positive economics and normative economics deal with respectively?
3. What are the two polar categories of economy? Please cite an example for both.
4. Does the U. S. government play an important role in the American economy? And in what way?
5. Which category of economy does the Chinese economy fall into?

Ⅱ **Write out the equivalents of the following words and expressions.**

1. centrally planned economy
2. consumption goods
3. command economy
4. profits and losses
5. property incomes
6. mixed economics
7. 实际经济学

8. 规范经济学
9. 自由贸易
10. 市场经济
11. 财产所有权
12. 稀有资源
13. 生产资料

Ⅲ **Translate the following into Chinese.**

Every human society—whether it is an advanced industrial nation, a centrally planned economy, or an isolated tribal nation—must confront and resolve three fundamental economic problems. Every society must have a way of determining what commodities are produced, how these goods are made, and for whom they are produced.

Indeed, these three fundamental questions of economic organization—what, how and for whom—are as crucial today as they were at the dawn of human civilization.

Unit 3

The Principle of Comparative Advantage

It is only common sense that countries will produce and export goods for which they are uniquely qualified. But there is a deeper principle underlying all trade—in a family, within a nation, and among nations—that goes beyond common sense. The principle of comparative advantage holds that a country can benefit from trade even if it is absolutely more efficient (or absolutely less efficient) than other countries in the production of every good. Indeed, trade according to comparative advantage provides mutual benefits to all countries.

Uncommon sense

Say that the United States has higher output per worker (or per unit of input) than the rest of the world in making both computers and grain. But suppose the United States is relatively more efficient in computers than it is in grain. For example, it might be 50 percent more productive in computers and 10 percent more productive in grain. In this case, it would benefit the United States to export that good in which it is relatively more efficient (computers) and import that good in which it is relatively less efficient (grain).

Or consider a poor country like Mali. How could impoverished Mali, whose workers use handlooms and have productivity that is only a fraction of that of industrialized countries, hope to export any of its textiles? Surprisingly, according to the principle of comparative advantage, Mali can benefit by exporting the goods in which it is relatively more efficient (like textiles) and importing those goods which it produces relatively less efficiently (like turbines and automobiles).

The principle of comparative advantage holds that each country will benefit if it specializes in the production and export of those goods that it can produce at relatively low cost. Conversely, each country will benefit if it imports those goods which it produces at relatively high cost. This simple principle provides the unshakable basis for international trade.

The logic of comparative advantage

To explain the principle of comparative advantage, we begin with a simple example of specialization among people and then move to the more general case of comparative advantage among nations.

Consider the case of the best lawyer in town who is also the best typist in town. How should the lawyer spend her time? Should she write and type her own legal briefs? Or should she leave the typing to her secretary? Clearly, the lawyer should concentrate on legal activities, where her relative or comparative skills are most effectively used, even though she has absolutely greater skills in both typing and legal work.

Or look at it from the secretary's point of view. He is a fine typist, but his legal briefs are likely to lack sound legal reasoning and be full of errors. He is absolutely less efficient than the lawyer both in writing and in typing, but he is relatively or comparatively more efficient in typing.

In this scenario, the greatest efficiency will occur when the lawyer specializes in legal work and the secretary concentrates on typing. The most efficient and productive pattern of specialization occurs when people or nations concentrate on activities in which they are relatively or comparatively more efficient than others; this implies that some people or nations may specialize in areas in which they are absolutely less efficient than others. But even though individual people or countries may differ in absolute efficiency from all other people and countries, each and every person or country will have a definite comparative advantage in some goods and a definite comparative disadvantage in other goods.

Ricardo's analysis of comparative advantage

Let us illustrate the fundamental principles of international trade by considering America and Europe of a century ago. If labor (or resources, more generally) is absolutely more productive in America than in Europe, does this mean that America will import nothing? And is it economically wise for Europe to "protect" its markets with tariffs or quotas?

These questions were first answered in 1817 by the English economist David Ricardo, who showed that international specialization benefits a nation. He called this result the law of comparative advantage.

For simplicity, Ricardo worked with only two regions and only two goods, and he chose to measure all production costs in terms of labor-hours. We will follow his lead here, analyzing food and clothing for Europe and America.

In America, it takes 1 hour of labor to produce a unit of food, while a unit of clothing requires 2 hours of labor. In Europe the cost is 3 hours of labor for food and 4 hours of labor for clothing. We see that America has absolute advantage in both goods, for it can produce them with greater absolute efficiency than can Europe. However, America has comparative advantage in food, while Europe has comparative advantage in clothing, because food is relatively inexpensive in America while clothing is relatively less expensive in Europe.

From these facts, Ricardo proved that both regions will benefit if they specialize in their areas of comparative advantage—that is, if America specializes in the production of food while Europe specializes in the production of clothing. In this situation, America will export food to pay for European clothing, while Europe will export clothing to pay for American food.

　　To analyze the effects of trade, we must measure the amounts of food and clothing that can be produced and consumed in each region (1) if there is no international trade and (2) if there is free trade with each region specializing in its area of comparative advantage.

　　Before Trade. Start by examining what occurs in the absence of any international trade, say, because all trade is illegal or because of a prohibitive tariff. **Table** shows the real wage of the American worker for an hour's work as 1 unit of food or 1/2 unit of clothing. The European worker earns only 1/3 unit of food or 1/4 unit of clothing per hour of work. Clearly, if perfect competition prevails in each isolated region, the prices of food and clothing will be different in the two places because of the difference in production costs. In America, clothing will be 2 times as expensive as food because it takes twice as much labor to produce a unit of clothing as it does to produce a unit of food. In Europe, clothing will be only 4/3 as expensive as food.

American and European Labor Requirements for Production

Product	Necessary labor for production (labor-hours)	
	In America	In Europe
1 unit of food	1	3
1 unit of clothing	2	4

TABLE　Comparative Advantage Depends Only on Relative Costs

　　After Trade. Now suppose that all tariffs are repealed and free trade is allowed. For simplicity, further assume that there are no transportation costs. What is the flow of goods when trade is opened up? Clothing is relatively more expensive in America, and food is relatively more expensive in Europe. Given these relative prices, and with no tariffs or transportation costs, food will soon be shipped from America to Europe and clothing from Europe to America.

　　As European clothing penetrates the American market, American clothiers will find prices falling and profits shrinking, and they will begin to shut down their factories. By contrast, European farmers will find that the prices of foodstuffs begin to fall when American products hit the European markets; they will suffer losses, some will go bankrupt, and resources will be withdrawn from farming.

　　After all the adjustments to international trade have taken place, the prices of clothing and food must be equalized in Europe and America (just as the water in two connecting pipes must come to a common level once you remove the barrier between them). Without further knowledge about the exact supplies and demands, we cannot know the exact level to which prices will move. But we do know that the relative prices of food and clothing must lie somewhere between the European price ratio (which is 3/4 for the ratio of food to clothing prices) and the American price ratio (which is $1/2$). Let us say that the final ratio is $2/3$, so 2 units of clothing trade for 3 units of food. For simplicity, we measure prices in American dollars and assume that the free-trade price of food is $2 per unit, which means that the free-trade price of clothing is $3 per unit.

With free trade, the regions have shifted their productive activities. America has withdrawn resources from clothing and produces food, while Europe has contracted its farm sector and expanded its clothing manufacture. Under free trade, countries shift production toward their areas of comparative advantage.

The economic gains from trade

What are the economic effects of opening up the two regions to international trade? America as a whole benefits from the fact that imported clothing costs less than clothing produced at home. Likewise, Europe benefits by specializing in clothing and consuming food that is less expensive than domestics produced food.

We can most easily reckon the gains from trade by calculating the effect of trade upon the real wage of workers. Real wages are measured by the quantity of goods that a worker can buy with an hour's pay. Using **Table**, we can see that the real wages after trade will be greater than the real wages before trade for workers in both Europe and America. For simplicity, assume that each worker buys 1 unit of clothing and 1 unit of food. Before trade, this bundle of goods costs an American worker 3 hours of work and a European worker 7 hours of work.

After trade has opened up, as we found, the price of clothing is $3 per unit while the price of food is $2 per unit. An American worker must still work 1 hour to buy a unit of food; but at the price ratio of 2 to 3 the American worker needs to work only 1.5 hours to produce enough to buy 1 unit of European clothing. Therefore the bundle of goods costs the American worker 2.5 hours of work when trade is allowed—this represents an increase of 20 percent in the real wage of the American worker.

For European workers, a unit of clothing will still cost 4 hours of labor in a free-trade situation, for clothing is domestically produced. To obtain a unit of food, however, the European worker needs to produce only $2/3$ of a unit of clothing (which requires $2/3 \times 4$ hours of labor) and then trade that $2/3$ clothing unit for 1 unit of American food. The total European labor needed to obtain the bundle of consumption is then $4 + 2\frac{2}{3} = 6\frac{2}{3}$, which represents an increase in real wages of about 5 percent over the no-trade situation.

When countries concentrate on their areas of comparative advantage under free trade, each country is better off. Compared to a no trade situation, workers in each region can obtain a larger quantity of consumer goods for the same amount of work when they specialize in the areas of comparative advantage and trade their own production for goods in which they have a relative disadvantage.

In a hypothetical example, America has lower labor costs in both food and clothing.

American labor productivity is between 2 and 3 times Europe's (twice in clothing, thrice in food).

Notes to the Text

1. brief: a short spoken or written statement giving facts about a law case 案情摘要, 辩护状

2. scenario: a situation that could possibly happen but has not happened yet 事态, 局面

3. David Ricardo: 大卫·李嘉图(1772—1823), 英国著名经济学家, 是最早使经济学系统化的思想家。其代表作为《政治经济学及赋税原理》。他进一步发展了亚当·斯密的"地域分工论", 提出了以"比较成本学说"为核心的国际贸易理论。这一学说及其以后对该学说的补充、发展, 被称为"国际贸易纯粹理论"或"一般理论"。

4. go bankrupt: to be unable to pay your debts and to have to sell your property and goods 破产, 倒闭

Exercises

I **Answer the following questions.**

1. Could you cite an example to explain the principle of comparative advantage briefly?

2. How can different nations benefit from the principle of comparative advantage?

3. Do you think a country can produce all the goods it needs? What makes international trade possible?

4. What can ordinary workers gain from specialization?

II **Write out the equivalents of the following words and expressions.**

1. comparative advantage   6. 配额
2. industrialized country   7. 实际工资
3. prohibitive tariff   8. 生产成本
4. economic gains   9. 商品流动
5. price ratio   10. 消费品

III **Translate the following into Chinese.**

We can most easily reckon the gains from trade by calculating the effect of trade upon the real wage of workers. Real wages are measured by the quantity of goods that a worker can buy with an hour's pay. Using Table, we can see that the real wages after trade will be greater than the real wages before trade for workers in both Europe and America. For simplicity, assume that each worker buys 1 unit of clothing and 1 unit of food. Before trade, this bundle of goods costs an American worker 3 hours of work and a European worker 7 hours of work.

After trade has opened up, as we found, the price of clothing is $ 3 per unit while the price of food is $ 2 per unit. An American worker must still work 1 hour to buy a unit of food; but at the price ratio of 2 to 3 the American worker needs to work only 1.5 hours to produce enough to buy 1 unit of European clothing. Therefore the bundle of goods costs the American worker 2.5 hours of work when trade is allowed—this represents an increase of 20 percent in the real wage of the American worker.

Unit 4

What Is Logistics

In the early part of 1991 the world was given a dramatic example of the importance of logistics. As a precursor to the Gulf War it had been necessary for the United States and its allies to move huge amounts of material great distances in what were thought to be impossibly short time-frames. Half a million people and over half a million tons of material and supplies were airlifted 12,000 kilometers with a further 2.3 million tons of equipment moved by sea—all of this achieved in a matter of months.

Throughout the history of mankind wars have been won and lost through logistics strengths and capabilities—or the lack of them. It has been argued that the defeat of the British in the American War of Independence can largely be attributed to logistics failure. The British Army in America depended almost entirely upon Britain for supplies. At the height of the war there were 12,000 troops overseas and for the most part they had not only to be equipped, but fed from Britain. For the first six years of the war the administration of these vital supplies was totally inadequate, affecting the course of operations and the morale of the troops. An organization capable of supplying the army was not developed until 1781 and by then it was too late.

In the Second World War logistics also played a major role. The Allied Forces' invasion of Europe was a highly skilled exercise in logistics, as was the defeat of Rommel in the desert. Rommel himself once said that, "... before the fighting proper, the battle is won or lost by quartermasters."

However while the Generals and Field Marshals from the earliest times have understood the critical role of logistics, strangely it is only in the recent past that business organizations have come to recognize the vital impact that logistics management can have in the achievement of competitive advantage. This lack of recognition partly springs from the relative level of understanding of benefit of integrated logistics. Arch Shaw, writing in 1915, pointed out that:

> The relations between the activities of demand creation and physical supply... illustrate the existence of the two principles of interdependence and balance. Failure to co-ordinate any one of these activities with its group fellows and also with those in the other group, or undue emphasis or outlay put upon any one of these activities, is certain to upset the equilibrium of forces which means efficient distribution.
>
> The physical distribution of the goods is a problem distinct from the creation of

demand... Not a few worthy failures in distribution campaigns have been due to such a lack of co-ordination between demand creation and physical supply...

Instead of being a subsequent problem, this question of supply must be met and answered before the work of distribution begins.

It has taken a further 70 years or so for the basic principles of logistics management to be clearly defined.

What is logistics management in the sense that it is understood today? There are many ways of defining logistics but the underlying concept might be defined as follows:

Logistics is the process of strategically managing the procurement, movement and storage of materials, parts and finished inventory (and the related information flows) through the organization and its marketing channels in such a way that current and future profitability are maximized through the cost-effective fulfillment of orders.

This basic definition will be extended and developed as the book progresses, but it makes an adequate starting point.

It is through the logistical process that materials flow into the manufacturing capacity of an industrial nation and products are distributed to consumers. The recent growth of global commerce and the introduction of e-commerce have expanded the size of complexity of logistical operations.

Logistics adds value to the supply chain process when inventory is strategically positioned to achieve sales. Creating logistics value is costly. Although difficult to measure, most experts agree that the annual expenditure to perform logistics in the United States was approximately 10.1 percent of the $9.96 billion Gross Nation Product (GNP) or $1.006 billion. The logistics of business is truly big business!

Despite the sheer size of logistical expenditure, the excitement of lean logistics is not cost containment or reduction. The excitement generates from understanding how select firms use logistical competency to achieve competitive advantage. Firms that have developed world-class logistical competency enjoy competitive advantage as a result of providing important customers superior service. Leading logistical performers typically implement information technology capable of monitoring global logistical activity on a real time basis. Such technology identifies potential operational breakdowns and facilitates corrective action prior to delivery service failure. In situations where timely corrective action is not possible, customers can be provided advance notification of developing problems, thereby eliminating the surprise of an unavoidable service failure. In many situations, working in collaboration with customers and suppliers, corrective action can be taken to prevent operational shutdowns or costly customer service failures. By performing at above industry average with respect to inventory availability, speed and consistency of delivery, and operational efficiencies, logistically sophisticated firms are ideal supply chain partners.

Notes to the Text

1. time-frames：the length of time that is used or available for something（事情发生或安排发生的）时间范围，时限

2. morale：the level of confidence and positive feelings, especially among a group of people who work together 士气

3. physical distribution：the process of transporting goods from the producers to the consumers, including transportation and storage 实物分销

4. Rommel：艾尔温·隆美尔（1891—1944），第二次世界大战期间德国陆军元帅，外号"沙漠之狐"，有惊人的军事才能，1944年因被控参与谋杀希特勒而被迫服毒自杀。

5. field marshal：an officer of the highest rank in the British army 陆军元帅

6. Arch Shaw：阿克·肖，美国市场营销研究的先驱，是最早提出物流概念并进行实际探讨的学者；1915年出版《市场流通中的若干问题》一书，是物流理论与实践的基础。

7. equilibrium：a state of balance, especially between opposing forces or influences 平衡，均势

8. cost-effective：giving the best possible profit or benefits in comparison with the money that is spent 有成本效益的，划算的

9. select：carefully chosen out of a large group of people or things 杰出的，优秀的

10. at above industry average：at a level above the average of a certain industry 超出行业平均水平的

Exercises

I Answer the following questions.

1. Could you cite an example to illustrate the importance of logistics in the war?

2. When did the basic principles of logistics take shape?

3. How do select firms use logistical competency to achieve comparative advantage?

4. Do you think the business of logistics big business?

II Write out the equivalents of the following words and expressions.

1. integrated logistics

2. demand creation

3. manufacturing capacity

4. Gross National product

5. annual expenditure

6. 存货

7. 信息流

8. 营销渠道

9. 供应链

10. 成本控制

11. 操作故障

III Translate the following into Chinese.

Firms that have developed world-class logistical competency enjoy competitive advantage as a result of providing important customers superior service. Leading logistical performers typically implement information technology capable of monitoring global logistical activity on a real time basis. Such technology identifies potential operational breakdowns and facilitates corrective action prior to delivery service failure. In situations where timely corrective action is not possible, customers can be provided advance notification of developing problems, thereby eliminating the surprise of an unavoidable service failure. In many situations, working in collaboration with customers and suppliers, corrective action can be taken to prevent operational shutdowns or costly customer service failures. By performing at above industry average with respect to inventory availability, speed and consistency of delivery, and operational efficiencies, logistically sophisticated firms are ideal supply chain partners.

Unit 5

Logistical Operation

The internal operational scope of integrated logistic operations is illustrated by the shade area of **Figure**. Information from and about customers flows through the enterprise in the form of sales activity, forecasts, and orders. Vital information is refined into specific manufacturing, merchandising, and purchasing plans. As products and materials are procured, a value-added inventory flow is initiated which ultimately results in ownership transfer of finished products to customers. Thus, the process is viewed in terms of two interrelated flows: inventory and information. While internal integrative management is important to success, the firm must also integrate across the supply chain. To be fully effective in today's competitive environment, firms must extend their enterprise integration to incorporate customers and suppliers. This extension reflects the position of logistics in the broader perspective of supply chain management.

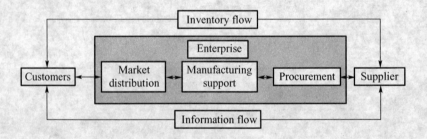

FIGURE   Logistical Integration

Inventory flow

The operational management of logistics is concerned with movement and storage of materials and finished products. Logistical operations start with the initial shipment of a material or component part from a supplier and are finalized when a manufactured or processed product is delivered to a customer.

From the initial purchase of a material or component, the logistics process adds value by moving inventory when and where needed. Providing all goes well, materials and components gain value at each step of their transformation into finished inventory. In other words, an individual part has greater value after it is incorporated into a machine than it had as a part. Likewise, the machine has greater value once it is delivered to a customer.

To support manufacturing, work-in-process inventory must be properly positioned. The cost of each component and its movement becomes part of the value-added process. For better understanding, it is useful to divide logistical operations into three areas: (1) market distribution, (2) manufacturing support, and (3) procurement.

1. Market distribution

The movement of finished product to customers is market distribution. In market distribution, the end customer represents the final destination. The availability of product is a vital part of each channel participant's marketing effort. Even a manufacturer's agent, who typically does not own inventory, must be supported by inventory availability to perform expected marketing responsibilities. Unless a proper assortment of products is efficiently delivered when and where needed, a great deal of the overall marketing effort will be jeopardized. It is through the market distribution process that the timing and geographical placement of inventory become an integral part of marketing. To support the wide variety of marketing systems that exist in a highly commercialized nation, many different market distribution systems are available. All market distribution systems have one common feature: they link manufacturers, wholesalers and retailers into supply chains to provide product availability.

2. Manufacturing support

The area of manufacturing support concentrates on managing work-in-process inventory as it flows between stages of manufacturing. The primary logistical responsibility in manufacturing is to participate in formulating a master production schedule and to arrange for its implementation by timely availability of materials, component parts and work-in-process inventory. Thus, the overall concern of manufacturing support is not how production occurs but rather what, when, and where products will be manufactured.

Manufacturing support is significantly different from market distribution. Market distribution attempts to service the desires of customers and therefore must accommodate the uncertainty of consumer and industrial demand. Manufacturing support involves movement requirements that are under the control of the manufacturing enterprise. The uncertainties introduced by random customer ordering and erratic demand that market distribution must accommodate are not typical in manufacturing operations. From the viewpoint of overall planning, the separation of manufacturing support from outbound market distribution and inbound procurement activities provides opportunities for specialization and improved efficiency. The degree to which a firm adopts a response strategy serves to reduce or eliminate the separation of manufacturing.

3. Procurement

Procurement is concerned with purchasing and arranging inbound movement of materials, parts and/or finished inventory from suppliers to manufacturing or assembly plants, warehouses or retail stores. Depending on the situation, the acquisition process is commonly identified by different names. In manufacturing, the process of acquisition is typically called purchasing. In government circles, acquisition has traditionally been referred to as procurement. In retailing and wholesaling, buying is the most widely used term. In many circles, the process is referred to as inbound logistics. For the purposes of this text, the term procurement will include all types of purchasing. The term material is used to identify inventory moving inbound to an enterprise, regardless of its degree of readiness for resale. The term product is used to identify inventory that is available for consumer purchase. In other words, materials are involved in the process of adding value through manufacturing whereas products are ready for consumption. The fundamental distinction is that products result from the value added to material during manufacture, sortation, or assembly.

Within a typical enterprise, the three logistics operating areas overlap. Viewing each as an integral part of the overall value-adding process creates an opportunity to capitalize on the unique attributes of each within the overall process. The overall challenge of a supply chain is to integrate the logistical processes of participating firms in a manner that facilitates overall efficiency.

Notes to the Text

1. shade area: the area with shade in it 阴影部分
2. jeopardize: to risk harming or destroying somebody or something 使危险，危害
3. overlap: to cover something partly and go beyond it. 与（某物）交搭，叠盖

I Answer the following questions.

1. What's the position of logistics in the broader perspective of supply chain management?
2. What are the three areas of logistical operations?
3. What is market distribution? What are the common features of market distribution system?
4. What's the difference between market distribution and manufacturing support?
5. Do you think the logistical operation a value-adding process? Why or why not?

II **Write out the equivalents of the following words and expressions.**

1. inventory flow
2. ownership transfer
3. internal integrative management
4. market distribution
5. response strategy

6. 制成品
7. 物流操作管理
8. 最终用户
9. 高度商业化国家
10. 增值税

III **Translate the following into Chinese.**

Procurement is concerned with purchasing and arranging inbound movement of materials, parts and/or finished inventory from suppliers to manufacturing or assembly plants, warehouses or retail stores. Depending on the situation, the acquisition process is commonly identified by different names. In manufacturing, the process of acquisition is typically called purchasing. In government circles, acquisition has traditionally been referred to as procurement. In retailing and wholesaling, buying is the most widely used term. In many circles, the process is referred to as inbound logistics. For the purposes of this text, the term procurement will include all types of purchasing. The term material is used to identify inventory moving inbound to an enterprise, regardless of its degree of readiness for resale. The term product is used to identify inventory that is available for consumer purchase. In other words, materials are involved in the process of adding value through manufacturing whereas products are ready for consumption. The fundamental distinction is that products result from the value added to material during manufacture, sortation, or assembly.

Unit 6

Tips to Establish Your Good Business Reputation

I have long believed that a good reputation is the most valuable asset you can have in business. By reputation, I mean that what people think of the way you do business and how they assess your character as a businessperson. Do you compete fairly? Do you run a nice, clean operation? Do you treat your employees well? Do you go around bad-mouthing other companies in the industry, or do you speak about them with respect?

Those are all factors that help to shape your business reputation, which in turn affects your ability to hire people, attract customers, get financing, make deals, and do everything else that goes into building a successful company.

What's interesting is the role your competitors play in the process. Their opinion, I believe, counts more than the view of any other group. Why? Because of their credibility within the industry and with potential customers. Competitors have a unique perspective on you and your company. They face the same pressures and have to make the same choices that you do. If you have the respect of your competitors, you probably deserve it. If they think you are a lowlife, you're headed for trouble.

So it's important to act in a way that's going to earn their respect. Not that you shouldn't compete as aggressively as possible, but you need to play by the rules. Which rules? I have three:

Never bad-mouth a competitor. When I compete for an account, I always ask which other suppliers the prospective customer is considering. Most prospects name the same two or three records-storage companies, our major competitors. "Those are all fine companies," I say, "and you are going to be happy if you choose any one of us. Of course, I think you'll be happiest with my company." Then I talk about our strong points, taking care not to say anything negative about the other companies.

To be sure, the customer occasionally includes on the list a company I don't hold in such high regard. In that case, I simply say, "Well, that firm isn't really a competitor of ours, but the others we compete against all the time, and they are very good. I just think we are better, and here's why."

Don't be a sore loser. It's always tough when a competitor takes a customer away from you, especially if the account is a big one. What happens? You get angry. You can't help it. But you have to remind yourself that you never know what the future holds. The people you deal with at the account may not agree with the decision to switch suppliers; if they go to work somewhere else, they could bring you another customer. Even the customer you just lost come back again someday, provided you keep yourself cool. In any case, you can only hurt yourself by letting your anger show.

So, no matter how upset I may feel inside, I make sure we treat our customers as well when they leave as we do when they come in. I want them to remember us as a class act all the way, and I want our competitors to hear about it.

Always be accommodating. There are times when we have to deal directly with competitors—for example, when a customer is moving into or out of our warehouse. That's an opportunity for us to send our competitors a message. Even if someone is taking a big account away from us, we're as nice as we can be. We acquiesce to the other company's schedule and handle the process however the competitor wants us to.

We are equally accommodating when we're moving a new customer out of a competitor's facility. We tell our drivers to be patient if they're kept waiting, as they often are. They can take all the day if they have to. We don't want to provoke any fights or arguments, and we don't want to rub salt in a competitor's wound.

Notes to the Text

1. bad-mouth: to speak badly of or criticize somebody 说人坏话,批评
2. lowlife: people who are outside normal societies, especially criminals 社会渣滓
3. account: a customer esp. one who has regular dealings with a company 老客户,老主顾
4. keep cool: to remain calm in a difficult situation（在困难情况下）保持冷静
5. accommodating: willing to help and do things for somebody 乐于助人的,与人方便的
6. acquiesce: to accept something without arguing, even if you do not really agree with it 默认,默许,勉强同意
7. rub salt in sb's wound: to make a bad situation even worse for someone 在某人的伤口上撒盐,雪上加霜

Exercises

I Answer the following questions.

1. What factors possibly help to shape the business reputation of a company?
2. How can your competitors help you to improve your business reputation?
3. What should you do when your competitor take a big account from you?

4. In your opinion, what is the proper way of treating your competitors?

5. What can a business do to attract and keep its customers?

II **Write out the equivalents of the following words and expressions.**

1. credibility   0. class act
2. make deals   7. 商业信誉
3. record-storage companies   8. 公平竞争
4. switch suppliers   9. 潜在顾客
5. company schedule   10. 融资

III **Translate the following into Chinese.**

It's always tough when a competitor takes a customer away from you, especially if the account is a big one. What happens? You get angry. You can't help it. But you have to remind yourself that you never know what the future holds. The people you deal with at the account may not agree with the decision to switch suppliers; if they go to work somewhere else, they could bring you another customer. Even the customer you just lost come back again someday, provided you keep yourself cool. In any case, you can only hurt yourself by letting your anger show.

So, no matter how upset I may feel inside, I make sure we treat our customers as well when they leave as we do when they come in. I want them to remember us as a class act all the way, and I want our competitors to hear about it.

Unit 7

Business Law

Business law refers to the branch of a law which consists of rules, statutes, codes and regulations established to provide a legal framework within which business may be conducted. Since every business must operate within the law, it is imperative for those involved in business to understand the basics of business law.

Contract law

A contract is a legally enforceable agreement between two or more parties and must contain the following five elements, namely, lawful purpose, competency of parties, voluntary agreement, consideration, and proper form.

Contracts with all the five elements listed above are legally enforceable. If you have such a contract and the other party fails to perform his duties as stipulated by the contract, he is said to be guilty of breach of contract. You, as the injured party, may cancel the contract, sue for damages, or ask for a court order forcing the other party to carry out the terms of the contract.

Tort law

Tort is a French word which means "wrong". In legal terminology, tort means a civil or private wrongful act by one party which results in injury to another party's body, property or reputation. Torts may come from negligence. Torts may also result from the deliberate actions by a person or a firm.

As there is a lot of uncertainties regarding the nature of torts, legislative bodies of many countries are working out new laws which will give torts clearer definitions. Both business firms and ordinary people should follow the development to better protect their rights and interests.

Property law

Property is anything of value that is owned by an individual or a business.
(1) Types of property

According to its attributes, property can be classified into three types. They are tangible real property, tangible personal property and intangible personal property. A special type of intangible personal property is intellectual property which includes trademarks, copyrights and patents.

（2）Title to property

When a consumer buys a T-shirt from a garment seller, the title to the T-shirt is transferred from the seller to the buyer. When goods of a more complex nature are shipped over long distance, however, problems concerning transfer of title often occur. To help you better deal with such problems, familiarize yourself with the following five rules.

First, if you have your goods delivered to a specific place, title passes to you when goods are delivered and arrive at that place. Second, if your purchase is on a trial basis, you become the owner if you pay for the goods or if you keep them for a reasonable long period. Third, if you buy an item on COD (cash on delivery) basis, title passes to you when the item is in transit after being delivered by the seller to the carrier. Fourth, if you purchase FOB (free on board) shipping point of shipment, title passes to you when the item is on board. Finally, if you purchase an item which requires installation as part of the purchase agreement, title will not pass to you upon delivery unless the installation is completed.

Agency law

Oftentimes, firms authorize people to act on their behalf. The firms are called principals and the authorized people are known as agents. And the law governing such relationships is called agency law, which forms an important part of business law.

Agents may be insiders (e.g. the partners of a partnership, the managers of a company) or outsiders who are hired and authorized to act on behalf of an organization. We'll focus our discussion on the latter.

If the authority given by the principal to the agent is based on a written contract, the authority is said to be expressed. On the other hand, if the authority of the agent is derived from business customers, it is said to be implied. There are also occasions when the agent does so, the agent is then said to act with apparent authority.

The principals, of course, have their responsibilities. They must give their agents equitable compensation, bear related business expenses, and inform the agents of the risks involved in the business. Principals are also responsible for the actions of their agents if they act within their terms of reference.

Bankruptcy laws

According to the bankruptcy laws in the US, a petition for bankruptcy can be filed with an appropriate court by the debtor, or by its creditors. If the debtor takes the initiative, the process is called voluntary bankruptcy; otherwise, it is referred to as involuntary bankruptcy. In either case, the debtor becomes bankrupt.

When a business goes bankrupt, most of its creditors can collect only a portion of the debt owed to them. Therefore, many creditors would rather work out an extension agreement with the debtor and give the latter an extension of payment terms. They hope that during the extension the debtor can be back on his feet again. Or the creditors can work out a composition agreement, in which case every creditor will take a cut on the debt owed to him. In either case, the creditors can demand some role in the debtor's management to make sure their interests are best protected.

Notes to the Text

1. statute: a law passed by a law-making body and formally written down 法令,法规;成文法

2. court order: a decision that is made in a court of law about what must happen in a particular situation 法庭命令,庭谕

3. tort: wrongful but not criminal act, that can be dealt with in a civil court of law 民事侵权行为

4. COD: cash on delivery 现金提货,货到付款

5. principal: a person for whom someone else acts as a representative, esp. in a piece of business 委托人

Exercises

Ⅰ Answer the following questions.

1. What's the function of business law?
2. If a party to a contract violates the contract terms, what should the other party do?
3. Could you give an example for tangible real property, tangible personal property and intangible personal property?
4. In what way do you think agent can help the principals in expanding business?

Ⅱ Write out the equivalents of the following words and expressions.

1. breach of contract
2. contract terms
3. legislative body
4. tangible real property
5. transfer of title
6. voluntary bankruptcy
7. 权利和利益
8. 知识产权
9. 合同法
10. 付款方式
11. 离岸价
12. 业务开支

Ⅲ Translate the following into Chinese.

First, if you have your goods delivered to a specific place, title passes to you when goods are delivered and arrive at that place. Second, if your purchase is on a trial basis, you become the owner if you pay for the goods or if you keep them for a reasonable long period. Third, if you buy an item on COD(cash on delivery) basis, title passes to you when the item is in transit after being delivered by the seller to the carrier. Fourth, if you purchase FOB (free on board) shipping point of shipment, title passes to you when the item is on board. Finally, if you purchase an item which requires installation as part of the purchase agreement, title will not pass to you upon delivery unless the installation is completed.

Unit 8

Everyday Etiquette for Office Life

Most bosses expect their employees to get along with one and another, and more important, to get along with clients and customers. This means that however important your job skills are, they may not count for much if you don't also have some people skills. Fortunately, getting along with people usually boils down to simple, everyday courtesy.

When you work for a company, you are its representative to the outside world. For this reason, everyone from a secretary to a CEO should know how to greet visitors and make them feel comfortable.

Both men and women should stand to greet visitors who come into their office. Co-workers also should be given a warm greeting, but you need not rise each time one comes into your office. For a visitor, though, your hand should be extended just as it would be if you were the host in your own home. Ask the person to sit down; and if there is a choice of seats, you may want to wave him into one.

Many managers and executives sit behind their desks when talking to co-workers and customers, but it is more gracious to move a conversation out to a sofa or two occasional chairs. Visitors should be asked whether they would like a beverage. If the answer is yes, the manager should get the drink or ask a secretary or assistant to get it.

Although corporate cultures vary from business to business and even from region to region, the exchange of daily greetings is a ritual everywhere. Co-workers usually say hello first thing in the morning and then simply smile when they pass each other the rest of the day. No further verbal greeting is called for, and no one should take offense when a colleague doesn't stop to chat. It is considered rude, though, not to acknowledge fellow workers when you see them, even if it is for the fifteenth time in one day. You can nod or smile, but don't look the other way when you see someone.

Beyond routine greetings, how much people chitchat during the day generally depends on the atmosphere of the work environment. A formal, rigidly organized workplace may allow little room for casual conversation, while one that is informal and loosely organized leaves room for this kind of socializing. Sometimes talk is encouraged or discouraged by the nature of the work. A assemble line that involves heavy equipment or noise, for example, doesn't promote collegial chitchat, while an under-worked sales staff may spend most of its work day talking.

In many workplaces, the chitchat—especially that of extracurricular nature—is frowned on by management, and with good reason, since workers do have jobs to perform. Then the problem for an employee who wants to appear friendly is how to disengage from the friendly chatter without alienating co-workers.

When you must cut short a conversation to get to work, it helps to announce your reason in a friendly manner. For example, you might say, "I'd love to talk more, but I've got to finish the year-end budget report," or "Can't talk right now. I have to finish these estimates."

If you disengage graciously, there should be no problem except for those relatively few workers who don't get the message. In these cases a little less friendliness is called for. Don't smile broadly; don't stop to initiate a conversation. When a talker walks by, quickly say, "Hi there," but don't look up from your work expectantly. With time, they should get the message.

Notes to the Text

1. CEO: Chief Executive Officer 首席执行官
2. chitchat: conversation about things that are not important 闲谈,聊天
3. frown on: to disapprove of somebody or something 不赞成,不同意
4. alienate: to make somebody become unfriendly or unsympathetic or unwilling to give support 使疏远,离间,使不友好

I Answer the following questions.

1. Is it enough to have job skills only? What other skills are essential for the success of one's career?
2. As representatives of a company, what should they do to make the guests feel at home?
3. What should you do in order to be both friendly and effective in a company?
4. What's the importance of everyday etiquette in business circle? Could you give more examples?

II Write out the equivalents of the following words and expressions.

1. Chief Financial Officer
2. rigidly organized workplace
3. year-end budget report
4. co-worker
5. socializing
6. 销售人员
7. 装配线
8. 工作环境
9. 办公室礼仪
10. 企业文化

III Translate the following into Chinese.

In many workplaces, the chitchat—especially that of extracurricular nature—is frowned on by management, and with good reason, since workers do have jobs to perform. Then the problem for an employee who wants to appear friendly is how to disengage from the friendly chatter without alienating co-workers.

If you disengage graciously, there should be no problem except for those relatively few workers who don't get the message. In these cases a little less friendliness is called for. Don't smile broadly; don't stop to initiate a conversation. When a talker walks by, quickly say, "Hi there," but don't look up from your work expectantly. With time, they should get the message.

Unit 9

A Brief Introduction to Accounting

Accounting information is used for decision making in all types of organizations—business and nonbusiness—as well as by both managers and individual citizens. Every person in society would benefit from some knowledge of accounting since it is used wherever economic resources are employed.

Accountancy is a professional field which can lead to careers in a variety of areas, including public accounting firms, business firms, and governmental organizations. The work of the accountant centers on systems design, interpretation of financial data, and the preparation or review of financial statements. Financial statements show the results of an organization's operations over a given period of time, its current financial condition, and changes in its financial position.

The environment of accounting

Many decisions are made daily in our society that have economic consequences, such as whether our savings should be invested in savings account in a bank, in government bonds, or in the shares of stock issued by business corporations. We may feel that our savings can be quite safely invested in a savings account or in a government bond. But we are far less certain about the outcome of an investment in shares of stock. To make an informed decision, we need information about the economic activity of corporations that issue such shares. And it is here that accounting enters the picture, since accounting is a primary source of information on economic activity.

Since economic activity includes the production, exchange, and consumption of scarce goods, it is found everywhere in our society. Accounting is nearly as extensive. Accounting is needed to show what was accomplished at what cost. This is true whether resources are used by individuals, business firms, or not-for-profit entities such as churches, units of government, and hospitals. Although accounting is used in all types of organizations, our attention here will center on the accounting and re-porting by business firms.

Accounting is the process used to measure and report to various users relevant financial information regarding the economic activity of an organization or unit. Relevant information has some bearing upon a decision to be made. This information is primarily financial in nature that is, it is stated in money terms.

When persons first study accounting, they often confuse bookkeeping and accounting.

Bookkeeping involves the recording of business activities and is a very mechanical process. Accounting includes bookkeeping but goes well beyond it in scope. Among other functions, accountants prepare financial statements, conduct audits, design accounting systems, prepare special studies, prepare forecasts and budgets, do income tax work, and analyze and interpret financial information.

In performing their work, accountants observe the economic scene and select (or identify) those events they consider evidence of economic activity. (The purchase and sale of goods and services are examples.) Then they measure these selected events in financial terms. Next, they record these measurements to provide a permanent history of the financial activities of the organization. In order to report upon what has happened, accountants classify their measurements of recorded events into meaningful groups. The preparation of accounting reports will require that accountants summarize these measurements even further. Finally, accountants may be asked to interpret the contents of their statements and reports. Interpretations involve explanations of the uses, meanings, and limitations of accounting information. Attention may also be drawn to significant items through trend or ratio analysis.

Accounting may also be defined as an information system designed to provide, through the medium of financial statements, relevant financial information. In designing the system, accountants keep in mind the types of users of the information(owners, creditors, etc.) and the kinds of decisions they make that require financial information. Usually, the information provided relates to the economic resources owned by an organization, the claims against these resources, the changes in both resources and claims, and the results of using these resources for a given period of time.

Employment opportunities in accounting

In our society, accountants typically are employed in(1) public accounting, (2) private industry, or (3) the not-for-profit sector. Within each of these areas, specialization is possible; an accountant may, for example, be considered an expert in auditing, systems development, budgeting, cost accounting, or tax accounting.

Public accounting

A certified public accountant(CPA) must have passed a rigorous national examination prepared and graded by the American Institute of Certified Public Accountants(AICPA)—the accounting equivalent of the American Bar Association or the American Medical Association. Having passed the CPA examination and having met certain other requirements, such as having a certain number of years of experience, an individual may be licensed by the state to practice as a certified public accountant. As an independent professional, a CPA may offer clients auditing, management advisory, and tax services. Clients may be business firms, individuals, or not-for-profit organizations.

Auditing

When a business seeks a loan or seeks to have its securities traded on a stock exchange, it is usually required to provide statements on its financial affairs. Users of these statements may accept and rely upon them more freely when they are accompanied by an auditor's opinion(or report). The auditor's opinion pertains to the fairness of the statements. In order to have the knowledge necessary for an informed opinion, the CPA conducts an audit (examination) of the accounting and related records and seeks supporting evidence from external sources.

Management advisory services

Often from knowledge gained in an audit, CPAs offer suggestions to their clients on how to improve their operations. From these and other contacts, CPAs may be engaged to provide a wide range of management advisory services. Such services tend to be accounting related; for example, they may include the design and installation of an accounting system or services in the areas of electronic data processing, inventory control, budgeting, or financial planning.

Tax services

CPAs also provide expert advice for the preparation of federal, state, and local tax returns. The objective is to determine the proper amount of taxes due. Of equal importance, because of high tax rates and complex tax laws, is tax planning. Proper tax planning requires that the tax effects, if any, of every major business decision be known and considered before the decision is made.

Private or industrial accounting

Accountants employed by a single business are referred to as private or industrial accountants. They may be the employer's only accountant, or one of many. They may or may not be CPAs. If they have passed a rigorous examination prepared and administered by the National Association of Accountants—an organization for accountants employed in private industry—they will possess a Certificate in Management Accounting(CMA).

Industrial accountants may specialize in providing certain services. For example, they may be concerned with recording events and transactions involving outsiders and in the preparation of financial statements. Alternatively, they may be engaged in accumulating and controlling the costs of goods manufactured by their employer. Still others may be specialists in budgeting—that is, in the development of plans relating to future operations. Many private accountants become specialists in the design and installation of systems for the processing of accounting data. Others are internal auditors and are employed by a firm to see that its policies and procedures are adhered to in its departments and divisions. These latter individuals may earn the designation, certified internal auditor(CIA), granted by the Institute of Internal Auditors.

Accounting in the not-for-profit sector

Many accountants, including CPAs, are employed by not-for-profit organizations, including governmental agencies at the federal, state, and local levels, and other organizations. The governmental accountant is likely to be concerned with the accounting for and control of tax revenues and their expenditure. Accountants are also employed by governmental agencies whose function is the regulation of business activity—for example, the regulation of public utilities by a state public service commission.

Some accountants are also employed in the academic arm of the profession. Here attention is directed toward the teaching of accounting, to research into its uses and limitations, and to the improvement of accounting information and the theories and procedures under which it is accumulated and communicated.

Internal decisions

In most companies, people at various levels of management make decisions that require accounting information. These decisions can be classified into four major types.

1. Financing decision—deciding what amounts of capital are needed and whether it is to be secured from owners or creditors.

2. Resource allocation decisions—deciding how the total capital of a firm is to be invested, such as the amount invested in machinery.

3. Production decisions—deciding what products are to be produced, by what means, and when.

4. Marketing decisions—setting selling prices and advertising budgets; determining where a firm's markets are and how they are to be reached.

Managerial accounting provides information for such management decisions.

Managerial accounting

Managerial accounting provides special analyses and other information for internal purposes. The information ranges from the very broad(long-range planning) to the quite detailed(why costs varied from their planned levels). The information must meet two tests. It must be useful, and it must not cost more to gather than its worth. It generally relates to a part of a firm, such as a plant or a department, because this is where most of the decisions are made. It is used to measure the success of managers in, for example, controlling costs and to motivate them to help a firm achieve its goals. And it is forward looking, often involving planning for the future.

External users and their decisions

The external users of accounting information and the types of questions for which answers are sought can be classified as follows:

1. Owners(stockholders) and prospective owners and their advisers—financial analysts and investment counselors. Should an ownership interest be acquired in this firm? Or, if one is now held, should it be increased, decreased, or retained at its present level? Has the firm earned satisfactory profits?

2. Creditors and lenders. Should a loan be granted to the firm? Will the firm be able to pay its debts as they become due?

3. Employees and their unions. Does the firm have the ability to pay increased wages? Can it do so without raising prices? Is the firm financially able to provide permanent employment?

4. Customers. Will the firm survive long enough to honor its product warranties? Can the firm install costly pollution control equipment and still remain profitable? Are profit margins reasonable?

5. Governmental units. Is this firm, a public utility, earning a fair profit on its capital investment? How much tax does it pay? In total, is business activity at a desired level for sound growth without inflation?

6. The general public. Are profit margins too high? Are they an increasing or decreasing part of national income? Are the firms in this industry contributing to inflations?

Except for uses by governmental units, the information needs of the above users are met by providing a set of general-purpose financial statements. These statements are the end products of a process known as financial accounting.

Financial accounting

Financial accounting provides statements which describe a firm's financial position, changes in this position, and the results of operations(profitability). Many companies publish these statements in an annual report. This report contains the auditor's opinion as to the fairness of the financial statements, as well as other information about the company's activities, products, and plans.

Financial accounting information is historical in nature, being a report upon what has happened. Because interfirm comparisons are often made, the information supplied must conform to certain standards or principles, called generally accepted accounting principles (GAAP).

It would be a mistake to assume that a clear-cut distinction can be drawn between financial accounting information and managerial accounting information. Management officials are keenly aware of the fact that their jobs may depend upon how the figures come out in the annual report. Also, much of what is called managerial accounting information is first accumulated in an accounting system designed with financial reporting in mind.

Notes to the Text

1. bond: certificate issued by a government or a company acknowledging that money has been lent to it and will be paid back with interest（政府或公司发行的）有息债券

2. bookkeeping: keeping an accurate recording of the accounts of a business 簿记

3. audit: an official examination of business and financial records to see that they are true and correct 审记；稽核

4. Certificate in Management Accounting：美国注册管理会计师，简称 CMA，是美国

管理会计师协会(The Institute of Management Accountants,简称 IMA)于 1972 年推出的针对管理会计领域的全球专业认证。成立于 1919 年的美国管理会计师协会(IMA)是全球最大的致力于发展管理会计和金融管理的专业机构,是国际管理会计学界最具权威的机构之一。

5. certified internal auditor:国际注册内部审计师,简称 CIA,它不仅是国际内部审计领域专家的标志,也是目前国际审计界唯一公认的职业资格。CIA 需经国际内部审计师协会(Institute of Internal Auditors,简称 IIA)组织的考试取得。IIA 1941 年成立于美国纽约,在联合国经济和社会开发署享有顾问地位。中国内部审计学会 1987 年加入该协会,成为国家分会。

6. public utility:public service such as the supply of gas,water,electricity,a bus or rail network to the public 公用事业

7. warranty:a written agreement in which a company selling something promises to repair or replace it if there is a problem within a particular period of time (商品)保修单

8. profit margin:the difference between the cost of buying or producing something and the price that it is sold for 利润率;利润幅度

9. generally accepted accounting principles(GAAP):一般公认会计准则。指被普遍接受或承认的下列内容:哪些经济资源和义务应被记为资产和负债;哪些资产和负债的变动应予以记录;资产、负债及其变动应如何计量;什么样的信息应被披露和怎样记录以及财务报表如何出具等。

Exercises

I Answer the following questions.

1. What's the purpose of accounting?
2. How many ways are there for people to deal with their earnings? What are the advantage and disadvantage of each of them? Which do you prefer?
3. What's the differencc between bookkeeping and accounting?
4. In what areas of social life can accountants offer services and make contributions?
5. What characteristics make a qualified accountant?

II Write out the equivalents of the following words and expressions.

1. system design
2. financial position
3. decision making
4. savings account

8. 经济资源
9. 注册会计师
10. 电子数据处理
11. 金融分析师

5. income tax

6. accountancy

7. profitability

12. 投资顾问

13. 股票交易所

III **Translate the following into Chinese.**

Accounting may also be defined as an information system designed to provide, through the medium of financial statements, relevant financial information. In designing the system, accountants keep in mind the types of users of the information (owners, creditors, etc.) and the kinds of decisions they make that require financial information. Usually, the information provided relates to the economic resources owned by an organization, the claims against these resources, the changes in both resources and claims, and the results of using these resources for a given period of time.

Unit 10

Basic Principles of Accounting

In view of the basic assumptions of accounting, what are the principles or guidelines that the accountant follows in recording transaction data? These principles can be classified as (1) the historical cost principle, (2) the revenue recognition principle, (3) the matching principle, and(4) the full disclosure principle. The principles relate basically to how assets, liabilities, revenues, and expenses are to be identified, measured, recorded, and reported.

Historical cost

Traditionally, preparers and users of financial statements have found that cost is generally the most useful basis for accounting measurement and reporting. As a result, existing GAAP requires that most assets and liabilities be accounted for and reported on the basis of acquisition price. This is often referred to as the historical cost principle. Cost has an important advantage over other valuations; it is reliable. To illustrate the importance of this advantage, let us consider the problems that would arise if we adopted some other basis for keeping records. If we were to select current selling price, for instance, we might have a difficult time in attempting to establish a sales value for a given item without selling it. Every member of the accounting department might have his or her own opinion of the proper valuation of the asset, and management might desire still another figure. And how often would we find it necessary to establish sales value? All companies close their accounts at least annually, and some compute their net income every month. These companies would find it necessary to place a sales value on every asset each time they wished to determine income—a laborious task and one that would result in a figure of net income materially affected by opinion on sales value of the many assets involved. Similar objections have been leveled against current cost(replacement cost, present value of future cash flows) and any other basis of valuation except cost.

Cost is definite and verifiable. Once established, it is fixed as long as the asset remains the property of the company. These two characteristics are of real importance to those who use accounting data. To rely on the information supplied, both internal and external parties must know that the information is accurate and based on fact. By using cost as their basis for record keeping, accountants can provide objective and verifiable data in their reports.

The question "What is cost?" is not always easy to answer because of other questions that follow in its wake. If fixed assets are to be carried in the accounts at cost, are cash discounts to be deducted in determining cost? Does cost include freight and insurance? Does it include cost of installation as well as the price of a machine itself? And what of the cost of reinstallation if the machine is later moved? When land purchased for a building site is occupied by old structures, is the cost of razing these structures part of the cost of the land? These and similar questions must be considered and answered in arriving at cost figures for assets purchased.

The basic financial statements include liabilities and assets. We ordinarily think of cost as relating only to assets, and so it may seem strange that liabilities too are accounted for on a basis of cost. If we convert the term "cost" to "exchange price", we will find that it applies to liabilities as well. Liabilities, such as bonds, notes, and accounts payable, are issued by a business enterprise in exchange for assets, or perhaps services, upon which an agreed price has usually been placed. This price, established by the exchange transaction, is the "cost" of the liability and provides the figure at which it should be recorded in the accounts and reported in financial statements.

Revenue recognition principle

Revenue is generally recognized when(1) the earning process is virtually complete, and (2) an exchange transaction has occurred. This approach has often been referred to as the revenue recognition principle. Generally, an objective test-confirmation by a sale to independent interests—is used to indicate the point at which revenue is recognized. Usually, only when an exchange transaction takes place is there an objective and verifiable measure of revenue—the sales price. Any basis for revenue recognition short of actual sale opens the door to wide variations in practice. Conservative individuals might wait until sale of their securities; more optimistic individuals could watch market quotations and take up gains as market prices increased; yet others might recognize increases that are only rumored; and unscrupulous persons could "write up" their investments as they are pleased to suit their own purposes. To give accounting reports uniform meaning, a rule of revenue recognition comparable to the cost rule for asset valuation is essential. Recognition through sale provides a uniform reasonable test.

There are, however, exceptions to the rule, and at times the basic rule is difficult to apply.

Percentage-of-completion approach

Recognition of revenue is allowed in certain long-term construction contracts before the contract is completed. The advantage of this method is that revenue is recognized periodically on the basis of the percentage that the job has been completed instead of only when the entire job has been finished.

End of production

At times, revenue might be considered recognized before sale, but after the production cycle has ended. This is the case where the price is certain as well as the amount.

Receipt of cash

Receipt of cash is another basis for revenue recognition. The cash basis approach should be used only when it is impossible to establish the revenue figure at the time of sale because of the uncertainty of collection.

Revenue, then, is recorded in the period in which an exchange takes place and the earning process is virtually complete. Normally, this is the date of sale, but circumstances may dictate application of the percentage-of-completion approach, the end-of-production approach, or the receipt-of-cash approach. Conceptually, the proper accounting treatment for revenue recognition should be apparent and should fit nicely into one of the conditions mentioned above, but often it does not. For example, how should motion picture companies such as Metro-Goldwyn-Mayer, Inc., Warner Bros., and United Artists account for the sale of rights to show motion picture films on television networks such as ABC, CBS, or NBC? Should the revenue from the sale of the rights be reported when the contract is signed, when the motion picture film is delivered to the network, when the cash payment is received by the motion picture company, or when the film is shown on television? The problem of revenue recognition is complicated because the TV networks are often restricted in regard to the number of times the film may be shown and over what period of time.

For example, Metro-Goldwyn-Mayer Film Co. (MGM) sold CBS the rights to show *Gone With The Wind* for $35 million. For this $35 million, CBS received the right to show this classic movie twenty times over a twenty-year period. MGM contended that revenue reporting should coincide with the right to telecast on first and subsequent showings as included in the license agreement. They argued that the right to show *Gone With The Wind* twenty times over a twenty-year period was a significant contract restriction and, therefore, revenue recognition should coincide with the showings. The accounting profession on the other hand argued that when (1) the sales price and cost of each film are known, (2) collectibility is assured, and (3) the film is available and accepted by the network, revenue recognition should occur. The restriction that *Gone With The Wind* be shown only once a year for twenty years was not considered significant enough or appropriate justification for deferring revenue recognition. It is interesting to note that MGM, Inc., in the first quarter of 1979 reported essentially the entire $35 million in revenue in one period as the following headline in the *Wall Street Journal* reported, "MGM Net Tripled in the First Quarter that Ended Nov. 30."

Matching principle

In recognizing expenses, accountants attempt to follow the approach of "let the expense follow the revenues. " Expenses are recognized not when wages are paid, or when the work is performed, or when a product is produced, but when the work(service) or the product actually makes its contribution to revenue. Thus, expense recognition is tied to revenue recognition. In some cases it is difficult to determine the period in which an expense contributes to as the generation of revenues but many expenses can be associated with particular revenues. This practice is referred matching principle because it dictates that efforts(expenses) be matched with accomplishment(revenues) whenever it is reasonable and practicable to do so.

For those costs for which it is difficult to adopt some type of rational association with revenue, some other approach must be developed. Often the accountant must develop a "rational and systematic" allocation policy that will approximate the matching principle. This type of expense recognition pattern involves assumptions about the benefits that are being received as well as the cost associated with those benefits. The cost of a long-lived asset, for example, must be allocated over all of the accounting periods during which the asset is used because the asset contributes to the generation of revenue throughout its useful life. Some costs are charged to the current period as expenses(or losses) simply because no future benefit is anticipated or no connection with revenue is apparent. Examples of these types of costs are officers' salaries and advertising and promotion expenses.

Summarizing, we might say that costs are analyzed to determine whether a relationship exists with revenue. Where this association holds, the costs are expensed and matched against the revenue in the period when the revenue is recognized. If no connection appears between costs and revenues, an allocation of cost on some systematic and rational basis might be appropriate. Where, however, this method does not seem desirable, the cost may be expensed immediately. Notice that costs are generally classified into two groups: product costs and period costs. Product costs such as material, labor, and overhead attach to the product and are carried into future periods if the revenue from the product is recognized in subsequent periods. Period costs such as officers' salaries and selling expense are charged off immediately because no direct relationship between cost and revenue can be determined.

The problem of expense recognition is as complex as that of revenue recognition. For example, at one time a large oil company spent a considerable amount of money in an introductory advertising campaign in Hawaii. The company obviously hoped that this advertising campaign would attract new customers and develop brand loyalty. Over how many years, if any, should this outlay be expensed? For another example, Delta Air Lines depreates its planes over 10 years, while American Airlines writes off its jet fleet over periods as long as 16 years. Does the revenue flow from these two fleets justify that much of a difference in the expense recognition?

The conceptual validity of the matching principle has been a subject of debate. A major concern is that matching permits certain costs to be deferred and treated as assets on the balance sheet when in fact these costs may not have future benefits. If abused, this principle permits the balance sheet to become a "dumping ground" for unmatched costs. In addition, there appears to be no objective definition of "systematic and rational". For example, Hartwig, Inc. purchased an asset for \$100,000 that will last five years. Various depreciation methods (straight-line, accelerated, units of production, all considered systematic and rational) might be used to allocate this cost over the five-year period. What criteria should guide the accountant in determining what portion of the cost of the asset should be written off each period? New solutions to the expense recognition issue are currently being studied by the FASB as part of the conceptual framework project.

Full disclosure principle

In deciding what information to report, accountants follow the general practice of providing information that is of sufficient importance to influence the judgment and decisions of an informed user. Often referred to as the full disclosure principle, this principle recognizes that the nature and amount of information included in financial reports reflects a series of judgmental trade-offs. These trade-offs strive for (1) sufficient detail to disclose matters that make a difference to users, and (2) sufficient combination and condensation to make the information understandable, keeping in mind costs of preparing and using it. The accountant can place information about financial position, income, and cash flows in one of three places: (1) within the main body of financial statements, (2) in the notes to those statements, or (3) as supplementary information.

Notes to the Text

1. securities: 有价证券
2. Metro-Goldwyn-Mayer, Inc.: 米高梅电影公司,简称 MGM。美国五大电影公司之一,1924 年由三家公司合并而成,旗下云集了克拉克·盖博、斯宾塞·屈塞、加里·格兰特、琼·克劳馥、凯瑟琳·赫本、葛丽泰·嘉宝、伊丽莎白·泰勒等多位巨星,制作了多部好莱坞经典影片,如《大饭店》、《绿野仙踪》、《乱世佳人》、《魂断蓝桥》、《宾虚》等,多次获得奥斯卡电影金像奖。2005 年底被索尼公司高价收购。
3. Warner Bros.: 华纳兄弟电影公司;1923 年 4 月由 H.B. 华纳和 J. 华纳两兄弟建立。当时总部设在美国纽约,制片厂设在好莱坞附近的伯班克。1927 年摄制、发行了电影史上第一部有声影片《爵士歌手》,从而使华纳公司于 20 世纪 30 年代初进入了好莱坞八大电影公司[米高梅公司(MGM)、派拉蒙公司(Paramount)、二十世纪福克斯公司(20th Century Fox)、华纳兄弟公司(Warner Brothers)、雷电华公司(Radio Keith Orpheum,简称 RKO)、环球公司(Universal)、联美公司(United Artists)、哥伦比亚公司(Columbia Pictures)]的行列。1988 年与美国时代公司合并成立了时代华纳公司,是世界上最强的传媒企业之一。
4. United Artists: 联美公司,1919 年由四位著名导演及演员卓别林、范朋克、毕克馥、格里菲斯出资创建,逐步发展成为控制美国电影生产和发行的八大公司之一。在 1981 年并入米高梅公司，改称为米高梅——联美娱乐公司，以出品"007
系列"电影知名。

5. ABC：美国广播公司，全称 American Broadcasting Company，总部在纽约。1995
年该公司被美国迪斯尼公司收购。

6. CBS：美国哥伦比亚广播公司，全称 Columbia Broadcasting System，美国三大全
国性商业广播电视网之一，成立于 1927 年。哥伦比亚广播公司是一个多元化的
信息传播企业，1987 年拥有直属电视台 5 家、电台 14 家，联属电视台 200 家、电
台 400 家。此外还经营音乐唱片、乐器、玩具、电化教育资料、戏剧影片、家用电
脑软件、图书杂志出版等业务。其电视新闻节目颇具特色，如《晚间新闻》、《CBS
报道》、《60 分钟》、《人物介绍》等都是美国名牌电视栏目。

7. NBC：全国广播公司，全称 National Broadcasting Company，是美国一家主流广播
电视网络公司，总部设在纽约洛克斐勒中心，以孔雀为标记。

8. Gone With the Wind：《乱世佳人》(又译《飘》、《随风而逝》)，好莱坞电影史上最值
得骄傲的旷世巨片。1939 年由米高梅电影公司出品，由克拉克·盖博和费雯丽
主演，在第十二届奥斯卡金像奖中荣获八项大奖：最佳影片奖、最佳艺术指导奖、
最佳编剧奖、最佳导演奖、最佳摄影奖、最佳女主角奖、最佳女配角奖和最佳剪辑
奖。本片根据女作家玛格丽特·米切尔的畅销小说《飘》改编而成，既是一部人
类美好爱情的绝唱，又是一部反映当时政治、经济、道德诸多方面的巨大而深刻
变化的历史画卷。

9. matching principle：配比原则

10. outlay：the money that you have to spend in order to start a new project or to
save yourself money or time later（必要的）开支，费用

11. Delta Air Line：美国三角洲航空公司，总部设在亚特兰大，是全美第三大航空
公司。

12. dump：to get rid of goods by selling them at a very low price, often in another
country（向国外）倾销，抛售

13. depreciation：the state of being less valuable over a period of time 贬值，跌价

14. FASB：（美国）财务会计准则委员会，全称 Financial Accounting Standards Board。

15. trade-off：the act of balancing two things that you need or want but which are
opposed to each other 权衡，协调

Exercises

I Answer the following questions.

1. Should accountants follow some principles in recording transaction data? Please
name some influential ones.

2. How do you understand the principle of historical cost?

3. When is revenue recognized generally? Are there any exceptions? Could you cite an example?

4. What's the essence of the matching principle? Why has the conceptual validity of this principle been a subject of debate?

5. Are there any connections among the four basic principles of accounting?

Ⅱ Write out the equivalents of the following words and expressions.

1. liabilities and assents
2. percentage of completion approach
3. full disclosure principle
4. conceptual framework project
5. period costs
6. overhead
7. collectibility
8. 净收入
9. 资金流动
10. 市场报价
11. 资产估价
12. 资产负债表

Ⅲ Translate the following into Chinese.

To illustrate the importance of this advantage，let us consider the problems that would arise if we adopted some other basis for keeping records. If we were to select current selling price，for instance，we might have a difficult time in attempting to establish a sales value for a given item without selling it. Every member of the accounting department might have his or her own opinion of the proper valuation of the asset，and management might desire still another figure. And how often would we find it necessary to establish sales value? All companies close their accounts at least annually，and some compute their net income every month. These companies would find it necessary to place a sales value on every asset each time they wished to determine income—a laborious task and one that would result in a figure of net income materially affected by opinion on sales value of the many assets involved. Similar objections have been leveled against current cost（replacement cost，present value of future cash flows）and any other basis of valuation except cost.

Unit 11

How Bank Works?

Profits and spreads

Commercial banks, like many other companies, are in business to make money for their shareholders. They do this by borrowing money at interest rates that are lower than the rates they earn on the loans and investments they make with that money. The spread between these two types of rates has to be large enough to cover the operating costs banks incur. Hence, a bank's principal activities revolve around gathering deposits and placing this money in either loans or investments of various kinds. Virtually everything else a bank does is intended to make it more attractive to depositors and borrowers.

The deposit side of the bank

The banking industry handles millions of deposit transactions every day, ranging from multimillion-dollar transfers to those involving less than a dollar. Some transactions pass through the hands of tellers; others are automated, like the computer-to-computer deposits of payroll or Social Security payments to personal accounts. All of these transactions are nothing more than transfers of money from one account to another.

In recent years, there has been an explosion in the variety of deposit accounts available to customers. In addition to the traditional savings and non-interest-bearing checking accounts, banks now offer a variety of interest-bearing checking accounts, certificates of deposit, IRAs, repurchase agreements, sweep accounts, statement savings accounts—all with rules, rates, and maturities that differ from one bank to the next. To make matters more confusing, these similar deposit vehicles are called by different names from bank to bank. Consequently, bank customers find it difficult to make comparisons; instead, they must study features thoroughly and make selections based upon their particular needs.

Deposit pricing

The interest rate paid on a bank's deposits follows closely the rate of return the bank can generate through investment, and the rate offered the largest depositors may be very close to the bank's own rate of return. Not surprisingly, the bigger a deposit account is, the more vigorously it is pursued by banks; deposits from corporations with excess funds are aggressively solicited, as are those from state and municipal agencies. Typically, these deposits, generally $ 1 million or more, are used by the bank to finance its own investments of an equal amount at a rate that is just a little bit higher than the rates it must pay to the company, state, or municipality. Thus, the rate paid to the depositor depends largely upon the investment rates that are available to the bank at the time. Because the competition for this kind of deposit business is so keen, spreads may be as little as a sixteenth or an eighth of a percent. Even so, small spreads add up quickly. Furthermore, this banking activity can be handled by a small staff; one person can easily generate many times his or her salary in the profit these transactions produce.

Rates on smaller deposits are determined by a variety of factors, such as the size of the bank and the community it serves. In many small banks, the president is the primary or sole rate setter, using a variety of sources of published rates, including newspapers and rate sheets from bigger banks in nearby cities. Rates at many larger banks are set by what are known as asset and liability committees(ALCOs), which evaluate rates and other information on loan demand and deposit supply gathered from the banks in the community.

Although antitrust laws prohibit banks from jointly agreeing on the interest rates to be set, many banks do call their competitors in the guise of customers to find out what's being offered. Some banks adjust, or at least review, their rates daily. Others do it weekly or even less frequently, waiting until customer complaints, major rate shifts, or some other occurrence dictates a change.

A bank wants to pay no more than necessary to gather deposits sufficient to achieve its financial goals. Consequently, a bank with a heavy loan demand is likely to pay better rates than a nearby bank with little or no demand for loans. Many banks, in fact, peg their interest rates directly to the demand for loans, in order to assure themselves of the funds they need. Nearly all banks have some customers who are "rate sensitive" and move their money around from one bank to another as rate opportunities suggest. But most customers are not like that. For example, many leave their money in low-rate savings accounts or in non-interest-bearing checking accounts when they could be earning much more on this money invested in, say, a certificate of deposit.

Check clearing

A very important part of any bank's activities is the conversion of checks into interest-earning assets. That happens when checks are physically delivered to the banks on which they are drawn and funds are transferred to the banks of deposit. Thanks to computers, the magnetic ink now used to encode checks, and a highly efficient system of check transfer, more than 90 percent highly efficient system of check transfer, more than 90 percent of all check deposits can be drawn on just one business day later.

A process called check truncation promises to simplify matters even further by temporarily storing, then destroying, all checks at the bank of deposit. How long it will be before this system is widespread is hard to say, since there is a good deal of customer resistance to doing away with the physical return of canceled checks. It will doubtless be a gradual process, much as the substitution of statement for passbook savings accounts has been slow.

The loan side

Consumer loans

The loan side of banking can be divided into two broad categories: consumer loans and commercial loans. Consumer loans are those that are repaid through monthly installments. At some banks, the term also encompasses demand loans and loans that mature every ninety days or so. Consumer loans are either secured(that is, backed by collateral) or unsecured, and are used mainly for financing major purchases and consolidating debt. Most consumer loans mature anywhere from six months to five or ten years from the time they are granted.

Mortgage loans

Mortgage loans, like consumer loans, lend themselves to formularization, and bank personnel who evaluate mortgage applications follow certain mathematical rules of thumb that don't vary too much from one bank to another. Commercial banks and thrifts(savings banks and savings-and-loan associations) offer fixed rate mortgages, variable-rate mortgages, and, frequently, both. As a rule, mortgage loans with long-term fixed rates are not kept by the bank but are sold off to long-term investors such as insurance companies and pension and profit-sharing plans.

Commercial loans

Commercial loans are entirely different from consumer loans. Every commercial loan represents a unique situation, one that cannot be analyzed using simple formulas like those associated with consumer loans. There are broad rules used in the analysis of commercial credits, but they are normally viewed against the history and prospects of the company requesting the loan. Not surprisingly, this kind of analysis can be performed only by personnel with special training and skills. In many smaller banks, the president is the only one who handles such loans. Most larger banks employ officers specially trained to handle commercial loans. These officers usually handle most of the borrower's other banking business as well.

Commercial loan departments of many larger banks are divided into groups that specialize in companies of a certain size, industry, or geographical location. They may even have high net worth groups that minister to the financial needs of only the wealthiest of the bank's customers.

Interest rates on commercial loans can be fixed or floating, and the life of the loans can vary from one day to five or ten years? Because interest rates have fluctuated considerably since World War II, most commercial banks today are not interested in fixing rates for more than three to five years; most prefer to use a rate that is pegged to the prime rate, a nationwide rate banks charge their better customers. Whether the rate is fixed or floating and whether it's at prime or above prime are matters that are negotiated separately for each loan. Loan rates are usually set within well-established guidelines, by individual loan officers. Frequently, a loan officer's rate is changed during the approval process.

Other banking services
Investments

Banks would prefer to put all of their money into loans if they could, because most loans produce a higher rate of return, even after allowing for losses on loans that go sour, than any other option. The problem is that there just isn't enough demand for loans to use up the cumulative capital of all the banks in business; in addition, loan demand fluctuates with seasons and business cycles. The bank has yet another group of people, usually called the Investment Department that spends its time putting the rest of the bank's money to work at the best rates it can find. That job is complicated by the fact that the amount of money available for investment in bonds and other non-loan financial vehicles fluctuates seasonally, monthly, weekly, daily, and even by the hour because of changes in loan demand and deposit levels as bank customers move their money. To deal with this, the bank keeps part of its investment portfolio highly liquid, ready to be sold off the moment the need arises.

But there's a price to liquidity. As a rule, the greater an investment's liquidity, the lower the interest it returns. So banks usually keep in their portfolios a few highly liquid investments, supplemented by less liquid, but higher-yielding, securities. Federal deposit insurance has virtually eliminated a major need for liquidity; the need to provide funds in the event of a run on the bank. Consequently, the primary purpose of investment portfolios has become putting to work excess funds—namely, the money that a bank has not been able to float in the form of higher-yielding loans.

Rate levels move up and down not only because of changes in current basic economic conditions but because of changes in people's expectations about future conditions. The changes in rates alter the prices of stocks (which banks do not invest in for their own account), bonds, and any other instrument whose rate of interest is fixed. (For instance, if interest rates decline, the market value of existing bonds will rise.) Some banks buy U. S. Treasury bills(T-bills) or government bonds and simply hold them until they mature; others trade in and out of them as opportunities arise. There is a wide variety of instruments banks use to sop up excess funds, including fed funds (so called because they used to represent money left over in accounts at the Federal Reserve Bank), repurchase agreements(repos), reverse repos, T-bills(which mature in less than one year), and government notes(which mature in one to five years) and bonds(which mature in more than five years). A repo is the purchase of a security with the understanding that the seller will buy it back by some agreed-upon date, usually one day later.

The complexity and unpredictability of investing leftover bank funds makes it a challenging job. It is an important banking activity, a bank's alternative to making loans. Of course, the latter is attractive only when loan losses aren't excessive, which hasn't been the case for many banks in recent years. For example, losses have been overwhelming for a large number of thrifts, primarily savings-and-loan associations. Losses have been disconcertingly high for a number of commercial banks as well.

In 1989, bad loans charged off by commercial banks averaged about six-tenths of one percent of all loans. In better times, that percentage is closer to three-tenths of a percent or less. If you consider those losses as a cost of doing business and then take that cost away from the interest rates earned on loans, you can see that the net yield is still much better than that on Treasury bills, government notes and bonds, and on other investments available to banks. A quick look at rates in The Wall Street Journal will confirm that for you.

The trust department

Many larger banks have trust departments and regard them as yet another service that helps attract deposit and loan customers. Some of these departments are profitable; many are not. The trust department is a department with which you should become familiar. It won't add a thing to your current profitability, but it can make a tremendous difference to your family if you should die. Despite the fact that the bank, like your accountant and your lawyer, can make money by planning your estate and handling it when you die or become incapacitated, you should hear what they have to say then act accordingly.

Trust departments can also help you in other ways. For example, they can help you take care of profit-sharing and pension plans, ESOPS(employee stock ownership plans), Keogh and H R 10 plans(pension plans for the self-employed), and investment matters you may be too busy to properly care for.

The international department

International departments of banks provide services such as letters of credit(either import or export), handle inquiries about conditions or companies in foreign countries, and offer advice about foreign currencies and exchange risks. Generally speaking, only large, metropolitan-area banks have international departments, though some of the functions of an international department are found at smaller banks, where they are handled by commercial loan officers. If a small bank doesn't have a certain service itself, it normally will work with larger correspondents in nearby cities to get the services its customers need.

Many large banks have not only sizable international operations here in this country but extensive branch and correspondent bank networks abroad. Through those networks, they can provide a domestic company operating abroad with virtually all the bank services available in this country or help it locate such services. Here again, though, the purpose is to provide customers with the services they need so that they will keep their loan and deposit business with the bank.

Other services

There are a variety of other services offered by banks, such as safe-deposit boxes, buying and selling of bonds, and discount brokerage services. Other banking services include check cashing, handling credit inquiries, and offering drive-in facilities, night-deposit drops, payroll services, and equipment leasing.

Regulation

Because of the importance of money to our economy, banks are subject to a considerable and growing amount of regulation. This regulation is designed to promote the well-being of the banking system and the overall economic health of the country. It is aimed at avoiding the financial panics that periodically racked the nation during the 1800s and the early 1900s. The Federal Reserve System, founded in 1913 to deal with such panics and otherwise guide the economy, functions today as one of the industry's principal regulators. It also serves the national economy by providing a money-transfer system for the banking industry.

Equally important to the nation's overall economic health is the safety of depositors' money. The stock-market crash of 1929 and the wide-spread bank problems that followed resulted in the creation of the Federal Deposit Insurance Corporation, tinder which the federal government provides insurance that guarantees virtually all depositors that the money they put in a bank up to specified limits will always be immediately available to them.

A third layer of regulation is concerned with the rights of particular groups of consumers. It has grown to the point that its paperwork alone, especially in the area of consumer lending, is believed to add something more than half a percent to the cost of making a loan.

While there has been talk about regulatory simplification, few in the banking industry believe it will actually come about. The fact is that banks are often a handy way of furthering social goals. A current example is the war against drugs; regulators are developing increasingly complex methods to cut down on the laundering of drug money. The goal is fine-funnel more money into underprivileged areas. But who should bear the expense? Shareholders? Depositors? Or the government?

Notes to the Text

1. spread: the difference between two rates or prices（两种比率或价格的）差额
2. IRA: 全称 individual retirement accounts，个人退休账户
3. repurchase agreement: 回购协议，简称 repos
4. sweep accounts: 过夜投资账户，平整账户
5. solicit: to ask somebody for something, such as support, money or information 索求；请求……给予（援助、钱或信息）
6. asset and liability committees: 资产负债委员会，简称 ALCOs
7. antitrust law: 反托拉斯法
8. peg: to fix or keep something at a particular level 使……固定于某水平；钉住……
9. truncation: the act of making something shorter especially by cutting off the top or end 截去，缩短
10. passbook: a small book containing a record of the money you put into and take out of account at a building society or bank 银行存折；房屋建筑协会借贷簿

11. rule of thumb：a practical method of doing or measuring something, usually based on past experience rather than on exact measurement 实用的估算方法，经验工作法

12. thrift：互助储蓄银行，储蓄借贷协会

13. portfolio：a set of shares owned by a particular person or organization（个人或机构持有的）有价证券财产目录

14. The Wall Street Journal：《华尔街日报》。是美国乃至全世界影响力最大，侧重金融、商业领域报导的日报，创办于 1889 年。

15. ESOPS：全称 employee stock owner plans，职工拥有股票计划

16. Keogh and H R 10 plans：养老金计划

17. discount brokerage services：贴现经纪业务

18. drive-in facilities：（银行）免下车服务，上门服务

19. night-deposit drops：过夜存款再贷业务

20. Federal Reserve System：（美国）联邦储备体系，始创于 1913 年，是一种带有制约和平衡特点的制度，即在地区之间、私人部门和政府部门之间以及银行家、工商业者和公众之间实行分权。联邦储备体系包括以下实体：联邦储备银行、联邦储备体系理事会、联邦公开市场委员会、联邦咨询委员会以及大约 4 000 家会员商业银行。

21. Federal Deposit Insurance Corporation：（美国）联邦存款保险公司，简称 FDIC，中文又译作"美国联邦储蓄保险公司"；成立于 1933 年。如果会员银行发生破产或无法偿还债务的危机时，FDIC 将为这个会员银行的每个储户提供最高限额为 $100 000 的存款保险。

22. launder：to move the money that has been obtained illegally into foreign bank accounts or legal businesses so that it is difficult for people to know where it came from 洗钱

23. underprivilieged：having less money and fewer opportunities than most people in society 贫苦的；底层的

Exercises

Ⅰ Answer the following questions.

1. How can banks own money by absorbing deposits and granting loans?

2. What are the differences between consumer loans and commercial loans?

3. How do American banks fix the interest rates for loans?

4. What kinds of roles do banks play in the economy of a country?

Ⅱ **Write out the equivalents of the following words and expressions.**

1. Social Security
2. non-interest-bearing checking accounts
3. certificate of deposit
4. demand loan
5. consolidating debt
6. cumulative capital
7. liquidity

8. 优惠利率
9. 开户银行
10. 抵押贷款
11. 回报率
12. 美国短期国库券
13. 净收益
14. 汇兑风险
15. 银行保险箱

Ⅲ **Translate the following into Chinese.**

The interest rate paid on a bank's deposits follows closely the rate of return the bank can generate through investment, and the rate offered the largest depositors may be very close to the bank's own rate of return. Not surprisingly, the bigger a deposit account is, the more vigorously it is pursued by banks; deposits from corporations with excess funds are aggressively solicited, as are those from state and municipal agencies. Typically, these deposits, generally $1 million or more, are used by the bank to finance its own investments of an equal amount at a rate that is just a little bit higher than the rates it must pay to the company, state, or municipality. Thus, the rate paid to the depositor depends largely upon the investment rates that are available to the bank at the time. Because the competition for this kind of deposit business is so keen, spreads may be as little as a sixteenth or an eighth of a percent. Even so, small spreads add up quickly. Furthermore, this banking activity can be handled by a small staff; one person can easily generate many times his or her salary in the profit these transactions produce.

Unit 12

The Evolution of Money

Barter

In an early textbook on money, when Stanley Jevons wanted to illustrate the tremendous leap forward that occurred as societies introduced money, he used the following experience:

> Some years since, Mademoiselle Zélie, a singer of the Théatre Lyrique at Paris, gave a concert in the Society Islands. In exchange for an air from *Norma* and a few other songs, she was to receive a third part of the receipts. When counted her share was found to consist of three pigs, twenty-three turkeys, forty-four chickens, five thousand cocoa-nuts, besides considerable quantities of bananas, lemons and oranges.... In Paris this amount of live stock and vegetables might have brought four thousand francs, which would have been good remuneration for five songs. In the Society Islands, however, pieces of money were scarce; and as Mademoiselle could not consume any considerable portion of the receipts herself, it became necessary in the mean time to feed the pigs and poultry with the fruit.

This example describes barter, which consists of the exchange of goods for other goods. Barter contrasts with exchange through the use of money, which is anything medium of exchange or means of payment. Although barter is better than no trade at all, it operates under grave disadvantages because an elaborate division of labor would be unthinkable without the introduction of the great social invention of money.

As economics develop, people no longer barter one good for another. Instead, they sell goods for money and then use money to buy other goods they wish to have. At first glance this seems to complicate rather than simplify matters, as it replaces one transaction with two. If you have apples and want nuts, would it not be simpler to trade one for the other rather than to sell the apples for money and then use money to buy nuts?

Actually, the reverse is true: two monetary transactions are simpler than one barter transaction. For example, some people may want to buy apples, and some may want to sell nuts. But it would be a most unusual circumstance to find a person whose desires exactly complement your own—eager to sell nuts and buy apples. To use a classical economic phrase, instead of there being a "double coincidence of wants", there is likely to be a "want of coincidence". So, unless a hungry tailor happens to find an undraped farmer who has both food and a desire for a pair of pants, under barter neither can make a direct trade.

Societies that traded extensively simply could not overcome the overwhelming handicaps of barter. The use of a commonly accepted medium of exchange, money, permits the farmer to buy pants from the tailor, who buys shoes from the cobbler, who buys leather from the farmer.

Commodity money

Money as a medium of exchange first came into human history in the form of commodities. A great variety of items have served as money at one time or another: cattle, olive oil, beer or wine, copper, iron, gold, silver, rings, diamonds, and cigarettes.

Each of the above has advantages and disadvantages. Cattle are not divisible into small change. Beer does not improve with keeping, although wine may. Olive oil provides a nice liquid currency that is as minutely divisible as one wishes, but it is a bit messy to handle. And so forth.

By the nineteenth century, commodity money was almost exclusively limited to metals like silver and gold. These forms of money had intrinsic value, meaning that they had use value in themselves. Because money had intrinsic value, there was no need for the government to guarantee its value, and the quantity of money was regulated by the market through the supply and demand for gold or silver. But metallic money has shortcomings because scarce resources are required to dig it out of the ground; moreover, it might become abundant simply because of accidental discoveries of ore deposits.

The advent of monetary control by central banks had led to a much more stable currency system. The intrinsic value of money is now the least important thing about it.

Modern money

The age of commodity money gave way to the age of paper money. The essence of money is now laid bare. Money is wanted not for its own sake but for the things it will buy. We do not wish to consume money directly; rather, we use it by getting rid of it. Even when we choose to keep money, it is valuable only because we can spend it later on.

The use of paper currency has become widespread because it is a convenient medium of exchange. Currency is easily carried and stored. The value of money can be protected from counterfeiting by careful engraving. The fact that private individuals cannot legally create money keeps it scarce. Given this limitation in supply, currency has value. It can buy things. As long as people can pay their bills with currency, as long as it is accepted as a means of payment, it serves the function of money.

Most money today is bank money—deposits in a bank or other financial institution. Checks are accepted in place of cash payment for many goods and services. In fact, if we calculate the total dollar amount of transactions, nine-tenths take place by bank money, the rest by currency.

Today there is rapid innovation in developing different forms of money. For example, some financial institutions will now link a checking account to a savings account or even to a stock portfolio, allowing customers to write checks on the value of their stock. Traveler's checks can be used for many transactions and are included in the money supply. Many companies are devising "smart cards" that allow people to pay for small items by simply passing the card through an electronic reader.

Components of the money supply

Let us now look more carefully at the different kinds of money that Americans use. The major monetary aggregates are the quantitative measures of the supply of money. They are known as M_1 and M_2, and you can read about their week-to-week movements in the newspaper, along with sage commentaries on the significance of the latest wiggle. Here we will provide the exact definitions as of 1997.

Transactions money

One important and closely watched measure of money is transactions money, or M_1, which consists of items that are actually used for transactions. The following are the components of M_1:

- Coins. M_1 includes coins not held by banks.
- Paper money. More significant is paper currency. Most of us know little more about a $1 or $5 bill than that it is inscribed with the picture of an American statesman, that it bears some official signatures, and that each has a numeral showing its face value.

   Examine a $10 bill or some other paper bill. You will probably find that it says "Federal Reserve Note". But what "backs" our paper currency? Many years ago, paper money was backed by gold or silver. There is no such pretense today. Today, all U. S. coins and paper currency are fiat money. This term signifies something determined to be money by the government even if it has no value. Currency and coins are legal tender, which must be accepted for all debts, public and private.

   Coins and paper currency(the sum known as currency) add up to about one-third of total transactions money, M_1.

- Checking accounts. There is a third component of transactions money—checking deposits or bank money. These are funds, deposited in banks and other financial institutions that you can write checks on. They are technically known as "demand deposits and other checkable deposits".

   If I have $1,000 in my checking account at the Albuquerque National Bank, that deposit can be regarded as money. Why? For the simple reason that I can pay for purchases with checks drawn on it. The deposit is like any other medium of exchange. Possessing the essential properties of money, bank checking-account deposits are counted as transactions money, as part of M_1.

   Table shows the dollar values of the different components of transactions money, M_1.

Kinds of money	Billions of dollars		
	1959	1973	1997
Currency (outside of financial institutions)	25.8	61.7	403.7
Demand deposits (exclude government deposits)	113.8	209.7	403.6
Other checkable deposits	0.4	0	257.9
Total transactions money (M_1)	140.0	271.4	1 065.2
Savings accounts, small time deposits, and other	158.8	300.2	2 838.9
Total broad money	298.8	571.6	3 904.1

TABLE   Components of the Money Supply of the United States

Two widely used definitions of the money supply are transactions money(M_1)and broad money(M_2). M_1 consists of currency and checking accounts. M_2 adds to these certain "near-monies" such as savings accounts and time deposits. (Source: Federal Reserve Board, Federal Reserve Bulletin, February 1997)

Broad money

Although M_1 is, strictly speaking, the most appropriate measure of money as a means of payment, as second closely watched aggregate is broad money, or M_2. Sometimes called asset money or near-money, M_2 includes M_1 as well as savings accounts in banks and similar assets that are very close substitutes for transactions money.

Examples of such near-monies in M_2 include deposits in a savings account in your bank, a money market mutual fund account operated by your stock-broker, a deposit in a money market deposit account run by a commercial bank, and so on.

Why are these not transactions money? Because they cannot be used as means of exchange for all purchases; they are forms of near-money, however, because you can convert them into cash very quickly with no loss of value.

There are many other technical definitions of money that are used by specialists in monetary economics. But for our purposes, we need master only the two major definitions of money.

Money is anything that serves as a commonly accepted medium of exchange. The most important concept is transactions money, or M_1, which is the sum of coins and paper currency in circulation outside the banks, plus checkable deposits. Another important monetary aggregate is broad money(called M_2), which includes assets such as savings accounts in addition to coins, paper currency, and checkable deposits.

The demand for money

The demand for money is different from the demand for ice cream or movies. Money is not desired for its own sake; you cannot eat nickels, and we seldom hand $ 100 bills on the wall for the artistic quality of their engraving. Rather, we demand money because it serves us indirectly, as a lubricant to trade and exchange.

Money's functions

Before we analyze the demand for money, let's note money's functions:

- By far the most important function of money is to serve as a medium of exchange. Without money we would be constantiy roving around looking for someone to barter with. We are often reminded of money's utility when it does not work properly, as in Russia in the early 1990s, when people spent hours in line waiting for goods and tried to get dollars or other foreign currencies because the Ruble ceased functioning as an acceptable means of exchange.

- Money is also used as the unit of account, the unit by which we measure the value of things. Just as we measure weight in kilograms, we measure value in money. The use of a common unit of account simplifies economic life enormously.

- Money is sometimes used as a store of value; it allows value to be held over time. In comparison with risky assets like stocks or real estate or gold, money is relatively riskless. In earlier days, people held currency as a safe form of wealth. Today when people seek a safe haven for their wealth, they put it in assets like checking deposits (M_1) and money market mutual funds(M_2). However, the vast preponderance of wealth is held in other assets, such as savings account, stocks, bonds and real estate.

Notes to the Text

1. Stanley Jevons：威廉姆·斯坦利·杰文斯(1835—1882)，生于利物浦，英国著名的经济学家和逻辑学家。他在《政治经济学理论》(1871年)中提出了价值的边际效用理论。

2. Society Islands：社会群岛，太平洋东南部法属波利尼西亚的主要岛群，由塔希提、莫雷阿、华希内等15个火山岛组成；陆地面积1 647平方公里，人口9.9万，主要为波利尼西亚人，余为华侨、法国人和英国人；主产椰油、香料、椰干、蔗糖、珍珠贝和磷灰石等；帕皮提是其主要城市和港口。

3. air：(often used in the title of a piece of music) a tune (乐曲的)曲调，旋律

4. Norma：意大利作曲家贝利尼(1801—1835)的歌剧代表作《诺尔玛》。《诺尔玛》的剧本源自古希腊神话美蒂亚的故事，但贝利尼将神话故事中美蒂亚血刃亲生子的残酷结局转化成女祭司诺尔玛为爱牺牲自判火刑的终极宽恕。贝利尼在《诺尔玛》中铺陈出华丽而浑然天成的抒情旋律，以强烈对比的剧情张力展现爱情、仇恨与宽恕的角力，提前一个半世纪预告了女性主义的到来。剧中由诺尔玛演唱的《圣洁的女神》(Costa Diva)一曲，成为一百多年来最受乐迷喜爱的名曲之一，被多部经典电影采用为插曲。

5. undraped：not covered with cloth or drapery; naked 无覆盖物的;裸体的

6. counterfeit：(of money or goods for sale) made to look exactly like something in

order to trick people into thinking that they are getting the read thing（钱币或商品）伪造的；假冒的

7. fiat：an official order given by somebody in authority, a formal authorization or decree 法令；授权，批准

8. Albuquerque：阿尔布开克，美国新墨西哥州中部城市

9. preponderance：the quality or fact of being greater in number, quantity, or importance（数量、重要性等）优势；多数

Exercises

I Answer the following questions.

1. What is barter? Why was this form of transaction gradually replaced by monetary transactions?

2. What kinds of commodities had been used as money before paper currency was used? Why were they replaced by paper currency?

3. What are the two important measures of money? What components consist of these two measures of money?

4. What are the functions of money in the present world?

5. What do you think are the disadvantages of paper currency? Will it be replaced by some other forms of money in the future?

II Write out the equivalents of the following words and expressions.

1. barter
2. monetary transactions
3. intrinsic value of money
4. bank money
5. traveler's checks
6. broad money
7. time deposits
8. near-money
9. counterfeiting
10. 支付方式
11. 商品货币
12. 货币制度
13. 活期存款
14. 面值
15. 智能卡（灵通卡）
16. 法定货币

III Translate the following into Chinese.

Actually, the reverse is true：two monetary transactions are simpler than one barter transaction. For example, some people may want to buy apples, and some may want to sell nuts. But it would be a most unusual circumstance to find a person whose desires exactly complement your own—eager to sell nuts and buy apples. To use a classical economic phrase, instead of there being a "double coincidence of wants", there is likely to be a "want of coincidence". So, unless a hungry tailor happens to find an undraped farmer who has both food and a desire for a pair of pants, under barter neither can make a direct trade.

Societies that traded extensively simply could not overcome the overwhelming handicaps of barter. The use of a commonly accepted medium of exchange, money, permits the farmer to buy pants from the tailor, who buys shoes from the cobbler, who buys leather from the farmer.

Unit 13

The Stock Market

A stock market is a place where the shares in publicly owned companies, the titles to business firms, are bought and sold. In 1996, the value of these titles was estimated at thirty trillion in the United States. Sales in a single year might total $3 trillion. The stock market is the hub of our corporate economy.

The New York Stock Exchange is the main stock market, listing more than a thousand securities. Every large financial center has a stock exchange. Major ones are located in Tokyo, London, Frankfurt, Hong Kong, Toronto, Zurich, and, of course, New York. A stock exchange is a critical part of modern market economies. When the countries of Eastern Europe decided to scrap their centrally planned systems and become market economies, one of their first acts was to introduce a stock market to buy and sell ownership rights in companies.

Bubbles and crashes

The history of finance is one of the most exciting, and sobering, parts of economics. As Burton Malkiel writes in his survey of bubbles, panics, and the madness of crowds, "Greed run amok has been an essential feature of every spectacular boom in history."

Investors are sometimes divided into those who invest on firm foundations and those who try to outguess the market psychology. The firm-foundation approach holds that assets should be valued on the basis of their intrinsic value. For common stocks, the intrinsic value is the expected present value of the dividends. If a stock has a constant dividend of £2 per year and the appropriate interest rate to discount dividends is 5 percent, the intrinsic value would be £2/0.05 = $40 per share. The firm foundation approach is the slow but safe way of getting rich.

Impatient souls might echo Keynes, who argued that investors are more likely to worry about market psychology and to speculate on the future value of assets rather than wait patiently for stocks to prove their intrinsic value. He argued, "It is not sensible to pay 25 for an investment which is worth 30, if you also believe that the market will value it at 20 three months hence." The market psychologist tries to guess what the average investor thinks, which requires considering what the average investor thinks about the average investor, and so on, ad infinitum.

When a psychological frenzy seizes the market, it can result in speculative bubbles and crashes. A speculative bubble occurs when prices rise because people think they are going to rise in the future—it is the reverse of Keynes' dictum just cited. A piece of land may be worth only $1,000, but if you see a land-price boom driving prices up 50 percent each year, you might buy it for $2,000 hoping you can sell it to someone else next year for $3,000. A speculative bubble fulfills its own promises. If people buy because they think stocks will rise, their act of buying sends up the price of stocks. This causes people to buy even more and sends the dizzy dance off on another round. But, unlike people who play cards or dice, no one apparently loses what the winners gain. Of course, the prizes are all on paper and would disappear if everyone tried to cash them in. But why should anyone want to sell such lucrative securities? Prices rise because of hopes and dreams, not because the profits and dividends of companies are soaring.

History is marked by bubbles in which speculative prices were driven up far beyond their intrinsic value. In seventeenth-century Holland, a tulip mania drove tulip prices to levels higher than the price of a house. In the eighteenth century, the stock of the South Sea Company rose to fantastic levels on empty promises that the firm would enrich its stockholders. In more recent times, similar bubbles have been found in biotechnology, Japanese land, "emerging markets", and a vacuum-cleaning company called ZZZZ Best, which turned out to have profited from laundering money for the Mafia.

The most famous bubble of them all occurred in the American stock market in the 1920s: The "roaring twenties" saw a fabulous stock market boom, when everyone bought and sold stocks. Most purchases in this wild bull market were on margin. This means a buyer of $10,000 worth of stocks put up only part of the price in cash and borrowed the difference, pledging the newly bought stocks as collateral for the purchase. What did it matter that you had to pay the broker 10 percent per year on the borrowing when Bethlehem Steel might jump 10 percent in value overnight?

The great crash

Speculative bubbles always produce crashes and sometimes lead to economic panics. One traumatic event has cast a shadow over stock markets for decades—the 1929 panic and crash. This event ushered in the long and painful Great Depression of the 1930s.

The crash came in "black October" of 1929. Everyone was caught, the big-league professionals as well as the piddling amateurs—Andrew Mellon, John D. Rockefeller, engineer-turned-President Herbert Hoover in the White House, and America's greatest economist, Irving Fisher.

When the bottom fell out of the market in 1929, investors, big and small, who bought on margin could not put up funds to cover their holdings, and the market fell still further. The bull market turned into a bear(or declining) market. By the trough of the Depression in 1933, the market had declined 85 percent.

Trends in the stock market are tracked using stock-price indexes, which are weighted averages of the prices of a basket of company stocks. Commonly followed averages include the Dow-Jones Industrial Average(DJIA) of 30 large companies and Standard and Poor's index of 500 companies(the "S&P 500"), which is a weighted average of the stock prices of the 500 largest American corporations.

Figure shows the history since 1920 of the Standard and Poor's 500. The lower curve shows the nominal stock-price average, which records the actual average during a particular year. The upper line shows the real price of stocks; this equals the nominal price divided by an index of consumer prices that equaled 1 in 1996.

Note the experience of the 1980s, which illustrates both the perils and rewards of "playing the market", Beginning in 1982, the stock market surged steadily upward for 5 years, gaining almost 140 percent. Those who had the luck or vision to put all their assets into stocks made a lot of money. The market peaked in the summer of 1987. On October 19, 1987—"black Monday"—the stock market lost 22 percent of its value in 6 hours. The shock to securities markets was a vivid reminder of the risks you take when you buy stocks. Nevertheless, 35 million Americans own stocks; 3 million of them are people with incomes under $10,000. Only a small fraction of the shares is held by low-income households, but the fact that so many people are willing to invest their wealth this way attests to the lure of prospective gains from stock ownership.

Where will it all end? Is there a crystal ball that will foretell the movement of stock prices? This is the subject of modern finance theory.

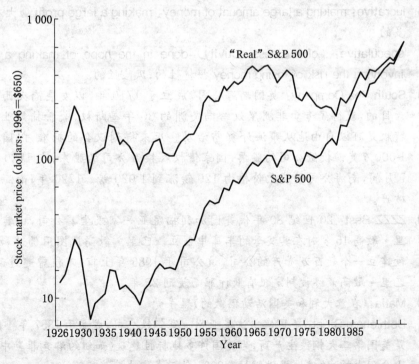

FIGURE   The Only Guarantee about Stock Prices Is That They Will Fluctuate

Stock prices in nominal terms, shown in the bottom line, tend to rise with inflation. The Standard and Poor's index (the S&P 500) shown here tracks the value-weighted average of the stock prices of the 500 largest American companies.

The top line shows the "real" S&P 500, which is the S&P 500 corrected or movements in the consumer price index.

Notes to the Text

1. New York Stock Exchange：纽约股票交易所，简称 NYSE；是美国和世界上最大的证券交易市场。交易所经营对象主要为股票，其次为各种国内外债券。除节假日外，交易时间每周五天，每天五小时。自 20 世纪 20 年代起，它一直是国际金融中心，这里股票行市的暴涨与暴跌都会在其他资本主义国家的股票市场产生连锁反应，引起波动。现在它还是纽约市最受欢迎的旅游名胜之一。

2. Burton Malkiel：伯顿·麦基尔，美国普林斯顿大学教授，著有《漫步华尔街》一书，曾任美国总统经济咨询委员会委员及美国金融协会主席。

3. amok：to suddenly become very angry or excited and start behaving violently, especially in a public place（尤指在公共场所）发狂，疯狂

4. outguess：猜透……的意图（或行动等）

5. dictum：a statement that expresses something that people believe is always true or should be followed 名言，格言

6. lucrative：making a large amount of money, making a large profit 赚大钱的，获利多的

7. speculative：（of business activity）done in the hope of making a profit but involving the risk of losing money 投机性的；风险性的

8. South Sea Company：英国南海公司，成立于 1710 年，以发展南大西洋的贸易为目的，获得了专卖非洲黑奴给南美洲的 30 年垄断权，兼营捕鲸业。它最大特权是可以自由地从事海外贸易活动。后来得到议会的批准，以国家公债约 1 000 万英镑换做公司的股票，国家债权人换做公司的股东，在 1720 年 4 月～7 月间，南海公司的股票价格由 120 镑涨到 1 020 镑。1720 年，南海公司宣告破产。

9. ZZZZ Best：20 世纪 80 年代美国加利福尼亚一家吸尘器公司，由其创始人巴里·敏高 15 岁时在其父母的车库中创立。巴里·敏高试图用伪造和偷窃等手段建立一个数百万资产的公司，该公司于 1986 年上市，市值曾超过两亿美元。巴里·敏高最终被判定犯有欺诈罪而获刑 25 年。

10. Mafia：（在意大利和美国活动猖獗的）黑手党

11. Bethlehem Steel：美国宾夕法尼亚州一家钢铁公司，成立于 1857 年 4 月 8 日，曾是美国第二大钢铁生产商，为美国许多地标性建筑（如纽约洛克菲勒中心和旧金山金门大桥）的建造提供钢材。2001 年正式宣告破产。

12. Andrew Mellon：安德鲁·梅隆，是美国历史上权力最大的财长，其财长生涯达 12

年,贯穿了上世纪整个 20 年代。他执掌过哈定、柯立芝和胡佛三位总统的财政大权,其空前的影响力被戏称为"三个总统为梅隆打过工"。梅隆旗下的"梅隆银行"是华尔街的金融巨头之一、"海湾石油公司"控制着美国石油的进出口、"美国铝业公司"则垄断了整个北美的铝生产。

13. John D. Rockefeller:约翰.D.洛克菲勒(1839—1937),美国标准石油公司创始人,美国石油大王,现代商业史上最富争议的人物之一。一方面,他创建的标准石油公司,在巅峰时期曾垄断全美 80% 的炼油工业和 90% 的油管生意。另一方面,他笃信基督教,以他名字命名的基金会,秉承"在全世界造福人类"的宗旨,捐款总额高达 5 亿美元。1870 年他创立了标准石油公司,1882 年开创了史无前例的联合事业——托拉斯,标准石油公司两年后成为全世界最大的石油集团企业,公司也更名为美孚石油公司。

14. Herbert Hoover:赫伯特·胡佛(1874—1964),美国第 31 任总统,生于衣阿华州,毕业于斯坦福大学。1921 年任商业部长。1928 年接受共和党总统候选人的提名并在大选中获胜。胡佛上台后,正赶上世界性的经济危机,美国经济坠入深渊,这使他原来希望依靠美国科学潜力来开辟一个"新时代"的愿望破灭。尽管他进行了不少努力,但危机一天天加重,终无力回天。1932 年大选中,他被罗斯福击败。退休后,著书立说,著作颇丰。

15. trough:a period of time when the level of something is low, especially a time when a business or the economy is not growing 低谷;(企业或经济的)低潮,萧条阶段

16. Fisher:理查德·费舍尔,美联储理事,达拉斯联邦储备委员会主席。

17. Dow-Jones Industrial Average:道琼斯工业指数,简称 DJIA,是由《华尔街日报》和道琼斯公司创建者查尔斯·道创造的几种股票市场指数之一;是道琼斯指数四组中的第一组,首次公布于 1896 年 5 月 26 日,它象征着美国工业中最重要的 12 种股票的平均数。

18. Standard and Poor's index of 500 companies:标准普尔 500 指数,简称 S&P 500 Index,是记录美国 500 家上市公司的一个股票价格指数,由标准普尔公司于 1957 年创建并维护。与道琼斯指数相比,标准普尔 500 指数包含的公司更多,因此风险更为分散,能够反映更广泛的市场变化。

19. play the market:to buy and sell stocks and shares in order to make a profit 买卖证券和股票

20. black Monday:"黑色星期一"。1987 年 10 月 19 日,道琼斯指数狂跌 508 点,日跌幅达 22.61%,由于该日是星期一,因此被称为美国股市的"黑色星期一"。美国爆发的这一"股灾",也引发了全球股市的同步暴跌。

21. attest:to show or prove that something is true 证实

Exercises

I Answer the following questions.

1. Why did the Eastern European countries begin their implementation of market economies with the introduction of stock market?
2. What are the reasons for so many people to play the market?
3. What would happen to the national economy and stock holders if there was a great crash in the stock market? Please take an example to prove your opinion.
4. In your opinion, how can people make money in the stock market?

II Write out the equivalents of the following words and expression.

1. collateral
2. cash in
3. the Great Depression
4. stock-price index
5. bull market
6. big-league
7. 股票经纪人
8. 经济恐慌
9. 熊市
10. 现代金融理论

III Translate the following into Chinese.

When a psychological frenzy seizes the market, it can result in speculative bubbles and crashes. A speculative bubble occurs when prices rise because people think they are going to rise in the future—it is the reverse of Keynes' dictum just cited. A piece of land may be worth only $1,000, but if you see a land-price boom driving prices up 50 percent each year, you might buy it for $2,000 hoping you can sell it to someone else next year for $3,000. A speculative bubble fulfills its own promises. If people buy because they think stocks will rise, their act of buying sends up the price of stocks. This causes people to buy even more and sends the dizzy dance off on another round. But, unlike people who play cards or dice, no one apparently loses what the winners gain. Of course, the prizes are all on paper and would disappear if everyone tried to cash them in. But why should anyone want to sell such lucrative securities? Prices rise because of hopes and dreams, not because the profits and dividends of companies are soaring.

Unit 14
Foreign Exchange

Both the currency of a foreign country and the process of exchanging it for the currency of another country are referred to as foreign exchange.

Just as nations developed differing languages, they also established various systems of money with a wide range of names: dollar, pound, crown, mark, franc, yen, peso, peseta, etc. Banks become involved in foreign exchange trading because it is necessary to translate one money to another so that people in one country can buy and sell goods and services with people in another country.

The trading of one currency for another arises from the various elements that make up a nation's balance of payments: movement of international trade, investment made, dividends on previous investments, loans, interest the payment for services, and the movements of tourists and immigrants. Whenever any international transaction takes place, there is eventually an exchange of one currency for another. The trading of foreign exchange is similar to trading any other commodity, such as wheat or cotton. Many of the major problems in international business begin first with establishing a value of one currency in terms of another, and second, obtaining sufficient quantities of each.

Today there are broad areas in which governments permit international trading of their money. In many countries such as the United States and the nations of Western Europe, there are few restrictions on foreign exchange trading. At the other extreme are such countries as the Soviet Union which prohibit foreign exchange trading.

Factors affecting exchange rates

Commercial transactions are concerned with exports and imports of both goods and services which give rise to the balance of trade and balance of payments on current account. If there is an adverse balance of payments on current account because we have imported more goods and services than we have exported, foreign exchange rates will have been affected in two ways. Firstly, the increase in imports will have created extra demand for foreign currencies and secondly, in order to buy these currencies additional sterling will have been placed on the market. The extra demand for foreign currencies will cause their values to appreciate and the increased supply of sterling will reduce its value in terms of foreign currencies. A favorable movement in the balance of payments would, of course, have the opposite effects upon exchange rates.

Another factor affecting the values of currencies is investment. When a British company constructs or acquires assets overseas or a British firm or resident acquires foreign stocks or shares(this is called indirect or portfolio investment) a demand for foreign currency is created. This export of capital therefore has a similar effect upon the value of sterling as an import of merchandise for in both cases, unless payment is to be made in sterling, foreign currencies have to be acquired through the market. Where foreigners invest in Britain, the opposite will apply, in other words the effect upon the market value of sterling will be the same as that of an export of goods. Foreigners will be demanding sterling and its value will tend to rise.

Movements of short-term capital affect the spot rates for currencies in the same way as movements of long-term capital. But an inflow or outflow of short-term capital affects the forward values as well. Furthermore the fact that the capital is invested on only a short-term basis means that its existence has a far more disturbing effect upon exchange rates than long-term capital.

Spot rates

Foreign exchange rates are determined by supply and demand in the same way that prices of ordinary commodities are determined by supply and demand. It is perhaps easier to understand how exchange rates are determined if the individual currencies are regarded as separate commodities. If the dollar/sterling exchange rate is $4 = £1, then the price of the commodity called the pound is $4 and the price of the commodity called the dollar is, £ $-$ T=25p. If there is an increased demand for dollars(perhaps because more American goods are being imported into Britain), then this will tend to increase the value of the dollar, e. g. it may rise to, say, 33p. To buy the extra dollars, more sterling will have to be put on the market and this will cause its value to fall from, say, $4 to S 3.

Although exchange rates fluctuate with supply and demand in this way, the extent to which they are allowed to fluctuate without government intervention is rather limited. Until recently Britain has had a system of fixed exchange rates, established when the International Monetary Fund was formed in 1946. Fixed parity rates are laid down between each individual currency and the U. S. dollar and gold, but day-to-day fluctuations around the parity rates are permitted up to a modest extent.

The majority of transactions in the market are "spot" transactions. This means that the currencies are bought and sold for immediate delivery. In actual fact, such transactions are completed two days after the agreement to buy and sell, to allow time for cable instructions to be sent to the foreign bank holding the currency concerned to pay it over to the bank nominated by the purchaser. If, for example, Barclays Bank sells $250,000 to the Midland Bank and this represents part of Barclays Bank's deposit with the First National City Bank in New York, then the bank in New York must be notified that it is to credit the $250,000 to a bank which Midland nominate, and to debit Barclays' account. The date for completion(i. e.

two days later in the case of spot transactions) is known as the value date. Where a bank buys foreign currency direct from a customer, the value date is the same day, there being no need for cable transactions, and the rate used will be the spot rate currently quoted in the market.

Spot rates are also T. T. rates, i. e. telegraphic transfer rates, for, as has been shown, spot transactions involving the movement of foreign balance necessitate the use of cables to send out the instructions. All other rates quoted in the foreign exchange market are based on the T. T. rate. For instance, the rate of exchange at which a bill of exchange will be bought by a bank will be the T. T. rate with an adjustment reflecting an allowance for interest to the date of maturity, based on the rates of interest in the centre in which it is sold. In calculating the rate for the purchase of a bill, the bank would adopt the maxim "the better the bill, the better the rate". In other words, the bank will pay a better price to the seller for a bill which involves only a small loss of interest than for one which involves a greater loss. Furthermore, a bill which carries the signature of a firm of repute will attract a better price than one drawn or accepted by a person or firm of lesser standing.

Forward exchange

Although the I. M. F. system of fixed exchange rates ensures that, apart from devaluations and revaluations, exchange rates can fluctuate only with narrow margins, it is nevertheless possible for those who have transactions to carry out in foreign currencies to lose through movements in rates of exchange during the time lag that occurs between the shipment of goods and the payment for them. When the value of sterling in terms of the U. S. dollar was fixed at $2.40, the exporter who had contracted to sell goods for $242,000 when the pound was at its lower support point of $2.38 = £1 would have reckoned to receive £101,680 for them(ignoring exchange commission and other expenses). If, before payment was received, the pound appreciated to its upper support point of $2.42 then only £100,000 would have been received for the dollars. The reduction of S 1,680 in the sterling proceeds might have represented a goodly proportion of his profit.

Exchange risks can be avoided by covering in the forward exchange market. Through this market, an exporter who is to receive payment for his goods in a foreign currency at some future date can fix immediately the rate of exchange at which he is to sell the currency when he receives it. If the value of the currency concerned depreciates before the settlement of the transaction, then a loss will be avoided. If the currency appreciated in value during the lapse of time between shipping the goods and receiving payment, the exporter would receive less for his currency under the forward contract than he would do in the spot market, but he cannot have the best of both worlds. If he wishes to protect himself against the risk of loss through fluctuations in exchange rates, then he cannot expect to receive the benefits that would have accrued to him had he not protected himself. The vital point is that he has been able to determine how much he is to receive in his own currency and is assured that his profit on the transaction remains intact.

Similarly, a forward exchange contract is invaluable to an importer. He knows in advance how much he is to pay out in foreign currency in the near future and will want to know how much this will be in terms of his own currency. If he can determine this in advance, he is better able to fix his prices for the resale of the goods at level that will provide a satisfactory profit margin. This margin might well be lost(if he did not cover himself) through an appreciation of the foreign currency in the spot market.

Forward exchange deals between bank and customer are entered into by way of formal contract. This is to protect the bank, for it may lose by fluctuations in exchange rates through having bought or sold currency in order to meet the customer's requirements which is subsequently not taken up by the customer. Even with a formal contract, there is always the risk that the customer may not be able to carry it through and, therefore, the bank may insist on a cash margin. This is kept on a special account on which interest is paid, with an understanding that the balance be maintained at a fixed percentage(usually between 10 per cent and 25 percent) of the current sterling value of the currency to be purchased or supplied by the bank.

Notes to the Text

1. International Monetary Fund：国际货币基金组织，是政府间的国际金融组织。它是根据1944年7月在美国新罕布什尔州布雷顿森林召开联合国和联盟国家的国际货币金融会议上通过的《国际货币基金协定》而建立起来的。1945年12月27日正式成立，1947年3月1日开始办理业务。其主要业务有:向成员国提供贷款、在货币问题上促进国际合作、研究国际货币制度改革的有关问题、研究扩大基金组织的作用、提供技术援助和加强同其它国际机构的联系。

2. Barclays Bank：巴克莱银行，成立于1862年，总部设在伦敦，从事银行金融服务已经有超过300年的历史，1998年总资产为3 652亿美元。巴克莱银行在全球约60个国家经营业务，在英国设有2 100多家分行。曾是位于汇丰银行和苏格兰皇家银行之后的英国第三大银行公司，2007年4月收购荷兰银行后跃升为英国第二大银行。

3. Midland Bank：英国米兰银行，成立于1836年，并于1974年收购曾享有100多年历史的萨穆尔蒙塔古商人银行，1991年1月并入汇丰银行。

4. First National City Bank：花旗银行，总部设在美国纽约，是华盛顿街最古老的商业银行之一，成立于1812年7月16日，其前身是1812年6月16日成立的纽约城市银行(City Bank of New York)；经过近两个世纪的发展、并购，已成为美国最大的银行，在全球近五十个国家及地区设有分支机构。

5. time lag: the period of time between two connected events（两件相关事件的）时间间隔，时滞

Exercises

I **Answer the following questions.**

1. By what are foreign exchange rate determined? What will happen to the value of the dollar if there is an increased demand for dollars? What will happen to the value of sterling if the U.K. imports more that it exports?

2. How do you understand the respective meaning of the first "better" and the second "better" in the maxim "the better the bill, the better the rate."?

3. Please tell the difference between depreciation and devaluation.

4. How can an exporter avoid exchange risks? If an exporter has protected himself in the forward foreign exchange market, can he still receive benefits in case of the appreciation of the foreign currency?

II **Write out the equivalents of the following words and expressions.**

1. foreign exchange rate
2. current account
3. spot rates
4. value date
5. forward exchange
6. firm of repute

7. 间接投资
8. 电汇
9. 升值
10. 到期日
11. 货物的发运
12. 利润率

III **Translate the following into Chinese.**

Exchange risks can be avoided by covering in the forward exchange market. Through this market, an exporter who is to receive payment for his goods in a foreign currency at some future date can fix immediately the rate of exchange at which he is to sell the currency when he receives it. If the value of the currency concerned depreciates before the settlement of the transaction, then a loss will be avoided. If the currency appreciated in value during the lapse of time between shipping the goods and receiving payment, the exporter would receive less for his currency under the forward contract than he would do in the spot market, but he cannot have the best of both worlds. If he wishes to protect himself against the risk of loss through fluctuations in exchange rates, then he cannot expect to receive the benefits that would have accrued to him had he not protected himself. The vital point is that he has been able to determine how much he is to receive in his own currency and is assured that his profit on the transaction remains intact.

Unit 15

Exchange Rates

Spot rate(S)

Rate of two currencies today: £1＝＄1.60

Appreciation and depreciation

If S falls from £1＝＄1.60 to £1＝＄1.55 the pound is now worth less in terms of ＄ it has depreciated(NB the ＄ is now worth more £ therefore the ＄ has appreciated).

If the £ rises in value against the ＄ it has appreciated. If the pound falls in value against the ＄ it has depreciated. Appreciation and depreciation are the price of exports and imports.

If S is £1＝＄1.60

With no transaction costs a good that is priced at £30 in the UK will be priced in the USA at ＄48(30×1.60＝48). A good that is priced at ＄100 in the USA will be priced in the UK at £62.50(100/1.60＝62.50).

If S depreciates to £1＝＄1.55

The UK good priced at £30 will now be priced in the USA at ＄46.5(30×1.55＝46.5). The US good priced at ＄100 will now be priced in the UK at £64.52(100/1.55＝64.52). The depreciation of the £ has made UK exports cheaper(in the USA) and US imports more expensive(in the UK). Therefore, UK exports will rise and imports will fall.

A depreciation will increase exports and reduce imports. From the US point of view the ＄ has appreciated against the £ and US exports have become more expensive and US imports are cheaper. An appreciation will reduce exports and increase imports.

Foward rate(F)

£1＝＄1.58 rate 6 months from today

If the future rate is less than spot rate F＜S—A discount exists on forward rate and the spot rate is expected to depreciate.

If the future rate is greater than the spot rate F＞S—A premium exists on the forward rate and the spot rate is expected to appreciate.

Nominal exchange rates—The rate at which currencies actually trade.

Effective exchange rate—A weighted-average of a currency against a basket of currencies.

Real exchange rates—A bilateral exchange rate adjusted for price changes.

Exchange Rate Systems

1. Floating exchange rates—market demand and supply determines the exchange rate;
2. Fixed exchange rates—governments fix exchange rate and take steps to keep the rate at the set parity;
3. Managed exchange rates—governments intervene in the markets to influence the exchange rate.

The purchasing power parity theorem

Suppose that the rate of inflation in the USA was 3% and in the UK it was 5% per annum. At the end of the year prices in the UK would have risen—relative to those in the USA—by a margin of 2%. If the exchange rate is fixed—UK goods will rise in price in the USA by 2% more than the rise in US goods. Therefore, with fixed exchange rates UK goods would become relatively more expensive in the USA and the demand for them in the USA would fall. At the same time US goods would become relatively cheaper in the UK and the demand for them in the UK would rise.

Law of one price

If all goods and services were homogeneous and were traded(with no barriers) the difference in price caused by differences in inflation would lead to people buy in the cheaper country(in this case the USA) and resell in the more expensive market(in this case the UK). This push the price up in the USA and push it down in the UK, which would continue until the price difference was eliminated—the law of one price.

However, in a system with floating exchange rates the demand from the UK for US goods and services would rise and the demand from the USA for UK goods and services would fall. Therefore the demand for £ (to buy UK goods and services) would fall and the supply of £ (to buy US goods and services) would rise. In these circumstances the £ would depreciate until the price difference between US and UK goods and services due to the differences in inflation was eliminated. There exists a new exchange rate at which the difference in inflation rates is exactly compensated and the law of one price will hold.

$Er1 \times Puk/Pusa = Er2$

$Er1$ = old exchange rate $Er2$ = new exchange rate

Puk = price level in UK $Pusa$ = price level in the USA

The purchasing power parity theorem implies that(if all goods and services are homogenous, are traded without barriers and exchange rates are floating) differences in inflation will lead to changes in exchange rates until the law of one price holds.

Empirical evidence does not support the purchasing power theorem(in the short run) because goods and services are not homogenous, trade barriers exist and there are interventions and imperfections in exchange rate markets that limit the applicability of the Purchasing Power Parity Theorem. Nevertheless, differences in inflation do have the influence on exchange rates that are suggested by the Purchasing Power Theorem.

Interest rate changes

With the removal of capital and exchange controls from most developed economies it became possible for very large amounts of short-term capital flows to cross frontiers to take advantage of interest rate differences.

These flows have large effects on exchange rates because they alter the demand and supply of currencies.

For example, if the rate of interest is higher in the UK (or is expected to rise) than in the USA capital will flow from the US to the UK. However, if the exchange regime is floating, these flows will alter the exchange rate (will lead to an appreciation of the £) which will lead to less $ per £. Therefore, the return (in $) from investing in the UK will decline.

Consequently, capital will flow leading to alteration to exchange rates until it is no longer worthwhile investing in the UK (even with higher interest rates in the UK).

Interest rate differences are therefore the main determinant of short-run exchange rates in floating exchange rate regimes.

In the long-run differences in inflation is the main determinant of exchange rate—the purchasing power parity theorem.

Three types of risk

1. Economic exposure—changes in the volume of sales and hence revenues as exchange rates vary
2. Translation risk—accounting problems when converting revenues and costs into different currencies
3. Transaction risk—uncertainty about the value of payments and receipts

Can you hedge against translation and transaction risk by buying at the forward rate or use option to buy at a given exchange rate. Economic risk can be hedged against by diversification of production plants in different countries.

Pricing decisions

Firms must decide what to do about export prices when exchange rates alter. Suppose a good is priced at £36,000 in the UK at an exchange rate of £1= $1.60, it would sell for $57,600 in the USA.

If the £ depreciated to £1= $1.55, the good if the UK price remained at £36,000 would sell in the USA for $55,800.

The firm could however, keep the price at $57,600 leading to a UK price of £37,161.29. This would lead to more revenue if the good is price inelastic in demand.

Cost of borrowing

A firm could face an interest rate on borrowing of 5% in the USA and 7% in the UK. Should the firm borrow in the cheaper US market?

The firm could speculate that the exchange rate would not move in an adverse direction and not cover for risk by buying on the forward exchange market. However, if the exchange rate did move in an adverse direction the firm would make losses if it borrowed abroad.

However, in the longer run(over two or three years) it is not possible to hedge against currency fluctuations. Hence the decision to take advantage of interest rate differences by borrowing in foreign markets is a risky business.

Notes to the Text

1. nominal exchange rate：名义汇率
2. effective exchange rate：有效汇率
3. real exchange rate：实际汇率
4. parity：the fact of the units of money of two different countries being equal（两国货币的）平价
5. theorem：a rule or principle, especially in mathematics, that can proved to be true（尤指数学的）定理
6. homogeneous：consisting of things or people that are all the same or all of the same type 同类的
7. hedge：以套期保值避免或减轻损失

Exercises

I **Answer the following questions.**

1. How do you understand the two types of exchange rates, spot rate and forward rate? What's the relationship between them?

2. What's the effect of exchange rate fluctuation on the prices of export and import goods?

3. Which currency should be used for the exporters to make quotations and the importers to make payment?

4. What is the law of one price?

5. What are the two main elements which determine the fluctuation of exchange rate in the short run and in the long run? Could you offer a brief explanation on this?

II **Write out the equivalents of the following words and expressions.**

1. depreciation
2. forward rate
3. discount
4. a basket of currencies
5. translation risk

6. 交易成本
7. 通货膨胀率
8. 浮动汇率
9. 外汇管制
10. 投资回报

III Translate the following into Chinese.

The purchasing power parity theorem implies that（if all goods and services are homogenous, are traded without barriers and exchange rates are floating）differences in inflation will lead to changes in exchange rates until the law of one price holds.

Empirical evidence does not support the purchasing power theorem（in the short run）because goods and services are not homogenous, trade barriers exist and there are interventions and imperfections in exchange rate markets that limit the applicability of the Purchasing Power Parity Theorem. Nevertheless, differences in inflation do have the influence on exchange rates that are suggested by the Purchasing Power Theorem.

Unit 16

International Trade

As we go about our daily lives, it is easy to overlook the importance of international exchange. America ships enormous volumes of food, airplanes, computers, and construction machinery to other countries; and in return we get vast quantities of oil, VCRs, cars, kiwi fruits, and other goods and services. Even more important for most countries are the new products and services that have over the years derived from other regions. While we may produce most of our national output, it is sobering to reflect how much our consumption— including clocks, railroads, accounting, penicillin, radar, and the Beatles—originates in the ingenuity of long-forgotten people in faraway places.

What are the economic forces that lie behind international trade? Simply put, trade promotes specialization, and specialization increases productivity. Over the long run, increased trade and higher productivity raise living standards for all nations. Gradually, countries have realized that opening up their economies to the global trading system is the most secure road to prosperity.

In this final part, we survey the principles governing international trade and finance, which is the system by which nations export and import goods, services, and financial capital. International economics involves many of the most controversial questions of the day: Why does the United States benefit from importing almost one-quarter of its automobiles and half of its petroleum? What are the advantages to the United States, Canada, and Mexico of a free-trade region? Is there wisdom in the European countries' adopting a common currency? And why has the United States become the world's largest debtor country in the last decade? The economic stakes are high in finding wise answers to these questions.

International vs. domestic trade

How does the analysis of international trade differ from that of domestic markets? There are three differences:

1. Expanded trading opportunities. The major advantage of international trade is that it expands trading horizons. If people were forced to consume only what they produced at home, the world would be poorer on both the material and the spiritual planes. Canadians could drink no wine, Americans could eat no bananas, and most of the world would be without jazz and Hollywood movies.

2. Sovereign nations. Trading across frontiers involves people and firms living in

different nations. Each nation is a sovereign entity which regulates the flow of people, goods, and finance crossing its borders. This contrasts with domestic trade, where there is a single currency, trade and money flow freely within the borders, and people can migrate easily to seek new opportunities. Sometimes, political barriers to trade are erected when affected groups objects to foreign trade and nations impose tariffs or quotas. This practice is called protectionism.

3. Exchange rates. Most nations have their own currencies. I want to pay for a Japanese car in dollars, while Toyota wants to be paid in Japanese yen. The international financial system must ensure a smooth flow of dollars, yen, and other currencies—or else risk a breakdown in trade.

Economic basis for international trade

Trends in foreign trade

An economy that engages in international trade is called an open economy. A useful measure of openness is the ratio of a country's exports or imports to its GDP. **Figure** shows the trend in the shares of imports and exports for the United States. It shows the dip in the trade share during the trade wars of the 1930s, followed by the steady expansion of trade with lower trade barriers over last three decades. Still, the United States is a lively self-sufficient economy. Many nations, particularly in Western Europe and East Asia, are highly open economies and export and import more than 50 percent of their GDP.

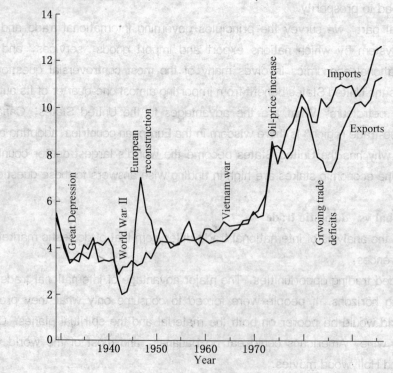

FIGURE   Growing U. S. Openness

The degree of openness is much higher in the U. S. industries, such as steel, textiles, consumer electronics and autos, than it is for the U. S. economy a whole. **Table** shows the commodity composition of U. S. foreign trade for 1996. The data reveal that despite being an advanced industrial economy, the United States exports surprisingly large amounts of primary commodities(such as food) and imports large quantities of sophisticated, capital-intensive manufactured goods(like automobiles and telecommunications equipment). Moreover, we find a great deal of two-way, or intra-industry, trade. Within a particular industry, the United States both exports and imports at the same time because a high degree of product differentiation means that different countries tend to have niches in different parts of a market.

U. S. Merchandise Trade, 1996

Commodity classification	Share of each commodity as percent of total	
	Exports	Imports
Industrial supplies:		
Food and beverages	9	4
Petroleum and petroleum products	1	8
Other	22	15
Manufactures:		
Capital goods		
Computers and related equipment	7	7
Civilian aircraft and related equipment	5	1
Other capital goods	27	19
Automotive vehicles and parts	10	16
Consumer goods	5	5
Other	14	25
Total		

TABLE   The United States Exports Surprising Amounts of Primary Goods and Imports Many Manufactures

The sources of international trade in goods and services

What are the economic factors that lie behind the patterns of international trade? Nations find it beneficial to participate in international trade for several reasons: because of diversity in the conditions of production, because of decreasing costs of production, and because of differences in tastes among nations.

Diversity in natural resources

Trade may take place because of the diversity in productive possibilities among countries. In part, these differences reflect endowments of natural resources. One country may be blessed with a supply of petroleum, while another may have a large amount of fertile land. Or a mountainous country may generate large amounts of hydroelectric power which it sells to its neighbors, while a country with deep-water harbors may become a shipping center.

Differences in tastes

A second cause of trade lies in preferences. Even if the conditions of production were identical in all regions, countries might engage in trade if their tastes for goods were different.

For example, suppose that Norway and Sweden produce fish from the sea and meat from the land in about the same amounts, but the Swedes have a great fondness for meat while the Norwegians are partial to fish. A mutually beneficial export of meat from Norway and fish from Sweden would take place. Both countries would gain from this trade; the sum of human happiness is increased, just as when Jack Sprat trades fat meat for his wife's lean.

Decreasing costs

Perhaps the most important reason for trade is differences among countries in production costs. For example, manufacturing processes enjoy economies of scale; that is, they tend to have lower average costs of production as the volume of output expands. So when a particular country gets a head start in a particular product, it can become the high-volume, low-cost producer. The economies of stale give it a significant cost and technological advantage over other countries, which find it cheaper to buy from the leading producer than to make the product themselves.

Take consumer electronics as an example. No doubt a company such as GE or IBM could make a videocassette recorder(VCR) in the United State if it wanted to. But it could not make one cheap enough to compete with Japanese manufacturers like Sony, which have the advantages of enormous volumes and long experience in making consumer electronics. As a result, the United States imports almost all of its VCRs.

The shoe is on the other foot when it comes to civilian aircraft, where the United States dominates the world market. Boeing, the leading exporter in the United States, has two important advantages. First, Boeing has a long track record in building reliable and safe passenger jets. This is not an easy task for a competitor to match. Because modern planes are complicated and technologically sophisticated, it takes time and practice to learn how to build reliable planes at an affordable price.

Large scale is often an important advantage in industries with large research and development expenses. As the leading aircraft maker in the world, Boeing can spread the enormous cost of designing, developing, and testing a new plane over a large sales volume. That means it can sell planes at a lower price than competitors with a smaller volume. Boeing's only real competitor, Airbus, got off the ground through large subsidies from several European countries to cover its research and development costs.

The example of decreasing cost helps explain the important phenomenon of extensive intra-industry trade shown in **Table**. Why is it that the United States both imports and exports computers and related equipment? The reason is that the United States has exploited the economies of scale in microprocessors and is specialized in that area, while Japan enjoys a cost advantage in memory chips and video screens for notebook computers and tends to specialize and export in that part of the market. Similar patterns of intra-industry specialization are seen with cars, steel, textiles, and many other manufactured products.

Like all major market economies, the United States has increasingly opened its borders to foreign trade over the last half-century. The result is a growing share of output and consumption involved in international trade. In the late 1980s, imports far outdistanced exports, causing the United States to become the world's largest debtor nation. (*Source*: *U. S. Department of Commerce*)

The United States exports a large volume of primary commodities, especially food and coal, mainly because of its ample natural resources. At the same time, it imports many manufactured goods, like cars and cameras, because other countries specialize in different market niches and enjoy economies of scale. (*Source*: *U. S. Department of Commerce*)

Notes to the Text

1. kiwi fruits: a small fruit with thin hairy brown skin, soft green flesh and black seeds, originally from New Zealand 猕猴桃；奇异果
2. Beatles：甲壳虫乐队（又译披头士乐队），由约翰·列侬，保罗·麦卡特尼，乔治·哈里森和林戈·斯塔尔创建于英国利物浦，是英国乃至世界音乐史上的奇迹。乐队最初创建于 1956 年，1960 年起定名为 Beatles，1967 年解散。乐队的代表曲目有：Please Please Me，Yesterday，Yellow Submarine，Let It Be 等等。
3. Hollywood：好莱坞，位于美国加利福尼亚州洛杉矶市西北部，是美国和世界电影业的中心。好莱坞在美国文化中具有重大的象征意义，它的发展史就是美国电影的发展史。好莱坞生产的影片不仅满足美国电影市场的需要，还出口到世界各地，不仅输出了美国的文化，更为好莱坞投资人带来了丰厚的利润。
4. niches：an opportunity to sell a particular product to a particular group of people 商机
5. Jack Sprat：英国著名童谣中的人物。原文如下：Jack Sprat could eat no fat/His wife could eat no lean/And so between the two of them/They licked the platter clean.
6. GE：美国通用电气公司（General Electricity），总部设在纽约，是世界上最大的多元化服务性公司，同时也是高质量、高科技工业和消费产品的提供者。
7. IBM：国际商业机器公司（International Business Machines），总部设在纽约，1914 年创立于美国，是世界上最大的信息工业跨国公司，目前拥有全球雇员 30 多万人，业务遍及 160 多个国家和地区。
8. videocassette recorder：盒式录音机（简称 VCR）
9. Boeing：波音公司，美国及世界主要民用飞机制造商，成立于 1961 年，总部最先

设在华盛顿州西雅图市, 2001 年 9 月迁至伊利诺伊州芝加哥市。该公司在军用飞机、卫星、人类太空飞行和运载火箭等领域始终处于领先地位。目前, 波音公司的用户遍布全球 140 多个国家和地区。

10. Airbus：欧洲空中客车公司, 创建于 1970 年, 是一家集法国、德国、西班牙与英国公司为一体的欧洲集团, 总部设在法国图卢兹, 由欧洲四家主要的宇航公司共同拥有——法国宇航公司、德国戴姆勒-奔驰宇航空中客车公司、英国宇航公司和西班牙飞机制造公司。

Exercises

I Answer the following questions.

1. What are the advantages and disadvantages of export and import?
2. Please explain in you own words the differences between international trade and domestic trade?
3. What factors make international trade possible and necessary?
4. Why is the U.S. the most advanced country and the biggest debtor nation at the same time?

II Write out the equivalents of the following words or expressions.

1. self-sufficient economy
2. primary commodities
3. capital-intensive manufactured goods
4. two-way intra-industry trade
5. consumer electronics
6. memory chips
7. endowment
8. 全球贸易系统
9. 金融资本
10. 债务国
11. 国内贸易
12. 电信设备
13. 航运中心

III Translate the following into Chinese.

An economy that engages in international trade is called an open economy. A useful measure of openness is the ratio of a country's exports or imports to its GDP. Figure shows the trend in the shares of imports and exports for the United States. It shows the dip in the trade share during the trade wars of the 1930s, followed by the steady expansion of trade with lower trade barriers over last three decades. Still, the United States is a lively self-sufficient economy. Many nations, particularly in Western Europe and East Asia, are highly open economies and export and import more than 50 percent of their GDP.

Unit 17

Classical Theories of Trade

Mercantilism

Maximize inflow of money from trade—implies minimize imports and maximize exports and therefore maximize balance of payments surplus.

However it is impossible for all nations to run a balance of payments surplus because if one country has a surplus at least one other country must have a deficit. Therefore the pursuit of mercantilism leads to protectionism and conflict between trading nations.

Moreover if a country persistently exports more than it imports there will be a net inflow of money into that country and a net outflow from deficit countries. This will increase demand in the surplus country（thereby tending to increase prices）. In deficit countries the reverse will occur leading to a tendency for prices to fall. As prices rise in surplus countries and fall in deficit countries this will tend to increase imports and reduce exports in surplus countries （vice versa in deficit countries）. Consequently mercantilism tends to be self-defeating.

However, if a country can run a persistent surplus, this reduces the ability of trading partners to buy products from surplus countries; and this hampers the growth of trade.

This dispute was what lay behind the free trade movement in 19 century Britain and led to the free trade movement.

Absolute and comparative advantage

These theories were developed by Adam Smith（Absolute advantage）and David Ricardo （Comparative advantage）to provide a theoretical basis for free trade.

These theories are based on the following assumptions.

1. No transport costs.
2. No transaction costs—no costs involved in conducting transactions.
3. Competitive markets—every trader is a price taker.
4. Goods and services can be traded across frontiers but capital and labor can not be traded across frontiers.
5. Full employment—all resources used in the production of goods and services are fully employed and they can be transferred between different types of production at zero cost.

All of these assumptions can be relaxed. Relaxing assumptions 1 and 2 simply requires the addition of these costs to the cost and therefore the price of the products relaxing the other assumptions makes it impossible to prove that free trade will be mutually beneficial.

Conclusions on classical theories of trade：

1. Free trade is mutually beneficial.

2. Countries that engage in free trade will specialize in those products for which they have an absolute or comparative advantage—i. e. they specialize in those goods and services in which they are relative best at producing.

3. Classical trade theory explains inter-industry trade—trade between different industries—e. g. one country specializes in computers，the other on clothing and they trade computers for clothing.

4. Classical trade theory can not explain intra-industry trade—trade within the same industry—e. g. buy and sell computers from each other.

5. If the assumption of full employment is dropped free trade gives rise to adjustment costs as resources made unemployed are transferred to other uses.

6. If the assumption of no mobility of capital and labor across frontiers is dropped the classical theory is unable to prove that free trade will be mutually beneficial.

Modern theories of trade have been developed to answer the questions left unanswered by classical theory. In particular why does intra-trade exist and what is the importance of the movement of labor and particularly capital across frontiers.

Notes to the Text

1. mercantilism：重商主义；赢利主义

2. self-defeating：causing more problems and difficulties instead of solving them；not achieving what you wanted to achieve but having an opposite effect 事与愿违的；适得其反的；弄巧成拙的

3. costs：此处指上文提到的运输成本和交易成本

4. cost：此处指总成本

Exercises

Ⅰ Answer the following questions.

1. Taking the all-round growth of the globe into consideration，is it good for a country to run a persistent surplus in international trade?

2. In your opinion，is absolute free trade possible in the present world? If not，what do you think are the obstacles to free trade?

3. Can the theory of comparative advantage be applied to the inter-industry trade within a particular country?

4. What are the contributions and shortcomings of classical theories of trade?

II **Write out the equivalents of the following words or expressions.**

1. classical theories of trade
2. balance of payment surplus
3. mobility of capital
4. movement of labor across frontiers
5. 逆差国

6. 比较劣势
7. 贸易伙伴
8. 互利
9. 行业内贸易

III **Translate the following into Chinese.**

However it is impossible for all nations to run a balance of payments surplus because if one country has a surplus at least one other country must have a deficit. Therefore the pursuit of mercantilism leads to protectionism and conflict between trading nations.

Moreover if a country persistently exports more than it imports there will be a net inflow of money into that country and a net outflow from deficit countries. This will increase demand in the surplus country (thereby tending to increase prices). In deficit countries the reverse will occur leading to a tendency for prices to fall. As prices rise in surplus countries and fall in deficit countries this will tend to increase imports and reduce exports in surplus countries (vice versa in deficit countries). Consequently mercantilism tends to be self-defeating.

Unit 18

Free Trade or Fair Trade

Gains from lower trade barriers

Reduced trade barriers have been key elements in the increased prosperity the world has seen in the post-1945 era. These lower barriers have allowed greater specialization of production, with consequent gains in cheaper goods enjoyed by all parties. At the present time, the average tariff on imports into Australia is 3.8 per cent. In 1984/1985 the tariff equivalent averaged 21 per cent for agricultural products and 13 per cent for manufactures. The rapid reduction in Australian tariffs did not cause high levels of unemployment. Present levels of unemployment are lower now than they were during the mid-1980s.

Drivers for liberalization

Multilateral agreements under the GATT and WTO have been the leading arrangements bringing greater liberalization, but narrower agreements such as the European Union and Canada-US bilateral free trade have also been significant. For Australia, the bilateral agreements with New Zealand have made important contributions by allowing Australia and New Zealand to become, in substance, a single economy.

Unilateral, non-reciprocated trade reform also offers benefits—indeed, Australia's liberalization has in the main been of this nature, with tariff and other barriers being reduced following reports of the Productivity Commission or its predecessors. These unilateral reductions have then been used as bargaining coin to seek concessions from other countries in trade negotiations.

Although trade liberalization works best if all parties participate, consumers gain from unilateral liberalizations even where others do not reciprocate. Such unilateral liberalizations also bring economy wide gains by inducing a relative contraction or improved efficiency of the tariff reducing country's less competitive businesses. These outcomes allow more to be produced with the same labor, capital and other resources.

Benefits of liberalization

Traditionally, trade benefits have been seen most clearly where countries have vastly different economic structures. Comparative advantage in different areas of production allows both countries to gain as a result of specialization. This view of trade gains has been at the heart of the process over a long period—England sent manufactures to Australia and received primary products in return. More recently, the increased income levels stemming from the European Union(EU) have highlighted different forms of gains or, perhaps more accurately, a different view of the same gains. The EU gains were realized by countries with structurally similar economies. The gains came from intra-industry trade—the trading partners appeared to be buying and selling goods that they already made in their home countries. The gains from this intra-industry trade following liberalizations between countries that have similar economic profiles have come from two directions:

- increased competitive pressures on suppliers that previously went less heavily challenged in their home markets; businesses facing increased competition usually lift their performance to the benefit of consumers in all participating countries;

- a variation of the traditional comparative advantage gains but one that takes advantage of the increased specialization of modern production and the increased number of stages through which materials are put prior to reaching the final consumer.

Fair trade

Over the years, there have always been calls for trade liberalization conditional on some measure of "fairness". After all, it could be said that those countries that pay very low wages are at a trade advantage with high-wage countries such as Australia. But a moment's thought shows the deficiencies of this approach. For a start, it would deny market opportunities to countries with low income levels, opportunities that have been crucial to the subsequent growth and high income levels of countries ranging from Japan to southern Europe. And as we have seen, trade liberalization has been accompanied by increased, not decreased, employment all round.

Moreover, once embarked upon, this road leads to a reversal of the trade liberalization that has served us so well. Thus it might be said that, with our vast agricultural land resources, Australian farmers have unfair advantages over European farmers in broad area crops like wheat. Similarly, with its abundance of easily won mineral wealth, Australia is not on a level playing field with mining operations in other countries. In both cases, many in importing countries would seek to equalize the competition by placing a penalty on Australian exports

More recently, some people have sought to use environmental or worker safety standards as conditions for permitting other countries to export to us. Although many championing such causes do so out of strong convictions, it means paternalistically imposing our own standards on other countries. And often supporting measures to restrict trade on safety or environmental grounds are those with a vested interest in maintaining a cushion against more competitive suppliers. But the protected suppliers' gain is the consumer's loss. Even seeking to use the fair trade weapon as a lever on manufacturers to lift employment conditions in poor countries where they operate is likely to hack fire on the workers in those countries. Forcing higher wages is likely to mean industries migrate to other countries which are less susceptible to such pressures. The outcome is lost jobs in the targeted country, with the displaced workers having to accept far inferior conditions than those they previously experienced.

The way forward

The call for fair trade is one of the factors thwarting further progress in dismantling trade impediments in global negotiations. The EU is a leader in using this negative weapon. In addition, under French influence, it has resisted any attempts to dismantle its notorious agricultural policies. These policies deny European market access to efficient producers such as Australia. The EU guarantees its own farmers high prices which also bring massive surpluses in many agricultural products. These are dumped on world markets and depress prices.

These developments have brought a hunt for alternative ways forward. Australia, like other countries, is exploring possible free trade agreements with individual countries. In our case, one with Thailand is on the cards, but the most important prospect is the USA.

This would integrate the Australian economy with the world's largest and most technologically advanced economy. Free access to the US market offers our manufactures and service providers the economies of scale they need to keep their costs down. For consumers, it means cheaper goods and services. These cheaper goods and services will in part be due to direct imports from the USA. But overwhelmingly they will be cheaper domestic supplies resulting from producers achieving lower costs that competition forces them to pass on.

Australia's opportunity for a free trade agreement with the USA is the envy of many countries. Nevertheless, there is a usual chorus of dissent from vested interests. Some vested interests, for example, the actors' union, want to see continued restraints on the employment of foreign artists in Australia. At present, there is a highly complex set of requirements on television stations and on those making TV advertisements to increase the Australian content from the levels that Australian consumers would otherwise opt for. This local content system is creaking at the edges because of technology advances and is likely to come under pressure in any case as the number of TV stations available to each household expands to the hundreds. Undeterred, the Australian Writers' Guild even wants to see the government forcing double the current requirements of locally produced drama onto the consumer.

Understandably, these protectionist dinosaurs see free trade with the US as a threat and would treat multilateral free trade with even greater hostility. Yet, the internationalization of Australian artists has opened up unheard-of opportunities for our local talent. Led by Russell Crowe and Nicole Kidman, our acting profession has achieved a global identity that nobody would have anticipated 10 years ago. Special privileges for Australian artists and TV programmers are unnecessary. They also bring increased costs that are passed on to

Australian consumers in dearer products and services.

Because the international liberalization process in trade is being stymied, bilateral avenues for liberalization are the best way forward. But bilateral agreements do bring dangers of reducing efficiency by diverting trade from the lowest cost supplier if another supplier is given an advantage. Fortunately, the nature of Australia's production makes this unlikely in the case of a trade agreement with the US. Nonetheless, a proliferation of bilateral treaties automatically brings a greater complexity in the rules. For example, the proliferation of free trade agreements in the United States has contributed to government procurement rules amounting to 300 pages compared to just seven pages for Australia.

Concluding comments

Australia's transformation into an internationally oriented economy with reduced trade barriers has turned us into one of the world's strongest and most prosperous economies. Further reductions in our trade restraints are the way forward.

The preferred route, multilateral trade agreements, is being shut off by those who seek to use trade negotiations as a tool of social and environmental policy. To accept this means stagnation, setting a criterion of "fairness" in trade means that the trade has to be managed. Some bureaucracy would need to sift through literally thousands of trade items across two hundred countries to give each product the elephant stamp of approval. Its decisions would contain the inevitable compromises and tit-for-tat favors which characterize all such negotiations. This would grind commerce down and, with it, living standards would fall in affluent and poor countries alike.

With the impasse in multilateral trade negotiations, free trade treaties with individual countries, especially with the USA, provide the optimal policy.

Notes to the Text

1. manufactures: manufactured goods 工业品
2. GATT: 关税及贸易总协定(简称"关贸总协定",General Agreement on Tariffs and Trade),是关于关税和贸易准则的多边国际协定和组织。第二次世界大战之后,国际经济严重萧条,国际贸易秩序混乱,1944 年 7 月在美国的布雷顿森林召开的国际货币与金融会议(44 个国家参加)建议成立国际货币基金组织、国际复兴开发银行(即世界银行)和国际贸易组织,作为支撑全球经济的三大支柱来调节世界经贸关系,推动全球经济的复苏和发展。1947 年 4 月至 10 月,在日内瓦召开的第二次筹委会会议同意将正在起草中的国际贸易组织宪章草案中涉及关税与贸易的条款抽取出来,构成一个单独的协定,并把它命名为《关税及贸易总协定》,它于 1948 年 1 月 1 日起正式生效。1995 年,关贸总协定 128 个缔约方在日内瓦举行最后一次会议,宣告关贸总协定的历史使命完结。根据乌拉圭回合多边贸易谈判达成的协议,从 1996 年 1 月 1 日起,由世界贸易组织(World Trade Organization—WTO) 取代关贸总协定。

3. European Union：欧洲联盟，简称欧盟(EU)，成立于 1993 年，是当今世界一体化程度最高的区域政治、经济集团组织，其总部设在比利时首都布鲁塞尔。欧盟现有 25 个成员国，分别为法国、德国、意大利、荷兰、比利时、卢森堡、丹麦、爱尔兰、英国、希腊、西班牙、葡萄牙、奥地利、芬兰、瑞典、波兰、匈牙利、捷克、斯洛伐克、爱沙尼亚、拉脱维亚、立陶宛、斯洛文尼亚、马耳他和塞浦路斯。其面积逾 100 万平方公里，人口 4.5 亿，生产总值超过 10 万亿美元。欧盟的前身为 1958 年成立的欧洲经济共同体(EEC)。欧盟共有 5 个主要机构：欧洲理事会、欧盟理事会、欧盟委员会、欧洲议会、欧洲法院。其他重要机构还有欧盟审计院、欧洲中央银行、欧洲投资银行、经济和社会委员会、地区委员会、欧洲警察局和欧洲军备局等。欧盟理事会(简称理事会)是欧盟的主要决策机构，由来自欧盟各成员国政府的部长组成。主席由成员国轮任，任期 6 个月。

4. reciprocate：to behave or feel towards somebody in the same way as they behave or feel towards you 回报；回应

5. vested interest：a personal reason for wanting something to happen, especially because you get some advantage from it 既得利益

6. thwart：to prevent somebody from doing what they want to do 阻止；阻挠

7. impediment：something that delays or stops the progress of something 阻碍；障碍；妨碍

8. Russell Crowe：拉塞尔·克劳，好莱坞当红男影星，1964 年生于新西兰，2000 年和 2001 年凭借《角斗士》和《美丽心灵》连续获得奥斯卡最佳男演员奖。

9. Nicole Kidman：妮可·基德曼，好莱坞当红女影星，1967 年生于澳大利亚，2003 年因影片《时时刻刻》(The Hours)荣膺第 60 届美国电影奥斯卡最佳女主角奖。

10. stymie：to prevent something from happening 阻挠；妨碍

11. proliferation：the sudden increase in the number or amount of something 激增；涌现

12. stagnation：the state of stopping developing or making progress 停滞

13. tit-for-tat：a situation in which you do something bad to somebody because they have done something bad to you 针锋相对；以牙还牙

Exercises

I Answer the following questions.

1. Could you list some types of trade barriers in international trade? Why do the governments of many countries impose trade barriers on the trade with other countries?

2. What can the international traders benefit from the trade liberalization?

3. Do you think there is absolute fairness in international trade? Please take

Australia as an example to illustrate you opinion.

4. What is the right way for Australia to become one of the world's strongest economies?

5. What's the difference between free trade and fair trade? Can they co-exist with each other?

II **Write out the equivalents of the following words and expression.**

1. specialization of production
2. worker safety standard
3. displaced workers
4. optimal policy
5. 多边协议
6. 贸易自由化
7. 本国市场
8. 贸易谈判

III **Translate the following into Chinese.**

Because the international liberalization process in trade is being stymied, bilateral avenues for liberalization are the best way forward. But bilateral agreements do bring dangers of reducing efficiency by diverting trade from the lowest cost supplier if another supplier is given an advantage. Fortunately, the nature of Australia's production makes this unlikely in the case of a trade agreement with the US. Nonetheless, a proliferation of bilateral treaties automatically brings a greater complexity in the rules. For example, the proliferation of free trade agreements in the United States has contributed to government procurement rules amounting to 300 pages compared to just seven pages for Australia.

Unit 19

International Institutions

In the early part of the twentieth century, even nations which were ostensibly at peace engaged in debilitating trade wars and competitive devaluations. After World War II, international institutions were developed to foster economic cooperation among nations. These institutions continue to be the means by which nations coordinate their policies and seek solutions to common problems. This section surveys the major international institutions and examines the issues raised by interdependencies among nations.

The United States emerged from World War II with its economy intactable and willing to help rebuild the countries of friends and foes alike. The postwar international political system responded to the needs of war-torn nations by establishing durable institutions that facilitated the quick recovery of the international economy. The major international economic institutions of the postwar period were the General Agreement on Tariffs and Trade (rechartered as the World Trade Organization in 1995), the Bretton Woods Exchange-rate System, the International Monetary Fund, and the World Bank. These four institutions stand as monuments to wise and far-sighted statecraft.

The bretton woods system

The major economists of die 1940s, particularly John Maynard Keynes, were greatly affected by the economic crisis of the prewar period. They were determined to avoid the economic chaos and competitive devaluations that had occurred during the Great Depression.

Under the intellectual leadership of Keynes, nations gathered in 1944 at Bretton Woods, New Hampshire, and hammered out an agreement that led to the formation of the major economic institutions. For the first time, nations agreed upon a system for regulating international financial transactions. Even though some of the rules have changed since 1944, the institutions established at Bretton Woods continue to play a vital role today.

Those who attended the Bretton Woods conference remembered well how the gold standard was too inflexible and served to deepen economic crises. To replace the gold standard, the Bretton Woods system established a parity for each currency in terms of both the U. S. dollar and gold. Currencies were defined in terms of both gold and the dollar, and exchange rates among currencies were determined in much the same way as they had been under the gold standard. For example, the parity of the British pound was set at £ 12.5 per ounce of gold. Given that the gold price of the dollar was $ 35 per ounce, this implied an official exchange rate between the dollar and the pound of $\$35 / £12.5 = \$2.80$ per $£1$, which was thereby set as the official parity on the pound. The revolutionary innovation of the Bretton Woods system was that exchange rates were fixed but adjustable. When one currency got too far out of line with its appropriate or "fundamental" value, the parity could be adjusted. The ability to adjust exchange rates when fundamental disequilibrium arose was the central distinction between the Bretton Woods system and the gold standard. Ideally, exchange-rate changes would be worked out among countries in a cooperative way.

By creating a fixed but adjustable system, the designers of Bretton Woods hoped to have the best of two worlds. They could maintain the stability of the gold standard, a world in which exchange rates would be predictable from one month to the next, thereby encouraging trade and capital flows. At the same time, they would simulate the adjustment of flexible exchange rates, under which persistent relative-price differences among countries could be adjusted to by exchange-rate changes rather than by the painful deflation and unemployment necessary under the gold standard.

The international monetary fund(IMF)

An integral part of the Bretton Woods system was the establishment of the International Monetary Fund (or IMF), which still administers the international monetary system and operates as a central bank for central banks. Member nations subscribe by lending their currencies to the IMF; the IMF then relends these funds to help countries in balance-of-payments difficulties. In recent years, the IMF has played a key role in organizing a cooperative response to the international debt crisis and in helping formerly communist countries make the transition to the market.

How would the IMF accomplish this objective? Suppose, for example, that Russia's transition to the market is in trouble because of a rapid inflation and an inability to raise funds in private markets. The country is having trouble paying interest and principal on its foreign loans. The IMF might send a team of specialists to pore over the country's books. The IMF team would come up with an austerity plan for Russia, generally involving reducing the budget deficit and tightening credit; these measures would slow inflation and increase confidence in the Russian ruble. When Russia and the IMF agree on the plan, the IMF would lend money to Russia, perhaps $\$5$ billion, to "bridge" the country over until its balance of payments improved. In addition, there would probably be a debt restructuring, wherein banks would lend more funds and stretch out payments on existing loans.

If the IMF program was successful, Russia's balance of payments would begin to improve, and the country would resume economic growth.

The world bank

Another international financial institution created after World War II was the World Bank. The Bank is capitalized by rich nations that subscribe in proportion to their economic importance in terms of GDP and other factors. The Bank makes low-interest loans to countries for projects which are economically sound but which cannot get private-sector financing. As a result of such long-term loans, goods and services flow from advanced nations to developing countries. In 1996, the World Bank made new loans of $ 21 billion.

If the projects are selected wisely, production in the borrowing lands will rise by more than enough to pay interest on the loans; wages and living standards generally will be higher, not lower, because the foreign capital has raised GDP in the borrowing countries. In addition, as the loans are being paid back, the advanced nations will gain by enjoying somewhat higher imports of useful goods.

Demise of the bretton woods system

For the first three decades after World War II, under the Bretton Woods arrangements, the U. S. dollar was the key currency. Most international trade and finance were carried out in dollars, and payments were most often made in dollars. Exchange-rate parities were quoted in dollar terms, and private and government reserves were kept invested in dollar securities. This was a period of unprecedented growth and prosperity. The industrial nations began to lower trade barriers and to make all their currencies freely convertible. The economies of Western Europe and East Asia recovered from war damage and grew at spectacular rates. During this period, the world was on a dollar standard. In essence, the U. S. dollar was the world currency because of its stability, convertibility, and widespread acceptability.

But recovery contained the seeds of its own destruction. U. S. trade deficits were fueled by an overvalued currency, budget deficits to finance the Vietnam War, and growing overseas investment by American firms. Dollars consequently began to pile up abroad as Germany and Japan developed trade surpluses. Dollar holdings abroad grew from next to nothing in 1945 to $ 50 billion in the early 1970s.

By 1971, the stock of liquid dollar balances had become so large that governments had difficulty defending the official parities. People began to lose confidence in the "almighty dollar". And the lower barriers to financial rows meant that billions of dollars could cross the Atlantic in minutes and threaten to overwhelm existing parities. On August 15, 1971, President Nixon formally severed the link between the dollar and gold, bringing the Bretton Woods era to an end. No longer would the United States automatically convert dollars into other currencies or into gold at $ 35 per ounce; no longer would the United States set an official parity of the dollar and then defend this exchange rate at all costs. As the United States abandoned the Bretton Woods system, the world moved into the modern era.

Today's hybrid system

Unlike the earlier uniform system under either the gold standard or Bretton Woods, today's exchange-rate system fits into no tidy mold. Without anyone's having planned it, the world has moved to a hybrid exchange-rate system. The major features are as follows：

- A few countries allow their currencies to float freely，as the United States has for some periods in the last two decades. In this approach，a country allows markets to determine its currency's value and it rarely intervenes.

- Some major countries have managed but flexible exchange rates. Today，this group includes Canada，Japan，and more recently Britain. Under this system，a country will buy or sell its currency to reduce the day-to-day volatility of currency fluctuations. In addition，a country will sometimes engage in systematic intervention to move its currency toward what it believes to be a more appropriate level.

- Many countries，particularly small ones，peg their currencies to a major currency or to a "basket" of currencies. Sometimes，the peg is allowed to glide smoothly upward or downward in a system known as a gliding or crawling peg.

- Some countries join together in a currency bloc in order to stabilize exchange rates among themselves while allowing their currencies to move flexibly relative to those of the rest of the world. The most important of these blocs is the European Monetary System. In addition，almost all countries tend to intervene either when markets become "disorderly" or when exchange rates seem far out of line with die "fundamentals"，that is，with exchange rates that are appropriate for existing price levels and trade flows.

Notes to the Text

1. World Trade Organization：世界贸易组织（WTO），成立于 1995 年，其前身是关税和贸易总协定（GATT）。WTO 是世界上最大的多边贸易组织，总部在瑞士日内瓦。WTO 与世界银行、国际货币基金组织被并称为当今世界经济体制的"三大支柱"。WTO 的最高决策权力机构是部长大会。部长大会下设总理事会和秘书处，负责 WTO 日常会议和工作。总理事会设有货物贸易、服务贸易、知识产权三个理事会和贸易与发展、国际收支、行政预算三个委员会。秘书处设总干事一人。

2. the Bretton Woods System：布雷顿森林体系，是指战后以美元为中心的国际货币体系。1944 年 7 月，44 个国家或政府的经济特使聚集在美国新罕布什尔州的布雷顿森林，商讨战后的世界贸易格局。会议通过了《国际货币基金协定》，决定成立一个国际复兴开发银行（即世界银行）、国际货币基金组织以及一个全球性的贸易组织。1945 年 12 月 27 日，参加布雷顿森林会议的国家中的 22 国代表在《布雷顿森林协定》上签字，正式成立国际货币基金组织和世界银行，从此开始了布雷顿森林体系。两机构自 1947 年 11 月 15 日起成为联合国的常设专门机构。

3. World Bank：国际复兴开发银行（the International Bank for Reconstruction and Development），简称为世界银行（the World Bank），它是联合国属下的一个专门负责长期贷款的国际金融机构。其主要业务活动是对发展中成员国提供长期贷款；为成员国政府或经政府担保的私人企业提供贷款和技术援助，资助他们兴建某些建设周期长、利润率偏低，但又为该国经济和社会发展所必需的建设项目。

4. GDP：全称 gross domestic product，国内生产总值；它是对一国（地区）经济在核算期内所有常住单位生产的最终产品总量的度量，常常被看成显示一个国家（地区）经济状况的一个重要指标。

5. balance of payments：a detailed record of a country's financial and economic transactions with other countries 国际收支

6. European Monetary System：欧洲货币体系

7. the Vietnam War：越南战争（1954—1975）

Exercises

I Answer the following questions.

1. What is the Bretton Woods system?

2. How does the IMF work?

3. How does the World Bank help its member nations with their economic development?

4. What is today's exchange rate system?

II Write out the equivalents of the following words and expressions.

1. currency devaluation
2. liquid dollar balance
3. financial transaction
4. the gold standard
5. gliding peg
6. far-sighted statecraft

7. 可兑换货币
8. 国际收支
9. 通货紧缩
10. 贸易赤字/贸易盈余
11. 汇率体系
12. 平价

III Translate the following into Chinese.

Another international financial institution created after World War II was the World Bank. The Bank is capitalized by rich nations that subscribe in proportion to their economic importance in terms of GDP and other factors. The Bank makes low-interest loans to countries for projects which are economically sound but which cannot get private-sector financing. As a result of such long-term loans, goods and services flow from advanced nations to developing countries. In 1996, the World Bank made new loans of $21 billion.

Unit 20

Institutional Pillars of International Business

World trade organization(WTO)

Trade issues, including trade in goods and services, investments and intellectual property, may be extended to environmental, labor market, industrial and competition policies.

GATT—General Agreement on Trade and Tariffs

GATS—General Agreement on Trade in Services

TRIPS—Agreement on Trade-Related Aspects of Intellectual Property Rights

TRIMS—Agreement on Trade-Related Investment Measures

World bank

Development issues, debt issues, policies to reduce obstacles to development, a small amount of lending to aid development. Information and reports on developing matters.

International monetary fund(IMF)

Banking, currency and financial matters. Debt problems and currency crises. With World Bank plans and implements polices to stop crises in developing countries, can lend funds to crises countries. Has in the past lent to developed countries. Information and reports on banking, currency and financial matters.

United nations commission for trade and development(UNCTAD)

Codes of conduct for business transactions between developed and developing countries. Information and reports on development issues.

World intellectual property organization(WIPO)

UN organization for discussions about the protection of intellectual property.

Organization for economic cooperation and development(OECD)

Organization of rich countries provides information and reports on a variety of economic, social and business matters and issues codes of conduct. Tried to get an agreement on trade related investment Multinational Agreement on Investment(MAI).

Bank of international settlements(BIS)

Organization of central bankers involved with rules for international banking, codes of conduct and technical matters connected to banking.

Regional trade blocs

Groups of countries involved with removing barriers to trade in goods and services and in the case of the capital and labor. Issuing of rules governing many aspects of trade within blocs and with third parties.

Means of protection

Tariffs—tax on imports.

Quotas—physical limitation on imports.

Non-Tariff Barriers(NTBs)—technical regulations(e. g. health and safety regulations), government policies(e. g. public procurement rules, taxes and subsidies that favour domestic producers).

Government Policies—environmental, social, and industrial and competition polices that restrict trade.

Tariffs and quotas have been significantly reduced by the GATT system except for agricultural products and textiles.

Problem with countries that are not members of WTO.

NTBs—very little progress in many areas getting worse because of health and safety regulations and taxes and subsidies. Some progress in some regional trade blocs notably the EU.

Government policies—practically no progress as most of these are not covered by WTO or other international institutions.

WTO

Established in 1995 as the umbrella organization governing world trade. Did not replace GATT rather the secretariat of GATT became the WTO. Based in Geneva where it used the agreements GATT, GATS, TRIPS and TRIMS as the basis to govern world trade and trade-related issues.

WTO principles

Most Favoured Nations clause. The best trade liberalization offer to any WTO member must be extended to all members.

If a WTO member breaks the agreements a disputes settlement panel rules on the case. Since the WTO was formed the panels are based more firmly on the text of the agreements, scientific evidence, and international law whereas the GATT secretariat often took a diplomatic route to dispute settlement. A dispute panel ruling against a country can lead to retaliatory measure including tariffs and quotas.

WTO also provides reports based on monitoring of the conduct of trade polices in WTO member states.

Single undertaking provision—WTO members must accept all of the agreements and cannot adopt, for example, GATT but reject TRIPS.

Series of trade rounds to develop existing agreements and to make new agreements. Meetings of all the members of WTO but bulk of the work done beforehand by WTO officials in negotiations with WTO members especially the large economies, USA and EU.

Exemptions

General system of preferences(GSP)—trade preferences can be granted to developing countries without them having to reciprocate.

Safeguard provisions—temporary protection for an industry suffering from large and rapid loss of market from imports—has to apply to WTO for permission.

Balance of payments protection—temporary quotas to help to prevent balance of payments crises.

Regional trade blocs—exemption from granting liberalization measures to non-members, but cannot increase protection against WTO members.

Problem areas

Liberalization of agriculture and textiles. Agreement on textiles has been agreed but not being implemented in accordance with original timetable. No agreement on new timetable.

Slow progress to reach agreements on GATS. Problem of prudential rules and consumer protection. Complex company law that governs many areas of services, especially in banking and financial services. IMF and BIS are also involved with this problem.

Large-scale problems with TRIPS as many developing countries are opposed to what they regard as unfair protection systems.

Problems with TRIMS to reach agreement on similar problems(but more pronounced) to GATS.

Slow and complex to obtain rulings for disputes panels.

Problems of enforcement—EU and US often disregard rulings from disputes panel. Banana protocol dispute lasted for over ten years. EU continues to refuse to accept WTO ruling on beef hormones.

Protection of intellectual property

Patents—temporary protection of techniques, process and technical aspects of products.

Trademarks—temporary but renewable protection of logos, words attached to products.

Patents and trademarks based on Paris Convention of 1883.

Copyright—temporary protection of authorship of books, music, art, graphics, multimedia and software. Based on Berne Convention of 1886.

Mask work—temporary protection of semiconductors and biotechnology. Based on Washington Treaty 1989.

TRIPS

All WTO members comply with Paris and Berne Conventions and Washington Treaty. The WTO has expanded on these conventions and treaties and any new agreement in these areas are binding on all WTO members.

Strategic Implications

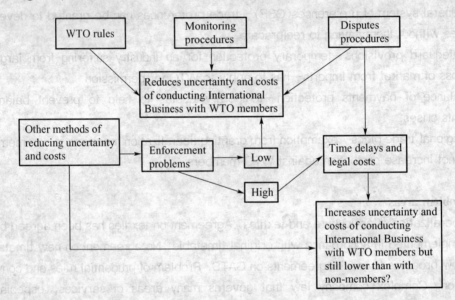

Scenario

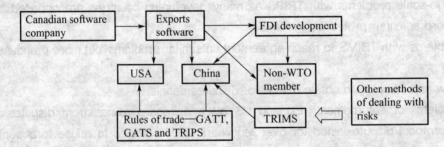

Notes to the Text

1. GATS:《服务贸易总协定》,是世界贸易组织 WTO 管辖的一项多边贸易协议,其核心是最惠国待遇、国民待遇、市场准入、透明度及支付的款项和转拨的资金的自由流动。《服务贸易总协定》的宗旨是在透明度和逐步自由化的条件下,扩大全球服务贸易，并促进各成员的经济增长和发展中国家成员服务业的发展；根据协定的规定，WTO 成立了服务贸易理事会，负责协定的执行。

2. TRIPS：《与贸易有关的知识产权协议》，世贸组织（WTO）前身关贸总协定（GATT）的乌拉圭回合谈判结束时达成 TRIPS，从此知识产权走入"世界贸易"框架。该协议内容涉及知识产权各个领域，不仅在很多方面超过了国际条约对知识产权保护水平的规定，而且把有形商品贸易的基本原则和一些具体规定引入知识产权领域，强化了执行措施和争端解决机制；TRIPS 要求全体成员必须遵守并执行 4 个国际公约，即《保护工业产权巴黎公约》、《保护文学艺术作品伯尔尼公约》、《保护表演者、录音制品制作者与广播组织公约》和《关于集成电路知识产权条约》。

3. TRIMS：《与贸易有关的投资措施协议》，在乌拉圭回合谈判中达成；与贸易有关的投资措施是指能够对国际贸易引起扭曲或限制作用的投资措施，并不是泛指所有的与贸易有关的投资措施。

4. United Nations Commission for Trade and Development（UNCTAD）：联合国贸易及发展会议，成立于 1964 年，是联合国唯一综合处理发展和贸易、资金、技术、投资和可持续发展领域相关问题的政府间机构，总部设在瑞士日内瓦。

5. World Intellectual Property Organization（WIPO）：世界知识产权组织，是联合国的一个专门机构，致力于发展兼顾各方利益、便于使用的国际知识产权（IP）制度，以奖励创造，促进创新；总部设在瑞士日内瓦。

6. Organization for Economic Cooperation and Development（OECD）：经济合作与发展组织，简称经合组织，是由 30 个市场经济国家组成的政府间国际经济组织，旨在共同应对全球化带来的经济、社会和政府治理等方面的挑战；成立于 1961 年，其前身是欧洲经济合作组织（OEEC）。

7. Bank of International Settlements（BIS）：国际清算银行，是一家办理中央银行业务的金融机构，成立于 1930 年 2 月，由美国摩根和花旗银行组成的银行团与英、法、意、德、比、日 6 国的中央银行共同投资设立，行址在瑞士巴塞尔。该行的宗旨是促进各国中央银行之间的合作，为国际金融活动提供更多的便利，在国际金融清算中充当受托人或代理人；它是各国"中央银行的银行"，向各国中央银行并通过中央银行向整个国际金融体系提供一系列高度专业化的服务，办理多种国际清算业务。

8. secretariat：an administrative unit responsible for maintaining records and other secretarial duties; especially for international organizations 秘书处

9. panel：a group of people gathered for a special purpose as to plan or discuss an issue or judge a contest etc 专门委员会（小组）

10. General system of preferences：普遍优惠制，简称普惠制；是指发达国家承诺对从发展中国家或地区输入的商品，特别是制成品和半制成品，给予普遍的、非歧视的和非互惠的关税优惠待遇，这种税称为普惠税。

11. reciprocate：give or take mutually; interchange, make a return for something given or done 交换，互给，报答，酬答，互换

12. Paris Convention of 1883：《保护工业产权的巴黎公约》(Paris Convention for the Protection of Industrial Property，简称《巴黎公约》)，于 1883 年 3 月 20 日在巴黎签订，1884 年 7 月 6 日生效；《巴黎公约》保护的对象是专利、实用新型、外观设计、商标、服务标记、厂商名称、货源标记、原产地名称等。

13. Berne Convention of 1886：《保护文学和艺术作品伯尔尼公约》，10 世纪西欧尤其是法国涌现出许多大文学家、大艺术家，他们创作的大量脍炙人口的作品流传到世界各地，这些国家开始相应地也就重视版权的国际保护。1878 年，由雨果主持在巴黎召开了一次重要的文学大会，建立了一个国际文学艺术协会。1883 年该协会将一份经过多次讨论的国际公约草案交给瑞士政府。瑞士政府于 1886 年 9 月 9 日在伯尔尼举行的第三次大会上予以通过，定名为《保护文学和艺术作品伯尔尼公约》，1887 年 12 月生效。这是世界上第一个国际版权公约。1992 年 7 月 1 日中国决定加入该公约，10 月 5 日成为该公约的第 93 个成员国。

14. Mask Work：世界知识产权组织于 1989 年在华盛顿制定了《关于集成电路知识产权条约》(The Treaty on Intellectual Property in Respect of Integrated Circuits, IPIC)，集成电路知识产权保护的对象即为集成电路布图设计，在美国称为"掩膜作品"(Mask Work)。

15. Washington Treaty 1989：《保护集成电路知识产权的华盛顿公约》(Treaty on Intellectual Property in Respect of Integrated Circuits)，简称《华盛顿公约》(Washington Treaty)，1989 年 5 月 26 日缔结于美国华盛顿，1989 年中国成为《华盛顿公约》的成员国。

Exercises

I Answer the following questions.

1. What's your understanding of the words "institutional pillars" in the title?

2. How does IMF help the world's economic development?

3. What are intellectual property rights? Do you think China has done enough to protect the rights?

4. Can you name some important regional trade blocs in the world?

5. How do you think nations might deal with the "problem areas" still existing in the world trade today?

II Write out the equivalents of the following words and expressions.

1. labour market
2. intellectual property rights
3. Non-Tariff Barriers

6. 政府补助，政府补贴
7. 最惠国
8. 专利

4. member state   9. 半导体

5. 关税与配额

III **Translate the following into Chinese.**

Most Favoured Nations clause. The best trade liberalization offer to any WTO member must be extended to all members.

If a WTO member breaks the agreements a disputes settlement panel rules on the case. Since the WTO was formed the panels are based more firmly on the text of the agreements，scientific evidence，and international law whereas the GATT secretariat often took a diplomatic route to dispute settlement. A dispute panel ruling against a country can lead to retaliatory measure including tariffs and quotas.

WTO also provides reports based on monitoring of the conduct of trade polices in WTO member states.

Unit 21

The World Trade Organization

As new protectionism took hold, GATT became increasingly constrained by the narrow tariff-focused agenda. Since its inception in 1947, trade issues had not only advanced but negotiations were taking longer to arrive at recommendations acceptable to the members. The Uruguay Round, for example, took eight years to reach completion in 1994. However, significant steps were taken towards expanding the coverage of GATT under the auspices of a new body, the World Trade Organization. The WTO came into being on 1 January 1995 with 81 founder members, the numbers increasing to 134 members by 1999, of which 100 were developing countries. Whereas GATT was a provisional treaty and concerned only with trade matters, the Geneva-based WTO has official status and increased scope.

The Uruguay Round set out a number of WTO Agreements, binding on the WTO members, which cover a continued commitment to the elimination of tariffs, plus the protection of intellectual property rights, trade in services, the promotion of liberalized unfair trade standards, harmonisation of health and an attack on safety standards, rules of origin and government procurement and the elimination of technical standards as barriers to trade. The decision-making process inside the WTO seeks to achieve decision by consensus, but if this fails, a three-quarter majority voting procedure on a one-country, one-vote basis is applied, subject to time limits and the right of appeal.

Members of the WTO have agreed not to take unilateral action against rule violations. To discourage such action a dispute resolution process, in which a panel of the WTO's Dispute Settlement Body investigates complaints, was designed to settle disputes quickly, that is, within one year. In the event of non-compliance with a panel's decisions, the aggrieved country may apply tariffs on imports from the offending country or region to provide compensation for damages sustained. But the WTO has no power to stop countries procrastinating or taking unilateral action—opportunities that have been exploited to the full by the triad countries.

Opponents of the WTO, who feel that the WTO contributes to the widening gap between developed and developing countries, favour their version of fair trade, which includes improved market access for developing countries, proactive discrimination in favour of female labour ethical tourism and trade discrimination against abuses of child labour and human rights. But the WTO does not accept this contentious concept of fair trade, which seriously challenges the backbone of the WTO, namely, a commitment to trade liberalisation, reciprocity and the most favoured nation clause as the basis for equitable treatment for all countries, so that the WTO will not even sanction trade discrimination against countries that abuse human rights. For example, the WTO argues that countries with high labour standards cannot use these to prevent imports from countries with lower standards, such as the payment of below-subsistence wages and the employment of child labour. The WTO view is that standards will improve with the increases in economic growth and development that will be the consequence of a more liberal international trade and investment regime.

A major advance in the scope of the GATT/WTO agenda has been the introduction of measures to regulate Trade-Related Intellectual Property Rights (TRIPS), Trade-Related Investment Measures (TRIMS) and the General Agreement on Trade in Services (GATS). Despite the emphasis on trade in the descriptors of these agreements, the fact is that foreign direct investment is part and parcel of these agreements because such investment is a primary vehicle through which international trade, via intra-firm trade, and technology transfer (at the heart of intellectual property issues) take place. For example, the opening up and internationalisation of the telecommunications industry owes a debt to the provisions for investment made in the GATS, and motor manufacturers can now source components from abroad without meeting local content requirements as a consequence of TRIMS.

Trade-Related Intellectual Property Rights (TRIPS)

Among developed countries a serious issue concerns the rapid growth of parallel imports and the emergence of grey markets. At the centre of the issue is the adoption by firms of price discrimination strategies between cross-border markets to exploit the monopoly power granted to them as owners of branded goods protected by patents or trademarks. Parallel imports occur when retailers of branded goods in high-priced market are able to buy in the cheap locations and sell at discounted prices in their own outlets. A grey market is said to exist when the proprietors of the branded goods disapproves of parallel imports in their products. Parallel imports and grey markets are particularly prevalent in the EU with its mix of high—and relatively low—priced markets for individual products. Solutions to the problem are typically sought at national and regional level (for example, the EU), but whether parallel imports give expression to free trade or is an example of "unfair" trade gives some of the flavour of the more general concern for the potential abuse of intellectual property rights.

Issues between developed and developing countries concerning the abuse of intellectual property rights cover a wider range of issues than parallel importing. These include counterfeiting (poor-quality counterfeiting or otherwise) of branded products "protected" by trademarks, the illegal use of expropriated trade marks, false country of origin claims and the pirating of industrial designs and manufacturing processes. Badly affected sectors in western nations include the arts and entertainment books, records, CDs, software, pharmaceuticals, perfumery, wines, fashion-ware, industrial components and industrial goods.

The World Intellectual Property Organization (WIPO), established in 1967 to adjudicate on multilateral agreements on intellectual property rights, has been recognized as a specialised United Nations agency since 1974. During the Uruguay Round, most members of GATT felt that WIPO, not GATT, was the appropriate arbiter of agreements and rules, but the EU, Japan and the USA were keen to have intellectual property issues included in the Uruguay Round and succeeded in doing so. When the TRIPS Agreement was introduced in January 1995, it signified a major, but controversial, addition to the responsibilities of the WTO compared to GATT. The developing countries are concerned that rules to strengthen intellectual property rights serve to perpetuate the technological advantage that developed countries already have. Many developing countries, lacking the innovative and entrepreneurial capacity of the west, regard the stiffer protection of intellectual property as an obstacle to economic development, which is dependent on cheap access to innovations and technology. In western nations, protection of intellectual property, and therefore the creation of temporary monopoly power, is seen as essential to encourage innovation and entrepreneurial risk taking. In time, as the protection runs out, as with patent protection, ownership takes on the characteristics of a universally free good. The issue, therefore, concerns the optimum length of protection and encouragement of commercial innovation versus the socially optimum timing of knowledge diffusion, over which there are serious differences of opinion between developed and developing countries.

Whatever the differences, the TRIPS Agreement aims to strengthen, protect and enforce intellectual property rights. WTO members are required to treat nationals of other member states no less favourably than their own and, should privileges be granted, treat all nations the same. In other words, the most favoured nation clause is evoked. Members are expected to observe a policy of non-discrimination when granting patents, to protect organisations and individuals against the disclosure of commercial secrets and to offer compensation and legal remedies against abuse. The basic purpose of the TRIPS Agreement is to enhance the flow of technology and proprietary knowledge to the developing world via foreign direct investment. Developing countries are encouraged to participate in technical cooperation and training programmes organized by the WIPO to make their economies more receptive to the inflow of western technology. Nevertheless, many developing countries believe that they are not ready or strong enough to accept the consequences of stronger and effective intellectual property laws.

Trade-Related Investment Measures (TRIMS)

The TRIMS Agreement, by specifically focusing on foreign direct investment for the first time on the WTO agenda, introduced a timescale for the elimination of trade-related investment measures that were already disallowed under the GATT but generally ignored.

The Agreement clarifies the investment measures applying to manufacturing enterprises that are inconsistent with the liberalisation of international trade and investment and seeks their removal over two years for developed countries, five years for developing countries and seven years for least developing countries. These include measures by governments to dictate the behaviour of firms with respect to local content requirements and export/output ratios.

The attempt by the WTO, through TRIMS, to seek to free foreign direct investment from controls that are not imposed on domestic firms is another contentious issue between developed and developing countries. Note, for example, how the failure of the Organization for Economic Cooperation and Development (OECD) to construct a set of guidelines was effectively sidelined by the weight of opposition to the proposals.

The general agreement on grade in services

Through the GATS, the WTO proposes to match in services the progress made by GATT to eliminate tariff barriers to trade in manufactures and by TRIMS and TRIPS to reduce controls on foreign direct investment in manufacturing. The supply of many services requires the physical presence of the supplier in the market. Indeed, the growth of foreign direct investment is growing more rapidly in services than in other sectors. The purpose of the GATS is to increase the international mobility of services and to remove cross-border obstacles to service providers which international firms depend on to manage their multinational operations. Although not a specific investment agreement, the GATS recognises that foreign investment is one of several ways in which a service can gain access to a market. The services covered in the agreements include communications, professional services, business services such as consulting and advertising, distribution, including franchising, and financial services.

Notes to the Text

1. inception: the beginning, the start 开始,开端,初期
2. Uruguay Round: "乌拉圭回合"谈判。1986 年 9 月在乌拉圭的埃斯特角城举行了关贸总协定部长级会议,决定进行一场旨在全面改革多边贸易体制的新一轮谈判,故命名为"乌拉圭回合"谈判。这是迄今为止最大的一次贸易谈判,历时 7 年半,于 1994 年 4 月在摩洛哥的马拉喀什结束。谈判几乎涉及所有贸易,参加方从最初的 103 个,增至谈判结束时的 125 个。
3. under the auspices of: with the support, help or approval of 在……的支持(帮助、赞助、同意)下
4. Dispute Settlement Body: WTO 争端解决机构。争端解决机构有权成立专家组,采纳专家和上诉机构的报告,监督规则和建议的实施情况,授权中止各协议所规定的特许权与义务。
5. optimum: most likely to bring successor advantage; most favourable 最适宜的,最佳的,最有利的

Exercises

I Answer the following questions

1. What do the WTO agreements cover?
2. How do the member countries deal with rule violation?
3. What is the parallel import? How does it occur?
4. Why do the developing countries regard the stiffer protection of intellectual property as an obstacle to economic development?
5. What is the purpose of the GATS?

II Write out the equivalents of the following words and expressions.

1. government procurement
2. founder members
3. technology transfer
4. country of origin
5. grey market
6. 知识产权

7. 市场准入
8. 多边协议
9. 最不发达国家
10. 商业秘密
11. 价格歧视

III Translate the following into Chinese.

Members of the WTO have agreed not to take unilateral action against rule violations. To discourage such action a dispute resolution process, in which a panel of the WTO's Dispute Settlement Body investigates complaints, was designed to settle disputes quickly, that is, within one year. In the event of non-compliance with a panel's decisions, the aggrieved country may apply tariffs on imports from the offending country or region to provide compensation for damages sustained. But the WTO has no power to stop countries procrastinating or taking unilateral action—opportunities that have been exploited to the full by the triad countries.

Unit 22

The Product Life Circle

The word "product" covers a lot more than the obvious tangible, physical articles available for sale. A product can be a service, like dry-cleaning or management consulting. A product can also be a concept you would like an audience to believe. You might be selling support for a person, place, event, organization, or idea.

Your "product" will most likely be a combination of tangible items, services, and beliefs. That is why I like to use the word offering. What you offer customers will almost certainly contain elements of each. A haircut is a product, but it results from the service of cutting hair. A political candidate is in many ways a product, promising to function in a way that solves problems for you if you elect the candidate to office. Non-profit agencies sell feelings, asking us to support activities that make us feel good about doing good. Each of these examples represents a discreet offering someone is asking an audience to buy or buy into. As a marketer, you must understand something about the life cycle of your products. If one product is slipping in popularity, you need to have something else in the pipeline. How do you develop new products? Are there innovations you can bring to current products, to make them new and improved?

The basic product life cycle goes like this: you introduce a product. If it's halfway successful, it passes from introduction into a growth phase. Eventually it reaches maturity, which is then followed by a nearly inevitable stage of decline. Products not only go through this cycle, but whole product categories do as well. Think about wine coolers, a classic marketing flash in the pan. The category was created by wine manufacturers, looking for an alternative to beer to offer young drinkers. The first products were created by Seagrams and Gallo, names of long-standing with deep pockets to draw on and mature products else-where in their families.

Once the big boys had used their muscle to introduce the concept of sweet, fruity, slightly alcoholic drinks, other upstarts came on the scene. But the crowd they appealed to, the 20-something drinkers, are notoriously fickle consumers. Wine coolers lost their fizz after only a couple of years on the market. At the bitter end of the category's life cycle, Coors introduced Zima, a "clear beer". Sales were disappointing. To invigorate the languishing brand, Busch added a sibling brew, now amber in color, called "Zima Gold". Are we backing to beer yet?

Your strategy as a company might involve being a market leader bringing new products on line early. Or you might prefer the more conservative "me-too" position, entering markets when they are more nearly mature. With the right price/value combination you can make money even on products that are in a declining phase. What's important is this: you should have products spread over several phases of the curve, to avoid uneven peaks and valleys in your sales—and profits.

When is a decline not a decline? Not every drop in sales indicates the end of your product's life cycle. Sometimes poor sales are indications of other problems, like mix-ups in the distribution channels, or activities of competitors. If a temporary down-slide in sales occurs, treat it as a warning sign, not a death knell.

Never forget our First Rule of Marketing: People don't buy products, they buy solutions to problems. If you can create a product offering that continually evolves, solving customer needs as those needs evolve, you will have a successful long-term product strategy.

Notes to the Text

1. Seagrams：一种金酒(杜松子酒)生产厂家。
2. Gallo：E. & J. Gallo 公司，是一家美国巨型家族企业，世界知名的葡萄酒生产商。
3. Coors：美国康胜啤酒公司，全球第五大啤酒酿造商。
4. Zima：美国康胜啤酒公司旗下品牌。

Exercises

I **Answer the following questions.**

1. What are tangible products?
2. What is the basic product life cycle?
3. How does the product life cycle influence a company's business strategy?
4. Do you agree with the writer that "People don't buy products, they buy solutions to problems"?

II **Write out the equivalents of the following words and expressions.**

1. tangible goods
2. non-profit agency
3. mature product
4. market leader

5. 销售渠道
6. 产品生命周期
7. 销售下滑
8. 产品组合

III Translate the following into Chinese.

The basic product life cycle goes like this: you introduce a product. If it's halfway successful, it passes from introduction into a growth phase. Eventually it reaches maturity, which is then followed by a nearly inevitable stage of decline. Products not only go through this cycle, but whole product categories do as well. Think about wine coolers, a classic marketing flash in the pan. The category was created by wine manufacturers, looking for an alternative to beer to offer young drinkers. The first products were created by Seagrams and Gallo, names of long-standing with deep pockets to draw on and mature products else-where in their families.

Unit 23

The Quality Imperative

The global environment of business is so important that we show it as surrounding all other environmental influences. It affects all of them. Perhaps the number one global environmental change is the growth of international competition and the opening of free trade among nations. In the recent past, Japanese manufacturers like Honda and Sony won much of the market for automobiles, videocassette recorders, TV sets, and other products by offering global consumers better-quality products than U.S. manufacturers. This competition hurt many U.S. industries and many jobs were lost.

Today, manufacturers in countries such as China, India, South Korea, and Mexico can produce high-quality goods at low prices because their workers are paid less money than U.S. workers and they've learned quality concepts from Japanese, German, and U.S. producers.

U.S. manufacturers have been analyzing and many have implemented the more advanced quality methods and skills the Japanese have developed. In fact, U.S. workers in many industries are now more productive than ever.

The consequence of global competition is that no country dares fall behind other countries in providing high-quality products. Quality production techniques have been in place for over a decade in countries such as Japan, the United States, and Germany. That means that top-quality manufacturers, such as Motorola, are able to make products with almost no defects and to make them quickly. Global consumers will fast become accustomed to such quality.

At IBM, for example, quality is defined as "meeting the requirements of our customers, both inside and outside the organization, for defect-free products, services, and business processes." *Fortune* magazine devoted its Autumn/Winter 1993 edition to "The Tough New Consumer / Changing Demands". It said that consumer and industrial buyers (buyers who buy goods from other businesses) are getting used to high standards of quality buy; being squeezed by merciless budgetary constraints, they aren't willing to pay top dollar for it. In other words, consumers are increasingly demanding the best quality at the lowest prices. Much of Wal-Mart's success is that it provides such value. Companies that can't provide this combination will be less able to compete in the 21st century.

In the United States, a new standard was set for quality with the introduction of the Baldrige Awards in 1987. To qualify for this award, a company has to show quality as measured three ways: (1) by customer satisfaction, (2) by product and service quality, and (3) by quality of internal operations. Among other things, the Baldrige Award requires companies to increase employee involvement, measure themselves against industry leaders, and shorten the time it takes to introduce products. A major criterion for the award is that customer wants and needs are being met, and customer satisfaction ratings are better than those of competitors. As you can see, focus is shifting away from just making quality goods and services to providing top-quality customer service in all respects.

The new global measures for quality are called ISO 9000 standards. Prior to the establishment of such standards in 1987, there were no international standards of quality with which to measure companies. Now ISO standards, established in Europe, provide a "common denominator" of business quality accepted around the world.

What makes ISO 9000 so important is that the European Union—the group of European countries that are establishing free-trade agreements—is demanding that companies that want to do business with the EU be certified by ISO standards. There are several accreditation agencies in Europe and in the United States. They certify that a company meets standards for all phases of its operations, from product development through production and testing to installation. Many European companies have already been certified, but only a few in the United States.

Those companies that qualify for the Baldrige Award will have little trouble passing the certification process for ISO 9000, but most U. S. companies have a long way to go to qualify. It's no longer enough to have a total quality program to compete in certain areas of the world. Now in order to do so that program must be certified by international standards.

Notes to the Text

1. Honda：日本本田汽车公司（Honda Motor Co., Ltd）。1948 年以生产自行车助力发动机起步，发展成为从小型通用发动机、踏板摩托车乃至跑车等各个领域都拥有独创技术，并不断研发、生产新产品的企业；在全世界 29 个国家拥有 120 多个生产基地，生产和销售摩托车、汽车和通用产品。

2. Sony：日本索尼公司，是视听产品、游戏产品、通讯产品和信息技术等领域的先导之一。

3. Motorola：美国摩托罗拉公司，创立于 1928 年，是世界《财富》百强企业之一，全球通信行业的领导者，为客户提供无线移动通信产品和解决方案；业务范围涵盖了宽带通信、嵌入式系统和无线网络等。

4. *Fortune*：《财富》杂志，1929 年由美国人亨利·卢斯创办，隶属于美国时代华纳公司（Time Warner）旗下的出版机构时代公司（Time）；该杂志每年评出世界五百强。

5. Wal-Mart：美国沃尔玛公司，由美国零售业的传奇人物山姆·沃尔顿先生于 1962 年在阿肯色州创立；现已成为世界上最大的连锁零售商。

6. Baldrige Awards：美国马尔科姆·波德里奇质量奖。近年来，通过推行国家质量奖计划来提升企业的管理水平已成为许多国家强化和提高产业竞争力的重要途径。影响最大的有日本爱德华·戴明质量奖(Edward Deming Prize)、美国马尔科姆·波德里奇质量奖(Malcolm Baldrige Award)和欧洲质量奖(European Quality Award)。这三大质量奖被誉为卓越管理与绩效模式的创造者和经济奇迹的助推器。

7. ISO：国际标准化组织(International Organization for Standardization)，是一个全球性的非政府组织，是国际标准化领域中一个十分重要的组织；1947年2月23日正式成立，总部设在瑞士的日内瓦。

Exercises

Ⅰ **Answer the following questions.**

1. What is the biggest change of the global business environment?
2. How does a company qualify itself for the Baldrige Awards?
3. What makes ISO 9000 so important?
4. Do you think the "made-in-China" goods are competitive on the world market?

Ⅱ **Write out the equivalents of the following words and expressions.**

1. quality imperative
2. customer satisfaction
3. internal operation
4. product development
5. defect-free product

6. 消费品
7. 预算限制
8. 业内标准
9. 客户服务
10. 贸易协议

Ⅲ **Translate the following into Chinese.**

To qualify for this award, a company has to show quality as measured three ways：(1) by customer satisfaction，(2) by product and service quality, and (3) by quality of internal operations. Among other things, the Baldrige Award requires companies to increase employee involvement，measure themselves against industry leaders，and shorten the time it takes to introduce products. A major criterion for the award is that customer wants and needs are being met，and customer satisfaction ratings are better than those of competitors. As you can see, focus is shifting away from just making quality goods and services to providing top-quality customer service in all respects.

Unit 24

Product Brands and Trademarks

A brand is a way of identifying a product through a unique name or design that sets the product apart from those offered by competitors. Tide and Oldsmobile are brand names. McDonald's golden arches, the Jolly Green Giant, the Pillsbury doughboy and the AT&T globe are brand symbols.

Brand names may be owned by producers of a product as well as by wholesalers and retailers. Sears Roebuck, for example, buys appliances from many manufacturers and sells all of them under its Kenmore brand. A&P, the supermarket chain, purchases canned fruits, jellies, rice, household cleaning products, and frozen foods from hundreds of suppliers and offers them under the A&P or Ann Page brand names. Brands owned by national manufacturers are called national brands. Brands owned by wholesalers and retailers, such as Sears and A&P, are private brands.

Brand names and brand symbols may be registered with the United States Patent and Trademark Office as trademarks. A trademark is a brand that has been given protection so that its owner has exclusive rights to its use. Because a well-known name is a valuable asset and generates more sales than an unknown name, manufacturers zealously protect their trademarks. The Coca-Cola Company, for example, employs 40 people whose job is to look out for improper use of the names Coke and Coca-Cola.

Brand loyalty

A well-known and respected brand name provides immediate identification for a product and suggests a certain level of quality and dependability that consumers are often willing to pay more for. Nevertheless, a company has to think carefully about the benefits before spending $80 million or more on a huge promotion campaign to establish a national brand name. The cost of such a campaign may drive up the price of the product, making it possible for other companies to sell unbranded or less-known brand products at a substantially lower price.

Before deciding to build a brand, marketers need to evaluate whether the payoff will be worth the investment. Often the answer depends on the type of the product. People are more loyal to some types of branded products than others. Mundane products designed to handle tedious chores are less likely to inspire loyalty than products associated with an individual's personal image.

Brand loyalty may be measured in degrees. The first level is brand recognition, which means that people are familiar with the product. They are likely to buy it because they recognize it. The next level is brand preference. At this level, people will habitually buy the product if it is available. However, they may be wiling to experiment with alternatives if they have some incentive to do so. The ultimate in brand loyalty is brand insistence, the stage at which the buyer will accept no substitute.

One of the most intriguing examples of brand loyalty occurred in 1985, when the Coca-Cola Company attempted to discontinue traditional Coke and replace it with a new formula. Although a $4 million taste test of 200,000 consumers had demonstrated that people preferred the new flavor, the company was deluged with protests when it made the switch. People were incensed that anyone would tamper with Coke, which had become an American institution in its 99 years. Within months, the company admitted that it had goofed and brought back the old formula, calling it Coca-Cola classic and selling it alongside the new Coke.

Brand strategies

Companies take various approaches to building brands. The traditional approach is to create a different identity for each product that a company sells, so that if a problem develops with that product, the other items in the line will not suffer. This approach has the added advantage of allowing a company to create different product images for various market segments. Take the American automobiles companies for example, with their varied product lines aimed at different types of buyers. The person who likes a Corvette and the person who wants a Cadillac are looking for completely different things, even though both want a General Motors car.

If a brand appeals to a certain group of customers, trying to broaden the appeal to other customers may be tricky, as General Motors recently discovered. The company has been trying to attract younger buyers for Cadillac by downsizing the cars, but in the process it is losing its traditional older customers who prefer a big, luxury car. GM might have been better off to maintain the Cadillac image and create a new brand aimed at the younger group.

Although individual branding has its advantages, in the past few years an increasing number of companies have been using family branding to add to their product lines. Procter & Gamble, for example, has launched Liquid Tide, building on the reputation of powdered Tide. Building on the name recognition of an existing brand enables companies to cut both costs and risks associated with introducing new products.

Another way to reduce the cost of building a new brand is to buy the rights to specific names and symbols that are already well known and then to use these licensed labels to help sell products. Licensing is quite common among manufacturers of children's products, who license popular cartoon or movie characters and affix them to everything from toys to clothing to presweetened breakfast cereals. The approach may backfire, of course, if the popularity of the licensed character declines. Pepperidge Farm learned this lesson the hard way when it lost $ 3 million on Star Wars cookies. Despite this risk, however, licensing in on a roll. Retail sales of licensed goods have soared to $ 50 billion, up from just $ 6.5 billion in 1979.

Notes to the Text

1. Oldsmobile：奥尔兹汽车。Olds 奥尔兹(1864—1950)，是美国发明家、汽车制造商，设计了奥尔兹汽车，首创流水线装配法。

2. Pillsbury：Pillsbury is a brand name used by Minneapolis-based General Mills and the the J. M. Smucker Company. The Pillsbury brand might have disappeared if not for the iconic Pillsbury Doughboy. 品食乐公司（"哈根达斯"冰淇淋为其著名产品），英国饮品国际集团 Grand Metropolitan PLC 旗下一员。

3. Procter & Gamble：美国宝洁公司，成立于 1837 年，是世界著名的日用消费品生产厂商；在国内主要知名品牌有潘婷、海飞丝、沙宣、玉兰油、舒肤佳等。

4. Liquid Tide：汰渍牌洗衣液，宝洁公司洗衣粉产品品牌之一。

5. Sears Roebuck：美国西尔斯百货公司，全球 500 强企业之一，是一家拥有百年历史的大型零售企业，销售额名列同行业前茅。

6. Kenmore：a brand name of household appliances produced mainly by Whirlpool in the USA 美国惠而浦公司生产的家用电器的一个品牌。

7. A & P：全称 Great Atlantic & Pacific Tea Company，太平洋和大西洋大茶叶公司。

8. Corvette：（雪佛莱）考维特汽车

9. Pepperidge Farm：（培柏莉农场出品的）饼干

Exercises

I **Answer the following questions.**

1. Can you cite examples to show the difference between a brand and a trademark?

2. What should a company take into consideration before carrying on a promotion campaign to establish a national brand name?

3. There are three levels of brand loyalty according to the text. Give examples to illustrate these levels.

4. What are the approaches to building brands mentioned in the text? Which do you think is the best? Why?

II **Write out the equivalents of the following words and expressions.**

1. appliances
2. brand loyalty
3. mundane product
4. downsize
5. Cadillac

6. 超市连锁
7. 罐装水果
8. 冷冻食品
9. 结果（报偿）
10. 通用汽车公司

III **Translate the following into Chinese.**

Brand loyalty may be measured in degrees. The first level is brand recognition, which means that people are familiar with the product. They are likely to buy it because they recognize it. The next level is brand preference. At this level, people will habitually buy the product if it is available. However, they may be willing to experiment with alternatives if they have some incentive to do so. The ultimate in brand loyalty is brand insistence, the stage at which the buyer will accept no substitute.

Unit 25

The Joint International Venture

The term *joint international business venture*, joint venture for short, has come to mean many things to many people. It sometimes is taken to mean any joint relationship between one or more foreign firms and one or more local firms. Such a broad definition is excluded here. Joint venture will be taken to mean joint ownership of an operation in which at least one of the partners is foreign based.

Joint ventures can take many forms. A foreign firm may take a majority share, a minority share, or an equal share in ownership. While it is not necessary to have financial control or to have operating control, some firms refuse to use the joint venture form if it is not possible to have a majority position in ownership. There are firms that have few qualms about holding minority position, however, so long as they can have operating control. They achieve this through technical aid, management, or supply contract.

It should be recognized that maintaining operating control is sometimes difficult if one does not have financial control too. Objectives of the participants may diverge; when they do, financial control becomes important. Management may wish to reinvest earnings while the majority of the board may wish earnings distributed as dividends. Unless policy issues of this kind can be settled amicably, lack of financial control can prove to be very unsatisfactory, if not fatal.

Many joint ventures emerge as matters of necessity: that is, no single firm is willing to assume the risks entailed, while a consortium of firms is. Large, capital-intensive, long-lived investments are natural candidates for the joint venture. Exploitation of resource deposits often is done by a consortium of several petroleum or mining firms. Roles are parceled out even though each phase of the operation is owned jointly. One firm does the actual mining, another provides transportation, and still another does the refining and extraction. There is a wide variety of combinations. However, increasingly, joint ventures are an extension of nationalism and are undertaken as a condition of entry rather than as a permissive arrangement between firms. Several countries now require that there be local ownership participation in new ventures involving foreign equity capital. In some instances, national governments insist on local financial control in a few industrial sectors. In others, almost all new investments must have at least 50 percent local participation. Countries that currently require local equity participation in some industries and in some forms include India, Peru, Mexico, the Philippines, Malaysia, and Indonesia.

As noted, the joint ventures can pose problems, especially if it is an enforced marriage of partners. For many ventures in small countries, it is difficult to find a suitable local partner, that is, one with sufficient capital and know how to be able to contribute to the partnership. In some developing countries, a small handful of families control the entire locally-owned part of the industrial structure. Under these circumstances, a joint venture merely insulates them further from independent, foreign-owned plants that would compete against them. For this and other reason, the only suitable partner may end up being the government itself. Most multinational firms, however, shy away from such arrangements where possible.

The Japanese multinational firms are much more likely to engage in joint ventures than are European and American firms. One explanation for this is that the Japanese are the new comers on the international scene and have had to enter most countries under more stringent conditions than did the European and American firms. Also, the large bulk of Japanese investments（55 percent of the total and 72 percent of manufacturing investments）are located in developing countries where joint ventures are preferable to wholly-owned subsidiaries. U. S.-based firms, by contrast, have only 21 percent of their investments in developing countries and 79 percent in advanced countries. Also, over 60 percent of U. S.-owned investments in manufacturing in developing countries are concentrated in high-tech fields, whereas Japanese firms have about two-thirds of their manufacturing investment in developing countries located in relatively low-tech industries. Since Japanese firms may have less to protect in the way of technology, they may be more willing to share ownership. Also, they compete in the same industries as do local firms and hence may feel compelled to use joint ventures as a form of protective coloration.

Notes to the Text

1. joint ownership：a partnership of two or more persons who invest jointly in a firm 联合所有权
2. Management may wish to reinvest earnings："Management" refers to people who are in charge of a firm, industry, considered as one body 资方，管理方
3. Consortium of firm：联营公司
4. capital-intensive, long-lived investments：资本密集型的，长期存在的投资

I **Answer the following questions.**

1. What does a joint venture mean?

2. What forms can joint ventures take?

3. What are the roles of a large joint venture?

4. Could you say something about the growth of joint ventures in China and their impacts on Chinese economy?

II **Write out the equivalents of the following words and expressions.**

1. qualm

2. diverge

3. parcel out

4. equity capital

5. equity participation

6. 红利

7. 劳动密集型

8. 全资分公司

9. 强迫联姻

10. 合作伙伴关系

III **Translate the following into Chinese.**

   It should be recognized that maintaining operating control is sometimes difficult if one does not have financial control too. Objectives of the participants may diverge; when they do, financial control becomes important. Management may wish to reinvest earnings while the majority of the board may wish earnings distributed as dividends. Unless policy issues of this kind can be settled amicably, lack of financial control can prove to be very unsatisfactory, if not fatal.

Unit 26

Multinational Corporations

One of the most significant international economic development of the postwar period is the proliferation of multinational corporations（MNCs）. These are firms that not only own, control, or manage production facilities but carry on financial and sales activities in several countries. Today MNCs account for over 20 percent of world output, and intra-firm trade is more than 25 percent of world trade in manufacturing. Some MNCs, such as Exxon and General Motors, are truly giants with yearly sales in the tens of billions of dollars and exceeding the total national income of all but a handful of nations.

The basic reason for the existence of MNCs is the competitive advantage of a global network of production and distribution. This competitive advantage arises in part from vertical and horizontal integration with foreign affiliates. By vertical integration, most MNCs can ensure their supply of foreign raw materials and intermediate products and avoid the imperfections often found in foreign markets. They can also provide better distribution and service networks. By horizontal integration through foreign affiliates, MNCs can better protect and exploit their monopoly power, adapt their products to local conditions and tastes, and ensure consistent product quality.

The competitive advantage of MNCs is also based on economies of scale in production, financing, research and development（R&D）, and the gathering of market information. The large output of MNCs allows them to carry division of labor and specialization in production much further than smaller national firms. Product components requiring only unskilled labor can be produced in low-wage nations and shipped elsewhere for assembly. Furthermore, MNCs and their affiliates usually have greater access at better terms to international capital markets than do purely national firms, and this puts MNCs in a better position to finance large projects. They can also concentrate R&D in one or a few advanced nations best suited for these purposes because of the greater availability of technical personnel and facilities. Finally foreign affiliates funnel information from around the world to the parent firm, placing it in a better position than national firms to evaluate, anticipate, and take advantage of changes in comparative costs, consumers' tastes and market conditions generally.

While MNCs, by efficiently organizing production and distribution on a worldwide basis, can increase world output and welfare, they also create serious problems in both home and host countries. The most controversial of the alleged harmful effects of MNCs on the home nation is the loss of domestic jobs resulting from foreign direct investment. That some domestic jobs are so lost is beyond doubt. These are likely to be unskilled and semiskilled production jobs in which the home nation has a comparative disadvantage.

In addition, through transfer pricing and similar practices, and by shifting their operations to lower-tax nations, MNCs reduce tax revenues and erode the tax base of the home nation. This results from common international taxing practice. Specifically, the host country taxes the subsidiary's profits first. To avoid double taxation of foreign subsidiaries, the home country then usually taxes only repatriated profits (if its tax rate is higher than in the host country), and only by the difference in the tax rates.

Finally, because of their access to international capital markets, MNCs can avoid domestic monetary policies and make government control over the economy in the home nation more difficult. These alleged harmful effects of MNCs are of crucial importance to the United States, since it is home for more than half of the largest MNCs. In general, home nations do impose some restrictions on the activities of MNCs, either for balance of payments reasons or, more recently, for employment reasons.

Home countries have even more serious complaints against MNCs. First and foremost is the allegation that MNCs dominate their economies. This is certainly true for Canada, where almost 60 percent of the total capital in manufacturing is owned or controlled by foreigners (40 percent by Americans). It is also true for some of the smaller developing countries.

Another harmful effect of MNCs on the host country is the siphoning off of R&D funds to the home nation. While this may be more efficient for the MNCs and the world as a whole, it also keeps the host country technologically dependent. This is especially true and serious for developing nations. MNCs may also absorb local savings and entrepreneurial talent, thus preventing them from being used to establish domestic enterprises that might be more important for national growth and development. In developing nations, foreign direct investment by MNCs in mineral and raw material production have often given rise to complaints of foreign exploitation in the form of low prices paid to host nations.

Whether MNCs are advantageous or disadvantageous, they have been mushrooming all over the world. That is a fact.

Notes to the Text

1. intrafirm trade: trade among the parent firm and its foreign affiliates 公司内部贸易
2. Exxon: (formerly Esso) Standard Oil Company (U.S.A.) 美国标准石油公司(美孚公司)
3. Vertical integration: a joining of business enterprises in which the integrating members are involved in the same product lines but at different stage of the manufacture 纵向联合,纵向一体化(不同生产环节合并,实行一体化)
4. intermediate product (goods): a product which is used at some point in the production process of other products 中间产品
5. comparative cost: in international trade, each country specializes in producing

those products at less cost than the other countries 比较成本

6. home country：country in which a parent firm is situated 母国；投资国

   host country：country in which the subsidiary of a MNC is situated 所在国；东道国

7. transfer price：the price fixed and charged by one section（affiliate）of the same firm（multinational corporation）内部调拨价；转移价

8. repatriated profits：profits made in foreign countries and sent back to home country 汇回本国的利润

Exercises

I Answer the following questions.

1. Could you explain in detail the advantages that vertical and horizontal integrations bring to MNCs?

2. What are the advantages that economies of scale has brought to MNCs in production，financing and R & D?

3. Why do you think foreign direct investment of the home country leads to the decrease of domestic employment for ordinary workers?

II Write out the equivalents of the following words and expressions.

1. proliferation   6. 规模经济

2. facility   7. 横向一体化

3. allegation   8. 货币政策

4. entrepreneurial talent   9. 课税

5. 跨国公司

III Translate the following into Chinese.

While MNCs，by efficiently organizing production and distribution on a worldwide basis，can increase world output and welfare，they also create serious problems in both home and host countries. The most controversial of the alleged harmful effects of MNCs on the home nation is the loss of domestic jobs resulting from foreign direct investment. That some domestic jobs are so lost is beyond doubt. These are likely to be unskilled and semiskilled production jobs in which the home nation has a comparative disadvantage.

Multinational Enterprises Are Regional, Not Global

We find that MNEs have a large proportion of intra-regional sales and assets. As MNEs are the vehicles of international business, it is apparent that the more aggregate data on trade and FDI reported elsewhere merely reflect the activities of these MNEs. Overall, international business is primarily regional business. Indeed, if we extend the data back over the last 20 years, there is no significant change in triad regional patterns of business activity.

The best evidence on the current nature of international strategy comes from examination of the activities of the 500 largest multinational enterprises (MNEs), as listed annually in the Fortune 500. These 500 MNEs account for well over 90% of the world's stock of foreign direct investment and over half of the world's trade. The top 500 include, for example, all the major automobile producers—the world's largest manufacturing sector accounting for one third of all U. S. -Canadian trade.

For a variety of reasons, it is not possible to find the foreign operations of all the top 500. In the best attempt to do so, the Templeton Global Performance Index (TGPI) has assembled information on 246 of these firms, ranked by foreign assets.

Only one of these 49 MNEs was found to be "global". The world's largest MNE is Wal-Mart, but over 90% of its sales are in the NAFTA region.

Trade business activity

The world is becoming less domestic oriented as firms look to increase profits by growing beyond their own borders. They do this in two ways: exports and/or foreign direct investment. For the last several years, economists and international business scholars have commented on this development, which they have labeled "globalization" and the associated concept of "global strategy".

This approach to doing business is particularly associated with the world's largest 500 companies, which are all multinational enterprises (MNEs), i. e. they produce and /or distribute products and/or services across national borders. Yet, very few MNEs are "global" firms with a "global" strategy—defined as the ability to sell the same product and/ or service around the world. Instead, the data indicate that most MNEs are regionally based in their home-triad market of either, North America, the E. U. , or Asia (principally Japan). In other words, most MNEs are internationally active in their home-triad regions but are not global.

A major reason for the success of these regionally-based strategies is that they permit the MNE to achieve all the economic advantages of scale and scope without the additional business risks of operating far from its home base. This occurs if the MNE sells the same product and/or service in the same manner within the home-triad region. This allows the MNE to gain all the potential economies of scale and scope and/or differentiation advantages within its home-triad market. The additional scale, scope or differentiation advantages to be gained by going global are not sufficient to compensate for the enhanced risks.

When MNEs have exhausted their growth opportunities in the home-triad and go into other regions, they then face a liability of foreignness and other additional risks by this global expansion. In other words, all of the advantages of homogeneity can be achieved within the home-triad, especially if the home-triad pursues policies of an internal market such as social, cultural and political harmonization (as in the EU) or economic integration (as in NAFTA and Asia). This requires that a "triad" dimension be added to the global/local split.

A related development is that such regional trade agreements tend to inhibit inter-block business by government-imposed barriers to entry. The E.U. and the United States are likely to fight trade wars and be responsive to domestic business lobbies seeking shelter in the form of subsidies and/or protection. These will remain cultural and political differences between members of the triad, but there will be fewer of these within each triad block. Thus, there are European MNEs. They will continue to earn 70% or more of their profits in the home-triad. There will only be a handful of purely "global" MNEs in the Fortune 500 listing. Globalization will remain a distant goal for most MNEs. The triad of regionalism will continue to dominate international business.

The home-triad base of MNE activity

A powerful indicator of triad/regional economic activity is the concentration of the world's largest MNEs in the "triad" economies of the US, EU and Japan.

These 500 MNEs dominate international business. They account for over 90% of the world's stock of FDI and nearly 50% of the world trade. This was also the situation in 1981, as documented in earlier studies of MNE economic activity. These MNEs are the "unit of analysis" for research in international business. They are the key vehicles for both FDI and trade. Furthermore, recent research reveals that the majority of these sales, on average, are intra-regional. And, for the great majority of them, this intra-regional trade is concentrated in their home-triad. Very few of these 500 large MNEs actually have any significant presence in all three parts of the triad. (In fact, only a handful such as Nestle and Unilever qualify as such "global" MNEs.)

A somewhat larger sub-set of the 500 have a strong presence in at least one other part of the triad in addition to the home-triad. In the following pages, these three types of MNEs are examined:

1. home-triad based MNEs: these are labeled home-based MNEs;
2. MNEs in two parts of the triad: these are labeled "bi-regional" MNEs;
3. MNEs in all three parts of the triad: these are labeled "global" MNEs;

Home-triad bound MNEs are defined as those with over 50% of their sales within their home-triad. Bi-regional MNEs have less than 50% of their sales within their home-triad, but at least 20% of their sales in two parts of the triad. Global MNEs have at least 20% of their sales in all three parts of the triad.

It should be noted that MNEs in all three groups are international, but not necessarily global. Only group 3 MNEs are actually global. Group 2—bi-regional MNEs—may be regarded as on the way to becoming global. Clearly, group 1 MNEs are not global by any definition.

There are several viable alternative ways to evaluate international business activity. The most useful, across all the 500 largest MNEs, is by looking at sales revenues. It is possible to calculate the ratio of Foreign-to-Total sales (F/T). Ideally, only sales by foreign affiliates should be included but often the exports of the home firm are also included as "foreign" sales in the consolidated accounts of many of the companies listed.

To summarize, of the 20 MNEs, 13 have over half of their sales within their home triad, and five of these 13 are entirely home-triad based. Then, of the potentially 12 bi-regional MNEs (those that have at least 20% of their sales in two parts of the triad), 10 are European-owned, with activities also in North America; one is Japanese (Yamaha); and one is American (Manpower). Only one MNE, Philips, is a true global MNE. The other 19 MNEs break out as is listed:

Global(1)
    Philips

Bi-regional(5):
    Astrazeneca
    Invensys
    DaimlerChrysler
    Manpower
    BP

Home-triad base (12):
    Thomson
    Nortel Networks
    Norsk Hydro
    Adecco
    RMC Group
    Peninsular & Oriental

Interbrew
Totalfinaelf
Yahama Motors
Skanska
Vouerone
BMW

Host-triad base(2)：

News Corp
Standard Chartered Group

Conclusions：

These data do not provide any evidence for globalization. Indeed only Philips needs to bother with a global strategy. The majority of these MNEs（a total of 15）are European home-triad based or bi-regional with some presence in North America. Two are host-triad based（News Corp. in America and Standard Chartered in Asia）. Two of the three North American MNEs are Canadian owned（Thomson and Northel）. Of these Nortel has followed a "double diamond" strategy with the US as its key market. The remainders are home-triad based.

Notes to the Text

1. Templeton Global Performance Index（TGPI）：Templeton 全球绩效指数,由 Templeton College, University of Oxford 提出,即从 the foreign assets, revenues and earnings 三个方面来评价一个跨国企业的绩效。

2. NAFTA：北美自由贸易协议（The North American Free Trade Agreement）,是美国、加拿大及墨西哥三国在 1992 年 8 月 12 日签署的关于三国间全面贸易的协议,该协议于 1994 年 1 月 1 日正式生效。

3. Nestle：雀巢公司。年销售额达 477 亿美元以上,其中大约 95％来自食品的销售,因此雀巢是世界上最大的食品制造商,也是最大的跨国公司之一。

4. Unilever：联合利华公司。1930 年,联合利华由荷兰人造黄油公司与英国利华兄弟制皂公司合并成立;今天,联合利华公司是世界最大的食品和饮料公司之一,冰淇淋、冷冻食品、茶饮料、调味品、人造奶油和食用油生产位于世界第一;也是全球第二大洗涤用品、洁肤产品和护发产品生产商;旗下品牌有和路雪、立顿、金纺、多芬、力士、旁氏、夏士莲等,为广大中国消费者熟悉。

5. Yamaha：日本雅马哈公司,是钢琴、电子乐器和吹管等乐器的制造商,也是供家庭影院使用的音频和视频产品和供移动电话使用的发声半导体的生产商。

6. Manpower：美国万宝盛华公司,为全球知名的人力资源公司,连续三年被美国

《财富》杂志(Fortune)及《福布斯》杂志(Forbes)评选为"最受赞赏企业"及"最佳管理企业"。

7. Philips：皇家飞利浦电子集团,是世界上最大的电子公司之一。

8. Astrazeneca：阿斯利康,全球领先制药公司之一,主要从事处方药品和医疗服务的研发、生产和销售业务,总部位于英国伦敦。

9. Invensys：英维思集团,由西比(Siebe)和BTR两大具有百年历史的专业自动化控制公司合并而成,是全球自动化及控制领域最大的公司之一,集团总部设在伦敦。

10. Daimler Chrysler：戴姆勒-克莱斯勒汽车公司,1998年由德国奔驰汽车公司与美国克莱斯勒汽车公司合并成立,业务范围包括轿车、商务车、航天航空、服务性业务、铁路系统、汽车电子以及柴油发动机等。

11. BP：全称British Petroleum,英国石油公司,是世界上最大的石油和石化集团公司之一。公司的主要业务是油气勘探开发、炼油、天然气销售和发电、油品零售和运输以及石油化工产品生产和销售;总部设在英国伦敦。

12. Thomson：全球领先的数字视频技术公司。

13. Nortel Networks：加拿大北电网络公司,成立于一个多世纪以前。目前,该公司为150多个国家的客户提供联网和通信服务以及基础设施,是世界上最大的全球供应商之一。

14. Norsk Hydro：海德鲁公司,挪威能源和铝业集团。

15. Adecco：艺珂公司,是在瑞士注册的全球最大的跨国人事顾问公司,财富500强之一,以提供最好的人才派遣及人才招募服务而闻名。

16. RMC Group：英国的RMC Group是全球最大的成品混凝土生产商。

17. Peninsular & Oriental：英国铁行轮船集团,英国历史最悠久的企业之一,全球著名的集装箱码头运营商。

18. Interbrew：比利时啤酒集团。

19. Totalfinaelf：法国一家石油公司,是法国道达尔菲纳石油公司与法国埃尔夫公司合并组建的一体化石油公司。

20. Skanska：瑞典建筑公司,全世界最大的建筑服务集团之一。

21. Vodafone：英国移动通信运营商。

22. BMW：宝马汽车股份公司,是世界上以生产豪华汽车、摩托车和高性能发动机而闻名的汽车公司;总部设在德国慕尼黑。

23. News Corp：澳大利亚新闻公司,是全球最大的媒介公司之一,《财富》500强之一,其产品及服务范围包括制作与分销电影、电视节目、电视、卫星和有线电视、报纸杂志和图书的出版、广告、数字广播系统的开发、有条件接入和订户管理系统的开发、大众在线节目的设计和分销等。

24. Standard Chartered：英国渣打银行,总部在伦敦。

Exercises

I Answer the following questions.

1. How do the companies increase profits today?

2. Why are those regionally-based strategies successful?

3. How is the international business activity evaluated?

4. Do you agree that "Multinational enterprises are regional, not global"?

II Write out the equivalents of the following words and expressions.

1. triad regional patterns   7. 海外经营
2. economic integration   8. 销售收入
3. subsidy   9. 关键市场
4. intra-regional trade   10. 贸易战
5. domestic oriented   11. 对外直接投资
6. differentiation advantages   12. 国内市场

III Translate the following into Chinese.

A major reason for the success of these regionally-based strategies is that they permit the MNE to achieve all the economic advantages of scale and scope without the additional business risks of operating far from its home base. This occurs if the MNE sells the same product and/or service in the same manner within the home-triad region. This allows the MNE to gain all the potential economies of scale and scope and/or differentiation advantages within its home-triad market. The additional scale, scope or differentiation advantages to be gained by going global are not sufficient to compensate for the enhanced risks.

Unit 28

Transfer Pricing in Multinational Companies

A transfer price is internal price charged by a selling department, division or subsidiary of a company for a raw material, component or finished good or service which is supplied to a buying department, division or subsidiary of the same company. The transfer price charged may be set by reference to the prices ruling in outside markets for inputs and products.

Alternatively, the transfer price may be set at a lower or higher level than the going market price according to some internal accounting convention and the desired "profit split" between the firm's activities and locations. Transfer pricing may be used both by a company which operates only in one national market and by multinational companies (MNCs) which produce and sell their products in a number of countries. In the case of MNCs transfer pricing across national borders provides additional opportunities to improve the company's competitive and profit position by enabling it, for example, to "manipulate" prices so as to ensure that most of the company's profits accrue in countries where company taxation rates are the lowest.

It is also possible, as the Nissan UK case below indicates, for transfer pricing to be used by a market intermediary (in this instance a distributor) to reduce its own tax bill without the knowledge of the supplier of the product (in this instance Nissan, Japan).

Objectives of transfer pricing: Maximizing global corporate profits, is often cited as a primary goal of an MNC. Given differences between countries, in terms of cost, tariff and tax structures, changes in exchange rates and in competitive pressures, internal transfer pricing as opposed to market-based transactions with intermediaries can provide an effective and flexible means of enhancing corporate profitability. Transfer pricing can be deployed in a number of contexts.

• Taxation: Minimization of the MNC 's global tax liability by using transfer pricing to move products at cost out of countries with high corporate taxes and the generation of profits in countries with low corporate taxes.

• Tariffs: Minimization of the MNC's exposure to tariffs by using transfer pricing to lower product prices sold to countries with high import tariffs.

• Exchange rates: Transfer pricing can be used to reduce the MNC's exposure to exchange rate risks by, for example, moving funds out of weak currencies into strong ones.

• Exchange controls: Transfer pricing can be used to move funds out of a country which operates exchange controls restricting the repatriation of dividends and capital.

　　• Competitive pressures: Transfer pricing can be used to enable subsidiaries to lower prices to match or undercut local competitors.

　　Transfer pricing methods: There are three basic methods of transfer pricing.

　　(a) Market based prices

　　With this method the MNC prices the goods and services it transfers between its business units at a price equal to that prevailing for those goods and services on the open market—a form of "arm's length" pricing insofar as intra-company transfers are priced the same as that charged to an external customer.

　　This method has two main advantages for the MNC. First, business units are able to operate as independent profit centers with the managers of these units being responsible for their own performance. This can increase the motivation of local managers while making it easier for headquarters to assess the actual operating performance results of its business units. Second, the market price method is usually favored by the tax and customs authorities of both host and home countries as they will receive a fair share of the profits made. In this case the international trading of the MNC is transparent, so avoiding potential conflict with the authorities.

　　In practice, however, the use of a market price as a benchmark is often difficult. There needs to be a competitive market which can provide a comparable price to which the transfer price can be matched. But for some items, e. g. complex capital equipment, an external market may not exist, and for others prices may be distorted by monopoly elements. Moreover, a definitive market price may be difficult to determine as prices for the same product may vary considerably from one country to another. Changes in exchange rates, transportation costs, local taxes and tariffs can result in large variations in the selling price. In addition, a company will want to set its prices in relation to the supply and demand conditions relevant to specific country conditions to ensure that a business unit can compete in that country. In sum, these factors mean that there is unlikely to be a unique market price for the MNC to follow.

　　(b) Cost-based prices

　　With this method, the cost of a good or service, with or without a profit element, is used as a basis to determine the transfer price. The costs of a good or service are generally available from within the company and can be determined from the MNC's own accounting systems. This method is generally acceptable to the tax and customs authorities since it provides some indication that the transfer price approximates to the real price of supplying the item and thus that the authorities will receive a fair share of tax and tariff revenues. Cost-based approaches are, however, not so transparent as to remove totally the suspicion that they have been "massaged", since the selection of a particular type of cost method can significantly alter the magnitude of the transfer price.

　　The issue is which cost approach to use—full actual costs, full standard costs, actual variable costs or only marginal costs. Should research and development costs be included? How should fixed costs be incorporated? And how should a profit element be entered into the calculation? Different cost permutations can yield widely differing transfer prices and hence raise a question mark over the legitimacy of such prices as viewed by the authorities. From the MNC's perspective, cost-based methods can create difficulties with the selling unit as there may be little incentive for it to remain cost effective if it knows that it can simply recover increased costs by raising the transfer price. Without an incentive to produce efficiently the transfer price may erode the competitiveness of the final product in the market place.

(c) Negotiated prices

In this approach, buying and selling business units are free to negotiate a mutually acceptable transfer price. Since each unit is responsible for its own performance this will encourage cost minimization and encourage the parties to seek a transfer price which yields them an appropriate profit return. However, this may result in sub-optimization overall since no account is taken of such factors as differences in tax and tariff rates between countries, and hence the scope to increase the profitability of the group as a whole by deploying transfer pricing to minimize the MNC's global tax bill.

Constraints

Transfer pricing can be a highly flexible tool in achieving benefits for the MNC but there are several constraints on its use, both internal and external.

(a) Internal constraints

The extent of decentralization or centralization may pose potential conflicts between the interests of the MNC and its various business units in terms of goal congruence, motivation and performance evaluation, decentralization and arm's length pricing may encourage attention to cost efficiency and boost local pre-tax profits but may undermine the MNC's overall after-tax profitability because of a failure to transfer the bulk of the company's profits to a tax haven. On the other hand, a centralization and "manipulative" transfer pricing may have negative effects on individual subsidiaries by harming local managers' morale and hiding operating inefficiencies, thus serving to undermine the company's longer-term competitive viability.

The mechanics of implementing and maintaining the less open forms of transfer pricing can be complex and time-consuming. A vast amount of information on product flows, tax and tariff rates in individual countries, and changes to these, need to be ascertained. A control system is needed to collect, analyze and transmit the obtained data and "masterminds" the network of transfer prices between subsidiaries and divisions.

(b) External constraints

The use of transfer pricing procedures by MNCs impacts on the countries between which intra-company trade takes place. National tax and customs authorities quite naturally wish to ensure that trade is conducted in a "fair" way and conforms to the country's legal requirements. The problem of the private interest of the MNC versus the public interest of the country can pose difficulties. The under-recording of local profits through the use of manipulative transfer prices which "transfer out" value added, for example, is one common area of confrontation between MNCs and host country governments. One way of combating this latter problem which has been widely canvassed (and is currently employed by the state of California) is the use of a unitary taxation system. Under a unitary tax system, local taxation is based on a proportion of the worldwide profits of a company calculated on the size of its assets etc. in that country instead of only on the profits actually declared in that country. **Table** shows a company having $ 1,000 m of assets both in country Y and country Z and total gross profits of $ 200 m. Country Y taxes corporate profits at 50 per cent and country Z at 20 per cent. Under the conventional taxation system, the company would pay a total of $ 40 m in tax to the authorities in country Z. Under a unitary taxation system, although the country has declared no profits in country Y the assets located there are assumed to have generated one-half of the worldwide profits of the company. In this case the company's tax bill is $ 90 m, i. e. $ 50 m payable on the "shadow" profits attributable to the company's assets in country Y plus $ 40 m on the actual profits declared in country Z.

	Country Y 50% tax rate Company assets = $ 1,000 m	Country Z 20% tax rate Company assets = $ 1,000 m	Tax liability
Taxation systems			
1 Conventional basis gross profits	0	$ 200 m	$ 40 m
2 Unitary basis gross profits	($ 100 m) plus	$ 200 m	$ 90 m

TABLE   Tax liabilities under conventional and unitary taxation systems

Some cases of transfer pricing abuse

Transfer pricing is often implemented in ways which are difficult to discern and evaluate by "outsiders" not privy to key corporate information and decision-making processes. This is particularly the case with manipulative transfer pricing which is conducted in a clandestine way. In some instances host country tax authorities need to rely on "whistleblowers" or a blatant transgression of national legal requirements to alert them to the possibility of abusive transfer pricing.

The USA and Japanese tax authorities have recently taken action against various foreign multinationals for suspected tax evasion: the USA against Nissan, and Japan against Coca-Cola, Roche, Ciba-Geigy and Hoechst. In addition to national litigations, the 17-year dispute between Barclays Bank and the State of California over the application of unitary taxation was ruled on by the US Supreme Court earlier this year. The Supreme Court upheld

California's right to apply penalty taxes on foreign companies. The verdict means that California is not now required to refund Barclays and a number of other foreign MNCs around $400 m (£267 m) It has already collected in penalty taxes and cancel another $500 m it has assessed and which is still awaiting collection.

Notes to the Text

1. Nissan：日本日产汽车公司，创立于 1933 年，是日本三大汽车制造商之一，也是第一家开始制造小型轿车和汽车零件的制造商。

2. Roche：瑞士罗氏制药公司，创立于 1896 年，总部位于瑞士巴塞尔。罗氏两大核心业务为药品和诊断，在众多领域已成为全球的领先者：全球诊断领域排名第一、全球肿瘤领域排名第一、移植学和病毒学领域的领先者、全球生物科技领域排名第二。

3. Ciba-Geigy：汽巴-嘉基公司，是瑞士一家医药公司。1996 年和山德士公司合并成立诺华公司（Novartis）。诺华与罗氏是瑞士两家最大的制药公司。

4. Hoechst：赫希斯特公司，德国三大化学工业公司之一。

Exercises

I Answer the following questions.

1. What is a transfer price?
2. Why do MNCs adopt the policy of transfer pricing?
3. What are the basic methods of transfer pricing?
4. What are the constraints of transfer pricing?

II Write out the equivalents of the following words and expressions.

1. transfer price
2. the going market price
3. taxation rate
4. market intermediary
5. marginal cost
6. 外汇管制
7. 垄断
8. 可变成本
9. 成本效益
10. 税前利润
11. 偷税漏税

III Translate the following into Chinese.

In practice, however, the use of a market price as a benchmark is often difficult. There needs to be a competitive market which can provide a comparable price to which the transfer price can be matched. But for some items, e.g. complex capital equipment, an external market may not exist, and for others prices may be distorted by monopoly elements. Moreover, a definitive market price may be difficult to determine as prices for the same product may vary considerably from one country to another. Changes in exchange rates, transportation costs, local taxes and tariffs can result in large variations in the selling price. In addition, a company will want to set its prices in relation to the supply and demand conditions relevant to specific country conditions to ensure that a business unit can compete in that country. In sum, these factors mean that there is unlikely to be a unique market price for the MNC to follow.

Unit 29

Insurance

One of the largest sectors of modern commercial life is the insurance business, of which there are four main branches: (a) Marine Insurance, (b) Fire Insurance, (c) Life Insurance and (d) Accident Insurance.

There is no real difference here between the words "insurance" and "assurance", but it has become customary to use the word "assurance" when referring to life policies. The event that is being insured against in the life policy will assuredly happen—for everyone dies at some time—but with all other insurances the loss insured against may never happen.

Marine Insurance usually covers the ship itself and the cargo, the crew and any passengers, as well as owner liabilities. It will cover loss by storm, fire, collision or other perils of the sea, but not such mishaps as oil escaping from a tanker into a sea. Such a case recently occurred near the British coast and three million pounds was eventually claimed from the owners of the vessel to cover the cost of cleaning the shores and beaches of oil. Events of this kind are usually covered by a Special Ship-owners' Liabilities Policy which relieves the owners of such risks so that they can carry on their business at sea with greater confidence.

Fire Insurance usually covers loss by fire of domestic and business premises and their contents, and often such a policy is extended to include what are termed "special perils", for example hurricanes, earthquakes, tornadoes, floods, and civil riots. Tied to this kind of policy is Consequential Loss Insurance which enables a company to receive reasonable payments in lieu of earnings while repair of damage and rebuilding is in progress.

Life Assurance is the most popular form of insurance and enables a man to guarantee an income to his family in the event of his early death, or, if he lives the normal span of years, it enables him to save for his retirement. When such a policy has matured, it is worth far more than the sum paid in over the years as it usually has profits added to it. A "with profits" Endowment Policy will bring the insured bonuses which depend on a share of the profits earned by the insurance policy.

General Accident Insurance is becoming more popular with the perils inherent in modern living. Car, rail, and air accidents are possibilities. Even accidents in the home can result in death, or perhaps temporary or permanent injury which can prevent the normal earning of a living. Also most industrial and commercial concerns are required to insure their staff against injury in the course of their work and on the business premises. A most important and relatively new area of insurance is "product liability", where a company can be held liable for any injury or damage caused by one of its products.

There is very little in the world today that can not be insured. All motorists must be insured not only against damage and injury to themselves and their own vehicle but against the same to other parties who may be involved with them in a motor accident. A world-famous sportsman can insure himself against injury and a highly paid concert pianist can insure his hands as they are the main source of his income and without them he could not earn his living. Parents may insure against the possibility of having twins; farmers against disease of their flocks and herds or damage to crops and woodlands; private householders or businessmen against burglary, loss or damage by vandalism or acts of God.

Insurance confers benefits on the insured who are thereby freed from a great deal of worry upon the payment of a relatively small premium. These benefits are also reflected in the economy of the nation. Insurance removes a great amount of uncertainty from business life and allows businessmen to take commercial risks which they might not otherwise attempt. This results in a higher level of business activity. In consequence of the regular sums of money from a large number of individuals and businesses, the insurance companies are able to invest in new developments in industry and technology. It is from these investments that they make profits which are eventually shared by holders of "with profits" policies.

Insurance companies are also among the most important assets to a nation, for by selling their services abroad they are contributing to the balance of payments position by earning foreign currency. A nation that has to import much of what it needs must export as much as possible to pay for the imports. When the cost of the imports exceeds the income from exports it is said to have "an adverse balance of trade". But the deficit is often made up by money earned on services which are sold overseas—what are normally called "invisibles" because they are not goods or commodities—and insurance is one of the most valuable sources of invisible earnings to any nation.

Notes to the Text

1. owner liabilities: matters for which the owner must take responsibility 拥有者(船主)责任
2. Consequential Loss Insurance: 间接损失险
3. Acts of God: natural disasters beyond the control of man, such as earthquakes, hurricanes, volcanoes and so on 天灾,(另一种说法是 force majeure)不可抗力
4. balance of trade: the difference between the value of exports and that of imports 贸易差额
5. invisible: referring to invisible exports which involve services rather than goods. Examples are freight, insurance, banking services, tourism, etc. 无形输出
6. invisible earning: 无形收益

Exercises

I **Answer the following questions.**

1. What are the four main branches of insurance?

2. Why is insurance necessary and important in people's lives?

3. Do you think insurance is beneficial to a country's national economy? Why?

4. What does a "with profit" endowment policy means?

II **Write out the equivalents of the following words and expressions.**

1. premium
2. deficit
3. "with profits" policy
4. in lieu of
5. product liability

6. 保（险）单
7. 养老保险
8. 贸易逆差
9. 贸易顺差
10. 资产

III **Translate the following into Chinese**

Insurance companies are also among the most important assets to a nation, for by selling their services abroad they are contributing to the balance of payments position by earning foreign currency. A nation that has to import much of what it needs must export as much as possible to pay for the imports. When the cost of the imports exceeds the income from exports it is said to have "an adverse balance of trade". But the deficit is often made up by money earned on services which are sold overseas—what are normally called "invisibles" because they are not goods or commodities—and insurance is one of the most valuable sources of invisible earnings to any nation.

Unit 30

Marine Insurance

It is customary to insure goods sold for export against the perils of the journey. According to the method of transportation, a marine or aviation insurance is effected.

The term "marine insurance" is somewhat misleading because the contract of marine insurance can, by agreement of the parties or custom of the trade, be extended so as to protect the assured against losses on inland waters or land which are incidental to the sea voyage. In the export trade it is usual to arrange an extended marine insurance in order to cover the transportation of goods from the warehouse of the seller to the port of dispatch, and from the port of arrival to the warehouse of the overseas buyer. Marine insurance is an institution of great antiquity; it was known in Lombardy in the fourteenth century, the first English statute dealing with it was passed in 1601, and Lloyd's Coffee House, the birthplace of Lloyd's London, is first mentioned in the records of 1688. The law relating to marine insurance is codified in the Marine Insurance Act 1906. This enactment provides a standard policy, known as Lloyd's S. G. policy, which the parties may adopt if they so desire whether they insure the risk with underwriters at Lloyd's or elsewhere.

The International Chamber of Commerce has prepared a publication entitled Tables of Practical Equivalents in Marine Insurance, in which the similarities and differences existing in marine insurance terms, clauses and covers in 13 important centers of the world are analyzed and compared from the marine insurance point of view.

In the law relating to insurance no standard policy has been developed yet and Lloyd's S. G. policy is used with suitable alterations.

Stipulations in the contract of sale

In an export transaction, the terms of the contract of sale provide normally whether the costs of marine insurance shall be borne by the seller or by the buyer. If the goods are sold on FOB terms, these costs have to be paid by the buyer and that is even true if the FOB seller, by request of the buyer, has taken out the policy. If the goods are sold on CIF terms, it is the duty of the seller to take out the policy and pay the costs of insurance. In a C&F contract the seller needs not insure, nor needs the buyer (at whose risk the goods travel), but if the C&F contract contains a clause "insurance to be effected by the buyer" or a clause in similar terms, that will normally place the buyer under a contractual obligation to insure and has not merely declaratory effect, the obligation to insure is thereby "put into the reverse", and the buyer must take out the same policy which the seller would have been obliged to obtain if the contract had been a CIF contract.

The marine insurance policy forms part of the shipping documents. Where goods are sold CIF the seller is obliged to take out a marine insurance policy which provides cover against risk customarily covered in the particular trade in respect of the cargo and voyage in question, but he is not required to do more. He need not take out an all risks policy unless the parties have agreed thereon or it is demanded by the custom of the trade.

The assured, the insurer and the broker

The parties to a contract of marine insurance are known as the assured and the insurer. Insurers are either underwriting members of Lloyd's or marine insurance companies. The "Society of Lloyd's" has underwriting and non-underwriting members. The former, known as the "names", form groups called "syndicates", which conduct the actual underwriting through an underwriting agent; every member of a syndicate is liable for a proportionate fraction of the risk, and thus the aim of all insurance is achieved, namely to spread the risk to many persons while, at the same time, providing indemnity for the assured if a loss occurs. The underwriting agent is usually, but not necessarily, a member of the syndicate or syndicates for which he acts. Insurance at Lloyd's is effected in "The Room", which is situated in London, and underwriting members accept only risks offered through Lloyd's brokers (who have access to The Room). A person who wishes to effect an insurance at Lloyd's has thus to employ the services of such a broker. The marine insurance companies have been early competitors of Lloyd's in the field of marine insurance, and can be approached directly or through an agent of the company (sometimes called an "underwriting agent" though his functions are different from those of an underwriting agent at Lloyd's), or through an insurance broker.

In the normal course of business the exporter, who wishes to have his goods insured, does not approach the insurer directly but instructs an insurance broker to effect the insurance on his behalf. Where the exporter is the regular client of the insurance broker, he forwards his instructions on a form supplied by a broker and gives the required particulars on that form. The broker, who is usually authorized to place the insurance within certain limits as to the rates of premium, writes the essentials of the proposed insurance in customary abbreviation on a document called "the slip" which he takes to Lloyd's or a marine insurance company. An insurer, who is prepared to accept part of the risk, writes on the slip the amount for which he is willing to insure and adds his initials; this is known as "writing a line". The broker then takes the slip to other insurers who successively likewise write lines until the whole risk is covered. It is important for the broker to secure a good "lead" because the second and following underwriters to whom the broker presents the slip are usually more ready to accept the risk if the lead is a well-known name.

When the risk is covered, the broker sends the assured a memorandum of the insurance effected which is conveniently executed on a duplicate form of the instructions. According to the nature of insurance which the broker was instructed to obtain, the memorandum assumes the form of a closed or open cover note. A closed cover note is sent if the assured, in his instructions, has given full particulars as to cargo and shipment and the insurance has, thus, been made definite. An open cover note is sent if the instructions of the assured are so general and indefinite that further instructions are required from him to define the cargo, voyage or interest shipped under the insurance; this happens where the assured requires a "floating policy" or an "open cover", or where he reserves the right to give "closing instructions".

The insurance broker should, as a matter of prudent business practice, notify the assured promptly of the terms of the insurance which he arranged for him and forward the cover note as soon as possible, but he is not under a legal duty to do so. In one case, the plaintiffs instructed the defendants, insurance brokers, to effect an open marine insurance on their goods, obtaining immediate cover. On April 2 the brokers reported that the cover was placed, and on April 4 they sent the assured the cover note which did not contain a clause covering the goods while at packers. In the night of April 4~5 goods of the value of £ 8,000 were destroyed by fire at a warehouse of packers. The action of the assured against the brokers for damages was dismissed. It was held that the brokers had no knowledge that the goods in the hands of the packers were uninsured and that the brokers were not negligent by not insuring them in the hands of the packers or not informing the assured that they had not so insured them. The learned judge likewise rejected the contention of the assured that the brokers were under a duty to notify the assured at once of the terms of the insurance:

It was, no doubt, prudent to do so, both to allay the client's anxiety and possibly to enable the client to check the terms of insurance, but that was very different from saying it was part of the broker's duty.

It may be added that at present no standard or approved clause has been devised to extend insurance cover while goods are in the hands of packers.

The position of the insurance broker is anomalous in two respects: he is the agent of the insurer and the assured but is paid by the insurer. Even more remarkable is the fact that he is personally and solely responsible to the insurer for payment of the premium while, as between insurer and assured, by a legal fiction the premium is regarded as paid. The historical origin of the rule is that underwriting members of Lloyd's refused, at an early date, to deal with assured persons directly, and accepted insurances only from brokers whom they knew personally as financially trustworthy. Today, the rules laid down, in respect of marine insurance effected at Lloyd's or elsewhere, in the Marine Insurance Act 1906.

The anomalous position of the insurance broker, in the second respect mentioned above, has been repeatedly commented on in an early case.

As between the assured and the underwriter the premiums are considered as paid. The underwriter, to whom in most instances, the assured are unknown, looks to the broker for payment, and be to the assured. The latter pays the premiums to the broker only, who is a middleman between the assured and the underwriter. But he is not merely an agent, he is a principal to receive the money from the assured, and to pay it to the underwriter.

The broker has a lien on the policy until the premium, commission and other charges due to him have been paid.

Notes to the Text

1. Lombardy：伦巴第区，意大利第一经济大区。主要有冶金、化工、机械制造、飞机制造、汽车制造、皮革加工、纺织、制衣及丝绸印染和加工等工业；交通方便，是连接欧洲大陆与地中海的枢纽，首府是米兰。

2. Lloyd's Coffee House：劳埃德咖啡屋。17 世纪伦敦金融城重要的海运地位使得当时商人对船只和船货的保险需求大大增加；1688 年，爱德华·劳埃德（Edward Lloyd）在伦敦金融城的塔街（Tower Street）开设了劳合社的前身——劳埃德咖啡屋（劳合社是世界上第一家保险市场，也是目前世界上最大的保险市场）。

3. Lloyd's London：英国劳合社。英国最大的保险组织，劳合社本身是个社团，更确切地说是一个保险市场，与纽约证券交易所相似，只向其成员提供交易场所和有关的服务，本身并不承保业务，伦敦劳合社是从劳埃德咖啡屋演变而来的，故又称"劳埃德保险社"。

4. The Marine Insurance Act 1906：英国 1906 年海上保险法，是一部对很多国家的海上保险立法都有重要影响的法律，被世界各国视为海上保险法的范本。

5. Lloyd's S.G. policy：劳合社保险单标准格式（Lloyd's ship & goods policy form）于 1779 年开始在伦敦保险市场上采用，1795 年在英国取代所有其他海上保险单，成为船舶与货物运输保险的标准海上保险单，英国 1906 年海上保险法把劳合社制订的 S.G.保险单作为标准保险单。

6. International Chamber of Commerce：国际商会（ICC），成立于 1919 年，是全球唯一代表所有企业的权威代言机构。国际商会推行开放的国际贸易、投资体系和市场经济，它所制定的用以规范国际商业合作的规章，如《托收统一规则》《跟单信用证统一惯例》《国际商会 2000 国际贸易术语解释通则》等被广泛地应用于国际贸易中，并成为国际贸易不可缺少的一部分。

7. C&F：全称 cost and freight，成本加运费价

8. CIF：全称 cost, insurance, freight，成本加保险费、运费价

9. Society of Lloyd's：劳合社。劳合社不仅是一家保险公司，而且是一个拥有会员的机构。构成劳合社保险和再保险市场的五大要素分别是：劳合社会员（Members of Lloyd's）、辛迪加（Syndicates）、管理中介（Managing Agents）、劳合社经纪人（Lloyd's Brokers）、本地经纪人（Local Brokers）。

10. syndicate：an association of people or firms authorized to undertake a duty or transact specific business 辛迪加

11. lien：the right to take another's property if an obligation is not discharged 扣押权，留置权

Exercises

I **Answer the following questions.**

1. What does marine insurance cover?
2. Who pays the insurance cost when the transaction is concluded on the FOB basis?
3. What are the parties to a contract of marine insurance?
4. How is insurance effected at Lloyd's?
5. What is an open cover note? What is a closed one?

II **Write out the equivalents of the following words and expressions.**

1. marine insurance
2. the assured
3. port of dispatch
4. standard policy
5. underwriter

6. 合同义务
7. 装运单据
8. 一切险（全险）
9. 保险费率
10. 委托人

III **Translate the following into Chinese.**

In an export transaction, the terms of the contract of sale provide normally whether the costs of marine insurance shall be borne by the seller or by the buyer. If the goods are sold on FOB terms, these costs have to be paid by the buyer and that is even true if the FOB seller, by request of the buyer, has taken out the policy. If the goods are sold on CIF terms, it is the duty of the seller to take out the policy and pay the costs of insurance. In a C & F contract the seller need not insure, nor need the buyer (at whose risk the goods travel), but if the C & F contract contains a clause "insurance to be effected by the buyer" or a clause in similar terms, that will normally place the buyer under a contractual obligation to insure and has not merely declaratory effect, the obligation to insure is thereby "put into the reverse", and the buyer must take out the same policy which the seller would have been obliged to obtain if the contract had been a CIF contract.

Unit 31

Elements of Communication

In business, as in most other areas of life, the best idea in the world can fail if it's not communicated effectively.

Communication is *both* situational (organizational) and personal (stylistic). Successful business communication depends on answering a few crucial questions: have you mastered and organized all the relevant information? Have you taken into account the personal and organizational context? Have you defined a clear, achievable goal? Have you considered the needs of your audiences? Have you expressed yourself as clearly, vividly, and forcefully as possible? Have you chosen the right communication channels?

Managers send messages through writing, speaking, actions, gestures, electronic media, graphics, the grapevine, and force of personality. Good business people devote tremendous attention to shaping their message and deciding how to deliver it. Experienced managers insist that success depends largely on effective communication.

A communicator, or source, sends a message to a receiver, or audience, provoking a response. Building on this model, which originates far back in the history of communication research, we suggest seven categories that will help you define and analyze any business communication situation.

1. Source: Who is initiating action, and why should she or he be believed?

2. Audience: What will move them to support you? Is their attitude toward your proposal positive, neutral, or negative? Are there any hidden audiences you haven't considered?

3. Goal: What result do you seek? Weigh it against the costs of achieving it. Can it stand on its own merits? Does it conflict with other goals of equal or greater importance? How, in short, will you measure success?

4. Context: Communication occurs in a specific environment. It can involve an effort to reach one person, or to reach millions. It can mean working within the norms of a particular corporate culture, its history, its competitive situation—or challenging those norms. Before you plan your communication strategy, be sure you know the territory.

5. Message: What message will achieve your goal with these particular audiences? Consider how much information they need, what doubts they're likely to have, how your proposal will benefit them, how to make your message convincing and memorable.

6. Media: Which medium will convey your message most effectively to each significant audience? Should you speak, write, call, send E-mail, meet, fax, produce a videotape, or

hold a press conference? Sending a memo to an office mate, for example, may express an unwillingness to talk face to face.

7. Feedback: Communication is not an act, but a process. A message provokes a response, which requires another message. The business communicator doesn't shoot an arrow at a target, but sets a process in motion designed to achieve a considered result. This means polling your audience at every stage of the communication and, more importantly, giving them an opportunity to respond. In that way you know what they think and can tailor your message accordingly.

Even a brief consideration of these seven analytical tools will reveal that any business communication task is really a management task. Many communication situations happen spontaneously to a manager rather than occur as planned events. Some of your key topics and goals may not be listed on any overt agenda. How can these realities be turned into an advantage? Considering the source, audience, goal, context, message, media, and feedback provides you with an economical framework for introspection in any business situation, whether you're planning a broad strategy or devising a particular communication effort.

Exercises

I **Answer the following questions.**

1. Do you agree that "Communication is both situational and personal"?
2. What are the elements to be considered in business communication?
3. What strategy do you adopt when communicating with your teacher or your classmates?

II **Write out the equivalents of the following words and expressions.**

1. business communication
2. introspection
3. electronic media
4. communication research
5. 交流渠道
6. 交流工具
7. 记者招待会
8. 会议日程

III **Translate the following into Chinese.**

Feedback: Communication is not an act, but a process. A message provokes a response, which requires another message. The business communicator doesn't shoot an arrow at a target, but sets a process in motion designed to achieve a considered result. This means polling your audience at every stage of the communication and, more importantly, giving them an opportunity to respond. In that way you know what they think and can tailor your message accordingly.

Unit 32
Main Forms of Communication in Business

The importance of communication in business becomes even more apparent when we consider the communication activities of an organization from an overall point of view. These activities fall into three broad categories: internal operational, external operational, and personal.

Internal-operational communication

All the communication that occurs in conducting work within a business is classified as internal operational. This is the communication among the business's workers that is done to implement the business's operating plan. Internal-operational communication takes many forms. It includes the orders and instructions that supervisors give workers, as well as oral exchanges among workers about work matters. It includes reports and records that workers prepare concerning sales, production, inventories, finance, maintenance, and so on. It includes the memorandums and reports that workers write in carrying out their assignments. Much of this internal-operational communication is performed on computer networks. Workers send electronic mail through networks to others throughout the business, whether located down the hall, across the street, or around the world, the computer also assists the business writer and speaker in many other aspects of communication.

External-operational communication

The work-related communication that a business does with people and groups outside the business is external-operational communication. This is the business's communication with its publics—suppliers, service companies, customers, and the general public. External-operational communication includes all of the business's efforts at direct selling — salespeople's "spiels", descriptive brochures, telephone callbacks, "follow-up service calls, and the like. It also includes the advertising the business does, what is advertising but communication with potential customers? Radio and television messages, newspaper and magazine advertising, and point-of-purchase display material obviously play a role in the business's plan to achieve its work objective. Also in this category is all that a business does to improve its public relations, including its planned publicity, the civic-mindedness of its management, the courtesy of its employees, and the condition of its physical plant. And of very special importance to our study of communication, this category includes all the letters that workers write in carrying out their assignments.

Technology assists workers with external-operational communication in both constructing and transmitting documents. For example, sales people can keep database information on customers; check their company's computers for new product information and inventory information, construct sales, order confirmation, and other letters for their customers. These letters can be transmitted by fax, electronic mail, or printed copy.

The importance of external-operational communication to a business hardly requires supporting comment. Every business is dependent on outside people and groups for its success. And because the success of a business depends on its ability to satisfy customers' needs, it must communicate effectively with them. In today's complex business society, businesses depend on each other in the production and distributional communication; external communication is vital to business success.

Personal communication

Not all the communication that occurs in business is operational. In fact, much of it is without purpose as far as the business is concerned. Such communication is called personal.

Personal communication is the exchange of information and feelings in which we human beings engage whenever we come together. We are social animals. We have a need to communicate, and we will communicate even when we have little or nothing to say.

We spend much of our time with friends in communication. Even total strangers are likely to communicate when they are placed together, as on an airplane flight, in a waiting room, or at a ball game. Such personal communication also occurs at the workplace, and it is a part of the communication activity of any business. Although not a part of the business's plan of operation, personal communication can have a significant effect on the success of that plan. This effect is a result of the influence that personal communication can have on the attitudes of the workers.

The workers' attitudes toward the business, each other, and their assignments directly affect their willingness to work. And the nature of conversation in a work situation affects attitudes. In a work situation where heated words and flaming tempers are often present, the workers are not likely to make their usual productive efforts. However, a rollicking, jovial work situation is likely to have an equally bad effect on productivity. Somewhere between these extremes lies the ideal productive attitude.

Also affecting the worker's attitudes is the extent of personal communication permitted. Absolute denial of personal communication could lead to emotional upset, for most of us hold dear our right to communicate. On the other hand, excessive personal communication could interfere with the word done. Again, the middle ground is probably the best.

Notes to the Text

1. spiel: a lengthy or extravagant speech or argument usually intended to persuade; plausible glib talk (especially useful to a salesperson) 流利又夸张的讲话；滔滔不绝的讲话；口若悬河

2. civic-mindedness: the quality of being mentally oriented toward the community or the people 公众意识；公民意识

3. physical plant: A physical plant or mechanical plant refers to the necessary infrastructure used in support of a given facility. This usually includes air conditioning (both heating and cooling systems) and other mechanical systems. It often also includes the maintenance of other systems, such as plumbing and lighting. The facility itself may be an office building, a school campus, military base, apartment complex, or the like. 物质设备，硬件（如空调、管道、照明、楼房等）

4. rollicking: carefree and high-spirited; boisterous; lively 欢乐的；欢快的

5. jovial: full of or showing high-spirited merriment; very happy 快活的，高兴的，愉快的

I Answer the following questions.

1. What is internal-operational communication?

2. What is external-operational communication?

3. Why is external-operational communication thought to be very important to a business?

4. What is personal communication? What effect does it have on the business activity?

II Write out the equivalents of the following words and expressions.

1. business operation

2. internal-operational communication

3. follow-up service

4. point-of-purchase display

5. 直销

6. 潜在客户

7. 公共关系

8. 工作环境

III Translate the following into Chinese.

The importance of external-operational communication to a business hardly requires supporting comment. Every business is dependent on outside people and groups for its success. And because the success of a business depends on its ability to satisfy customers' needs, it must communicate effectively with them. In today's complex business society, businesses depend on each other in the production and distributional communication; external communication is vital to business success.

Unit 33

The Changing Concept of Marketing

The terms *market* and *marketing* can have several meanings depending upon how they are used. The term *stock market* refers to the buying and selling of shares in corporations as well as other activities related to stock trading and pricing. The important world stock markets are in London, Geneva, New York, Tokyo, and Singapore. Another type of market is a grocery market, which is a place where people purchase food. When economists use the word market they mean a set of forces or conditions that determine the price of a product, such as the supply available for sale and the demand for it by consumers. The term *marketing* in business includes all of these meanings, and more.

In the past, the concept of marketing emphasized sales. The producer or manufacturer made a product he wanted to sell. Marketing was the task of figuring out how to sell the product. Basically, selling the product would be accomplished by sales promotion, which included advertising and personal selling. In addition to sales promotion, marketing also involved the physical distribution of the product to the places where it was actually sold. Distribution consisted of transportation, storage, and related services such as financing, standardization and grading, and the related risks.

The modern marketing concept includes all of the activities mentioned, but it is based on a different set of principles. It subscribes to the notion that production can be economically justified only by consumption. In other words, goods should be produced only if they can be sold. Therefore, the producer should consider who is going to buy the product—or what the market for the product is—before production begins. This is very different from making a product and then thinking about how to sell it.

Marketing now involves first deciding what the customer wants, and designing and producing a product that satisfies these wants at a profit to the company. Instead of concentrating solely on production, the company must consider the desires of the consumer, and this is much more difficult since it involves human behavior. Production, on the other hand, is mostly an engineering problem. Thus, demand and market forces are still an important aspect of modern marketing, but they are considered prior to the production process.

Because products are often marketed internationally, distribution has increased in importance. Goods must be at the place where the customer needs them or brought there. This is known as place utility, it adds value to a product. However, many markets are separated from the place of production, which means often both raw materials and finished products must be transported to the points where they are needed.

Raw materials requiring little or no special treatment can be transported by rail, ship, or barge at low cost. Large quantities of raw materials travel as bulk freight, but finished products that often require special treatment, such as refrigeration or careful handling, are usually transported by truck. This merchandise freight is usually smaller in volume and requires quicker delivery. Merchandise freight is a term for the transportation of manufactured goods.

Along all points of the distribution channel various amounts of storage are required. The time and manner of such storage depends upon the type of product. Inventories of this stored merchandise often need to be financed.

Modern marketing is therefore a coordinated system of many business activities, but basically it involves four things: (1) selling the correct product at the proper place, (2) selling it at a price determined by demand, (3) satisfying a customer's need and wants, and (4) producing a profit for the company.

Notes to the Text

1. Geneva: a city in Southwestern Switzerland 日内瓦
2. subscribe to: support, consent to 支持, 同意
3. place utility: the increase in value of a product because of its availabilities at a certain place 地方效用
4. bulk freight: goods or cargo carried in large quantities, usu. unpacked 大宗货物, 散货
5. barge: a large flat-bottomed boat 驳船, 平底货船

Exercises

I Answer the following questions.

1. How does modern marketing differ from the old ideas and practices of marketing?
2. Does the theory of modern marketing impact on production decisions?
3. Why are marketing problems more difficult to solve than production problems?
4. What is the concept of modern marketing?

II **Write out the equivalents of the following words and expressions.**

1. at a profit
2. figure out
3. encompass
4. prior to
5. personal selling

6. 多种销售渠道
7. 有效的促销措施
8. 机器零件的标准化
9. 股票交易与定价
10. 满足顾客的需求

III **Translate the following into Chinese.**

The modern marketing concept encompasses all of the activities mentioned, but it is based on a different set of principles. It subscribes to the notion that production can be economically justified only by consumption. In other words, goods should be produced only if they can be sold. Therefore, the producer should consider who is going to buy the product—or what the market for the product is—before production begins. This is very different from making a product and then thinking about how to sell it.

Unit 34

Market and Marketing

A market is commonly thought of as a place where commodities are bought and sold. Thus fruit and vegetables are sold wholesale at Covent Garden Market and meat is sold wholesale at Smithfield Market. But there are markets for things other than commodities, in the usual sense. There are real estate markets, foreign exchange markets, labor markets, short-term capital markets, and so on; there may be a market for anything which has a price. And there may be no particular place to which dealings are confined. Buyers and sellers may be scattered over the whole world and instead of actually meeting together in a marketplace they may deal with one another by telephone, telegram, cable or letter. Even if dealings are restricted to a particular place, the dealers may consist wholly or in part of agents acting on instructions from clients far away. Thus agents buy meat at Smithfield on behalf of retail butchers all over England; and brokers on the London Stock Exchange buy and sell securities on instructions from clients all over the world. We must therefore define a market as any area over which buyers and sellers are in such close touch with one another, either directly or through dealers that the prices obtainable in one part of the market affected the prices paid in other parts.

Modern means of communication are so rapid that a buyer can discover what price a seller is asking, and can accept it if he wishes, although he may be thousands of miles away. Thus the market for anything is, potentially, the whole world. But in fact things have normal markets. This's maybe because nearly the whole demand is concentrated in one locality. These special local demands, however, are of quite minor importance. The main reason why many things have not a world market is that they are costly or difficult to transport.

Marketing is the essential part of the entire process of management. They are not separate or independent functions. Marketing is not restricted to just buying and selling, or dealing with imports and exports; instead, it is a three-sided function, and each side is closely involved in the management process. Marketing research and product development are one side. Advertising and sales promotion are another, and sales services and administration are the third. The concept of management functions operates in each of these areas, and effective management in each must be coordinated with effective overall management to make the entire process successful.

Marketing research is not the same thing as market research. Market research is an analysis of a specific market. For example, how many potential customers there are and where they're located. Marketing research is much broader than that and refers to many functions of sales which, to be more specific, can be defined as gathering, recording and analyzing all facts about problems related to merchandising, including product planning, transport, services and communication, too. In the merchandising function, production plays a major role. There are very few products which will continue to be marketable over a long period of time without undergoing changes. This is where the function of research and development becomes important. Successful merchandising means that companies must stay abreast of changing markets and changing products. This is the essential role of research and development or product improvement.

Selecting and establishing the appropriate marketing channels at the beginning is vital. Once established, a good marketing channel will continue to function properly without the need for constant supervision. Thus advanced planning becomes important, especially when we consider both the time and quantity inputs which will be necessary to prime the marketing channel. A properly developed marketing channel will ensure the continuous flow of merchandise from producer to consumer with the minimum of problems or what we call a bottleneck.

Throughout the entire process of merchandising, attention should also be given to the role of image, public relations and advertising to better promoting sales.

Image, in essence, is a matter of establishing trust. This is all part of building reputation and establishing what we call good will. Indeed, good advertising is vital to call attention to a product and introduce new products. But in the long run it's image that really counts. The concept of image refers to product image and company image, both of which are largely determined by the quality of product and sales service, etc., and public relations come into play in either of the two images.

Notes to the Text

1. Covent Garden Market：科文特花园市场，伦敦一大菜场，原为一修道院花圃，故得名。

2. Smithfield Market：史密斯菲尔德市场（伦敦的肉类批发市场）

3. London Stock Exchange：伦敦证券交易所，世界第三大证券交易中心，是世界上历史最悠久的证券交易所。（世界四大证券交易所依次为：纽约证券交易所、东京证券交易所、伦敦证券交易所、法兰克福证券交易所）

4. bottleneck：the narrow part of a bottle near the top; a hindrance to progress or production 瓶颈；障碍

5. come into play：begin to be used or to have an effect on something 启用，使用，开始起作用

Exercises

I **Answer the following questions.**

1. What is a market?
2. Does marketing means the same as market?
3. What is the function of marketing?
4. In terms of the merchandising function, what plays a major role?
5. Do you agree with the writer that "in the long run it's image that really counts"? Why or why not?

II **Write out the equivalents of the following words and expressions.**

1. real estate
2. capital market
3. potential customer
4. sales promotion
5. stock exchange
6. 批发商
7. 外汇市场
8. 市场调研
9. 进出口贸易
10. 产品形象

III **Translate the following into Chinese.**

Marketing research is not the same thing as market research. Market research is an analysis of a specific market. For example, how many potential customers there are and where they're located. Marketing research is much broader than that and refers to many functions of sales which, to be more specific, can be defined as gathering, recording and analyzing all facts about problems related to merchandising, including product planning, transport, services and communication, too.

Unit 35

The Importance of Marketing

Financial success often depends on marketing ability. Finance, operations, accounting, and other business functions will not really matter if there is not sufficient demand of products and services so the company can make a profit. There must be a top line for there to be a bottom line. Many companies have now created a Chief Marketing Officer, or CMO, position to put marketing on a more equal footing with other C-level executives such as the Chief Executive Officer (CEO) and Chief Financial Officer (CFO). Press releases from organizations of all kinds—from consumer goods makers to health care insurers and from non-profit organizations to industrial product manufacturers—trumpet their latest marketing achievements and can be found on their Web sites. In the business press, countless articles are devoted to marketing strategies and tactics.

Marketing is tricky, however, and it has been the Achilles' heel of many formerly prosperous companies. Large, well-known businesses such as Sears, Levi's, General Motors, Kodak, and Xerox have confronted newly empowered customers and new competitors, and have had to rethink their business models. Even market leaders such as Microsoft, Wal-Mart, Intel, and Nike recognize that they cannot afford to relax. Jack Welch, GE's brilliant former CEO, repeatedly warned his company, "Change or die."

But making the right decisions is not always easy. Marketing managers must make major decisions such as what features to design into a new product, what prices to offer customers, where to sell products, and how much to spend on advertising or sales. They must also make more detailed decisions such as the exact wording or colour for new packaging. The companies at greatest risk are those that fail to carefully monitor their customers and competitors and to continuously improve their value offerings. They take a short-term, sales-driven view of their business and ultimately, they fail to satisfy their stockholders, their employees, their suppliers, and their channel partners. Skilful marketing is a never-ending pursuit.

The Scope of marketing

To prepare to be a marketer, you need to understand what marketing is, how it works, what is marketed and who does the marketing.

What is marketing?

Marketing deals with identifying and meeting human and social needs. One of the shortest definitions of marketing is "meeting needs profitably". When eBay recognized that people were unable to locate some of the items they desired most and created an online auction clearinghouse or when IKEA noticed that people wanted good furniture at a substantially lower price and created knock-down furniture, they demonstrated marketing savvy and turned a private or social need into a profitable business opportunity.

The American Marketing Association offers the following formal definition: *Marketing is an organizational function and a set of processes for creating, communicating, and delivering value to customers and for managing customer relationships in ways that benefit the organization and its stake holders*. Coping with the exchange processes calls for a considerable amount of work and skill. Marketing management takes place when at least one party to a potential exchange thinks about the means of achieving desired responses from other parties. We see **marketing management** as *the art and science of choosing target markets and getting, keeping, and growing customers through creating, delivering, and communicating superior customer value*.

We can distinguish between a social and a managerial definition of marketing. A social definition shows the role marketing plays in society. One marketer said that marketing's role is to "deliver a higher standard of living". Here is a social definition that serves our purpose: *Marketing is a societal process by which individuals and groups obtain what they need and want through creating, offering, and freely exchanging products and services of value with others*. For a managerial definition, marketing has often been described as "the art of selling products", but people are surprised when they hear that the most important part of marketing is not selling! Selling is only the tip of the marketing iceberg. Peter Drucker, a leading management theorist, puts it this way:

> *There will always, one can assume, the need for some selling. But the aim of marketing is to make selling superfluous. The aim of marketing is to know and understand the customer so well that the product or service fits him and sells itself. Ideally, marketing should result in a customer who is ready to buy. All that should be needed then is to make the product or service available.*

When Sony designed its Play Station, when Gillette launched its Mach III razor, and when Toyota introduced its Lexus automobile, these manufacturers were swamped with orders because they had designed the "right" product based on careful marketing homework.

Exchange and transactions

A person can obtain a product in one of four ways. One can self-produce the product or service, as when one hunts, fishes, or gathers fruit. One can use force to get a product, as in a hold-up or burglary. One can beg, as happens when a homeless person asks for food; or one can offer a product, a service, or money in exchange for something he or she desires.

Exchange, which is the core concept of marketing, is the process of obtaining a desired product from someone by offering something in return. For exchange potential to exist, five conditions must be satisfied:

1. There are at least two parties.
2. Each party has something that might be of value to the other party.
3. Each party is capable of communication and delivery.
4. Each party is free to accept or reject the exchange offer.
5. Each party believes it is appropriate or desirable to deal with the other party.

Whether exchange actually takes place depends on whether the two parties can agree on terms that will leave them both better off (or at least not worse off) than before. Exchange is a value-creating process because it normally leaves both parties better off.

Two parties are engaged in exchange if they are negotiating—trying to arrive at mutually agreeable terms. When an agreement is reached, we say that a transaction takes place. A **transaction** is a trade of values between two or more parties: A gives X to B and receives Y in return. Smith sells Jones a television set and Jones pays $400 to Smith. This is a classic monetary transaction; but transactions do not require money as one of the traded values. A barter transaction involves trading goods or services for other goods or services, as when lawyer Jones writes a will for physician Smith in return for a medical examination.

A transaction involves several dimensions: at least two things of value, agreed-upon conditions, a time of agreement, and a place of agreement. A legal system supports and enforces compliance on the part of the transactors. Without a law of contracts, people would approach transactions with some distrust, and everyone would lose.

A transaction differs from a transfer. In a transfer, A gives X to B but does not receive anything tangible in return. Gifts, subsidies, and charitable contributions are all transfers. Transfer behaviour can also be understood through the concept of exchange. Typically, the transferer expects to receive something in exchange for his or her gift—for example, gratitude or seeing changed behaviour in the recipient. Professional fund-raisers provide benefits to donors, such as thank-you notes, donor magazines, and invitations to events. Marketers have broadened the concept of marketing to include the study of transfer behaviour as well as transaction behaviour.

In the most generic sense, marketers seek to elicit a behavioural response from another party. A business firm wants a purchase, a political candidate wants a vote, a church wants an active member, and a social-action group wants the passionate adoption of some cause. Marketing consists of actions undertaken to elicit desired responses from a target audience.

To make successful exchanges, marketers analyze what each party expects from the transaction. Simple exchange situations can be mapped by showing the two actors and the wants and offerings flowing between them. Suppose John Deere, a worldwide leader in agricultural equipment, researches the benefits that a typical large-scale farm enterprise wants when it buys tractors, combines, planters, and sprayers. These benefits include high-quality equipment, a fair price, on-time delivery, good financing terms, and good parts and service. The items on this want list are not equally important and may vary from buyer to buyer. One of John Deere's tasks is to discover the relative importance of these different wants to the buyer.

John Deere also has a want list. It wants a good price for the equipment, on-time payment, and good word of mouth. If there is a sufficient match or overlap in the want lists, a basis for a transaction exists. John Deere's task is to formulate an offer that motivates the farm enterprise to buy John Deere equipment. The farm enterprise might in turn make a counteroffer. This process of negotiation leads to mutually acceptable terms or a decision not to transact.

What is marketed?

Marketing people are involved in marketing 10 types of entities: goods, services, experiences, events, persons, places, properties, organizations, information and ideas.

Goods. Physical goods constitute the bulk of most countries' production and marketing effort. Each year, U.S. companies alone market billions of fresh, canned, bagged, and frozen food products and millions of cars, refrigerators, television sets, machines, and various other mainstays of a modern economy. Not only do companies market their goods, but thanks in part to the Internet, even individuals can effectively market goods.

Services. As economies advance, a growing proportion of their activities is focused on the production of services. The U.S. economy today consists of a 70-30 services-to-goods mix. Services include the work of airlines, hotels, car rental firms, barbers and beauticians, maintenance and repair people, as well as professionals working within or for companies, such as accountants, bankers, lawyers, engineers, doctors, software programmers, and management consultants. Many market offerings consist of a variable mix of goods and services. At a fast-food restaurant, for example, the customer consumes both a product and a service.

Events. Marketers promote time-based events, such as major trade shows, artistic performances, and company anniversaries. Global sporting events such as the Olympics or World Cup are promoted aggressively to both companies and fans. There is a whole profession of meeting planners who work out the details of an event and make sure it comes off perfectly.

Experiences. By orchestrating several services and goods, a firm can create, stage, and market experiences. Walt Disney World's Magic Kingdom represents experiential marketing: Customers visit a fairy kingdom, a pirate ship, or a haunted house. So does the Hard Rock Cafe, where customers can enjoy a meal or see a band in a live concert. There is also a market for customized experiences, such as spending a week at a baseball camp playing with some retired baseball greats, paying to conduct the Chicago Symphony Orchestra for five minutes, or climbing Mount Everest.

Persons. Celebrity marketing is a major business. Today, every major film star has an agent, a personal manager, and ties to a public relations agency. Artists, musicians, CEOs, physicians, high-profile lawyers and financiers, and other professionals are also getting help from celebrity marketers. Some people have done a masterful job of marketing themselves— think of Madonna, Oprah Winfrey, the Rolling Stones, Aerosmith, and Michael Jordan. Management consultant Tom Peters, himself a master at self-branding, has advised each person to become a "brand".

Places. Cities, states, regions, and whole nations compete actively to attract tourists, factories, company headquarters, and new residents. Place marketers include economic development specialists, real estate agents, commercial banks, local business associations, and advertising and public relations agencies. To fuel their high-tech industries and spawn entrepreneurship, cities such as Indianapolis, Charlotte, and Raleigh-Durham are actively wooing 20 to 29-year-olds through ads, PR, and other communications. Louisville, Kentucky, spends $1 million annually on e-mails, events, and networking approaches to convince 20-somethings of the city's quality of life and other advantages.

Properties. Properties are intangible rights of ownership of either real property (real estate) or financial property (stocks and bonds). Properties are bought and sold, and this requires marketing. Real estate agents work for property owners or sellers or buy residential or commercial real estate. Investment companies and banks are involved in marketing securities to both institutional and individual investors.

Organizations. Organizations actively work to build a strong, favourable, and unique image in the minds of their target publics. Companies spend money on corporate identity ads. Philips, the Dutch electronics company, puts out ads with the tag line "Let's Make Things Better". In the United Kingdom, Tesco's "Every Little Bit Helps" marketing program has vaulted it to the top of the supermarket chains in that country. Universities, museums, performing arts organizations, and non-profits all use marketing to boost their public images and to compete for audiences and funds.

Information. Information can be produced and marketed as a product. This is essentially what schools and universities produce and distribute at a price to parents, students, and communities. Encyclopaedias and most non-fiction books market information. Magazines such as *Road and Track* and *Byte* supply information about the car and computer worlds, respectively. The production, packaging, and distribution of information is one of our society's major industries. Even companies that sell physical products attempt to add value through the use of information. For example, the CEO of Siemens Medical Systems, Tom McCausland, says, "Our product is not necessarily an X-ray or an MRI, but information. Our business is really health-care information technology, and our end product is really an electronic patient record: information on lab tests, pathology, and drugs as well as voice dictation."

Ideas. Every market offering includes a basic idea. Charles Revson of Revlon observed,

"In the factory, we make cosmetics; in the store we sell hope." Products and services are platforms for delivering some idea or benefit. Social marketers are busy promoting such ideas as "Friends Don't Let Friends Drive Drunk" and "A Mind Is a Terrible Thing to Waste".

Notes to the Text

1. Chief Marketing Officer(CMO)：首席营销官
2. Chief Financial Officer (CFO)：首席财务总监
3. the Achilles' heel：a fatal weakness, a vulnerable area. The term alludes to the Greek legend about the heroic warrior Achilles whose mother tried to make him immortal by holding the infant by his heel and dipping him into the River Styx. Eventually he was killed by an arrow shot into his undipped heel. 唯一致命的弱点，薄弱环节，要害。"Achilles' heel"直译是"阿基里斯的脚踵"，是个广泛流行的国际性成语。它源自荷马史诗《伊利亚特》(Iliad)中的希腊神话故事，Achilles 是希腊联军里最英勇善战的骁将，也是荷马史诗《伊利亚特》(Iliad)里的主要人物之一。传说他呱呱坠地后，母亲希望儿子健壮永生，把他放在火里锻炼，又捏着他的脚踵倒浸在冥河(Styx)圣水里，因此 Achilles 浑身钢筋铁骨、刀枪不入，只有脚踵部位被母亲的手捏住，没有沾到冥河圣水，成为他的唯一要害。在特洛伊战争中，Achilles 骁勇无敌，所向披靡，杀死了特洛伊主将——著名英雄赫克托耳(Hector)，而特洛伊的任何武器都无法伤害他的身躯。后来，太阳神阿波罗(Apollo)把 Achilles 的弱点告诉了特洛伊王子帕里斯(Paris)，Achilles 终于被帕里斯诱到城门口，遭暗箭射中脚踵，负伤而死。
4. Sears：美国西尔斯百货公司，是美国著名的百货公司，全球 500 强企业之一，是一家拥有百年历史的大型零售企业。
5. Microsoft：美国微软公司，创建于 1975 年，总部设在华盛顿州的雷德蒙市(Redmond, 邻近西雅图)，目前是全球最大的电脑软件提供商，其主要产品为 Windows 操作系统、Internet Explore 网页浏览器及 Microsoft Office 办公软件套件等。
6. Intel：英特尔公司，成立于 1968 年。1971 年，英特尔推出了全球第一个微处理器，微处理器所带来的计算机和互联网革命，改变了世界；英特尔公司是世界最大的芯片制造商，也是世界领先的个人电脑、网络和通讯产品制造商。
7. Nike：耐克公司，创建于 1975 年，总部位于美国俄勒冈州 Beaverton，是全球著名的体育用品制造商。
8. eBay：全球最大的 C2C 电子商务网站，任何人都可以在这里出售商品和参加拍卖，1995 年 9 月建立。2003 年 6 月 12 日，eBay 以 1.5 亿美元的价格收购中国电子商务网站易趣公司 67% 的股份，实现完全控股，从而打入中国电子商务市场。
9. IKEA：宜家，瑞典的全球最大的家居零售巨头，创建于 1943 年。
10. The American Marketing Association：美国营销协会
11. tip of the iceberg：a small evident part or aspect of something largely hidden; superficial evidence of a much larger problem 冰山一角，(事物的)表面小部分，端倪

12. Gillette：吉列公司，成立于 1901 年，总部设于波士顿，主要生产剃须产品、电池和口腔清洁卫生产品。2005 年 1 月，美国宝洁公司宣布并购吉列公司，两家公司合并后组成世界最大日用消费品生产企业。

13. Toyota：日本丰田汽车公司

14. map（v.）：plan, delineate, or arrange in detail, to work out and arrange the parts or details of 设计，计划

15. Walt Disney World's Magic Kingdom：迪斯尼世界的主题乐园"神奇王国"

16. Hard Rock Café：硬石餐厅，全球著名的美式连锁餐厅，于 1971 年 6 月 14 日正式开业。

17. Chicago Symphony Orchestra：芝加哥交响乐团，前身是芝加哥乐团，成立于 1891 年，现为美国历史上最为悠久的三个交响乐团之一。

18. Mount Everest：珠穆朗玛峰。西方人称之为 Mount Everest 是为纪念英国人占领尼泊尔时，负责测量喜马拉雅山脉的印度测量局局长乔治·额菲尔士（George Everest）。

19. Madonna：美国女歌手麦当娜

20. Oprah Winfrey：奥普拉·温芙瑞，美国著名脱口秀大师，美国最成功的企业家和电视节目主持人之一。

21. Rolling Stones：滚石乐队，流行乐史上最重要的乐队之一，摇滚史上最有影响的乐队之一。滚石乐队与 The Beatles（甲壳虫）、The Kinks（奇想）还有 The Who（谁人）等乐队一起开创了 20 世纪 60 年代英国摇滚文化的新纪元。

22. Aerosmith：史密斯飞船乐队。

23. Michael Jordan：迈克·乔丹，美国著名篮球运动员。

24. Tesco：英国第一大超市连锁店

25. *Road and Track*：美国专业汽车杂志

26. *Byte*：美国著名的计算机杂志

27. Siemens：西门子公司；是世界上最大的电气工程和电子公司之一。

28. X-ray：伦琴射线，又称"X 射线"，德国物理学家威尔海姆·伦琴 1895 年发现 X 射线，给医学和物质结构的研究带来了新的希望。

29. MRI：nuclear magnetic resonance imaging 核磁共振成像

30. Revlon：露华浓公司，创立于 1932 年，是一家在化妆品、护肤、香水和个人护理品等领域全球知名的公司，总部设在美国纽约。

Exercises

I **Answer the following questions.**

　　1. What is marketing?

　　2. What factors does a transaction involve?

3. Does a transaction mean the same thing as a transfer?

4. What are physical goods? What are intangible goods?

5. Do you agree that "Information can be produced and marketed as a product"?

II Write out the equivalents of the following words and expressions.

1. business model

2. target market

3. knock-down furniture

4. barter transaction

5. financing terms

6. financial property

7. 拍卖

8. 还盘

9. 无形资产

10. 机构投资者

11. 最终产品

III Translate the following into Chinese.

Properties are intangible rights of ownership of either real property (real estate) or financial property (stocks and bonds). Properties are bought and sold, and this requires marketing. Real estate agents work for property owners or sellers or buy residential or commercial real estate. Investment companies and banks are involved in marketing securities to both institutional and individual investors.

Unit 36

The Role and Activities of Promotion

Promotion is the aspect of marketing concerned with increasing sales. Marketing must be considered in making production decisions, and promotion must be considered in the overall marketing process. Promotion attempts to persuade and influence the customer's attitude in various ways. It is oriented toward producing a customer for the product rather than a product for the customer. Economists believe price should be determined by supply and demand. Promotion attempts to increase demand for a product and thereby increase sales. It wants to make the demand for the product inelastic when prices increase and elastic when prices decrease. In other words, through promotion, companies try to keep demanded sales constant when prices increase. They do not want an increase in the price of their product to result in lower sales; instead they want it to result in an increase in profits. However, if the price decreases, they want demand for the product to increase, hoping that an increase in sales volume will offset the decrease in price.

Three main promotional activities are advertising, personal selling, and sales promotion. Advertising is a non-personal presentation of goods, services, or ideas aimed at a mass audience. It is particularly suited for products that are widely distributed, such as convenience goods. There are several methods of advertising and several media. The method selected depend upon the product, the distribution of the market, and the type of information which the company wishes to convey about its product. For example, television advertising reaches a large audience. It has the advantage of appealing to the emotions of the audience through the senses of sight and sound. Television advertisements, on the other hand, can appear on a particular day in a particular geographic area. A newspaper advertisement can contain a lot of written retail that appeals to the logic of the reader. It explains why he should purchase a particular product or service.

In general, advertising works best when the demand for a product is increasing. It also works well when there are real differences between two or more similar products such as the different types of cars. Using advertising, a company can emphasize the differences between its product and that of its competitor. The purpose of advertising is to communicate information that convinces a customer to buy a specific product.

Personal selling involves a salesperson trying to customers directly to buy a product. Personal selling is very effective when there this a concentrated market for a product—in other words, the product is not for general consumption by the public. For examples, airplanes are purchased only by airlines, not by the general public. There would be little point in advertising them on television. The same is true for many industrial goods. A sales representative usually gets a commission. If the product has a high unit value, in other words each individual item is very expensive, the cost of the product justifies the commission paid to the sales representative for his or her work. If the product must be individually tailored to the purchaser, the sales person must be able to sell exactly what the customer needs. Sales staff are also needed to demonstrate a product. This is particularly important for new products which may be unfamiliar to the customer. Finally, personal selling is necessary when there is negotiation about the price of the product, for example, when a trade-in is involved.

Sales promotion involves several activities. It is becoming increasingly important in the self-service environment where there is often no sales staff. Sales promotion activities are of two types: information and stimulation. Examples of information promotion are a pamphlet or booklet about the product, a demonstration, market research information telling about the nature of customers, and dealer training and managerial advice from producers. Stimulation promotion can be accomplished by the distribution of the samples, reduced price promotions, premiums, and coupons. A premium is something that the customer receives as a bonus when he purchases a product. For example, a customer purchasing a razor might receive a free package of razor blades. A coupon is a certificate which entitles the customer to purchase the product at a reduced price. Sales promotions also involve displays of the products. Displays can increase sales as well. A customer might make a decision to buy a particular product like a convenience item simply on the basis of a display that makes the item easy to see and reach.

Basically there are two ways to increase sales of products: find new market and increase market share. A company seeking new markets can expand its geographical area or try to sell its product to a different segment of the population. In this case promotion may involve increased advertising to spread information about the product. Personal selling at the wholesale level can encourage additional retailers to carry the product.

A different market situation requires a different method of promotion. When a market is saturated, it means that there are no new customers to be found. A company then needs to lure customers from the competitors and gain a greater share of the total market. To increase market share, the marketing department of a company must design a total program of promotion for a particular product. Such a program may involve increased advertising to remind the customer of the name of the product. In advertising the company will also emphasize the superiority of its product by comparing it with the competitor's product. A program to increase market share may also include convincing a retailer to allow more shelf space in the store for the product. Sales promotions may include contests, coupons, and price discounting. Increasing market share involves more stimulation of the buyer's emotions than does finding new markets where simply furnishing information about the product may increase sales.

Notes to the Text

1. inelastic demand：无弹性需求（指商品购买率的变化小于价格的变化）
2. offset：balance or make up for 抵消
3. tailor：prepare for a special purpose 使适应,使适应特定需要
4. appeal（to）：be attractive or interesting（to somebody）对某人有吸引力;使某人感兴趣
5. saturate：supply（a market）beyond a point at which the demand for a product is satisfied（市场供应）饱和
6. lure：attract 吸引

Exercises

I Answer the following questions.

1. What are the three main promotional activities?
2. What's the purpose of advertising?
3. Can you say something about the two types of sales promotion as mentioned in the text?
4. When can the promotional activities be best carried out? Why?

II Write out the equivalents of the following words and expressions.

1. convenience goods
2. mass audience
3. trade-in
4. shelf space
5. 佣金
6. 演示
7. 小册子
8. 自助

III Translate the following into Chinese.

In general, advertising works best when the demand for a product is increasing. It also works well when there are real differences between two or more similar products such as the different types of cars. Using advertising, a company can emphasize the differences between its product and that of its competitor. The purpose of advertising is to communicate information that convinces a customer to buy a specific product.

Unit 37

Personal Selling

Personal selling is a process of informing potential buyers about and persuading them to purchase a product. It is the most flexible of all promotional methods because it allows marketers to communicate specific information that might trigger a purchase. Of all the promotional activities, only personal selling can zero in on a prospect and attempt to persuade the prospect to make a purchase. Although personal selling has a lot of advantages, it is one of the most costly forms of promotion. A sales call on an industrial customer in the U. S. can cost as much as $200 or $300. Many products require personal selling in order for the company to achieve sales results. A company must employ effective salespeople to describe a product's advantages and benefits to compete with the sales forces of competing firms.

Professional salespeople are professional communicators. They know their companies, products, competitors and customers. Many factors affect a marketer's selection of the type of salesperson to employ. The product's complexity, the type of market, and the general nature of distribution in a particular industry are all important considerations. Three distinct types of salespersons are order takers, creative salespersons, and support salespersons. Order takers are salespeople who execute sales for customers who have already decided to buy the product from a particular organization. Their major role is to make sure that supplies are adequate and there are no problems with the purchase. Inside order takers are located in sales offices and receive orders by mail or telephone. Outside order takers may engage in some important sales functions for the company by encouraging customers to increase the size of their orders or reminding them to purchase certain products. In many firms, order takers generate the majority of sales.

Creative salespersons are involved in informing and persuading a prospect to buy a product. The creative salesperson tries to increase the firm's sales by finding new customers and encouraging old customers to purchase. A key role of the creative salesperson is to find new prospects and convert them into customers. Products such as automobiles, insurance, furniture, and appliances require the skill of creative salespeople to maintain sales levels.

Support salespersons facilitate and assist in the selling function but usually do not take orders. They are used in markets where educating the customer, building good will, and providing service are important for supporting the overall sales volume of the company. Technical salespersons, for example, are support salespersons who provide engineering and other types of technical assistance. They help with product application, specific system design, and provide technical information about how a product will function best under particular environments or situations. Technical salespersons are often used for computers, machinery and equipment, and steel and chemicals.

Prospecting

The first step in personal selling is to identify potential buyers of the product that is being sold. This can be done by examining directories or trade lists that identify people who use various types of products. The salesperson concentrates his or her efforts on prospects who have needs and wants, financial ability, and authority to purchase the product.

Approaching

The salesperson finds and analyzes information about prospects' needs and desires for products. The information helps the salesperson approach the potential customer. There are different types of approaches. Using a referral, the salesperson explains to the prospect that an acquaintance or some other person has indicated that the prospect might be interested in the product. Using cold canvassing, the salesperson calls on potential customers without any prior notice or referral.

Presenting

After making the approach, the salesperson must make a presentation to get the prospect's attention and to persuade the prospect to buy the product. In making the presentation, it is important for the salesperson to use stimulating methods. Demonstrating the product and using visual aids such as a videotape or slides can assist greatly in the presentation. The salesperson should demonstrate what the product can do and the benefits associated with it.

Handling objections

Objections are reasons mentioned by the prospect for not buying the product. One of the best ways for a salesperson to handle an objection is to try to anticipate and counter it before it is expressed. Doing this is risky, however, because the salesperson may bring up an objection that the prospect had not thought of. At any rate, objections should be dealt with immediately when they arise. A good salesperson does not dodge objections but find out what the objections are and tries to deal with them. A successful sale may depend on how well the salesperson handles objections.

Closing

Closing is asking the prospect to buy the product. It is an important step in personal selling because a customer may actually be reluctant to volunteer to purchase a product.

Prospects usually need some encouragement or persuasion to make a purchase decision. This is the salesperson's last spurt and determines whether the sale will be consummated. A trial close involves asking questions that assume the customer is going to buy the product; its purpose is to get answers to identify objections. The trial close indicates what decision is going to be made. Trial closing questions relate to matters such as delivery dates and model colors.

Following up

A good salesperson follows up on a successful sale to make sure the customer is satisfied with the purchase. The salesperson may check to see whether the product was delivered on time and whether the buyer got exactly what he or she wanted. Waiters and waitresses often ask "How was your dinner?" This is a follow-up question to make sure that customers are leaving satisfied. Only a satisfied customer will return; therefore, the follow-up is necessary for the salesperson to have repeat business. The follow-up helps develop rapport with the buyer and ensure an ongoing relationship.

Notes to the Text

1. zero in on: direct one's attention to, concentrate or focus on 对……集中注意力

2. prospect: potential buyer of a product or service (who has not previously been a purchaser of that product or service) 潜在顾客

3. referral: name of a prospective customer (or member, donor) acquired from a current customer or other third party 被推荐人

4. follow-up: in general, any letter, telephone call, or personal call subsequent to a contact or communication intended to continue or to further evaluate the earlier contact; in marketing, step in a marketing plan that follows the implementation of an advertising campaign or promotion or the introduction of a new product, in order to evaluate the results 后续服务/措施

Exercises

I Answer the following questions.

1. What is personal selling?

2. What are the three distinct types of salespersons?

3. What are the steps to follow in personal selling?

4. Did you ever try this promotional method of personal selling?

II **Write out the equivalents of the following words and expressions.**

1. personal selling
2. potential buyer
3. promotional activity
4. industrial customer
5. sales force
6. repeat business

7. 销量
8. 技术支援
9. 行业名录
10. 经济能力
11. 交货日期

III **Translate the following into Chinese.**

A good salesperson follows up on a successful sale to make sure the customer is satisfied with the purchase. The salesperson may check to see whether the product was delivered on time and whether the buyer got exactly what he or she wanted. Waiters and waitresses often ask "How was your dinner?" This is a follow-up question to make sure that customers are leaving satisfied. Only a satisfied customer will return; therefore, the follow-up is necessary for the salesperson to have repeat business. The follow-up helps develop rapport with the buyer and ensure an ongoing relationship.

Unit 38
Branding and Brand Equity

For some organizations, the primary focus of strategy development is placed on brand building, developing, and nurturing activities. Factors that serve to increase the strength of a brand include (1) product quality when products do what they do very well (e. g. , Windex and Easy-Off); (2) consistent advertising and other marketing communications in which brands tell their story often and well (e. g. , Pepsi and Visa); (3) distribution intensity whereby customers see the brand wherever they shop (e. g. , Marlboro); and (4) brand personality where the brand stands for something (e. g. , Disney). The strength of the Coca-Cola brand, for example, is widely attributed to its universal availability, universal awareness, and trademark protection, which came as a result of strategic actions taken by the parent organization.

The brand name is perhaps the single most important element on the package, serving as a unique identifier. Specifically, a brand is a name, term, design, symbol, or any other feature that identifies one seller's good or service as distinct from those of other sellers. The legal term for brand is trademark. A good brand name can evoke feelings of trust, confidence, security, strength, and many other desirable characteristics. To illustrate, consider the case of Bayer aspirin. Bayer can be sold at up to two times the price of generic aspirin due to the strength of its brand image.

Many companies make use of manufacturer branding strategies in carrying out market and product development strategies. The line extension approach uses a brand name to facilitate entry into a new market segment (e. g. , Diet Coke and Liquid Tide). An alternative to line extension is brand extension. In a brand extension, a current brand name is used to enter a completely different product class (e. g. , Jello pudding pops, Ivory shampoo).

A third form of branding is franchise extension or family branding, whereby a company attaches the corporate name to a product to enter either a new market segment or a different product class (e. g. , Honda lawnmower, Toyota Lexus). A final type of branding strategy that is becoming more and more common is dual branding. A dual branding (also known as joint or cobranding) strategy is one in which two or more branded products are integrated (e. g. , Bacardi rum and Coca-Cola, Long John Silver's and A&W Root Beer, Archway cookies and Kellogg cereal, US Airways and Bank of America Visa). The logic behind this strategy is that if one brand name on a product gives a certain signal of quality, then the presence of a second brand name on the product should result in a signal that is at least as powerful as, if not more powerful than, the signal in the case of the single brand name, each of the preceding four approaches is an attempt by companies to gain a competitive advantage by making use of its or others' established reputation, or both.

Companies may also choose to assign different brand names to each product. This is known as multibranding strategy. By doing so, the firm makes a conscious decision to allow the product to succeed or fail on its own merits. Major advantages of using multiple brand names are that (1) the firm can distance products from other offerings it markets; (2) the image of one product (or set of products) is not associated with other products the company markets; (3) the product(s) can be targeted at a specific market segment; and (4) should the product(s) fail, the probability of failure impacting on other company products is minimized. For example, many consumers are unaware that Dreft, Tide, Oxydol, Bold, Cheer, and Dash laundry detergents are all marketed by Procter & Gamble. The major disadvantage of this strategy is that because new names are assigned, there is no consumer brand awareness and significant amounts of money must be spent familiarizing customers with new brands.

Increasingly, companies are finding that brand names are one of the most valuable assets they possess. Successful extensions of an existing brand can lead to additional loyalty and associated profits. Conversely, a wrong extension can cause damaging associations, as perceptions linked to the brand name are transferred back from one product to the other. Brand equity can be viewed as the set of assets (or liabilities) linked to the brand that add (or subtract) value. The value of these assets is dependent upon the consequences or results of the marketplace's relationship with a brand. **Figure** lists the elements of brand equity. Brand equity is determined by the consumer and is the culmination of the consumer's assessment of the product, the company that manufactures and markets the product, and all other variables that impact on the product between manufacture and consumer consumption.

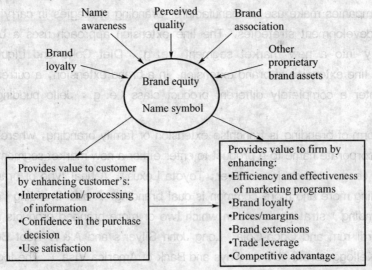

FIGURE   Elements of Brand Equity

Source: David A. Aaker, Managing Brand Equity. 1991, New York, by David A. Aaker.

Before leaving the topic of manufacturer brands, it is important to note that, as with consumer products, organizational products also can possess brand equity. However, several differences do exist between the two sectors. First, organizational products are usually branded with firm names. As a result, loyalty (or disloyalty) to the brand tends to be of a more global nature, extending across all the firm's product lines. Second, because firm versus brand loyalty exists, attempts to position new products in a manner differing from existing products may prove to be difficult, if not impossible. Finally, loyalty to organizational products encompasses not only the firm and its products but also the distribution channel members employed to distribute the product. Therefore, attempts to establish or change brand image must also take into account distributor image.

As related branding strategy, many retail firms produce or market their products under a so-called private label. For example, Kmart has phased in its own store-brand products to compete with the national brands. There's Nature's Classics, a line of fancy snacks and cookies; Oral Pure, a line of dental care products; Prevail house cleaners; B. E. , a Gap-style line of weekend wear; and Benchmark, a line of "made in the U.S. A" tools. Such a strategy is highly important in industries where middlemen have gained control over distribution to the consumer. The growth of the large discount and specialty stores, such as Kmart, Wal-Mart, Target, The Gap, Limited, and others, has accelerated the development of private brands. If a manufacturer refuses to supply certain middlemen with private branded merchandise, the alternative is for these middlemen to go into the manufacturing business, as in the case of Kroger supermarkets.

Private label products differ markedly from so-called generic products that sport labels such as "beer", "cigarettes", and "potato chips". Today's house brands are packaged in distinctively upscale containers. The quality of the products used a house brands equals and sometimes exceeds those offered by name brands. While generic products were positioned as a means for consumers to struggle through recessionary times, private label brands are being marketed as value brands, products that are equivalent to national brands but are priced much lower. Private brands are rapidly growing in popularity. For example, it only took JC Penney Company, Inc. , five years to nurture its private-label jeans, the Arizona brand, into a powerhouse with annual sales surpassing $500 million.

Consolidation within the supermarket industry, growth of super centres, and heightened product marketing are poised to strengthen private brands even further. However, these gains will not come without a fight from national manufacturers who are undertaking aggressive actions to defend their brands' market share. Some have significantly rolled back prices, while others have instituted increased promotional campaigns. The ultimate winner in this ongoing battle between private (store) and manufacturer (national) brands, not surprisingly, should be the consumer who is able to play off these store brands against national brands, thus giving them the best of both worlds: value and variety.

Notes to the Text

1. Windex：玻璃清洗剂品牌，美国庄臣公司（SC Johnson）产品。美国庄臣公司于1886年创建于美国威斯康辛州的瑞辛市，是家庭清洁用品、个人护理用品和杀虫产品的世界领先的制造商之一。

2. Easy-Off：（美国）厨房清洁剂品牌。

3. Bayer：（德国）拜尔公司，为世界500强，全球最大的化工和医药保健企业之一，业务范围包括医药、诊断器材、农作物保护产品、塑料及纤维等。

4. Diet Coke：健怡可乐，是一种无糖可乐，可口可乐公司外延品牌之一。

5. Jello pudding pops：一种冰淇淋品牌。

6. Bacardi rum：百加得朗姆酒，1862年源于古巴圣地亚哥的高档朗姆酒，陈年酿制，口感甘醇清新；可以和任何软饮料调和，直接加果汁或者冰块后饮用，被誉为"随瓶酒吧"。

7. Long John Silver's：美国最大的知名海鲜连锁餐厅，取名于著名小说《金银岛》的独脚海盗，全球有1 300多家分店。

8. David A. Aaker：艾克，美国著名的品牌管理大师、美国加州大学伯克利分校的市场营销教授。

9. Simon & Schuster：西蒙和舒斯特出版公司（美国著名出版社之一）

10. Kroger：克罗格公司，创建于1883年，如今在美国拥有两千余家大型超级商场，员工约17万人，年销售额约191亿美元。

Exercises

I Answer the following questions.

1. What is a brand?
2. What are the factors that help strengthen a brand?
3. What are the major advantages of using multiple brand names?
4. Why are brand names considered to be valuable assets?
5. How are the private label products different from generic products?

II Write out the equivalents of the following words and expressions.

1. brand building
2. marketing communications
3. franchise extension
4. dual branding
5. brand equity
6. trade leverage
7. discount store
8. 品牌形象
9. 品牌意识
10. 品牌延伸
11. 资产与负债
12. 品牌忠诚

Ⅲ Translate the following into Chinese.

Increasingly, companies are finding that brand names are one of the most valuable assets they possess. Successful extensions of an existing brand can lead to additional loyalty and associated profits. Conversely, a wrong extension can cause damaging associations, as perceptions linked to the brand name are transferred back from one product to the other. Brand equity can be viewed as the set of assets (or liabilities) linked to the brand that add (or subtract) value. The value of these assets is dependent upon the consequences or results of the marketplace's relationship with a brand.

Unit 39

Going Global

The word "globalization", minted not much more than a decade ago, has become the inescapable and admittedly useful axiom of the international economy. But as with all words, it has its limits. It defines a process—the internationalization of economic activities—that is crucial to today's business strategies. We were trying to convey something else, something larger than business and economics, though encompassing both: something pointed more toward the new century. Not a process, but the results of a process: a place, a condition, the situation that comes afterward.

I rolled into the Swiss ski village of Davos for the 29th annual World Economic Forum— the epicenter of the world's intellectual capital market—and discovered that the theme of this year's talkathon was "Responsible Globality." As Prof. Klaus Schwab, founder of the WEF, told *The Wall Street Journal*, "We wanted to look beyond the economic dimensions of what is happening. . . It is globality." The word seemed to fall off the lips of Davos panelists with an ease that suggested years of familiarity. "Globality is here to stay," said U.S. Sen. John Kerry. And so, it seems, is the word. Bill Gates told a Davos session that he "would have globality added to Microsoft's dictionary—much appreciated, as the spell checker on my computer would then stop underlining it as an error."

So, what is globality? It is the 24-hour interconnected, hyperactive, sleep-deprived, e-mail-fueled world. It is a world where governments have less leverage over their own economies. And where companies really do operate on a global basis—as Hewlett-Packard CEO Lewis Platt says, in "a seven-day, 24-hour workweek where things are changing rapidly." Nongovernmental organizations also increasingly project their influence globally. Esperanto is not going to make a comeback, but common vocabularies are adopted by increasing number of people around the world—whether in software and operating systems or one's daily news feed.

Three forces are interacting to create this new globality. The first is a move away from counting on governments to manage economies and toward a much greater confidence in the ability of markets to function fairly and deliver the goods. This is translated into deregulation and privatization.

The second spur to globality: borders are eroding as individual national economies are integrated. Think of the European Central Bank and the World Trade Organization. The rapid growth of trade, investment and capital markets is also tying countries together. International brands beat out national champions.

And third, add to all this the relentless force of technology, which provides the working foundation for globality. Cheap communications and information technology are fashioning a woven world, a global community—or, more precisely, a multitude of global communities. It's hard not to stay in touch—or get in touch.

Globality helps to explain the ceaseless wave of big mergers blurring national identities. Opportunities now exist that would have been unthinkable—or politically impossible—a few years ago. The ever more intense cross-border competition seems to require a new scale and broader capabilities, while shareholders increasingly demand high-caliber financial performance. Globality has some very nice features—such as higher incomes, wider choice. It also has some very unappealing aspects, such as the financial contagion that has swept around the world.

The heat of this year's Davos, at least for me, lay in its use of the world "responsible". Taking globality as a given, it asked, "What kind of globality?" That question underlies debates about everything from what to do about the tidal flows of capital, to the environment, to social justice and the reform of the warefare state, to the power and magic of media. What will be the rules of this new reality? How will the world manage itself? What happens to culture and national identity? How will this affect the billions of the world's poor? Inherent in all these questions is the underlying issue of legitimacy and acceptability. One sort of globality or another is inevitable. It will increasingly affect the lives of an ever-growing number of people. Its workings can bring many benefits and opportunities. It can also generate much disruption and discord.

Globality is not necessarily the most beautiful word. But it has two things going for it: it captures a new reality, and it's useful. Any day now, it'll show up in a dictionary.

Notes to the Text

1. Davos：达沃斯，瑞士东北部小镇。
2. World Economic Forum(WEF)：世界经济论坛,是由瑞士日内瓦大学教授施瓦布先生于 1971 年在瑞士创立的非盈利国际组织,原名欧洲管理论坛(European Management Forum),1987 年更名为世界经济论坛,总部设在日内瓦。
3. talkathon：a lengthy session of discussions, speeches, or debates 马拉松式的冗长演说
4. globality：the state of going global 全球性
5. Wall Street Journal：《华尔街日报》,创办于 1889 年,是美国乃至全世界影响力最大、侧重金融及商业领域报导的日报,同时出版亚洲版、欧洲版、网络版。《华尔街日报》是道琼斯公司的旗舰报纸,是全球最有影响的商务财经报纸。
6. spell checker：(计算机)拼写检查程序;拼写检查功能;拼写检查器
7. Hewlett-Packard：(美国)惠普公司(HP),成立于 1939 年,是一家全球领先的计算机成像解决方案与服务的供应商。

8. Esperanto：世界语,是波兰医生柴门霍夫博士于 1887 年创造的一种语言。他希望人类借助这种语言,达到民族间相互了解,消除仇恨和战争,实现平等、博爱的人类大家庭。柴门霍夫在公布这种语言方案时用的笔名是"Doktoro Esperanto"(意为"希望者博士"),后来人们就把这种语言称作 Esperanto。本世纪初,当世界语刚传入中国时,有人曾把它音译为"爱斯不难读"语,也有叫"万国新语"的。以后有人借用日本人的意译名称"世界语",一直沿用至今。世界语是在印欧语系的基础上创造出来的一种人造语,共有 28 个字母,书写形式采用拉丁字母。世界语的词汇尽量采用自然语言中的国际化部分,其基本词汇的词根大部分来自印欧语系的各自然语言,其中大部分来自拉丁语族,少部分来自日尔曼语族和斯拉夫语族。世界语的语法是在印欧语系的基础上加以提炼的。

9. European Central Bank：欧洲中央银行(ECB),于 1998 年 7 月 1 日正式成立,其前身是设在法兰克福的欧洲货币局。欧洲央行独立于欧盟机构和各国政府之外,是世界上第一个管理超国家货币的中央银行,它不接受欧盟领导机构的指令,不受各国政府的监督;它是唯一有资格允许在欧盟内部发行欧元的机构。

Exercises

Ⅰ Answer the following questions.

1. According to the writer, what is globality?
2. What are the three forces interacting to create this new globality?
3. What are the nice features of globality?
4. Do you agree with the writer that the word "globality" will appear in a dictionary one day?

Ⅱ Write out the equivalents of the following words and expressions.

1. capital market
2. nongovernmental organization
3. spur
4. merger
5. flows of capital
6. 福利国家
7. 国际化
8. 私有化
9. 信息技术
10. 国民经济

Ⅲ Translate the following into Chinese.

Globality helps to explain the ceaseless wave of big mergers blurring national identities. Opportunities now exist that would have been unthinkable—or politically impossible—a few years ago. The ever more intense cross-border competition seems to require a new scale and broader capabilities, while shareholders increasingly demand high-caliber financial performance. Globality has some very nice features—such as higher incomes, wider choice. It also has some very unappealing aspects, such as the financial contagion that has swept around the world.

Unit 40

Globalization Perspectives

Economic globalization

The economic debate centres on the decline of national markets and the rise of global markets as the focal points for major players, principally the multinational corporations. This trend is associated with the effects of technological change in reducing temporal and psychic distance between national markets. In addition, in consequence of globalization, it is generally assumed that the rules of competition are being redefined, to which firms and governments will have to learn how to adapt. The globalization of finance, as an example, is associated with the ability of unregulated global capital markets to accumulate global economic power and escape the confines of national regulations and controls. The creation of new mechanisms to shift around savings and investment renders ineffective the policy tools used by governments and policy makers to pursue nationally focused macroeconomic policies (Boyer, 1996; Palan et al., 1996). Thus, financial markets are reducing and gradually weakening the nation-state. Further, in the wake of globalization, the durability of nationally unique banking and regulative systems is called into question, as market forces can be expected to induce "best practice" models and strategies, which nation-states and firms must strive to accommodate.

Economic globalization also influences microeconomic phenomena because deregulation and technological developments serve to increase international competition—especially within the triad countries of Western Europe, North America, and Japan and South-East Asia—by creating national "level playing fields" that offer the same opportunities to domestic and foreign firms alike. These new parameters and a greater homogeneity of consumer tastes and attitudes worldwide are influencing the decision-making processes of multinational firms, which have become committed to global marketing strategies and global manufacturing chains.

With the increasing integration of economic activities, national firms find themselves more exposed to competitive pressures from MNCs (Multinational Corporations) and firms from other countries. Western firms, in particular, experience severe cost pressures from competitors who are able to source low-wage countries. In consequence, state policies that raise firm's costs, such as minimum wages and employment standards, are often condemned by industry for the detrimental effects they have on employment and the ability to compete in the world economy, a view that is held in developed and developing nation alike.

Cultural globalization

The globalization debate extends to whether there is a global culture or, at least, a set of universal cultural variables, and how globalization might overcome and displace embedded national cultures and traditions. Although the onset of a truly homogeneous global culture is fanciful, the intensification of cultural exchange has, nevertheless, had the effect of challenging the invincibility of traditional, often previously isolated cultures.

The impact, intensity and receptivity of global cultural flows can be expected to vary from region to region. One view is that cultural globalization has both homogenising and differentiating effects. This is because features previously unique to a particular locality can become universally dispersed, thereby increasing the impact of a particular culture on a wider scale. A process of hybridisation can occur in which local or regional cultural styles and traditions become detached from their original context to be embraced by other traditions.

Geographical globalization

Globalization implies a compression of time and space as a result of rapid electronic exchanges of information and reduced travel times between locations. The consequence is that distance matters to a far lesser extent than hitherto. In addition, due to dramatic advances in the transmission of information, knowledge that was confined to certain geographical areas is now far easier to access and is universally available and, as a consequence, less place bound. Issues within the globalization debate centre on the potential such a compression of space and time might have on the geographical configuration of the world economy.

A particularly important issue concerns the interplay between space and place, in the sense of cities and regions maintaining or losing significance. Advocates of a neo-liberal persuasion claim the "end of geography" (that is, location and place no longer matter) due to recent developments in technology and the ease with which "footloose" global capital can cross borders. Others, conversely, refer to the importance of the attributes of place in generating the potential for achieving competitive advantages (Porter, 1990; Sassen, 1995). For example, in international finance (banking and securities), arguably the most globalized of industries, there exists a global division and concentration of labour in three global cities, London, New York and Tokyo, and several smaller ones, Chicago, Paris, Hong Kong, Singapore and Frankfurt (Sassen, 1991). This global division is based on the respective strengths, competencies and contribution of these cities to international financial services.

Despite the continuing importance of place and location, there remains a danger that they will succumb to homogenising pressures as a direct result of their efforts to compete for footloose economic resources to secure their place within the world order (Peck and Tickell, 1994: 280 - 1). Homogeneity can occur because in "place-making" competition, places compete to offer the same kind of services and facilities, such as training and investment grants and a high-quality infrastructure. This uniformity of "local" strategies, in turn, reopens the debate concerning the significance of place and whether globalization will bring about an end to geographical and territorial distinctiveness.

Political globalization

The relationship between the power of markets and responsibilities of the state has undergone fundamental changes since the end of World War II. The period after the war, the so-called "golden age of capitalism", was characterised by national demand management and counter-cyclical policies and international cooperation to control economies. The 1970s witnessed the renaissance of a belief in the power of the price mechanism and market forces to allocate resources in an efficient manner and proposals to restrict the influence of governments on market behaviour. The contemporary dominant ideology, linked to the globalization process, emphasises wealth creation via competitive processes in the private sector, the endorsement of supply-side management and the gradual retreat of the state as an active manager of the economy. Globalization, however, is not seen to be a deterministic process inherent in the market economy, but a process that is conditioned by market players, particularly MNCs and financial institutions participating in the global economy and having a vested interest in the way it functions. Despite the ability of these players to defend their positions and the trends toward an ever more integrated world economy, questions remain about the durability and irreversibility of globalization and the direction of the interplay between markets and nation-states.

Political globalization focuses on the changing role and importance of the nation-state because, through globalization, political activity and the processes and exercise of political power and authority are no longer primarily defined by national boundaries. The globalization of politics encompasses old and new debates. An earlier debate was concerned with the power relationships between international markets and the state. A new debate centres on the supposed "hollowing out of the state" and the consequent "erosion of sovereignty" (Palan et al., 1996: 1), that is, whether globalization has actually outflanked and withered away the authority of the nation-state and any loss of national authority is unlikely to be substituted by effective control and governance mechanisms on an international or supranational level, with the effect that capitalism will be left without a home, a development that is seen as potentially destabilising (Peck and Tickell, 1994).

Since the march towards globalization strengthens the case for laissez-faire policies, it poses a serious threat to the "managed economy" and undermines the economic and political foundations of regulation and control. If this is to be the impact of globalization on the nation-state and national systems, it offers further support to free market propositions that a laissez-faire regime is superior to a Keynesian-style welfare state. Free market advocates claim that the state should concentrate on such matters as social stability and military safety but should hesitate to take measures to influence the structure and performance of the economy because they are likely to have harmful effects on the competitiveness of firms and markets. However, although the free market ideology, including deregulation and privatization, has taken hold around the globe for its promises of economic growth and wealth creation, it is heavily disputed for its lack of mechanisms to deal with unemployment, financial crises, continuing inequalities and under-investment in education and research (Boyer, 1996).

Notes to the Text

1. Boyer: 罗伯特·博奕(Robert Boyer),法国应用数理计划经济预测研究所教授,主要研究领域是宏观经济学、技术革新与成长的分析、劳动市场与工资的关系、管理方式的国际比较与欧洲一体化。

2. Porter: 迈克尔·波特(Michael E. Porter),当今全球第一战略权威,被誉为"竞争战略之父",是现代最伟大的商业思想家之一。2000 年 12 月,获得哈佛大学最高荣誉"大学教授"(University Professor)资格,成为哈佛大学商学院第四位得到这份"镇校之宝"殊荣的教授;他提出的"竞争五力模型"、"三种竞争战略"在全球被广为接受和实践,其竞争战略思想是哈佛商学院必修的科目课之一;主要著作有《竞争优势》、《竞争战略》、《竞争论》、《国家竞争优势》等。

3. Sassen: 萨森(Saskia Sassen),伦敦经济政治学院和芝加哥大学政治经济学教授,全球化和城市社会学研究的领军人物。

4. Keynesian-style welfare state: 凯恩斯(英国经济学家)主义模式的福利国家;认为贫困和失业是由社会不合理结构造成的,福利政策是促进国家的繁荣和发展、缓和社会矛盾、保障社会安全的必要措施。

5. invincibility: quality or state of being too strong to be defeated or overcome 不可战胜

6. homogeneity: quality of being alike 同种,同质

7. renaissance: revival, a renewed interest in something 再生,复兴

8. interplay: interaction, having an effect on each other 相互作用,相互影响

9. compression: compressing or being compressed 压缩

10. outflank: outwit, gain an advantage over somebody 胜过,出奇制胜

Exercises

❶ Answer the following questions.

1. What influences does the economic globalization have?

2. Do you think there is a global culture?

3. What roles does the geographical location play in globalization?

4. What does political globalization focus on?

II **Write out the equivalents of the following words and expressions.**

1. deregulation

2. hybridisation

3. price mechanism

4. detrimental effects

5. *laissez-faire* policy

6. 跨国公司

7. 金融市场

8. 市场力量

9. 最低工资

10. 宏观经济政策

III **Translate the following into Chinese.**

With the increasing integration of economic activities, national firms find themselves more exposed to competitive pressures from MNCs (Multinational Corporations) and firms from other countries. Western firms, in particular, experience severe cost pressures from competitors who are able to source low-wage countries. In consequence, state policies that raise firm's costs, such as minimum wages and employment standards, are often condemned by industry for the detrimental effects they have on employment and the ability to compete in the world economy, a view that is held in developed and developing nation alike.

Unit 41

Globalization versus Regionalization: Which Way for the Multinational? (1)

Flying in the face of conventional wisdom, the authors contend that multinationals need to pay more attention to strengthening regional competitiveness in their discussion of globalization. Increasingly, managers are confronted by calls for dramatic change in the way their businesses should compete internationally. Nowhere is this more apparent than in so-called "global" industries, where managers have been urged to introduce offshore manufacturing, cut costs through worldwide economies of scale, standardize products internationally, and subsidize national market-share battles through international cash flows or other support activities. These actions form the basis of "global strategies" that have been suggested as the emerging pattern of international competition.

Two fundamental assumptions drive this thinking. The first is that a sizable number of competitors are indeed using global strategies to compete; the second is that performance can be improved by pursuing global strategies, particularly in an industry that has global structural characteristics. For managers in global industries the message has been, "Either quickly adopt a global strategy or see your competitiveness diminish."

In fact, some observers have gone so far as to suggest that the imperatives to globalize are so great and the benefits are so pronounced that *globalization* is fast becoming the strategic norm rather than the exception. Although such comments are directed toward managers in the front-line global industries (for example, semiconductors, aircraft parts, pharmaceuticals, and heavy machinery), they are also being heard by senior managers in numerous other industries that are beginning to face greater and greater levels of international competition.

Ongoing challenges: environmental volatility

With few exceptions, there was widespread concurrence among the study's participants that environmental change had accelerated during the last half of the 1980s. To many managers, fundamental international changes—economic, political, technological, and social—were occurring in an independent manner, seemingly independent of each other. As a result, managers were often perplexed in their attempts to sort out opportunities from threats in the competitive environment. Corporate managers in particular faced myriad perspectives generated by far-flung operations in which managers must deal with their own unique challenges.

Managers have historically coped with uncertainty and complexity by constructing mental frameworks for interpreting phenomena. For U.S. managers, conventional wisdom held that the U.S. market was of paramount importance and that business practices successful at home would be successful overseas. Using this reasoning, many companies entered foreign markets either by exploring or by establishing overseas subsidiaries as "miniature replicas" of the U.S. parent. A miniature replica, which is a scaled-down version of the parent, basically produces the same products as those produced by the parent but in lower volumes for the smaller "domestic" market. Consider the following examples.

- In home appliances, General Electric established its Camco subsidiary in Canada in 1976 by merging the appliance division of GSW and GE Canada and subsequently acquiring Westinghouse's Canadian major appliance operations. Protected by Canadian tariff barriers averaging 12 percent and aided by considerable corporate resources, Camco established production facilities for refrigerators, ranges, dishwashers, stoves, and washers and dryers to serve Canadian demand. Although the scale of these facilities did not render them internationally cost-efficient, Camco has gone on to become Canada's largest major appliance manufacturer.

- In health-care products, the Kendall Healthcare Products Company established a German subsidiary to manufacture and market a wide line of products developed in the United States. A broad range of the parent's urological products, critical-care products, and vascular-care products are locally manufactured for German consumption. Localized manufacturing has historically made sense, given that product standards have varied considerably from country to country and that the German health-care system has been a major customer of the firm's products.

- In consumer electronics, Matsushita Electric Industrial Company paid $108 million in 1974 for an ailing Motorola television manufacturing facility in Illinois. Under the Quasar Electronics name, Matsushita channelled funds and designs to the upgraded, miniature replica of the parent with the objective of producing television sets in the United States that were similar in quality and price to those developed in Japan.

The management of international operations through either exports or miniature replicas was relatively easy for the parent. Minimal strategic input from local managers was required beyond the local market, thus reassuring head-office managers and encouraging their continued preoccupation with home-country competition. However, this arrangement often resulted in limited communication between parent and subsidiary and certainly restricted corporate advancement opportunities for the overseas managers. The end result in many companies was a perpetuation of the norm that international operations should be treated as appendages to home-country operations.

Unravelling home-country orientation: the rise of global mania

When this home-country orientation began to unravel in the late 1970s, the greatest effect was felt by U.S. managers. As U.S. economic dominance declined, many American managers began to realize that international markets were critically important and that, if they were to compete effectively, new international strategies would be required. This ushered in a new era of what we refer to as "global mania".

An interest in global management began to pick up in the early 1980s and was accelerated, in part, by the declining competitiveness of the United States vis-a-vis Japan. Within the emerging mind-set, managers began to perceive the world differently. Home-country competitive pressures, for example, were put in the context of broader international pressures.

Managers began to see a link between what happened at home and what happened overseas. As an indicator of the *globalization* of competition, experts pointed to a real shrinkage in differences from country to country—shrinkage brought on by rising monetary interdependence, transportation and communication efficiencies, various GATT (General Agreement on Tariffs and Trade) rulings, and so on.

By the mid-1980s, numerous academic articles were lauding the merits of pursuing global strategies. Key—and often strategic—industries were identified as having global structural characteristics. These characteristics included low tariff and non-tariff barriers to trade, high factor-cost differentials (i. e., in land, labor, and capital costs) between host countries, the possibility of achieving major economies of scale through worldwide production runs, and standardized product demand. Businesses were urged to respond by integrating operations around the world and by developing highly standardized products and marketing approaches.

To support these recommendations, observers noted that such companies as Caterpillar Inc., L. M. Ericsson, and Honda Motor Co., Ltd. had been highly rewarded for pursuing global integration strategies. Other observers pointed to the increasingly "stateless" world of manufacturing, in which dozens of the world's largest corporations generated more than half their sales outside their home country. Examples included ICI, which generated 78 percent of its sales outside the U.K.; Sony Corp., which produced 66 percent of total sales from outside Japan; and IBM, which received almost 63 percent of sales from activities not based in the United States.

The notion of a global strategy has had considerable appeal for corporate managers, largely because such strategies are best managed through tight central control. These strategies, like miniature replica strategies, let corporate managers ultimately determine what is produced and where it is produced. In other words, the center would continue to dominate the periphery. The global "solution" was also a concrete step—and concrete steps were called for in an era of cutthroat international competition.

However, despite the advice calling for pursuit of global strategies, our research failed to uncover widespread support for such an organizational response. The managers in our study generally did not see the world as an undifferentiated global marketplace. Interestingly, competitors in the U.S. regarded the U.S. as preeminently important in matters of investment, product development, position, and so on. A similar though somewhat less pronounced pattern was observed for British, German, French, Canadian, and Japanese firms with respect to their home markets.

Thus, though managers sensed that markets were becoming more competitive internationally, their loyalties remained primarily home-based. Even though they recognized that considerable international opportunities were slipping away, the vast majority of managers did not consider *globalization* the preferred approach for pursuing them. These managers simply viewed the advantages of *globalization* as being much more theoretical than real, particularly in view of some common problems that included the following:

- Industry standards remain diverse. In spite of talk about the convergence of standards—in the European television industry, for example—there are currently seven different technical standards governing such matters as voltage and broadcasting frequencies. To meet this diverse set of standards, Toshiba Corporation in 1981 acquired the assets of a local British consumer electronics firm and began manufacturing television sets for the European market. From a centralized plant in Plymouth, the company now produces 110 models of television sets from 14 "to 28" in size, "custom" manufactured for local country needs within Europe.

- Customers continue to demand locally differentiated products. In many industries in Europe, North America, and Japan, subsidiaries continue to focus on reformulations, blending, and packaging activities. In the pharmaceutical industry, for example, differences in standards, tastes, and perceived needs remain a major obstacle to *globalization*. Prescription dosages for many products can vary up to 100 percent between Europe and Japan. Medical training and health-care delivery systems, which vary considerably from country to country, significantly influence the types of prescriptions written and the delivery of both ethical and over-the-counter drugs. In response, Parke-Davis in France and both American Cyanamid Co. and Pfizer Inc. in Germany continue to focus much of their efforts on reformulating dosages and repackaging them.

- Being an insider remains critically important. In theory, one advantage of a global strategy is that world-scale production maximizes production efficiencies and underwrites heavy product-development expenses. The result is supposed to be a standardized, low-cost product that, when combined with local marketing input, produces a competitive advantage for the global competitor. In reality, however, such advantages have taken on mythical proportions. The example of Inmos provides a case in point. Formed in 1978, the semiconductor manufacturer based in Bristol, U.K. is now a subsidiary of S. G. S. -Thomson Microelectronics, Inc. Inmos produces a variety of fast static RAMs, high-performance microprocessors (transputers), and graphics components for the worldwide market. Inmos's products are intended for global customers, and some 90 percent of its revenues are generated outside the U.K. However, it has observed a definite bias in the industry in favor of hardware developed in Silicon Valley. Moreover, it has found that Japanese and, particularly, U.S. customers are often skeptical of European products—and that such skepticism is more psychological than based on rational assessments of the technology and costs involved. As a result, Inmos has joined with a host of other European and Japanese semiconductor producers to consider manufacturing locally in the United States. Being perceived as an insider is still a critical concern for many firms.

- Global organizations are difficult to manage. To effectively implement a global strategy, managers must find ways to coordinate far-flung operations. To do this, they must denationalize operations and replace home-country loyalties with a system of common corporate values and loyalties. This is particularly challenging because globalization by definition involves exposure to and linkages with broadly divergent national cultures. Globalization is also based on huge world-scale plants in which acculturation and communication become real challenges. Production economies also reach upper limits with size—limits that of course often restrict the benefits of globalization. Many companies face clear, often insurmountable operational obstacles to *globalization*. At Cyanamid's German subsidiary, for example, a critical shortage of labor makes it nearly impossible to run a plant 24 hours a day. Furthermore, the labor laws that forbid many women in Germany from working at night compound the staffing problem. Language is another simple, though very real, obstacle to *globalization*. In Germany, Cyanamid has determined that implementing a global strategy, which would require the insertion of technical product information into packages, would mean the proliferation of centralized packaging. To speed the packaging function and to give medical practitioners in the field timely backup support, the company estimates that it would need staff members with technical fluency in approximately 12 to 15 languages at global headquarters. They argue further that German law outlaws global market-share battles in which profits are artificially generated in one market to support operations in another. Clearly, the promises of *globalization* must be viewed in the context of very real organizational obstacles and costs to be overcome.

- Globalization often circumvents subsidiary competencies. Many global strategies are based on rationalizing operations so that subsidiaries contribute a portion of a finished product's value-added content. Subsidiaries, which in the past functioned as miniature replicas, face a role change that often involves a reduction in their strategic autonomy. A case in point is Alkaril Chemicals, Ltd. of Canada, which was recently acquired by Rhone-Poulenc. Alkaril had considerable skills in developing low-volume, specialty chemicals. For surfactants in particular, the company had developed a noteworthy reputation for customized product formulation and flexible production. With the acquisition，Alkaril has been left wondering what role it will play in Rhone-Poulenc's broader strategy，which emphasizes rationalized production and greater economies of scale. Although subsidiaries have typically responded promptly to corporate initiatives，globalization is being resisted by many subsidiary managers who fear the loss of autonomy and personal contribution that comes with globalization. Unless they handle this situation delicately，corporations risk losing many of the top managers who ran miniature replica subsidiaries. Another very real risk is that subsidiary managers may take initiatives that restrict the parent from making future moves to rationalize operations.

Notes to the Text

1. Kendall Healthcare Products Company：美国一家医疗器械和保健品公司。

2. Caterpillar：美国卡特彼勒公司，成立于 1925 年，是世界上最大的工程机械和矿山设备生产厂家，燃气发动机和工业用燃气轮机生产厂家之一，也是世界上最大的柴油机厂家之一。现已跻身身财富 100 强。

3. Matsushita Electric Industrial Company：日本松下电器产业株式会社。

4. L. M. Ericsson：爱立信公司，1876 年成立于北欧的瑞典，是全球领先的提供端到端的全面通信解决方案的供应商，其业务遍布全球 140 多个国家。

5. Toshiba Corporation：日本东芝集团，是一家有着 130 年历史的知名跨国企业集团，业务范围涉及能源电力、半导体、电子元器件、信息系统工程、IT 终端产品、家电等等，几乎囊括了生产生活的各个领域。

6. Parke-Davis：帕克戴维实验室，是华纳兰伯特制药公司（Warner-Lambert）的一个分支，而后者又在 2000 年被制药业巨人辉瑞公司（见 Note 8）并购。

7. American Cyanamid Co.：美国氰氨公司，2000 年 7 月被巴斯夫集团（BASF Corporation）收购。巴斯夫集团是世界第三位、德国第二位以化工为主体的大型跨国化学公司，其主要业务包括保健和营养品、染料和涂料、石油和天然气、化学品、塑料和纤维。

8. Pfizer Inc.：美国辉瑞公司，是一家拥有 150 多年历史的世界著名的研究开发型跨国制药企业，产品治疗领域包括心血管系统、内分泌系统、精神健康和神经系统疾病、泌尿和生殖系统疾病、感染性疾病、关节炎及疼痛、眼科、肿瘤及女性健康等。

9. S. G. S. -Thomson Microelectronics Inc.：意法半导体（ST）集团，于 1987 年 6 月成立，由意大利的 SGS 微电子公司和法国 Thomson 半导体公司合并而成。1998 年 5 月，将公司名称改为意法半导体有限公司（ST Microelectronics）。

10. RAM：全称 Random-Access Memory，随机存取存储器，一种存储单元结构，用于保存 CPU 处理的数据信息。Fast static RAM，快速静态随机存取存储器。

11. CPU：全称 Central Processing Unit，中央处理器，是计算机的心脏，包括运算部件和控制部件，是完成各种运算和控制的核心，也是决定计算机性能的最重要的部件。

12. Silicon Valley：硅谷。在美国加利福尼亚州旧金山市南端，有一条不足 1500 平方英里的狭长谷地,这就是硅谷的所在地。硅谷的英文是 Silicon Valley,这个词是 1971 年创造出来的。1971 年 1 月 11 号,"硅谷"这个词出现在《每周商业报》介绍电子新闻的系列文章中。之所以有一个"硅"字,是由于当地的多数企业都与高纯度硅制造的半导体和电脑有关。惠普、IBM、英特尔、苹果、施乐、雅虎、网景、亚马逊书店等一十批著名企业都诞生在这里,是众多科技界、企业界风云人物的荟萃之地;可以说,硅谷是当今美国乃至全世界信息产业的龙头。

13. Rhone-Poulenc:法国一制药公司。1999 年 12 月,该公司与德国的赫司特 (Hoechst)公司合并,创建了在生命科学领域居领先地位的巨型公司赛诺菲-安万特(Aventis Pharma)公司。公司业务主要集中在医药和农业方面,总部设在法国的斯特拉斯堡(Strasbourg)。

Exercises

Ⅰ Answer the following questions.

1. What forms the basis of "global strategies"?
2. How do companies enter foreign markets?
3. What is a miniature replica?
4. Why do some managers simply view the advantages of *globalization* as being much more theoretical than real?
5. What risks might confront the companies going global?

Ⅱ Write out the equivalents of the following words and expressions.

1. offshore manufacturing
2. miniature replica
3. tariff barrier/ non-tariff barrier
4. customized product
5. rationalized production
6. 地区竞争优势
7. 成本效率
8. 标准化产品
9. 制成品

Ⅲ Translate the following into Chinese.

Increasingly, managers are confronted by calls for dramatic change in the way their businesses should compete internationally. Nowhere is this more apparent than in so-called "global" industries, where managers have been urged to introduce offshore manufacturing, cut costs through worldwide economies of scale, standardize products internationally, and subsidize national market-share battles through international cash flows or other support activities. These actions form the basis of "global strategies" that have been suggested as the emerging pattern of international competition.

Unit 42

Globalization versus Regionalization：
Which Way for the Multinational? (2)

The regional alternative

The move toward the *globalization* of competition was paralleled in the latter half of the 1980s by a dramatic upsurge in regional competitive pressures. Although regional pressures come from a variety of sources, the most important developments are in the formalization of trading blocks. In North America, the Free Trade Agreement between Canada and the United States is having a far-reaching impact on the business environment. This Agreement, which was signed on January 2, 1988, promises to remove all tariffs for a wide variety of industries by 1998. Although trade barriers will remain in place in the areas of agriculture, culture, and maritime-related industries, virtually every other industry faces liberalized trade.

Within the European Community, 1992 looms as a pivotal year in eliminating trade barriers among the 12 member-nations. The goal of Europe 1992, as specified first in the 1985 White Paper and reaffirmed in the 1987 Single European Act, is to sweep away the non-tariff barriers that restrict the flow of goods, services, and capital throughout the trading block. Three categories of barriers are to be either eliminated or reduced: fiscal, physical, and technical barriers.

In 1989, 21 of the 22 richest industrialized nations in the world—the exception being Japan—belonged to regional trading groups. Japan, as the dominant economic power of the Pacific Rim, has long attempted to strengthen its position in the region. The countries of the Pacific Rim now have the fastest-growing economies in the world, caused in part by the huge influx of Japanese investment. Many Japanese companies, aided by the strong yen, have transferred whole manufacturing bases to such countries as Thailand and Singapore. Production in these newly industrialized economies is now increasingly being referred to as "JapaNIEs" manufacturing. Japanese economic aid to the region has shown similar growth; in 1989 it was almost 14 times greater than that supplied by the United States.

With all this investment, trade has skyrocketed. Trade within Pacific Asia is now growing at an annual rate of 30 percent and promises to surpass Pacific Asia-North American levels of $250 billion by 1991. Fearful of being left out of the development of the region, Australia and Thailand have proposed the establishment of formal Asian-Pacific consultative bodies with many similarities to the Canada-U.S. Free Trade Agreement and the Europe 1992 phenomenon.

The rise of regional trading blocks has led many companies to reassess the anticipated rise of *globalization*. Some are taking their cues from governments that established free-trade associations at least in part to encourage and control the economic adjustments that ultimately result in improved global competitiveness. Increasingly, *regionalization* is being viewed by managers as a stepping-stone to more effective global competition. This view is ably summarized by Wisse Dekker, chairman of the Supervisory Board of N. V. Philips, in an interview with Nan Stone that was reported in the Harvard Business Review (May-June, 1989, pp. 90~95):

> 〔We〕 need a single European market with common technical standards. Without it, we cannot achieve the optimum scale and the lower unit costs we need to be competitive worldwide.

This reasoning was shared by many managers in our study—namely, that regional strategies are increasingly providing the primary determinant of competitive advantage. In fact, according to the majority of companies surveyed, the evolution to true global competition is currently on hold. Instead of *globalization*, managers are finding that regional competitive pressures are taking on an ever-greater importance by introducing a set of distinct opportunities and threats.

Regional competition

A consequence of *regionalization* pressures, our research found, is that home-oriented parents and subsidiaries—whether in Europe, North America, or Japan—were pressured to become more regionally focused or face a competitive disadvantage, even in so-called global industries. Similarly, companies that had attempted to pursue global strategies were coming under intense pressure to scale back their efforts to meet regional competitive conditions.

Under a regional strategy, companies extend home-country loyalties to the entire region. Local markets are intentionally linked within the region where competitive strategies are formulated. It is within the region that top managers determine investment locations, product mix, competitive positioning, and performance appraisals. Managers are given the opportunity to solve regional challenges regionally.

The importance of responding to the upsurge in regional pressures was not going unnoticed in the companies we studied—witness the following examples:

- Thomson Consumer Electronics, Inc. has been trying for several years to regionalize its strategy for its television sets. To do so it has established four Thomson factories in Europe: EWD in Germany, Seipel in France, Cedosa in Spain, and Ferguson in the U.K. Each of these factories assembles specific types of television sets for the European market. EWD, for example, has a European mandate to produce high-feature, large television sets; Cedosa of Spain focuses on low-cost, small-screen sets. The marketing and distribution of the sets is handled by a separate Thomson division that has a similar regional mandate.

In North America, Thomson manufactures television sets under the RCA and GE nameplates. In spite of sourcing some common low-cost components from the Far East, the North American and European operations are run separately. Thomson has established a network of regional suppliers and subassemblers—largely in Mexico—to maintain the regional integrity of North American operations.

- Warner Lambert Co. has had operations in Europe since the 1920s through its Parke-Davis subsidiary. The company currently has manufacturing facilities in the U.K., France, Italy, Spain, Germany, Belgium, and Ireland. Historically, these plants have focused on blending and packaging to meet local needs.

In 1987, discussions were begun under the direction of the parent to dramatically restructure operations to maximize regional responsiveness. After three years of often heated discussions, a plan was adopted to cut the number of manufacturing units to less than half of 1990 levels and to specialize in each unit. Instead of producing a large number of products for each local market, each plant would produce fewer products for the entire European market.

To the majority of the companies studied, *regionalization* represented a compromise between the traditional strategies adopted by miniature replica subsidiaries and the global strategies currently being advocated. Regional production facilities have often proved to be as scale-efficient as global facilities while being more forgiving of the need to tailor key product features for local markets. Regional plants also avoid many of the very real staffing, communication, and motivational problems of huge global facilities.

By shifting operations and decision making to the region, the company is also better able to maintain an insider advantage. Many of the Japanese regional investments in the automobile and consumer electronics industries have, for example, been based on the objective of developing insider market advantages. Finally, *regionalization* allows corporations to more effectively leverage subsidiary competencies by encouraging affiliate involvement in activities that extend beyond local markets.

The *regionalization* of competition is occurring irrespective of the often very real opportunities to globalize certain aspects of company operations. Indeed, many of the companies studied were sourcing raw materials and commodity components across regions; others were sharing R&D between laboratories across regions. What *regionalization* does suggest is that even companies in so-called global industries should move to exploit strengths and determine competitive strategies separately on a region-by-region basis. To do so may require some macro, trans-regional facilitation, but strategic decision making should not unilaterally emanate from world headquarters.

New organizational challenges

The move toward regional competition brings with it significant changes in the tasks and responsibilities of both home-country and subsidiary managers. For many companies, the organizational obstacles are extensive, suggesting a bumpy road to change.

The challenge is all the more daunting in view of the sheer magnitude of overseas investment and the weak understanding of many company managers of the opportunities and threats at hand. In 1987, for example, the value of goods and services produced by American firms in the European Community exceeded $235 billion, a figure four times the value of U.S. exports to the region. The gap continues to widen, and similar trends have been observed in North America and Japan.

For the parent, often far removed from distant markets and operations, several tasks and responsibilities become critical. That is, the parent needs to:

- Stay abreast of local market conditions. In many instances, subsidiary managers felt that the parent dangerously misunderstood local or regional market conditions. Adjectives such as "naive" or "simplistic" were commonly used by subsidiary managers in describing their parents' understanding of local or regional conditions. A frequently stated belief was that the parent typically overestimates the similarities between markets and consequently pushes too hard and too fast for global consolidation. Subsidiaries often act in conjunction with one another to convince the parent to proceed more cautiously.

- Stay abreast of subsidiary strengths and weaknesses. Many of the subsidiary managers who participated in this study commented that the parent often has only superficial understanding of the strengths and weaknesses of their operations. Though it was not unusual for a parent to know the product/market mix and sales levels of a subsidiary, it was far less common for the parent to understand the subsidiary's competitiveness on a product-by-product basis. Parents too often assumed that the subsidiary was uncompetitive outside local markets—even though, in many cases, the subsidiary could have competed on equal ground with the parent in terms of product development and cost competitiveness.

- Prepare to shift autonomy to regional managers. For many a corporate parent, *regionalization* involves a greater leap of faith than it does for a subsidiary; after all, the parent is removed from decision making, while the subsidiary remains a central participant in the process. Our research found that the adjustment to regional decision making was easiest for European managers and most difficult for Japanese managers. The Japanese difficulties stemmed from two sources: a fairly thin cadre of Japanese managers with international training and experience, and a legacy of tight top-to-bottom control that seriously frustrated non-Japanese managers.

In one instance, the general manager of European operations for one of Japan's largest consumer electronics companies commented that he constantly felt like an outsider in the corporation. As a non-Japanese, he felt that his opportunities for further advancement were nil and that his contributions to corporate thinking were largely ignored. Unless this kind of situation changes, Japanese ability to respond to mounting regional pressures will be severely hampered.

North American corporate managers also face serious challenges. One recent assessment of corporate preparedness for Europe 1992 ranked Canadian managers at 39 and U.S. managers at 38 out of a possible maximum score of 100. Not surprisingly, European managers fared significantly better. American corporate managers have also been criticized for their lack of preparedness in penetrating the Japanese market and the Pacific Asian market.

For the subsidiary, a different set of tasks is important. Subsidiaries need to:

• Prepare to take strategic initiatives. Our research found that subsidiaries can and often do influence their future roles under *regionalization*. Take the example of Motorola Canada. Like managers at other subsidiaries, managers at Motorola Canada were somewhat apprehensive about the risks associated with the expected rationalization of operations that would come under the Canada-U.S. Free Trade Agreement. Although the subsidiary is U.S.-owned, it employs about 2,500 people—virtually all of whom are Canadians. These people feared that, under free trade, many of their jobs would become redundant.

In an effort to maintain some control over developments, managers began as far back as the late 1970s to take several important initiatives. First, they beefed up their R&D group; then they began looking for new products that would complement existing offerings while providing export potential independent of the parent. What resulted was a series of products—including land-mobile radios and systems, modems, and data multiplexers—for which the subsidiary was given product mandates. Such mandates have given the subsidiary considerable influence in corporate decision making while providing the parent with new sales and manufacturing resources.

In the case of Motorola, the Canadian subsidiary was granted product mandates that allowed it access to the parent's worldwide distribution system. However, in the drive toward *globalization*, only a tiny fraction of the subsidiary's export sales went outside the region. To have attempted to develop, manufacture, and market universal products to worldwide customers would probably have overwhelmed the subsidiary at a time when it was struggling to gain credibility in the eyes of its parent. The more realistic initiative taken was to move regionally before pursuing a global presence.

• Exploit existing competencies/build new strengths. Subsidiary managers need to look for opportunities to position themselves as "natural leaders" in selected products within the region. This implies a gradual build-up of competencies through small studies, pilot production in existing facilities, and so on. With expertise comes the influence that determines the subsidiary's position within the region.

The case of Cyanamid Canada is illustrative in this regard. Since 1907, Cyanamid has had Canadian operations that have benefited from high Canadian tariffs. In the early 1980s, however, the parent undertook a number of initiatives to strengthen itself as a company involved in biotechnology and specialty chemicals. What followed was a series of divestitures that caused the subsidiary to lose more than half its employees. With the movement toward free trade, concern mounted in the subsidiary that operations would be cut further as the parent rationalized operations on a regional basis.

In spite of these troubling conditions, however, subsidiary managers clearly believed that much could be done to reverse the situation. The feeling was that the subsidiary's competitive advantage lay in producing smaller-run products that required high levels of technological input. Consequently, beginning in 1988, Cyanamid Canada began focusing efforts on reaching out to new technologies in highly specialized fields where it could best exploit its unique strengths; this resulted in two recent acquisitions of Canadian biotechnology companies. Both acquisitions provided the subsidiary with considerable control over operations and an opportunity to strengthen its competencies in ways that will ensure its position in the ongoing restructuring of the parent's operations.

• Manage structural mechanisms more effectively. Although there was a strong awareness of changing parent and subsidiary roles in all the companies we studied, many subsidiary managers were concerned about how to proceed with the necessary changes. At some subsidiaries, a damaging "us versus them" attitude had emerged. In these subsidiaries, managers often attempted to quietly sabotage change, frequently by entrenching the subsidiary through long-term supply or service contracts. These elaborate measures often severely tied the parents' hands and 3 proved costly to both parent and subsidiary. In many of these organizations, morale was low and prospects for the future bleak.

Instead of avoiding inevitable integration, successful subsidiaries moved to preempt change through the artful use of a variety of structural mechanisms. These integrative mechanisms included a variety of such tools as personal contact between managers and the use of committees, task forces, and boards of directors. Knowing how and when to use appropriate structural mechanisms can maximize subsidiary influence while facilitating integration at multiple levels in the organization.

Structural mechanisms play a vital role because the move to a regional organization is a time-consuming and strenuous process. It was not uncommon for negotiations concerning a move toward *regionalization* to take three years or more; in many of the companies studied, negotiations that began in the mid-1980s were still ongoing five years later. Negotiations typically involved regular meetings of subsidiary managers and corporate executives and often served as the springboard for establishing more formal, regional decision-making bodies.

Conclusions: capability and flexibility are the keys

Few companies remain untouched by the complex environmental changes sweeping the world. In responding to these changes, however, managers have been urged to abandon the dated "miniature replica" approaches in favor of full-fledged global strategies. Although a global strategy promises in theory to be highly efficient, we found in this study that *globalization* is no panacea. In fact, global imperatives are being eclipsed by an upsurge in regional pressures. Companies are finding that the implementation of global strategies is often prohibitively costly in terms of morale, internal opposition, and lost opportunities to exploit key subsidiary strengths. As a consequence, both parents and subsidiaries are finding that regional strategies represent a safer, more manageable option.

In the course of our study, we also found that management of the *regionalization* process is often as important as design of the strategy. Flexibility is critical for both parents and subsidiaries as they negotiate roles and tasks in the restructuring of operations.

Here, however, managers are finding that flexibility is only as good as the competencies within the organization. As competitive pressures heat up, organizations that effectively nurture and exploit distinctive competencies stand the greatest chance of success. We suggest that *regionalization* provides a controlled approach to change and that it builds upon the distinctive competencies of the entire organization while responding to the legitimate pressures for greater integration.

Notes to the Text

1. Canada-U.S. Free Trade Agreement：美加自由贸易协定。1988 年 1 月 2 日，当时的美国总统里根和加拿大马尔罗尼总理所签署。根据《协定》，两国将在 1989 年 1 月 1 日《协定》正式生效后的 10 年内最终建成"美加自由贸易区"。1992 年 8 月 12 日，美国、加拿大及墨西哥三国签署了一项三边自由贸易协定——北美自由贸易协定（North America Free Trade Agreement，Nafta）。1994 年 1 月 1 日，该协定正式生效。

2. European Community：欧共体，欧洲共同体的简称，创立于 1957 年 3 月 25 日，是欧洲联盟 European Union（简称欧盟）的前身。1999 年 1 月 1 日起大多数成员国使用统一货币——欧元（euro）。

3. white paper：an authoritative report（White papers are used to educate customers, collect leads for a company or help people make decisions. They can also be a government report outlining policy.）白皮书

4. The 1987 Single European Act：1987 年单一欧洲法案。欧洲经济共同体（EEC）于 1987 年 7 月 1 日通过单一欧洲法案（Single European Act，SEA），希望自 1993 年起成为单一市场，废除所有贸易障碍，使所有的财货、劳务等在区域内自由移动。

5. Pacific Rim：Far Eastern countries and markets bordering the Pacific Ocean, including Hong Kong, South Korea, Singapore, Taiwan, China, Malaysia, Indonesia, the Philippines, New Zealand, and Australia. Japan, because of its singular economic importance, is not usually included in the definition. 环太平洋国家，太平洋周边国家。

6. Wisse Dekker：德克尔，1982 年—1986 年任飞利浦电子集团首席执行官（CEO）。Royal Philips 是世界上最大的电子公司之一，在欧洲名列榜首，在彩色电视、照

明、电动剃须刀、医疗诊断影像和病人监护仪以及单芯片电视产品领域世界领先。

7. Harvard Business Review：《哈佛商业评论》(简称 HBR)，创刊于 1922 年，是哈佛商学院的标志性刊物，也是全球顶尖的管理杂志；致力于创造和传播最新的管理理念和方法，帮助商界人士不断更新理念。

8. Thomson Consumer Electronics，Inc．汤姆逊消费电子有限公司，是法国最大的国家企业集团，位居全球第四大消费类电子生产商。汤姆逊公司创始人埃利胡·汤姆逊是个发明家，1879 年建立了自己的公司，1988 年并购通用电气(GE)的消费电子部门，并把自己的医疗器械业务置换给通用电气，从此成为一个专业的视讯产品商。2004 年中国 TCL 集团并购重组了法国汤姆逊彩电业务，缔造了全球彩电领先企业 TCL 汤姆逊电子有限公司(TTE)。

9. Warner Lambert Co.：华纳兰伯特制药公司，2000 年被制药业巨头辉瑞公司并购。

I Answer the following questions.

1. What is a trading block?
2. Why is *regionalization* being viewed by managers as a stepping-stone to more effective global competition?
3. How do companies enhance their regional competitiveness?
4. What do you think companies can do to respond to the environmental changes in the business world?

II Write out the equivalents of the following words and expressions.

1. structural mechanisms
2. industrialized nation
3. manufacturing base
4. economic adjustment
5. performance appraisal
6. task forces

7. 原材料
8. 成本竞争优势
9. 试生产
10. 董事会
11. 灵活性

III Translate the following into Chinese.

Under a regional strategy, companies extend home-country loyalties to the entire region. Local markets are intentionally linked within the region where competitive strategies are formulated. It is within the region that top managers determine investment locations, product mix, competitive positioning, and performance appraisals. Managers are given the opportunity to solve regional challenges regionally.

Unit 43

International Marketing

The essence of what constitutes international marketing emerged in the literature in the 1980s and the early 1990s. This work identifies the strategic and managerial issues connected to internationalisation as the major focus of research work in international marketing. A number of key issues emerged from this literature:

- Stage theories of internationalisation and the link to international marketing
- Networks in international marketing
- Segmentation or standardisation

Stage theories of internationalisation

The Uppsala internationalisation model suggests that internationalisation proceeds, by a process of learning, from exporting to the establishment of higher level activities including production sites and product development facilities. A similar developmental process is postulated in innovation-related internationalisation models. Stage models of internationalisation stress the importance of learning, often originating from exposure to similar but slightly different cultural environments, that induces the development of internationalisation strategies on a steady path towards more complex and deep involvement with foreign markets. However, these models are rather mechanistic and suggest that firms follow a rigid linear development of internationalisation that is often not verified by empirical work. Theories based on the development of networks have sought to clarify the complex factors that appear to determine the internationalisation path of firms. These theories adopt a less mechanical view of the process of internationalisation. The debate on how to best capture the many factors that influence the development of the internationalisation processes of firms notwithstanding, most of the theories and empirical evidence provides support for the view that internationalisation follows an evolutionary processes that develops over time. The time path and major characteristics of this evolutionary process seem to be influenced by a variety of factors, but it seems that firms normally follow a progression from simple to more complex activities. However, this is not a straightforward or a linear development and appears to be strongly influenced by sector and the characteristics of home and host countries.

The implications for international marketing of the view that the internationalisation process is a complex evolutionary process based on learning implies that marketing strategies and activities adjust in line with the acquisition of information and its conversion into useful knowledge. In these circumstances, marketing strategies may begin with simple exporting, alternatively more complex modes of entry such as DFI may begin early in the internationalisation process. The deciding factor is the knowledge that the firm possesses on matters such as market conditions and the means of producing, promoting and distributing products for foreign markets. In the complex evolutionary view of the internationalisation process firms may start with a small number of countries to which they are geographically and culturally close or with a wide range of countries that are geographically and culturally disparate from the host country. It is likely that most firms will begin with the simple marketing strategies and objectives but may rapidly move to more complex plans that miss out many of the intervening stages suggested in the more traditional models of internationalisation. Therefore, the key to the development of the international marketing strategy is the ability of firms to acquire knowledge about foreign markets and the supply conditions to these markets and to rapidly adjust their plans based on the acquired knowledge and this need not follow a linear path of development from exporting to more complex entry modes.

Networks and international marketing

The increasing focus on the importance of networks for international business activities is reflected in the international marketing literature. Research by the IMP Group emphasised the importance of learning in uncertain and competitive environments that leads to sophisticated buying behaviour by firms rather than the mechanistic approach that is expounded in traditional views of international marketing. In the IMP view of international marketing the main drivers of strategy are the interactions between buyers and sellers as they seek to establish networks for production, promotion, distribution and after-sales service that deliver outcomes that are acceptable in an environment that is fast changing because of changes in the competitive and technology environments. This type of approach is also evident in the relationship approach to marketing where strategic alliances, partnerships and joint ventures are used to achieve desirable outcomes. The importance of networks for international marketing is also highlighted in the phenomenon of "born global" firms and as a means to help small and medium sized enterprises (SMEs) internationalise. Clearly, networks and relationships within networks are important factors in international marketing for sales between firms and for arranging packages of products and distribution to final customers.

Segmentation or standardisation

The drive towards global standardisation was based on a view that the progressive removal of trade barriers plus the growth of global cultural values was creating an single economic system that could be supplied with global products and uniform marketing processes such as promotion and the use of common brand names. The advantages of mass production in terms of economies of scale and scope could be realised in the sort of world. However, the case that a single global economic system with very few economic, legal and cultural barriers is imminent has certainly been overstated. The persistence of economic, legal and especlally, cultural barrlers to mass production generated an approach from many marketers that markets should be segmented geographically according to cultural clusters and within countries by social and demographic groups. The focus on segmentation led in some cases to fragmentation of markets that were broken down into ever more complex and overlapping segments. Moreover, the use of continuous improvement by product development resulted in layers of production, sales and distribution systems with a consequent generation of a multitude of organisational systems. These developments added to the production and transaction costs often with little benefit in terms of extra sales. A study by McKinsey estimated that the costs of product differentiation and continuous improvement in the car industry for cars with limited demand amounted to $ 80 billion per year. Another example of the potential to waste resources by over-segmentation of markets is illustrated by Toyota when it reduced the product range by 25 percent when it discovered that 20 percent of its range accounted for 80 percent of its sales.

The solution to this problem is sought in build-to-order (BTO) systems whereby using sophisticated information from the Internet, specifications from customers are matched to the supply chain to assemble the components to customers' exact requirements. This type of approach is being pursued by major car companies such as GM, Ford, Nissan and Volkswagen that are seeking to develop BTO systems that can deliver a car to the customers' specification in three days. White goods manufacturers in the US such as Whirlpool and General Electric are also developing BTO systems to deliver products to customers' specifications (Economist, 2001). Operating BTO systems leads to lower production costs because of the reduced need for high levels of inventories of components, as BTO is a very lean and effective just-in-time system. Moreover, by customising the product, premium prices can be charged. BTO systems based on the use of the Internet also offer the prospects of customised promotion systems by use of common platforms for advertising and information dissemination that are tailored to the groups or even individuals that are targeted by e-business systems.

Financial services firms have been operating BTO packages in areas such as personal saving plans and financial packages for leasing systems for firms for many years. However, financial services do not require the assembling of physical components and they have zero or low logistical costs of assembling the components of a financial package. The pioneer of mass customisation using BTO for manufactured goods was Dell Computers. Dell's success was based on the use of standardised components that are slotted together according to customers' specification received via the Internet. The success of Dell Computers is largely due to the ability to use standardised components that can be assembled into different package by fairly minor modifications to the basic platform of the PC. Furthermore, Dell is able to sell and promote online to people who are computer literate and therefore do not need sophisticated advice and after-sales services. Dell also does not face significant legal, economic or cultural differences that require significant changes to organisational systems to use the standard Dell marketing model across a variety of countries. Using standardised BTO organisational systems for more complex products (that can be significantly different rather than have only minor changes to the same basic package and where there are legal, economic and cultural barriers) will present an all together more challenging task. Moreover, some products can be successfully standardised to generate the ability to charge a price relative to cost of supply that leads to higher profit than a BTO system. This process of standardisation is well advanced in the commoditization of components by using e-auctions by firms that sell to final customers.

BTO systems require the development of effective e-business and logistical systems that can deliver inputs and final products on very tight schedules. The problems of using such complex e-business systems for international business activities may hamper the use of this approach to mass customization. Moreover, the cost of segmenting markets to this level, in terms of developing effective BTO organisational and logistical systems, may lead to similar results to the attempts to mass customise by producing and marketing myriad different models by the car industry. Economic, legal and cultural differences across countries may also limit the use of global BTO systems because technical regulations and differences in rules and what is culturally and legally acceptable as means of promotion will require adaptation of the basic BTO marketing model. This will further complicate the organisational complexity of effectively operating BTO systems.

Clearly, the differentiation to mass production debate has not yet been resolved and a judicious mix of standardisation to differentiation, including in some cases mass customisation appears to be the way forward, the selection of the appropriate approach being determined by the nature of the product, minimum efficiency scale, ability to easily adapt basic product platforms, the extent of legal, economic and cultural barriers and the ability to construct organisational systems that deliver the largest difference between price that can be charged and the costs of differentiation (see **Exhibit**).

EXHIBIT   Standardisation, segmentation and build to order

Conditions		Standardisation	Segmentation	BTO
High resistance to	Yes	Undesirable	Desirable	Desirable
uniform products	No	Desirable	Undesirable	Undesirable
High barriers	Yes	Undesirable	Desirable	Undesirable[2]
to trade[1]	No	Desirable	No effect	Desirable
Low costs of adjustment	Yes	Undesirable	Desirable	Desirable
relative to price[3]	No	Desirable	Undesirable	Undesirable

(continued)

Conditions		Standardisation	Segmentation	BTO
Minimum efficiency	High	Desirable	Undesirable	Undesirable
scale	Low	Undesirable	Desirable	Desirable
Ability to adapt basic product	High	Undesirable	Undesirable	Desirable
platform	Low	Desirable	Desirable	Undesirable

1 Legal，economic and cultural barriers.

2 High barriers to trade requires BTO systems to be distinct in different countries in which the systems are used thereby leading to high organisational costs due to dissimilar systems in various countries.

3 Costs are organisational and logistical resources to product differentiate or to BTO relative to the higher price that can be charged for non-standard products.

Notes to the Text

1. The Uppsala internationalisation model：乌普萨拉国际化过程模型,是 20 世纪 70 年代一批北欧学者在瑞典的乌普萨拉大学提出的企业国际化模型。

2. McKinsey：麦肯锡公司,成立于 1926 年,在咨询业中占有主导地位。除了向全球大企业、商业银行、大型高科技公司提供服务外,还向教育、社会、环境及文化组织提供公众利益服务。

3. white goods：In retailing, all those heavy household appliances that were originally manufactured with a white enamel finish，such as refrigerators，freezers，washers and dryers，or stoves. Today the term applies to all such goods，even though they are available in a variety of decorator colors and finishes. (白色的)大型家用电器

4. Economist：《经济学家》,英国出版的一份主要刊载英国以及世界经济、政治时事评论、贸易与金融动态报道、统计资料等内容的周刊。

5. Dell Computers：戴尔计算机公司,1984 年由企业家迈克尔•戴尔创立,总部设在美国德克萨斯州。

Exercises

Ⅰ **Answer the following questions.**

1. What is the key to the development of the international marketing strategy?

2. Are networks important in international marketing?

3. What is the build-to-order（BTO）system?

4. How do you look at the segmentation strategy and the standardization strategy in international marketing?

II Write out the equivalents of the following words and expressions.

1. DFI
2. BTO
3. IMP Group
4. tight schedule
5. mass production
6. customization
7. product differentiation

8. 产品系列
9. 溢价
10. 中小企业
11. 售后服务
12. 产品开发
13. 最终用户

III Translate the following into Chinese.

BTO systems require the development of effective e-business and logistical systems that can deliver inputs and final products on very tight schedules. The problems of using such complex e-business systems for international business activities may hamper the use of this approach to mass customization. Moreover, the cost of segmenting markets to this level, in terms of developing effective BTO organizational and logistical systems, may lead to similar results to the attempts to mass customize by producing and marketing myriad different models by the car industry. Economic, legal and cultural differences across countries may also limit the use of global BTO systems because technical regulations and differences in rules and what is culturally and legally acceptable as means of promotion will require adaptation of the basic BTO marketing model. This will further complicate the organizational complexity of effectively operating BTO systems.

Unit 44

Marketing Planning

Introduction

Marketing planning is widely adopted by businesses from all sectors. The process of marketing planning encapsulates all elements of marketing management: marketing analyses, development of strategy and the implementation of the marketing mix. Marketing planning can, therefore, be regarded as a systematic process for assessing marketing opportunities, helping organisations to stay in touch with marketplace trends and to keep abreast of customer needs. In this respect, the process helps businesses to effectively develop, co-ordinate and control marketing activities. The broad objectives of the marketing planning process are as follows:

- Identifying the required resources for carrying out marketing activities so that a budget can be set.
- Specifying expected results so that the business can anticipate what its situation will be at the end of the current period of planning.
- Emphasising business strengths over rivals and clarifying any basis for competing/ differential advantage.
- Understanding key weaknesses to rectify and threats to pre-empt.
- Bringing about the implementation of the organisation's marketing strategy.
- Describing in sufficient detail the marketing tasks that must take place so that implementation responsibilities can be assigned and schedules specified.
- Enabling activities and results to be monitored so that an appropriate level of control can be exerted.
- Ensuring consistency between marketing activities, customer needs and market developments.

Marketing planning is able to achieve these objectives by driving the business through three kinds of activities: analyses, development of marketing strategy, and design and implementation of marketing programmes. These activities, which are considered in more detail in this paper, involve the following:

- Analysis of markets and the trading environment.
- Determination of core target markets.
- Identification of a basis for competing (differential advantage).
- Statement of specific marketing objectives and desired brand or product positioning.

- Development of marketing programmes to implement plans.
- Determination of required budgets and allocation of marketing tasks.
- Monitoring of performance and changing market conditions.

The Marketing Plan is the written document that businesses develop to record the output of the marketing planning process. This document provides details of the analysis and strategic thinking that have been undertaken and outlines the marketing objectives, marketing mix and plan for implementation and control. As such, the plan plays a key role in informing organisational members about the plan and any roles and responsibilities they may have within it. The plan also provides details of required resources and should highlight potential obstacles to the planning process, so that steps can be taken to overcome them. In some respects the Marketing Plan is a kind of road map, providing direction to help the business implement its strategies and achieve its objectives: the plan guides senior management and all functional areas within the organisation.

The Marketing Planning Process

Marketing planning can be thought of as an on-going process of analysis, planning and control. This process is sometimes depicted as a cycle. Best practice suggests that marketing plans should be updated on an on-going basis an annual or longer timeframe. The marketing planning process begins with a series of core analyses, which then form the basis for developing marketing strategy. Once the marketing strategy has been determined, detailed marketing programmes can be designed and implemented. The marketing planning literature encompasses a variety of academic and practitioner texts providing detailed guidance on all aspects of the process.

The marketing planning literature explains that companies adopting a marketing planning approach must first engage in a systematic review of the markets in which they are operating. This should include market size, structure and key trends; the needs and buying behaviour of customers; the wider marketing environment—encapsulating the main economic, political, social, technological, environmental, legal and regulatory trends—as well as the competitive environment where trading is taking place. The robustness level of detail provided in the marketing analyses impact and directly upon the appropriateness of the subsequently developed marketing strategy and programmes. When combined with a systematic review of company strengths and weaknesses, these analyses provide the foundation upon which the remainder of the planning process is built. By understanding these areas and adopting a sensible view of the company's strengths in the eyes of customers and vis-a-vis competitors, a realistic basis for competing can be determined. This can then be expressed in the brand positioning strategy and marketing programmes designed by the business.

Core Analyses

- Review of the existing situation

- ABC Sales-Contribution Analysis
- General market trends and the marketing environment
- Strengths, Weaknesses, Opportunities, Threats
- Customer needs, expectations and buying patterns
- Competitive positions/strategies
- Balance of the product portfolio
- Existing brand or product positioning

Strategy Development

- Determination of new or revised target segments
- Selection of new or revised target segments
- Determination of differential advantage—basis for competing
- Identification of brand or product positioning strategies
- Setting detailed marketing objectives
- Gap analysis

Programmes for Implementation

- *Marketing Mix Programmes*
  o Product range
  o Pricing and payment terms
  o Promotional strategy and tactics
  o Distribution channels and control
  o Service levels and personnel requirements
  o Sales force planning
  o Internal communication and organisation
- *Resources and Scheduling*
  o Budgets
  o People and responsibilities
  o Activities
  o Timing
- *On-Going Requirements*
  o Product/brand development
  o Marketing research and data collection
  o Training and recruitment
  o Communications
  o Monitoring performance

Weaknesses in any of the analyses can result in the development of inappropriate marketing programmes. For example, marketing activities in the airline industry are particularly susceptible to the wider marketing environment. As recent events have demonstrated, political pressures and periods of war and unrest substantially impact upon profitability. The marketing planning process must, therefore, address the likely impact of such trends. Similarly, a detailed understanding of customer needs and buying behaviour is at the heart of the marketing process. For example, fashion retailers must offer a range of clothing that fits current trends and projects the image desired by their consumers. In addition, their merchandise must meet certain quality standards and be practical to maintain. Failure to achieve these requirements will compromise retail sales and result in consumer dissatisfaction. Finally, a poor understanding of the competitive environment in which the business is operating can result in the pursuit of an inappropriate positioning or basis for competing strategy. Following the recent deregulation of the UK electricity industry, some of the regional electricity companies which had previously enjoyed monopoly status within their local areas, failed to adequately address the likely impact of future competition. Some of the companies were slow to accept that their existing customers might switch to alternative suppliers. Others adopted an overly narrow view about the future shape of competition in the industry and were ill-prepared for new entrants such as Virgin and the supermarket chains.

Notes to the Text

1. sector: a distinct part or branch of a nation's economy or society or of a sphere of activity such as education 部门,部分
2. encapsulate: express the essential features of (someone or something) succinctly 压缩
3. assess: evaluate or estimate the nature, ability, or quality of 评估,估定
4. pre-empt: take action in order to prevent (an event) from happening; forestall 先发制人
5. consistency: conformity in the application of something, typically that which is necessary for the sake of logic, accuracy, or fairness 连贯;各事物或各部分之间的一致性或逻辑上的连贯性
6. highlight: pick out and emphasize 突出,使显著
7. practitioner: a person actively engaged in a discipline, or profession, esp. medicine 从业者,从事专业技术的人员
8. review: a formal assessment or examination of something 回顾,评论
9. robustness: (of a process or system, esp. an economic one) able to withstand or overcome adverse conditions 强健,稳健,可靠性
10. remainder: a part, number, or quantity that is left over 剩余,存余者
11. be susceptible to: be likely or liable to be influenced or harmed by a particular thing 易受影响的
12. compromise: the acceptance of standards that are lower than is desirable 妥协
13. deregulation: removing regulations or restrictions 撤销规定,取消限制
14. Virgin: The Virgin Group Ltd. is a group of separately run companies that each

uses the Virgin brand of British celebrity business tycoon Sir Richard Branson. The core business areas are travel，entertainment and lifestyle among others.（英国）维珍公司

Exercises

I Answer the following questions.

1. What is marketing planning?
2. Can you make a brief account of the objectives of the marketing planning process?
3. What is a marketing plan according to the text?
4. What are those activities for a company to go through so that it can achieve?

II Write out the equivalents of the following words and expressions.

1. keep abreast of...
2. brand/product positioning
3. market size
4. buying pattern
5. product portfolio
6. product range

7. 营销组合
8. 竞争优势
9. 贸易环境
10. 职能部门
11. 消费者购买行为
12. 垄断地位

III Translate the following into Chinese.

Marketing planning is able to achieve these objectives by driving the business through three kinds of activities：analyses，development of marketing strategy，and design and implementation of marketing programmes. These activities，which are considered in more detail in this paper，involve the following：

• Analysis of markets and the trading environment.
• Determination of core target markets.
• Identification of a basis for competing（differential advantage）.
• Statement of specific marketing objectives and desired brand or product positioning.
• Development of marketing programmes to implement plans.
• Determination of required budgets and allocation of marketing tasks.
• Monitoring of performance and changing market conditions.

Unit 45

International Human Resource Management

Introduction

The globalization of business is forcing managers to grapple with complex issues as they seek to gain or sustain a competitive advantage. Faced with unprecedented levels of foreign competition at home and abroad, firms are beginning to recognise not only that international business is high on the list of priorities for top management but also that finding and nurturing the human resources required to implement an international or global strategy is of critical importance. Effective human resource management (HRM) is essential, especially perhaps for small and medium firms, where international expansion places extra stress on limited resources, particularly people. As Duerr (1986) points out:

Virtually any type of international problem, in final analysis, is either created by people or must be solved by people. Hence, having the right people in the right place at the right time emerges as the key to a company's international growth. If we are successful in solving that problem, I am confident we can cope with all others.

Writing in the mid-1980s on the state of the field of international human resource management (IHRM), Laurent (1986) concluded that "the challenge faced by the infant field of international human resource management is to solve a multidimensional puzzle located at the crossroad of national and organizational cultures". The aim of this paper is to examine developments in the field of IHRM and to determine if any progress has been made towards completing the puzzle noted by Laurent. Specifically, three issues are examined: first, the various approaches which have been taken to the study of IHRM; second, the variables which moderate differences between domestic and international HRM; and third, recent work which examines the topic of strategic human resource management in multinational enterprises (MNEs).

Approaches to international HRM

The field of international HRM has been characterised by three broad approaches. Early work in this field emphasised a cross-cultural management approach and examined human behavoiour within organisations from an international perspective (Adler, 1997; Phatak, 1997). A second approach developed from the comparative industrial relations and HRM literature seeks to describe, compare and analyse HRM systems in various countries (see for example, Brewster and Hegewisch, 1994). A third approach seeks to focus on aspects of HRM in multinational enterprises(see for example, Dowling, et al., 1999).

The approach taken in this paper reflects the third approach and our objective is to explore the implications what the process of internationalisation has for the activities and policies of HRM. In particular, we are interested in how HRM is practised in multinational enterprises (MNEs).

Each approach takes a somewhat different view of IHRM and it is the author's view that it is essential to identify the approach which a researcher is taking to the subject, as the approach taken influences what is *defined* as IHRM. One only has to look at the diversity in the programme at various international HRM conferences to see that there are multiple definitions of what constitutes international HRM.

Defining international HRM from the perspective of a multinational enterprise

Before offering a definition of international HRM, we should first define the general field of HRM. Typically, HRM refers to those activities undertaken by an organisation effectively to utilise its human resources. These activities would include at least the following:

- Human resource planning
- Staffing
- Performance management
- Training and development
- Compensation and benefits
- Labour relations

We can now consider the question of which activities change when HRM goes international. A paper by Morgan (1986) on the development of international HRM is helpful in considering this question. He presents a model of international HRM (shown in **Figure**) that consists of three dimensions.

1. The three broad human resource activities of procurement, allocation and utilisation. (These three broad activities can be easily expanded into the six HR activities just listed.)

2. The three national or country categories involved in international HRM activities: the host country where a subsidiary may be located, the home country where the firm is headquartered and "other" countries that may be the source of labour or finance.

3. The three types of employees of an international firm: *host country nationals* (HCNs), *parent country nationals* (PCNs), and *third country nationals* (TCNs). Thus, for example, IBM employs Australian citizens (HCNs) in its Australian operations, often sends US citizens (PCNs) to Asia-Pacific countries on assignment and may send some of its Singaporean employees on an assignment to its Japanese operations (as TCNs).

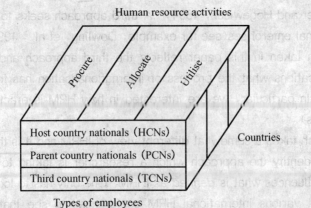

FIGURE   Model of international HRM in multinational enterprises

Morgan defines international HRM as the interplay among these three dimensions—human resource activities, types of employee and countries of operation. We can see that in broad terms international HRM involves the same activities as domestic HRM (e. g. procurement refers to HR planning and staffing). However, domestic HRM is involved with employees within only one national boundary.

It is argued that the complexities of operating in different countries and employing different national categories of workers is a key variable that differentiates domestic and international HRM, rather than any major differences between the HRM activities performed. Many firms underestimate the complexities involved in international operations and there is some evidence to suggest that business failures in the international arena may often be linked to poor management of human resources.

Increasingly, domestic HRM is taking on some of the flavour of international HRM as it deals more and more with a multicultural workforce. Thus, some of the current focus of domestic HRM on issues of managing workforce diversity may prove to be beneficial to the practice of international HRM. However, it must be remembered that management of diversity within a single national context may not necessarily transfer to a multinational context without some modification.

It is worthwhile examining in detail what is meant by the statement that international HRM is more complex than domestic HRM. Dowling (1988) has summarised the literature on similarities and differences between international and domestic HRM and argues that the complexity of international HR can be attributed to six factors, which differentiate international from domestic HRM. These factors are as follows:

1. More HR activities
2. Need for a broader perspective
3. More involvement in employees' personal lives
4. Changes in emphasis as the workforce mix of expatriates and locals varies
5. Risk exposure
6. More external influences

Each of these factors is now discussed in detail to illustrate its characteristics.

More HR activities

To operate in an international environment, a human resources department must engage in a number of activities that would not be necessary in a domestic environment: international taxation; international relocation and orientation; administrative services for expatriates; host government relations; and language translation services.

Expatriates are subject to *international taxation*, and often have both domestic (i. e. home country) and host country tax liabilities. Therefore, tax equalisation policies must be designed to ensure that there is no tax incentive or disincentive associated with any particular international assignment. The administration of tax equalisation policies is complicated by the wide variations in tax laws across host countries and by the possible time lag between the completion of an expatriate assignment and the settlement of domestic and international tax liabilities. In recognition of these difficulties, many multinational firms retain the services of a major accounting firm for international taxation advice.

International relocation and orientation involves arranging for pre-departure training; providing immigration and travel details; providing housing, shopping, medical care, recreation and schooling information; and finalising compensation details such as delivery of salary overseas, determination of various overseas allowances and taxation treatment. Many of these factors may be a source of anxiety for the expatriate and require considerable time and attention successfully to resolve potential problems—certainly much more time than would be involved in a domestic transfer/relocation such as New York to Dallas, Sydney to Melbourne, London to Cardiff or Frankfurt to Munich.

A multinational firm also needs to provide *administrative services* for expatriates in the host countries in which it operates. Providing administrative services can often be a time-consuming and complex activity because policies and procedures are not always clear-cut and may conflict with local conditions. For example, ethical questions can arise when a practice that is legal and accepted in the host country may be at best unethical and at worst illegal in the home country. For example, a situation may arise in which a host country requires an AIDS test for a work permit for an employee whose parent firm is headquartered in the USA, where employment—related AIDS testing remains a controversial issue. How does the corporate HR manager deal with the potential expatriate employee who refuses to meet this requirement for an AIDS test and overseas affiliate which needs the services of a specialist expatriate from headquarters? These issues add to the complexity of providing administrative services expatriates.

Host government relations represent an important activity for a HR department, particularly in developing countries where work permits and other important certificates are often more easily obtained when a personal relationship exists between the relevant government officials and multinational managers. Maintaining such relationships helps resolve potential problems that can be caused by ambiguous eligibility and/or compliance criteria for documentation such as work permits. US-based multinationals, however, must be careful in how they deal with relevant government officials, as payment or payment in kind such as dinners and gifts may violate the US Foreign Corrupt Practices Act.

Provision of *language translation services* for internal and external correspondence is an additional international activity for the HR department. Morgan (1986) notes that if the HR department is the major user of language translation services, the role of this translation group is often expanded to provide translation services to all foreign operation departments within the multinational.

Need for a broader perspective

HR managers working in a domestic environment generally administer programmes for a single national group of employees who are covered by a uniform compensation policy and taxed by one national government. Because HR managers working in an international environment face the problem of designing and administering programmes for more than one national group of employees (e. g. PCN, HCN and TCN employees who may work together in Zurich at the European regional headquarters of a US-based multinational), they need to take a broader view of issues. For example, a broader, more international perspective on expatriate benefits would endorse the view that all expatriate employees, regardless of nationality, should receive a foreign service or expatriate premium when working in a foreign location. Yet, some multinationals which routinely pay such premiums to their PCN employees on overseas assignment (even if the assignments are to desirable locations) are reluctant to pay premiums to foreign nationals assigned to the home country of the firm. Firms following such a policy often use the term "inpatriate" to describe foreign nationals assigned to the home country of the firm. Such a policy confirms the common perception of many HCN and TCN employees that PCN employees are given preferential treatment. Complex equity issues arise when employees of various nationalities work together and the resolution of these issues remains one of the major challenges in the international HRM field.

More involvement in employees' personal lives

A greater degree of involvement in employees' personal lives is necessary for the selection, training and effective management of both PCN and TCN employees. The HR department or professional needs to ensure that the expatriate employee understands housing arrangements, healthcare and all aspects of the compensation package provided for the assignment (cost of living allowances, premiums, taxes and so on). Many multinationals have an "international HR services" section that coordinates administration of these programmes and provides services for PCNs and TCNs such as handling their banking, investments, home rental while on assignment, coordinating home visits and final repatriation.

In the domestic setting, the HR department's involvement with an employee's family is limited. The firm may, for example, provide employee insurance programmes. Alternatively, if a domestic transfer is involved, the HR department may provide some assistance in relocating the employee and family. In the international setting, however, the HR department must be much more involved in order to provide the level of support required and will need to know more about the employee's personal life. For example, some governments require the presentation of a marriage certificate before granting a visa to an accompanying spouse. Thus, marital status could become an aspect of the selection process, regardless of the best intentions of the firm to avoid using a potentially discriminatory selection criterion. In such a situation, the HR department should advise all candidates being considered for the position of the host country's visa requirements with regard to marital status and allow candidates to decide whether they wish to remain in the selection process. Apart from providing suitable housing and schooling in the assignment location, the HR department may also need to assist children left behind at boarding schools in the home country. In more remote or less hospitable assignment locations, the HR department may be required to develop, and even run, recreational programmes. For a domestic assignment, most of these matters either would not arise or would be primarily the responsibility of the employee rather than the HR department.

Changes in emphasis as the workforce mix of PCNs and TCNs varies

As foreign operations mature, the emphases put on various human resource activities change. For example, as the need for PCNs and TCNs declines and more trained locals become available, resources previously allocated to areas such as expatriate taxation, relocation and orientation are transferred to activities such as local staff selection, training and management development. This last activity may require establishment of a programme to bring high-potential local staff to corporate headquarters for developmental assignments. The need to change emphasis in HR operations as a foreign subsidiary mature is clearly a factor that would broaden the responsibilities of local HR activities such as human resource planning, staffing, training and development and compensation.

Risk exposure

Frequently, the human and financial consequences of failure in the international arena are more severe than in domestic business. For example, expatriate failure (the premature return of an expatriate from international assignment) is a potentially high-cost problem for international companies. Direct costs (salary, training costs, and travel and relocation expenses) per failure to the parent firm may be as high as three times the domestic salary plus relocation expenses, depending on currency exchange rates and location of assignments. Indirect costs such as loss of market share and damage to overseas customer relationships may be considerable.

Another aspect of risk exposure that is relevant to international HRM is terrorism. Most major multinationals must now consider this factor when planning international meetings and assignments and it is estimated that they spend 1 to 2 percent of their revenues on protection against terrorism. Terrorism has also clearly had an effect on the way in which employees assess potential international assignment locations. The HR department may also need to devise emergency evacuation procedures for highly volatile assignment locations. The invasion of Kuwait and the ensuing Gulf War in 1991 is an example of a situation in which employees unexpectedly and very rapidly became at risk.

More external influences

The major external factors that influence international HRM are the type of government, the state of the economy and the generally accepted practices of doing business in each of the various host countries in which the multinational operates. A host government can, for example, dictate hiring procedures, as is the case in Malaysia. During the 1970s the government introduced a requirement that foreign firms comply with an extensive set of affirmative action rules designed to provide additional employment opportunities for the indigenous Malays who constitute the majority of the population but tend to be under-represented in business and professional employment groups relative to Chinese Malays and Indian Malays. Various statistics showing employment levels of indigenous Malays throughout the firm must be forwarded to the relevant government department.

In developed countries, labour is more expensive and better organised than in less developed countries and governments require compliance with guidelines on issues such as labour relations, taxation and health and safety. These factors shape the activities of the subsidiary HR manager to a considerable extent. In less developed countries, labour tends to be cheaper and less organised and government regulation is less pervasive, so these factors take less time. The subsidiary HR manager must spend more time, however, learning and interpreting the local ways of doing business and the general code of conduct regarding activities such as gift giving. It is also likely that the subsidiary HR manager may also become more involved in administering benefits either provided or financed by the multinational such as housing, education and other facilities not readily available in the local economy.

Notes to the Text

1. grapple with: struggle with or work hard to deal with or overcome (a difficulty or challenge) 苦战，设法解决，努力克服
2. nurture: care for and encourage the growth or development of 使发展；培养
3. infant field: a state in an early stage of its development 尚处于初创阶段的一个领域，新的领域
4. MNEs: multinational enterprises 跨国企业

5. staffing：provide（an organization，business，etc.）with staff 配备人员

6. operation：a business organization，a company 企业，组织，公司

7. dimension：an aspect or feature of a situation，problem or thing 方面

8. modification：partial or minor changes to（something），typically so as to improve it or to make it less extreme 改变，变化

9. the US Foreign Corrupt Practices Act：美国反海外腐败法

10. endorse：declare one's public approval or support of 认可，赞同，支持

11. volatile：liable to change rapidly and unpredictably，esp. for the worse 易变的，反复无常的，变坏的

Exercises

I **Answer the following questions.**

1. What is, in its final analysis, the key to a company's international growth?

2. What are the approaches to international HRM?

3. What does HRM refer to?

4. What are the factors that lead to the complexity of international HR?

5. What are the main aspects of "risk exposure" discussed in the text?

II **Write out the equivalents of the following words and expressions.**

1. expatriate premium
2. multidimensional puzzle
3. procurement
4. HCNs / PCNs
5. inpatriate
6. tax equalisation policy
7. ambiguous eligibility
8. a uniform compensation policy

9. 比较优势
10. 人力资源
11. 行前（出发前）培训
12. 费时的活动
13. 优惠待遇
14. 寄宿学校
15. 紧急情况撤预案（应急预案）
16. 行为准则

III **Translate the following into Chinese.**

The field of international HRM has been characterised by three broad approaches. Early work in this field emphasised a cross-cultural management approach and examined human behaviour within organisations from an international perspective（Adler，1997；Phatak，1997）. A second approach developed from the comparative industrial relations and HRM literature seeks to describe, compare and analyse HRM systems in various countries（see for example, Brewster and Hegewisch，1994）. A third approach seeks to focus on aspects of HRM in multinational enterprises（see for example, Dowling, et al.，1999）.

Unit 46

Mission Statement

What is a mission statement and why is it important

An effective mission statement describes the firm's fundamental, unique purpose. An important part of this description indicates how a firm is unique in its scope of operations and its product or service offerings. Thus, in simple yet powerful terms, a mission statement proclaims corporate purpose. This proclamation indicates what the organization intends to accomplish, identifies the market(s) in which the firm intends to operate, and reflects the philosophical premises that are to guide actions. Mission statements are also intended to provide motivation, general direction, an image of the company's character, and a tone, or set of attitudes, through which actions are guided. Furthermore, because mission statements embody a company's soul, they are often inspirational.

Levi Strauss & Company's mission statement provides an interesting example in terms of these issues. In the 1989 Annual Report (entitled "Crusaders of the Golden Needle"), the company's mission statement is described as follows:

> We seek profitable and responsible commercial success creating and selling jeans and casual clothing. We seek this while offering quality products and service—and by being a leader in what we do. What we do is important. How we do it is also important. Here's how: By being honest. By being responsible citizens in communities where we operate and in society in general. By having a workplace that's safe and productive, where people work together in teams, where they talk to each other openly, where they're responsible for their actions, and where they can improve their skills.

Thus, the firm has described its fundamental, unique purpose. Additionally, the mission statement indicates what the company intends to accomplish and describes the philosophical premises that guide peoples' actions.

Once completed, mission statements become the foundation on which other intended actions are built. Only after a mission statement has been developed can objectives and appropriate strategies be formed properly in all segments of a company. The following part of the mission statement of Anheuser-Busch Companies, Inc. demonstrates this point, "Anheuser-Busch's corporate mission statement provides the foundation for strategic planning for all subsidiaries."

Peter Drucker (1973) perhaps best described the general relationship and sequence between a mission statement and objectives. He noted that, "A business is not defined by its name, statutes, or articles of incorporation. It is defined by the business mission. Only a clear definition of the mission and purpose of the organization makes possible clear and realistic business objectives."

Today's complex environmental challenges

Today's challenges suggest the critical nature of effectively articulated mission statements. Included among the challenges confronting executives in the 1990s are:

1. complex and ambiguous decision conditions;
2. increasing levels of environmental turbulence and the difficulty of managing it;
3. increasing intensity in global market battles;
4. increasing numbers of hostile takeovers and the sophistication of manufacturing technologies; and
5. the need to constantly introduce high-quality, innovative products and services.

Having analyzed such environmental conditions, Walker Lewis, head of Strategic Planning Associates, proposed that "this may be a time of immense uncertainty, but it is a certainty that Western companies are in for ten years of competitive hell." These types of conditions clearly suggest the paramount importance of effective mission statements. A key outcome of mission statements is the determination of a firm's focus when coping with complex environments. Among other attributes, focus means "setting a clear, realistic mission and then working tirelessly to make sure everyone—from the chairman to the middle manager to the hourly employee—understands it."

Home Depot, America's largest warehouse chain selling do-it-yourself items, has remained focused. The company's CEO suggested that although Home Depot may be able to sell many products (including, for example, toys and food products), it has avoided the temptation to do so. The reason for retaining Home Depot's original focus is to prevent the customer from thinking the company is anything other than what it is—a highly successful purveyor of do-it-yourself products.

Various mission statements indicate different companies' intended focus. For example, the mission statement of Anheuser-Busch notes that "the fundamental premise of the mission statement is that beer is and always will be Anheuser-Busch's core business." Similarly, in reference to its mission, the Harley-Davidson company has stressed that, "Instead of pandering to trends, we'll stick with what got us here: remaining faithful to our heritage." Finally, Federal Express's Corporate Mission, as shown below, clearly describes the firm's intended focus:

Federal Express is committed to our PEOPLE-SERVICE-PROFIT philosophy. We will produce outstanding financial returns by providing totally reliable, competitively superior global air-ground transportation of high-priority goods and documents that require time-certain delivery. Equally important, positive control of each pack will be maintained utilizing real-time electronic tracking and tracing systems. A complete record of each shipment and delivery will be presented with our request for payment. We will be helpful, courteous, and professional to each other and the public. We will strive to have a satisfied customer at the end of each transaction.

The failure to develop mission statements

Evidence suggests that environmental complexity and turbulence create a need for effective mission statements. However, many organizations have not formed essential direction-setting statements. For example, one researcher found that 59 percent of the Chief Executive Officers of Business Weeks' top 1,000 firms run companies that do not have mission statements. Interestingly, some of these large firms had acquired other companies to diversify their scope of operations beyond the company's original core business or product areas. One researcher examined the performance of these types of diversified firms and concluded that his "data paint a sobering picture of the success ratio of these moves". In fact, Porter discovered that "on average, corporations divested more than half of their acquisitions in new industries and more than 60 percent of their acquisitions in entirely new fields." As noted previously, a mission statement is intended to provide a focus for all firms' efforts, including those that have diversified through acquiring other companies. Thus, it is possible that the lack of an effective mission statement and the necessity of restructuring have contributed to the number of divestitures that have occurred recently in some large diversified firms.

Failure to develop mission statements is not unique to large companies. In fact, mission statements are rarely developed in small firms. The results of failing to draft mission statements in small firms mirror those in large companies. For example, two researchers discovered that 20 percent of small firms that did not engage in any type of strategic planning failed, while failures occurred in only 8 percent of the companies engaging in sophisticated strategic planning. Thus, failure to articulate a firm's focus through a mission statement may partially account for the fact that approximately 50 percent of start-ups fail in the first year of operation, whereas 75 to 80 percent fail within their first three to five years.

Mission statements are often developed in small firms only during a crisis period. The experiences of Computer-Aided Design Group (CADG) illustrate this tendency. Initially, CADG was extremely successful. In fact, the CEO suggested that because "clients track us down", a mission statement and strategy were not necessary. However, after the first three years, this situation changed, partly because of CADG's entrance into different markets and the resulting loss of its original focus. Following a four-hour meeting between the CEO and other key individuals, a crisp mission statement was developed that provided the focus necessary for the firm to again become successful.

The evidence presented above suggests the following important question: Why are mission statements not developed in all types of organizations?

Factors ihibiting the development of mission statements

Several factors may account for the failure to develop mission statements. Here, we examine the following: 1) the number and diversity of organizational stakeholders; 2) the amount of work required to develop an effective mission statement; 3) the tendency for some stakeholders to become comfortable with a firm's current position (the status quo is viewed as being acceptable or preferable); 4) the belief that mission statements may reveal too much confidential, competitive information; 5) the controversy that can be created through development of a mission statement; 6) the difficulty that can be encountered when key upper-level personnel spend too much time on operational rather than strategic issues; 7) the requirement to think as a "generalist", not as a "specialist", when developing a mission statement; 8) some individuals' desire for excessive amounts of organizational autonomy; and 9) the historical formality of strategic planning processes.

Notes to the Text

1. in its scope of operations and its product or service offerings: 在公司经营范围或产品服务的范围内

2. proclamation: the public or official announcement of something 公告，宣告

3. philosophical premise: a philosophical statement or idea on which reasoning is based 哲学前提

4. motivation: the reason or reasons one has for acting or behaving in a particular way; the general desire or willingness of someone to do something 动机，动力；诱因，兴趣

5. Levi Strauss & Company: 李维服装公司，成立于 1853 年；以其"李维斯"牛仔服装闻名于世。

6. crusader: a person who lead or take part in a campaign concerning a social, political, or religious issue 改革者，社会改革运动的斗士

7. jeans and casual clothing: 牛仔休闲服

8. segments: each of the parts into which something is or may be divided 部分

9. Anheuser-Busch Companies, Inc.: 安休斯·布希公司，成立于 1979 年，总部设在美国密苏里州的路易斯市，是世界上最大的啤酒酿造企业，每年生产 1 亿桶啤酒，其主打品牌有"百威"牌啤酒等。

10. Peter Drucker: 彼得·德鲁克(1909—2005)，现代管理学之父、多产作家、企业顾问和演讲家。

11. articles of incorporation: regulations and rules of company 公司条例

12. critical: having decisive importance in the success or failure of something 重要的，关键的

13. articulated: (of an idea or feeling) expressed; put into words 表达清楚的

14. focus: the centre of interest or activity(注意、活动、兴趣)中心点，重点，宗旨

15. cope with: deal effectively with something difficult 处理，对付

16. attribute：a quality of feature regarded as a characteristic or inherent part of someone or something 品质，属性，特征

17. hourly employee：实行时薪的员工

18. Home Depot：家得宝，美国最大的零售公司，主要从事家庭装潢材料和建筑材料的零售以及仓储业务。

19. do-it-yourself：自己动手做（DIY）

20. CEO：Chief Executive Officer 执行总裁，首席执行官

21. other than：apart from, except 不同于；除了

22. purveyor：a person who provides or supplies（food, drink, or other goods）as one's business 供应者，提供者

23. Harley-Davidson：哈利·戴维森摩托车公司，1903年创建于美国密尔沃基，是美国摩托车产量最大的企业之一。

24. pander：gratify or indulge（an immoral or distasteful desire, need or habit or a person with such a desire, etc.）迎合，迁就

25. Federal Express：联邦快递公司

26. real-time electronic tracking and tracing systems：实时电子跟踪及跟踪系统

27. diversify：enlarge or vary the range of products or the field of operation of（a company）；spread（investment）over several enterprises or products in order to reduce the risk of loss 使多样化，做多样化投资

28. restructuring：reforming, organizing differently, making adjustment 改革，改组，调整

29. divestiture：the action or process of selling off subsidiary business interests or investments（母公司）抛售子公司的利润或投资；强制过户（处理）

30. account for：explain the cause of something 解释，说明原因

31. start-up：a newly established business 新兴公司，新创办的企业

32. track sb/sth down：find sb/sth by searching 跟踪，追踪到

33. stakeholder：a person with an interst or concern in something, esp. a business; a person who has a share in a business 股东

34. generalist：a person competent in several different fields or activities 通才，多面手

Exercises

Ⅰ **Answer the following questions.**

1. What is a mission statement?

2. What is a mission statement intended to do?

3. How do you understand the philosophical premises of Levi Strauss & Company's mission statement?

4. What are the challenges confronting executives today?

5. What's your understanding of Federal Express's PEOPLE-SERVICE-PROFIT philosophy?

6. Some companies failed because of their failure to develop their own mission statement. Do you agree to this point of view? Why or why not?

Ⅱ **Write out the equivalents of the following words and expressions.**

1. mission statement
2. high-priority goods
3. outstanding financial returns
4. market battles
5. takeover
6. competitive hell
7. organizational autonomy
8. 优质产品
9. 战略规划
10. 子公司
11. 供应商
12. 核心业务
13. 现状
14. 多种经营公司

Ⅲ **Translate the following into Chinese.**

We seek profitable and responsible commercial success creating and selling jeans and casual clothing. We seek this while offering quality products and service—and by being a leader in what we do. What we do is important. How we do it is also important. Here's how: By being honest. By being responsible citizens in communities where we operate and in society in general. By having a workplace that's safe and productive, where people work together in teams, where they talk to each other openly, where they're responsible for their actions, and where they can improve their skills.

Unit 47

E-commerce: A Kind of New Commercial Tool

In the early 1970s, with the innovation of electronic fund transfers (EFT), E-commerce (EC) applications began, for large companies, financial institutions, and some daring small businesses. Then came EDI, which enlarged the participating companies from financial institutions to manufacturers, retailers, services, and so on. Many other applications followed, ranging from stock trading to travel reservation systems. Such systems were described as Telecommunication Applications and their strategic value was widely recognized. The term Electronic Commerce appeared, and EC applications expanded greatly.

With the commercialization of the Internet in the early 1990s and its rapid growth to millions of potential customers, we believe that a large scale reform will happen, no matter how the economic structure changes and how the industry structure to be adjusted in the world. One reason for the rapid expansion of the technology was the increase in competition and other business pressures. The other reason was the development of networks, protocols, software, and specifications. So E-commerce will become the new big economic growth point.

Like so many popular words in use today, Electronic Commerce may mean different things to different people. The term *commerce* is viewed by someone as transactions conducted between business partners. Therefore, the term *Electronic Commerce* seems to be quite narrow to some people. However, many people use the term E-business. It refers to a broader definition of EC, not just buying and selling but also servicing customers, cooperating with business partners over networks, and conducting electronic transactions within an organization. E-business processes include not only online marketing and sales, but also supply-chain and channel management, manufacturing and inventory control, and financial operations across the entire organization. Essentially, E-business technologies empower customers, employees, suppliers, distributors, vendors and partners by giving them powerful tools for information management and communications.

E-commerce can be classified into the following types by the nature of transactions

(1) Business-to-business (B2B). This type is quite common today. It includes the IOS (Inter-organizational Information System) transactions and electronic market transactions

between organizations. B2B EC applications will enable companies to get the following kinds of information: product; customer; supplier; inventory; supply chain alliance; competitor; sales and marketing.

(2) Business-to-consumer (B2C). These are retailing transactions with individual shoppers. The typical shopper at *Ammazon com* is a customer, or consumer.

(3) Consumer-to-business (C2B). This type includes individuals who sell products or services to organizations, as well as individuals who seek sellers, negotiate with them, and conclude a transaction.

(4) Consumer-to-consumer (C2C). In this type a consumer sells directly to consumers. Individuals in classified ads can sell residential property, cars; advertise personal services on the Internet and sell knowledge as well as expertise.

(5) Intra-organizational EC. All internal organizational activities involved in exchange of goods, services, or information usually are performed on Intranets. Activities can range from selling corporate products to employees' online training.

(6) Non-business EC. An increased number of non-business institutions such as academic institutions, religious organizations, social organizations, not-for-profit organizations, and government agencies are using different types of EC to reduce their expenses or to improve their operations and customer services.

E-commerce has the following characteristics

(1) It is a global commerce. The commerce is conducted between different areas and countries. The bigger online market has been shaping. The producers and service providers will get more and more benefits from the expanding E-commerce market. We could use some words to express such changes, which are "Companies will become bigger and bigger", "Countries will become smaller and smaller" and "The commercial scope will go beyond the countries' borders".

(2) It reduces the operating costs of business process. It costs lower than the traditional one. The traditional one has been changing since E-commerce appeared.

(3) It is quicker and more suitable, and it makes the consumers realize their shopping desires in a short time. You could "go shopping at home".

(4) It is more efficient and offers your company a new distribution channel. The changes, such as visible trade changed to be invisible trade, paper trade changed to be the non-paper trade, have greatly changed the ways of working, living and thinking. In recent years, it is approved that the commercial efficiency rate has been increased dozens or even hundreds of times. It is more than just online shopping, being also about conducting business to business transactions with your customers, suppliers, vendors and others.

Above all, in today's competitive trading environment, you have to keep moving just to stay ahead and no matter what the size of your business is, E-commerce has gradually become a tool you can use daily.

Notes to the Text

1. EFT: electronic fund transfers 资金电子传递，资金电子过户

2. daring: bold or courageous in a new or unusual way 大胆的,具有冒险精神的,别出心裁的

3. range from   to   ,vary or extend between specified limits 在……之间变化或变动；从……延伸到……

4. protocol: a set of rules governing the exchange or transmission of data electronically between devices (计算机系统的)协议,规定

5. specifications: a detailed description of the design and materials used to make something 规格,规范

6. inventory: a quantity of goods held in stock 库存产(商)品

7. empower: enable somebody to do something 使能够,使有能力(干)

8. shape: develop in a particular way, progress 发展,进展

Exercises

I **Answer the following questions.**

1. E-Commerce is a kind of new commercial tool. Do you agree to this statement?
2. Could you explain EFT & IOS?
3. How many characteristics does E-Commerce have? What are they?
4. Are there any (potential) disadvantages about E-Commerce? If yes, what are they?

II **Write out the equivalents of the following words and expressions.**

1. stock trading system
2. travel reservation system
3. non-business EC
4. invisible trade
5. paper trade
6. 因特网商业化
7. 新的经济增长点
8. 分类广告
9. 非盈利性机构
10. 金融机构

III **Translate the following into Chinese.**

With the commercialization of the Internet in the early 1990s and its rapid growth to millions of potential customers, we believe that a large scale reform will happen, no matter how the economic structure changes and how the industry structure to be adjusted in the world. One reason for the rapid expansion of the technology was the increase in competition and other business pressures. The other reason was the development of networks, protocols, software, and specifications. So E-commerce will become the new big economic growth point.

Unit 48

Outline of E-business

Definition of e-commerce

E-commerce is the application of information and communication technologies (ICT) to the production and distribution of goods and services on a global scale.

Definition of e-business

E-business is using electronic information to improve performance, create value and enable new relationships between business and customers.

Main types of e-business

Business to business (B2B)

B2B Involves the use of ICT by firms to purchase supplies, distribute goods and services and to exchange information between firms and other types of organisation that provide information for firms. Electronic data interchange (EDI) systems enable firms to use ICT to issue purchasing orders, invoices and payments by electronic means. Traditional EDI systems are restricted to those firms that invest in the computer and linkage systems to allow EDI to operate. This limits the use of these types of EDI systems to large firms that can afford the large investment in computer-based ordering systems. Internet-based exchange can be provided by *extranets*—web-based platforms that can be accessed by any firm that has a web address or *intranets*—internet-based systems that can only be accessed by authorised users. Extranet and intranet systems permit the creation of large network of firms that can be used for purchasing goods and services and to manage supply chains.

Business to consumer (B2C)

Internet service providers (ISPs) such as AOL supplies access to the internet for a large number of households and individuals. These ISPs not only provide a link to the internet, they also connect potential customers to the web pages of firms that are offering to sell goods and services online. Potential customers that are searching for products can also access specialised search engines such as Lycos that enables searches to be made for desired products and information and links consumers to suppliers that provide online purchasing services. Online media companies such as Yahoo! provide a variety of free media services to customers and make revenue by selling advertising space on their web pages with hyperlinks to the web pages of firms wishing to sell products to consumers.

Consumer to business（C2B）

The internet provides a low-cost and quick method for consumers to convey information to firms, for example, bids to purchase product, complaints about products, queries about payment, information on delivery times and methods. Consumers can also use the internet to obtain information from firms, for example, information on prices, qualities and deliver dates for products. Firms may also use the internet to gather opinions from existing or potential customers on such matters as the attractiveness of their products and the quality of their after-sales service.

Consumer to consumer（C2C）

Online auctions permit consumers to bid for second-hand products from other consumers. The internet also provides a medium that consumers can use to exchange information about prices and qualities of products.

Peer to peer（P2P）

The internet is used to transmit computer files, codes and other types of digital information. Indeed, this was the original use of the internet when scientists, academics and computer enthusiasts swapped digital information by using the internet. These P2P systems allow transmission of software, music, visual images, and written text, indeed, anything that can be placed into digital codes. The most famous of these P2P operations is the transfer of music via the internet. This type of activity has important implications for copyright and the protection of intellectual property.

Information exchange systems

Firms can establish intranet systems that provide access via the internet to a network of computers within firms. These systems can contain sensitive information about suppliers, customers, prices and delivery dates that can be used by sales and purchasing staff to help them conduct their activities by providing current information on these matters from any place that has access to the internet. These systems can also be used for internal management communication purposes. For example, parent companies can monitor and assess financial, sales, output and other data to convey instructions and advice to their subsidiaries. Extranet system can also be used to exchange information across organizations to help to formulate strategies, overcome problems and to generate new business opportunities. These systems can involve firms, customers, governmental agencies, universities and other organizations that provide valuable information.

Notes to the Text

1. extranet: an intranet that can be partially accessed by authorized outside users, enabling businesses to exchange information over the Internet in a secure way 外联网

2. intranet: a local or restricted communications network, especially a private

network created using World Wide Web software 内部网络，内联网

3. AOL：美国在线；成立于 1985 年，曾是世界上最大的 ISP——互联网接入服务提供商，拥有超过 2200 万用户，1999 年 AOL 买下软件公司 Netscape 震惊业界，它还拥有网上最流行的聊天软件 ICQ 和虚拟社区数字城市 digital city。最近公司业务也由在线服务转入网络技术和电子商务领域，并同 SUN 等公司结成战略联盟对抗微软。2000 年，AOL 与时代华纳宣布合并，组成 AOL 时代华纳公司，成为媒体巨人。

4. Lycos：莱科斯公司，美国一家老牌网络公司，成立于 1995 年，总部在马萨诸塞州。

5. media service：service provided by television，radio and newspapers etc. including advertising etc 媒介服务

6. revenue：income（In the text，it refers to "money" or "profit".）；make revenue：挣钱

7. hyperlink：a link from a hypertext file or document to another location or file，typically activated by clicking on a highlighted word or image at a particular location on the screen 超级链接

8. query：a question，especially one addressed to an official or organization 问题，询问

9. academic：a teacher or scholar in a university or institute of higher education 大学教师；学者

10. swap：give something in exchange for something else 交换，交流

Exercises

I Answer the following questions.

1. What's e-commerce? What is, if any, the difference between e-commerce and e-business?
2. What's B2B? What's B2C?
3. How do "online media companies" make money?
4. Have you ever bought something online?
5. Do you think that e-commerce will one day replace all the commercial centres including those supermarkets, department stores and retail shops?

II Write out the equivalents of the following words and expressions.

1. ISP   7. 网址
2. intellectual property   8. 供应链

3. web-based platforms   9. 在线销售物品
4. internet-based systems   10. 搜索引擎
5. P2P   11. 售后服务
6. e-commerce

Ⅲ Translate the following into Chinese.

Firms can establish intranet systems that provide access via the internet to a network of computers within firms. These systems can contain sensitive information about suppliers, customers, prices and delivery dates that can be used by sales and purchasing staff to help them conduct their activities by providing current information on these matters from any place that has access to the internet. These systems can also be used for internal management communication purposes. For example, parent companies can monitor and assess financial, sales, output and other data to convey instructions and advice to their subsidiaries. Extranet system can also be used to exchange information across organizations to help to formulate strategies, overcome problems and to generate new business opportunities. These systems can involve firms, customers, governmental agencies, universities and other organizations that provide valuable information.

Unit 49

How the Credit Card Captured America

The proliferation of platinum American Express Cards in the 1980s created rumors of an ultimate, highly exclusive, never publicized "Black Card". Carried by billionaires, it reportedly allowed holders to demand private shopping service at the world's most exclusive shops and to call for helicopters in the middle of the Sahara.

American Express strongly denies the existence of such a card. But the persistence of the myth suggests the social importance credit cards have for so many Americans. As one business writer puts it, "To have one's credit cards cancelled now is akin to being excommunicated by the medieval church."

Americans today charge almost $500 billion a year. And nowadays there is almost nothing you can't use a credit card for. The Guinness record for cards held belongs to Walter Cavanagh of Santa Clara, Calif., who keeps many of the 1,381 different credit cards he holds in a custom-made wallet that stretches 250 feet.

America's love affair with the credit card began in 1949, when businessman Frank X. McNamara finished a meal in a New York restaurant and then discovered he had no cash. In those days, gasoline and store charge cards were common, but cash was standard for almost everything else. An embarrassed McNamara called his wife, who rushed over to bail him out. His predicament gave him the idea for Diners Club.

Within a year some 200 people carried the world's first multi-use credit card. For an annual fee of $5, these card holders could charge meals at 27 restaurants in and around New York City. By the end of 1951 more than a million dollars had been charged on the growing number of cards, and the company was soon turning a profit.

In 1953, a new idea struck upon McNamara. He sold out to his partners, Ralph Schneider and Alfred Bloomingdale, for about $200,000. People didn't believe that just by applying, they would get a credit card. They thought there had to be a catch. There was a catch, but it snared the merchant, not the customer. Diners Club charged retailers a "discount" of more than five percent on each sale. Despite the loss in their profits, merchants signed up, enticed by the argument that people with cards spend more than those without.

The problem was to persuade enough people to carry the cards. Diners Club turned to promotions. It gave away a round-the-world trip on a popular television show. The winners charged their expenses and made it "from New York to New York without a dime in their pockets".

By 1955 the convenience of charging was catching on in a big way. Diners Club was followed by a number of other credit cards including the American Express Card, which was introduced in 1958 and very soon dominated the field.

As the cards proliferated, so did advertising encourage consumers to charge up a luxurious life. Carte Blanche promised a 19-years-old, $73-a-week clerk named Joseph Miraglia that its card would open up a new and magical world. He used it for a $10,000 spending binge—visiting Montreal, Las Vegas, Miami Beach and Havana, and staying only in the best hotels.

"For a month I was somebody," Miraglia stated after he was finally arrested.

But banks, sensing among the less affluent a pent-up desire to spend, began issuing cards of their own. The first to turn a profit was Bank of America's BankAmericard today known as Visa. Its followers and competitors were MasterCard and Sears' Discover card. Airlines, car and insurance companies, even long-distance phone companies allied themselves with banks to offer credit cards, too. Experts estimate there are from 15,000 to 19,000 different cards available in this country.

The continuing competition has forced bank credit-card issuers to counter with imaginative marketing strategies. Gold and other premium cards caught on, many offering lower interest rates and higher credit limits—though the real attraction often is something else. People admit that they use a gold card because of the status it imparts.

To keep ahead in this, American Express came up with the Platinum Card, exclusively for "card members" who charged at least $10,000 a year. By 1985 over 50,000 people were paying $250 a year for the privilege. That fixed fee won holders a host of personal services. American Express representatives searched the world for hard-to-find gifts, picked up belongings left behind by travellers and arranged such members—only entertainment offers as Tony Awards parties with the stars. If the holder of a Platinum Card fell ill while travelling, he or she could request free assistance—even, if necessary, free medical evacuation home to America.

Of course, credit cards have not only replaced cash for many purposes, but also in effect have created cash by making it instantly available virtually everywhere. The credit card cash advance is becoming as ubiquitous as the automated teller machine (ATM). So the revolution that began in 1949 with an embarrassed businessman who was out of cash now seems complete. What Alfred Bloomingdale predicted seems to have come true: An America where "there will be only two classes of people—those with credit cards and those who can't get them".

Notes to the Text

1. American Express Card: 运通卡
2. the Guinness record: 吉尼斯世界纪录

3. Diners Club card：大莱卡

4. BankAmericard（Visa）：维卡，签证卡

5. MasterCard：万事达卡

6. Tony Awards：Tony was an American actress and producer. Tony Award is a medal awarded annually by a professional organization for notable achievement in the theatre. 托尼奖

7. excommunicate：exclude（as a punishment）from the privileges of a member of the church 剥夺教友权利；逐出教会

8. entice：attract by offering hope of reward or pleasure 诱惑，诱使

9. binge：a completely uncontrolled action；a happy and merry time 欢闹

10. the Sahara：撒哈拉沙漠（非洲北部大沙漠）

11. custom-made：made according to the customer's requirements 定做的，定制的

Exercises

I   Answer the following questions.

1. Why does the author say credit cards have not only replaced cash but also have created cash? Make comment on this.

2. How could you explain Alfred Bloomingdale's prediction：An America where "there will be only two classes of people—those with credit cards and those who can't get them"?

3. Could you explain the formalities of applying for a credit card and the way to use it?

4. Why do you think some people like to use a gold card or premium card?

II   Write out the equivalents of the following words and expressions.

1. evacuation

2. ubiquitous

3. bail somebody out

4. catch（n.）

5. a pent-up desire

6. 亿万富翁

7. 持卡人

8. 自动取款机

9. 困境，窘迫

10. 金卡与高档卡

III   Translate the following into Chinese.

To keep ahead in this，American Express came up with the Platinum Card，exclusively for "card members" who charged at least $ 10,000 a year. By 1985 over 50,000 people were paying $ 250 a year for the privilege. That fixed fee won holders a host of personal services. American Express representatives searched the world for hard-to-find gifts, picked up belongings left behind by travellers and arranged such members—only entertainment offers as Tony Awards parties with the stars. If the holder of a Platinum Card fell ill while travelling, he or she could request free assistance—even, if necessary, free medical evacuation home to America.

Unit 50

Will Cash Completely Vanish?

Anyone who has ever traveled to Britain knows the reassuring jangle of a £1 coin. It's weighty stuff, nearly twice the heft of an American quarter, and six times valuable. It's got a gilt-colored exterior and a serene-looking Queen Elizabeth Ⅱ on the face. It's thick coin, about three stacked quarters high, and the British Royal Mint has dressed up the edge with fancy-looking Latin inscriptions ("Spend me wisely," they seem to say). The pound feels like real money. It feels great.

Americans are about to get their own version of this metallic frisson. A smooth-edged, golden-hued 1 coin is working its way into circulation. The U. S. Mint hopes to have about 1 billion of the dollar coins bouncing in our pockets. It looks and feels like something you might see in an old West saloon, perfect for nation that worships its frontier past. (It's not accident that an Indian princess and scout decorate the face.)

But if the new coins feel so good—and fill such a giant need in our world of 1 vending machines—why has the Treasury spent 45 million advertising them? Why is the U. S. Mint distributing 5,000 of them in cereal boxes as a marketing gimmick? Because even in money, there is no such thing as a sure thing. How we feel about what we carry in our pockets says an awful lot about what we carry in our hearts and minds. The year before last a coalition of 11 European countries rolled out a brand new currency called the euro. Continental bankers hoped the euro would compete with the dollar as an international currency of choice. Instead, the euro has fallen more than 20% against the dollar, a poorer showing than even the most pessimistic predictions. Betting on what kind of money people want to use is a dangerous way to invest.

The most common conceit about our future, of course, is that the kind of cash we will most want to use will be digital. But the paperless wallet has proved as practical as the paperless office. In late 1997, two New York City banks tried an experiment on the Upper West Side of Manhattan. They spent millions installing special digital-cash-card machines in all kinds of retail sites—hairdressers, retail stores, even taxicabs. Then they distributed—for free—smart digital cards. Surely, if digital cash was this easy to use, people would stop using the green stuff. Wrong. It was just too hard to change people's habits. When it comes to cash, people don't want gimmicks. They want something that is universally accepted, convenient and easy. Bank researchers figured out the real problem was that wiring even 30% of the "spend points" in the area wasn't enough. They would need blanket coverage to make e-cards into everyday currency.

The power of electric cash, however, isn't simply as a digital replacement of an already refined analog technology. E-cash will eventually take off because what we can do with it. We have so much choice about where and what we are buying, that it's inevitable we will soon have plenty of leeway in choosing how we buy. If I want to purchase a case of Alpo from *Pets. com* using my American Airlines frequent-flyer miles, why shouldn't I be able to do so? If *Amazon. com* wants to issue special "Amazon dollars" that are worth 1. 20 a piece at selected merchants, why wouldn't I start changing my U. S. dollars for Amazon dollars at a furious pace?

For a new generation of e-bankers, this is exactly the future they have in mind, a place where money isn't universal but personal. My employers at *Time* could pay me, if they wished, in specialized T-dollars that fluctuate based on reaction to my articles. If they get lots of positive e-mails and letters about my work, the dollars get more valuable. I can spend them anytime, so there's room for me to do a little speculating: Should I hold on to the cash in the hope that this story ignites a flurry of flattery notes, or should I spend quickly in case it bombs?

A version of this kind of alternative-currency universe is up and running on the Internet. At *beenz. com*, users earn digital beenz for performing e-work—like telling advertisers about their buying habits. Beenz can be cashed in at about a hundred retail sites and wherever MasterCard is accepted online (at about 200 beenz to 1). And while the roughly 6 million worth of beenz in circulation today is no threat to the greenback, this hints at a future of nearly unlimited choice in currency. And because of the Net, you'll be able to exchange these e-currencies more easily than you can now change yen for dollars.

Bankers say they always get the same three questions about this emerging e-cash world: Are we still going to have pennies? Doesn't using e-cash mean giving up privacy? Won't this put the Federal Reserve Chairman out of work? The answers, in short, are: Pennies will keep turning up for the next decade at least. Some e-cash will be traceable, but much of it will be as anonymous as a wrinkled ten-spot. And with jillions of alternative currencies out there, it's possible that the Federal Reserve Chairman—who controls the economy by controlling dollars—may find his power tools are losing their torque. But as countries such as Argentina ponder dumping their own currencies in favor of the dollar, it seems likely the chairman's power will still last. So go ahead—stock up on your Sacajaweas.

Notes to the Text

1. jangle: harsh, usu. metallic, noise 刺耳的声音(通常指金属声)
2. quarter: (US, coin worth) 25 cents; fourth part of a dollar 两角五分(的硬币);四分之一元
3. British Royal Mint: 英国皇家造币厂

4. scout: person sent out to get information about the enemy's position, strength, etc. 侦察员

5. the Treasury: (in Britain and some other countries) government department that controls public revenue(英国及其他一些国家的)财政部

6. gimmick: (often derogatory) usual, amusing thing whose only purpose is to attract attention, and which has little or no value or importance of its own(常作贬义)为引人注意而无价值或不重要的小玩意儿，花招

7. coalition: action of uniting into one body or group 结合；联合

8. Upper West Side of Manhattan: (美国纽约)曼哈顿西上区

9. Alpo: 爱宝(商标名)宠物食品品牌，雀巢旗下 Ralston Purina 公司生产经营的猫粮狗食。

10. Pets. com: Pets. com is a former enterprise that sold pet accessories and supplies direct to consumers through Internet. It established in 1998 and ceased operations in November of 2000. Pet. com 成立于 1998 年，曾是一个网上经营宠物系列产品的公司。该公司于 2000 年 11 月倒闭。

11. beenz. com: beenz 是一种只在国际互联网上流通的"新货币"，既无硬币币种，也无纸币币种，被称作"网豆"，是 beenz. com 公司的产品，公司希望它能够成为在国际互联网上流通的货币。要使用网豆 beenz，消费者可以在 beenz. com 开一个免费账户。网站可以向购物或浏览的访问者发放网豆，作为各种形式的奖励。这样，消费者访问一家发放网豆的站点，就会有一笔大小不等的网豆转到自己的账户中。beenz. com 网站上时刻公布有关赚取网豆的机会，比如，只要在某投资网站登记成为一名免费会员，就能获得 50 个网豆。随着钱包里的 beenz 数量的增多，消费者就可以在近 200 家认可 beenz 支付方式的电子商务网站消费了。beenz. com 公司于 2001 年 8 月破产。

12. yen: unit of money in Japan 圆(日本的货币单位)

13. Argentina: 阿根廷(南美洲南部国家)，是拉丁美洲最发达的国家之一，经济基于农业及多样化工业。它于 1816 年宣布脱离西班牙而独立，首都是布宜诺斯艾利斯。

14. Sacajawea: 萨卡加维亚(1788—1884)北美肖肖尼印第安人妇女，携婴儿随 W. Clark 和 M. Lewis 的西征探险队[1804—1805]任向导和翻译，使探险队绝路逢生，其事迹富有传奇色彩。

Exercises

I Answer the following questions.

1. What does the author refer to when he (or she) mentions the "green stuff"?
2. How do you understand the power of e-cash?

3. Will cash completely vanish?

4. Do you use e-cash? Are there any disadvantages of e-cash?

II **Write out the equivalents of the following words and expressions.**

1. e-banker
2. frisson
3. bouncing
4. leeway
5. torque
6. ten-spot

7. 点燃，激起
8. 投机
9. 奉承
10. 匿名的
11. 美联储
12. 模拟计算机技术

III **Translate the following into Chinese.**

Bankers say they always get the same three questions about this emerging e-cash world: Are we still going to have pennies? Doesn't using e-cash mean giving up privacy? Won't this put the Federal Reserve Chairman out of work? The answers, in short, are: Pennies will keep turning up for the next decade at least. Some e-cash will be traceable, but much of it will be as anonymous as a wrinkled ten-spot. And with jillions of alternative currencies out there, it's possible that the Federal Reserve Chairman—who controls the economy by controlling dollars—may find his power tools are losing their torque. But as countries such as Argentina ponder dumping their own currencies in favor of the dollar, it seems likely the chairman's power will still last. So go ahead—stock up on your Sacajaweas.